BELLE AMI

EXPOSED

TIP OF THE SPEAR
THRILLER SERIES

CONTENTS

Published Internationally by Tema N. Merback
Calabasas, CA USA
belleamiauthor.com

PRINT ISBN 978-1-7359423-5-3

EBOOK ISBN 978-1-7359423-4-6

ACKNOWLEDGMENTS

Thank you to my parents Dina & Leo, my husband Joe, my children Natasha & Benjamin, my siblings Sarah, Joel, and Josh, my other children Julianna & Mitch, and my brother-in-law Steve.

A special thank you to Joanna D'Angelo, my editor, advisor, coach, and dear friend, without you there would be no books. Thank you, Fiona Jayde of Fiona Jayde Media for creating the most beautiful covers for the Tip of the Spear Series. Thank you, Teri Barnett for your elegant book design.

DEDICATION

To all the women warriors out there of every stripe who fight every day whether with quiet determination or with front line strength — you empower us.

PROLOGUE

12:00 a.m., January 3
Baghdad, Iraq

Hajj Qasem Solatani's prayers would soon be answered — the death of Cyrus Hassani, traitor and enemy to Iran.

With his thumb and index finger, Qasem rubbed his prayer beads as he trotted down the stairway of the Cham Wings Airbus. The amber beads released a soothing scent of pine-tree resin. The blue and yellow gems were old and rare, given to him by the Ayatollah twenty years ago when Qasem became the leader of the Quds Force. Calmed by the repetitive action of rolling the prayer beads, Qasem relaxed, focusing on what was important, his ever-evolving blueprint for attacks against his hated enemies, the United States and Israel.

Surrounding him, his protective ring of three bodyguards would gladly lay down their lives in his defense. Confident in their dedication, Qasem left his safety to his men — his life he placed in Allah's hands.

Qasem led his men from the frontlines. It was one of the reasons his army was so devoted to him. His reputation had grown to mythical proportions, his fearlessness in battle legendary. The silver fox, as his men called him, had survived dozens of battlefields and considered himself an invincible warrior. Regardless of the danger, the general, called "a living martyr," by the Ayatollah, never wavered in his devotion to the Supreme Leader of the Islamic Republic of Iran — and stood steadfast in his mission, which he believed was blessed by Allah.

Lines of fatigue shadowed Qasem's face, but even his weariness could not still the mind of the general who never slept. Following a lifetime practice after a victory or a loss, he contemplated his next move on the chessboard that was the Middle East. His meeting in Damascus between Syria's Bashar al-Assad and Vladimir Putin's envoy Alexei Belov had gone well. Assad was indebted to Solatani for saving his ass and keeping him in power. As for Putin, Solatani had forged a friendship with the Russian ruler and established a mutually fruitful relationship between Iran and Russia that was paying off in spades.

The U.S. delivery of a billion and a half dollars cash after the signing of the JCPOA agreement in 2015 had paid for the arms and rockets from Russia and North Korea. With the decreased American presence in Iraq, Qasem grabbed the opportunity to expand his mission. Now in 2020, with the great Bear's blessing, Qasem's Quds Force army dominated the Iraqi landscape, spreading its tentacles throughout the Middle East. Thanks to Qasem's friendship with Putin and North Korea's Kim Jong-un, stockpiles of rockets were stored deep underground below Iran's air force bases, ready for use. He planned to up the ante by escalating attacks and consolidating his growing power in the region.

Uranium was again being processed for Iran's ultimate goal of nuclear armament. Everything in preparation for the glorious day when Iran would unleash its arsenal and at long last fulfill its destiny. Qasem would never be satisfied until the American presence was banished from the Middle East and every Israeli driven into the sea.

But even with all the blessings that Allah had bestowed upon him, there was one failure that irked him and gave him sleepless nights. He'd failed to destroy the Iranian traitor Cyrus Hassani. The Mossad deep-cover agent had nearly single-handedly destroyed Iran's nuclear aspirations, and Qasem was bent on eliminating him. As of yet, revenge eluded him. To his great frustration, he'd lost two of his most trusted aides while trying to kill Hassani. Ali and Omar Zandi, brothers that were like sons to him, had both been martyred. The Zandi brothers had been lost in America when a mission to exact vengeance on Hassani and his family had failed. Another stitch in his side was the failed assassination attempt on Hassani's wife and daughter. Vengeance had slipped again through his fingers when Hezbollah General Amir Haddad blew up a bus in Israel. Although many infidels were slaughtered, Hassani's wife and child had survived. But Qasem was a patient man. He rubbed his prayer beads together — *All in good time. With your help, Allah, I will destroy our enemy.* He whispered a prayer to Allah for his martyred sons and took a moment to gaze up at the star-filled sky before getting into the armored SUV that waited for him on the tarmac. He nodded for his guards to follow in the second SUV. Jumping into the car, he closed the door.

"As-salamu alaikum," he was greeted by his friend, the commander of Iraq's Popular Mobilization Forces. The PMF was an official militia formed by the Iraqi government that had fought side-by-side with Solatani's Quds Force against the Islamic State of Iraq and the Levant. For a short period, the goal of destroying ISIL had led to an unlikely alliance between the Quds Force and the Americans. But now that the caliphate was all but defeated, it was time to consolidate and further Iran's control over the Middle East.

"Wa-alaikum-salaam," said Qasem. "Is everything ready in Baghdad?"

The two men embraced, and the convoy pulled away, leaving the plane behind. "Yes, everything is prepared for our next move."

Qasem sighed. "I have secured the full support of our friends."

"The first attack against the U.S. embassy was a mere precursor of things to come," said the leader of the PMF. "There is much incertitude in the capital. The time is ripe."

Thinking of the PMF's December 2019 revenge attack that had reignited U.S. enmity, Solatani rhapsodized. "We will not be cowered. We play for the end game."

"Alhamdulillah!"

Qasem glanced out the window of the SUV as they stopped for airport security. The guard nodded after barely looking at their papers, and they passed through the airport without incident. The two SUVs shadowed each other. Qasem knew his ever-faithful bodyguards were alert and ready to defend should the need arise. But something was not right. The years of battle and guerilla warfare had sharpened his instincts. A tingle crept up his spine, setting off an alarm. Perhaps it was the silence or maybe a premonition, but for some reason, Qasem's gaze rose to the roof of the car. The last thing he heard was the whoosh, whistle, and whine of the four Hellfire rockets seconds before they blew his car to smithereens. Both vehicles disappeared in a fiery explosion, their passengers incinerated.

As the two SUVs smoldered, the only recognizable human body part of the general lay on the tarmac—his hand and the glittering silver ring set with a red carnelian.

Twenty-thousand feet in the sky, the direct hits were recorded and transmitted instantly. Thunderous applause erupted in the war room in Washington.

CHAPTER ONE

Monday, February 3, evening
London, United Kingdom

They're all dead.

Jazmin Amin choked, swallowing the vomit that filled her throat. She didn't dare make a sound as she crouched beneath the outside windowsill of her family's home. The bitter taste of bile coated her tongue, and more than anything, she wanted to throw up and curl into a fetal ball. The image of bullets piercing flesh circled in her brain until she caught herself holding her breath. Dizzy, she inhaled softly and looked up, unable to breathe. Jazmin sensed the assassin's face pressed to the window, squinting, searching through the gloom of night, intent on finding and eliminating her.

Do murderers dream? Do they have families? Have they ever loved?

She had no answers. She heard the assassin curse and she shuddered. She thought about standing up tall in front of the window and screaming loud enough for the entire neighborhood to hear, "Kill me, too, you bastard!" Instead, she closed her eyes, hoping this was a nightmare. Praying that when she opened her eyes, she'd awaken once more to her happy life — everything would be as it had been.

This was not supposed to happen. How had a family dinner celebrating her marriage become a nightmare? Tomorrow she was to marry Darien, the man of her dreams, an intern specializing in emergency medicine at Royal London Hospital. Their future had seemed so bright. Jazmin swallowed the thickness in her throat. In an instant, a spray of bullets wiped out Darien and their life together.

How will I go on?

The minutes ticked away. Her thighs burned, and her stomach cramped. If she didn't move soon, she'd soil herself. It began to drizzle, and she could feel her hair frizzing in the cold moisture. *I am shameful. Forgive me, Allah.* How could she possibly think about her hair at a moment like this? But it made sense to think of anything other than cold-blooded murder. The way their bodies danced when the bullets riddled them. Would she ever remember her parents, her beloved, even her home, as they appeared without blood and bone spattering the white walls like a Pollack painting? What would Pollack name such an image? *Death of a Family*. Insane thoughts even for an art major. But easier to imagine Pollack than to face the truth — everyone she loved had disappeared in the blink of an eye? *I must survive. I'm the only one who knows what happened. The dead will never rest unless I live.*

"Inna Lillahi wa inna ilayhi raji'un," she whispered. "Indeed, to Allah, we belong, and to Him we shall return." The Muslim prayer for the dead and its mournful melody echoed in her mind.

Exhausted, she leaned her head against the brick. And then she felt it, the aftershock from the front door slamming. A tremble reverberated through the bones of the house. Instantly alert, she strained to hear anything, but the only sound came from a barking dog and the distant hum of traffic. The neighborhood was quiet except for the voices of the dead who called to her for vengeance. But now was not the time to listen. She must ignore the cries echoing in her head.

She stood slowly, every joint stabbing with pain. *What should I do?* Should she force herself to go into the house and call the police? *No I can't. I can't see them dead.* The gruesome thought made her double over. Her stomach convulsed, and she heaved up everything inside until only bile remained. Tears and snot streamed down her face. *Oh, God, oh, God. Please, God, this can't be real. Don't let it be real.*

Wiping her face on the sleeve of her blouse, she pressed her hands against the wall and stood. *Get away from the house. Get away from the house.* The words thrummed in her mind like a drumbeat. The voices of the dead or her own voice she could not say, but the urge for self-preservation kicked in. She made it as far as the stately old sycamore tree in the backyard, its branches leafless and barren, then crouched behind it. Jazmin stared at the ground and grabbed a handful of dirt. She crushed it in her fist, squeezing the damp, moist earth through her fingers. *I swear, Baba and Maman, I will avenge your deaths.*

Jazmin rose on shaky legs and leaned back against the tree. Her slender body stood invisible behind the massive trunk. She gulped frigid air, filling her lungs, fighting to squelch the despair that tore through her. The hair stood up on the back of her neck in warning, and she looked over her shoulder in terror as the townhouse exploded in a fiery blaze. The blast wave shook everything around her, and she was flung to the ground.

She covered her head, protecting herself from the projectiles that flew from the house with ballistic force and sliced into the tree. Blazing fireballs rained down on the lawn. Black smoke billowed. The roar of fire incinerating everything it touched sounded like screams, as if the souls of the dead inside screamed out the injustice of it all. Riddled with bullets and then blown to dust. Rage washed her and she trembled from head to toe. The bodies of her loved ones had been annihilated. No bodies remained to bury and pray over. Nothing but cinder and ash.

My life is ash. She crawled back to the safety of the tree trunk. Her head swam and her heart pounded hard and fast.

I'm going into shock.

The loud hum of police sirens snapped her back to her senses.

Her father's words replayed in her head. "There is only one person you can trust."

Taking a last look at the home that was now a towering inferno of flame, Jazmin stumbled across the yard and left through the back gate. She had to get away, and she had to trust her father's instructions. She prayed he was right or else no place on earth would be safe for her.

CHAPTER TWO

Monday, February 3, morning
Tel Aviv, Israel

Cyrus smiled as his five-year-old daughter Cerise sang along to *Frozen* while she ate her breakfast. He stood at the kitchen counter chopping tomato and cucumber for the Shirazi salad that was Cerise's favorite. The mundane activity soothed him as much as sipping a glass of scotch. Therapeutic, in fact. It gave him time to think. His wife Layla was away, and he was back on Mommy and Daddy duty.

After surviving two kidnappings and an attempt on her life and Cerise's, his wife, Layla, had made up her mind that she would never be a victim again. The head of Mossad had arranged for her to train for a month in martial arts and weapons at an IDF army base. Cyrus supported her decision and encouraged her to learn self-defense. As long as there was a price on his head, his family would never be entirely safe. General Solatani's obliteration by the Americans eliminated his most fearsome enemy, but until there was a regime change, he would never rest easy. He knew only too well that when you cut off the head of one snake, another slithered out of the ground to take its place. The world was full of murderous thugs, terrorists, and criminals, and that would never change.

His thoughts strayed to Iran, the country of his birth, a land of endless beauty, ancient civilizations, and artistic culture. He knew he would most likely never set foot in his homeland again. The beautiful house his architect father had designed and built, the loving home of his youth, was lost to him forever. Devasted by his father's suicide when he was only eighteen, Cyrus had struggled to hold onto his family home. It was a difficult time as he grappled to keep his mother and sister safe in an increasingly volatile political climate. His mother's secret Jewish heritage had set him on a different path. Recruited by Mossad while he was at university in Paris, Cyrus had acquired the means to get his mother and sister out of Iran by faking their deaths. He also made certain he could afford the upkeep of his childhood home. As a double agent in the employ of Oghab 2, Iran's secret nuclear watchdog, he'd been able to live in his home while working for Oghab 2. But after Mossad ordered him to blow his cover six years ago to rescue a red-haired spitfire who'd been kidnapped by the Quds Force, little did he know how much his life would change.

There's no going back.

All that remained were memories, the good and the bad. He and his sister were born years after the revolution. But even with the family's loss of wealth and status, their parents had worked hard to build a life. The love of a close-knit family had sustained them. As he prepared the tangy dressing for the colorful salad, he inhaled the sweet scent of citrus and felt transported back to the verdant hills that surrounded his parents' villa in Tehran. A bittersweet pain filled his chest. He still dreamed in Farsi. His words of love were always expressed in the language of his birth. He spoke five languages fluently, yet it was only Farsi that created a yearning in his heart.

Normally, he didn't indulge in sentimentality. For so many years, he had to live one step ahead of everyone else. Always thinking, always planning. With Layla's love, he'd learned to live in the moment, but he couldn't stop himself from falling into old habits. *Stop with the nostalgia and tears. Everything you love is here in Israel. Iran is a country controlled by evil men. Citrus trees and flowers bloom everywhere.* He grabbed another red onion and sliced it in half.

It didn't take a psychiatrist to tell him that without Layla, he'd be lost at sea. She was due back today, and Cyrus could hardly wait. Not that he didn't love caring for Cerise, he did. He chuckled to himself at how easily he'd adapted to domesticity. A spy and assassin, chopping vegetables and caring for a child. No one would ever believe it. He had trouble believing it, but Layla had worked that miracle. He'd never dreamed love was possible for him, but love had found him. Love was an unexplainable force that had changed him. More than anything in the world, he loved the woman who brought him out of the cold and gave meaning to his life. He may have rescued Layla from her kidnappers in Iran, but she was the one who had saved him.

From the corner of his eye, he saw Cerise move as stealthily as a spy making a drop. She slipped her hand under the table to feed Norit a bite of her eggs. He struggled to contain his amusement at the sounds of Norit's tongue slobbering and lapping at Cerise's fingers. When Cerise stole a glance at him, Cyrus pretended he hadn't heard or seen a thing. He said nothing and continued to chop. The yellow ball of fur had invaded his life and somehow managed to lay claim to his affection. He shook his head, one more chink in his armor brought down.

"*Aba,* when is mommy coming home? Norit misses her. And I want to show *Ima* Norit's new trick I taught her." In most things, Cerise was as impatient as he was, but when it came to Norit, Cerise had somehow found the patience of a prophet or a dog whisperer. He'd been reluctant to welcome the puppy into his life, but the last few months had changed his mind. He'd begun to understand that the fluffy ball of yellow fur provided invaluable lessons not only for his daughter but for him. It took a great deal of patience to housebreak a puppy and teach it obedience. Both Layla and Cerise were utterly entranced with Norit, but he had approached the idea of a four-legged creature invading his home with reticence.

Oddly, Norit had chosen him as her favorite human, which he

found bewildering. She jumped in his lap every chance she could and then wouldn't settle down until she'd licked his face clean. For his daughter, this represented an endorsement beyond question. For him, it required restraint and a whole lot of getting used to and adjustment. Kissing his wife and daughter was one thing, but kisses from a four-legged creature was another. He still held hope that the puppy would outgrow this licking compulsion, but he had a feeling that was wishful thinking.

"You ask me that every day, *aziz-am.*" Cerise had begun to claim that Norit missed Mommy, perhaps with the notion that it would produce the desired result of bringing Layla home sooner. "Mommy is coming home today, and we're going to visit your great-grandparents tomorrow for a welcome home Mommy party."

Cerise's green eyes gleamed. "Will we have cake? Can Norit come?"

"Yes, I'm sure Dina will make a cake, and Norit can come. But Cerise, you can't give Norit cake. It's very bad for dogs." He shot a significant glance her way, letting her know that he knew what she was up to under the table. But like the best of spies, Cerise proffered her most angelic, innocent face. How long, he wondered, before he would no longer be able to tell whether she was telling him the truth? The teenage years were down the road, but being a protective father, Cyrus already had fears about what trouble she might get into. He was convinced she'd turn him prematurely gray, or worse, he'd tear his hair out and become bald.

Cyrus carried the salad to the table and sat down. He served Cerise and petted Norit on her head. The affectionate puppy rubbed against his leg. "Eat your food, Cerise, or you won't grow up to be big and strong."

He filled his plate and dug in.

"Aba?"

"Ken."

"When are you and Mommy going to make another baby?"

The question caught him off guard, and he swallowed, choking on the bite that went down the wrong pipe. He poured a glass of juice, swigged it down, and cleared his throat. Cerise was, if anything, linear in her pursuit of knowledge. When a concept took hold of her, nothing could dissuade her. Since the accident, the notions of miscarriage and conception were first and foremost in her mind. The horrific terrorist attack when the bus blew up and she and Layla were nearly killed replayed in her psyche over and over again, much to Cyrus's dismay.

The trauma had brought about Layla's miscarriage. It had been a devastating loss for them. Cerise had seen her mother sink into depression in the aftermath. In Cerise's mind, the only cure was another baby, and she was determined to make it happen. She'd made clear her preference for a sister but had grudgingly agreed that if it were a boy, she'd find a way to accept him. "These things take time, sweetheart. A lot..." he paused as he considered the minefield ahead. "Things have to come together, and one of those is having your mommy home again." Explaining the birds and bees to a five-year-old was not about to happen, at least not from him. *Layla can have that pleasure.*

"If Mommy's coming home today, we can make a baby tomorrow. Right, Daddy?"

The thought of holding his woman again turned up the temperature in his body, causing Cyrus to chuckle. "We'll try."

Cerise was as stubborn as Layla and as focused and single-minded as her father. His laughter was cut short. Something caught his eyes through the window in their small back yard. Instinctually, his hand released the catch on his gun harness. Since the Ayatollah's *fatwa* calling for his death and the targeting of his family for elimination, he was always locked and loaded. He listened for any sound that might indicate an unwanted intruder.

Rising from the table, he tuned out Cerise's continuing chatter and moved to the back door, positioning himself behind it when it opened. He glanced at Cerise, who'd slipped out of her chair and was on the floor with Norit. The back door swung open, and Cerise screamed. Cyrus had his gun raised, ready to take down the intruder.

"*Ima!* You're home!" Cerise came bounding toward her mother, who knelt and opened her arms.

"Baby!" Cerise rushed into Layla's arms, causing her to lose her balance. They rolled over in a burst of giggles and kisses. Norit joined the happy ruckus, barking and frolicking into the mix of mother and child reunion.

Cyrus sighed, calming the adrenaline rush that surged through his veins. He returned his automatic safely to its harness. "Layla, you scared the living daylights out of me. You can't sneak up like that." He didn't say what he might have said had Cerise not been listening. He took a more diplomatic approach. "Why the subterfuge?"

Layla looked up at him and glanced down at his hand, still on his gun. "Sorry, I wanted to surprise Cerise." She tried to rise with Cerise clinging to her neck. Cyrus reached out and gave her his hand, pulling them both into his arms. He buried his face in Layla's hair, inhaling the scent of vanilla. He was so happy to see her, he quickly forgot the fact that he'd nearly shot her.

Norit jumped up and down on Layla's legs. "Sit, Norit," Cerise commanded. The puppy's rump hit the ground, her tail wagging back and forth. And then, with the focus of a laser, Cerise returned to her desire and commanded. "Daddy, kiss Mommy and make a baby."

"What —" Before Layla could finish the sentence, Cyrus silenced her with a breathless kiss. The mere touch of her lips on his ignited the fires that had remained dormant, awaiting her return. He'd missed her so badly that he could hardly control the ache of desire that raced through him. If his daughter wasn't there, he would already have picked Layla up in his arms and raced up the stairs to the bedroom for a passionate reunion. Reluctantly, he broke the kiss.

Cerise clapped her hands, delighted she'd accomplished her goal. "How long, Daddy, before the baby comes?"

Layla's brows rose in question. "Don't ask," said Cyrus.

"Don't ask what, *Aba*?"

"Layla, I'm not explaining to a five-year-old how babies are made. I give you that honor. The only thing I told her was that Mommy has to be here for it to happen." He grinned. "Should make for an interesting conversation."

Layla giggled. "My duffle's outside the door. Would you mind getting it, please? I'll spend some time with our daughter and try to address this void in her knowledge."

"You got it. I'll take Norit for a walk while you discuss the birds and the bees." He grabbed Norit's leash and made for the door. As the door swung closed, he heard Cerise ask.

"Mommy, what do birds and bees have to do with babies?"

LAYLA PRESSED a kiss to Cerise's forehead and sighed. Like Cyrus, Cerise was a master at falling asleep the instant her head hit the pillow. Smiling, she tucked the covers close around her child. Norit snored with her nose nuzzled into Cerise's armpit. Layla's plan of running Cerise and Norit up and down the sand in the sun for hours had worked its magic. Both child and puppy were exhausted from the beach. After dinner and a bath, they'd climbed into bed without protest. Love squeezed Layla's heart as she watched her daughter and Norit in slumber.

Being away for a month from her child had been difficult, especially after losing the baby. The painful loss was never far from her thoughts, nor was the near-death experience for both her and Cerise. A year had passed since the bombing, and the Ramsad's offer to train at the IDF base had come at a perfect time. She'd needed to get beyond her feelings of victimhood. She wanted to distance herself from the helplessness she'd felt in the hospital, with the loss of miscarriage all she could think about.

The first few days at the base had been overwhelming. But once she'd settled in, the training became empowering. Never again would she feel helpless and incapable of defending herself or those she loved. She'd grown in strength, not only physically but mentally.

Missing her "superman" was something else, though. Cyrus was her rock. He was her intellectual equal and loved her as she loved him, without condition. Yet knowing all this, she still felt like an empty shell without their physical passion. She knew it was the same for him, that in their union as one, the day-to-day became a magical journey. The bumps in the road of marriage and the demands of their careers were paved smooth when they made love. Being married to a spy was still difficult, but the boot camp she'd gone through in the past month had given her a better understanding of his dedication to protecting the world. She hated sharing him, but she accepted it was for the greater good.

Her spy had showered while she'd put Cerise and Norit to bed. He exited the bathroom as she opened the door to their bedroom. The sight of him made the adrenaline course through her veins. The years of living undercover had cemented his body with the grace and litheness of a predator. He moved soundlessly, like a beast without fear. Even with only a towel wrapped around his waist, he was intimidating and formidable. She shivered when she saw the hunger in his eyes as his gaze swept over her. His roguish smile set her heart racing. It excited her, and it was all she could do not to wrestle him to the bed. Instead, she provocatively brushed against him. The enjoyment of revving his engine was a high Layla couldn't resist.

"My turn, Superman." It was her endearment, the nickname that she'd bestowed on him when he'd burst through the door at Evin prison and rescued her from the guard who was hell-bent on raping her. What better way to define the man who seemed a superhero to her? Cyrus had risked his life numerous times protecting her and bore the scar of a knife wound across his belly to prove it — an injury that had nearly killed him. Nor would it be the last time that this man of honor would put his life on the line for her. She found the intensity of his love and passion for her mystifying. But mostly, she thanked the Lord he was hers.

"I can't wait, *eshgham.* Your prolonged absence was almost unbearable. How I ever lived before you is a mystery to me. I often think that my life began with you. Before that, I was a dead man pretending to be alive."

There was something so romantic when he spoke Farsi to her. The endearment of *eshgham,* "my love," was a sentimentality he used exclusively for her. The ease with which he admitted his love for her never failed to amaze her. She cupped his face with her hands. "I love you so much, Cyrus. Nothing will ever separate us." She stood on tiptoe and kissed him. After all they'd been through, it was important to remind him that their marriage meant everything to her.

A KITTENISH SMILE of satisfaction graced Layla's lips. Cyrus's chest felt damp beneath her cheek from their lovemaking. His heart pounded rhythmically against her face.

"That was a baby maker." He sighed contentedly.

She playfully slapped his chest. "Stop, you sound like Cerise. She thinks every time you kiss me, we're making a baby. If that were the case, we'd be on our way to creating an army of Hassanis."

His chuckle rumbled from his chest. "I guess more lovemaking and less kissing might be safer. Although, the idea of an army of Hassanis might be what the world needs to keep the bad guys in line."

"Even Superman can't stop all of the evil in the world." Would she ever get used to him being back in the field where his life was in constant danger? If she could, she would convince him to fight his battles sitting at a desk, but she knew if she did, she'd take from him everything that made him who he was. His purpose in life was to make the world a better place, a safer place. The man she'd fallen in love with was a spy, and regardless of the deadly situations he was placed in, she would have to suck it up and live with the risks that entailed.

"He can try." He hugged her closer.

"Just so you know, I failed miserably at dissuading our daughter from her belief that tomorrow I'll be pregnant." She ran her fingers across the breadth of his chest.

"Ha-ha, a few more liaisons like this last one, and maybe you will be pregnant. Maybe you are now." His playful smile told her the night was still young. "So, tell me about your basic training, *eshgham.* I can't wait to go to the gym and spar with you on the mats." His devilish grin sent a flash of delicious heat shooting through her.

"I'm good, but not that good," she laughed. "But seriously, your support means everything to me. I'm stronger and more confident. No more victim for me. If I'm ever in a life-threatening situation, I won't go down without a fight."

A shadow crossed his face. "It kills me to think the possibility still exists that you might have to use these skills someday." The lines around his eyes etched deeper. "Your safety and Cerise's safety will always be at risk because of me."

"We're a team. Because of me, you blew your cover in Iran. Because of me, there's a price on your head. Don't even think about blaming yourself. We all must face challenges in life. At least now, I'm more prepared to meet them."

Cyrus nodded, but his supportive smile couldn't hide the anguish in his eyes. She hoped that one day the constant fear he had for their safety would disappear. But she knew that day would not be anytime soon.

Cyrus's cell phone buzzed, and he glanced at the screen. "It's the office. I better take this."

She intended to slip out of bed to give him privacy, but he kept his arms wrapped snugly around her. "Hassani here." He leaned down to her ear at the same time. "I love you." Then he laughed. "No, I don't love you, Saul, I was talking to my wife." He listened, and the smile on his face faded. "Now? He wants to see me now?"

Layla froze. A call from the office demanding his presence was never good news.

"Okay. I'm on my way." He ended the call, dropped a kiss on her head and got up. Layla followed him into the walk-in closet.

"What's going on?"

"The Ramsad called an emergency meeting. I have to go." He buttoned his shirt and tucked it into his jeans. Pulling on socks and boots, he grabbed a leather jacket off a hanger.

"Did he say what it's about?"

Cyrus fastened his gun harness, and she tailed him out of the closet. From the nightstand, he picked up his Jericho pistol and slipped it into the harness. His gaze took her in from head to toe, and the devilish smile she loved returned to his eyes. "It's not easy to leave you under the best of circumstances, but naked, it's damn near impossible."

She looked down and realized she'd been so distracted she hadn't bothered to grab her robe. "The good news is if you're not gone too long, I'll still be naked, waiting for you in our bed." She nuzzled up against him enticingly.

Hugging her, he kissed the tip of her nose. "Do you think if I tell the Ramsad my wife is waiting naked in bed for me at home, he'll hurry up the meeting?"

"You tell him that your wife requires her husband back before morning. You needn't tell the old fox all of our secrets."

CHAPTER THREE

Monday, February 3, evening
Gilat Junction, North of Tel Aviv, Israel
Mossad headquarters

Cyrus arrived at the security gate of Mossad HQ on his Kawasaki Ninja H2 motorcycle. The motorcycle was one of the fastest in the world, and given the late hour and lack of traffic, he'd pressed the pedal to the metal and made it in record time. The wind in his hair and the exhilaration made up for the fact that Layla had protested his purchase of the powerful beast, considering it a dangerous temptation to fate. But Cyrus had held firm. There were few things Cyrus coveted. The Ninja was one of them.

The Kidon team sniper and arms procurer, Ash, had gotten the bike at a bargain price from one of his arms dealers in Japan. Kidon, or *tip of the spear*, was the secret group of spies and assassins who answered only to the head of Mossad and the prime minister. A year ago, Cyrus had led the team's last mission, a covert operation to prevent a nuclear electromagnetic pulse – or EMP – attack by Hezbollah emanating from the Beqaa Valley. To Cyrus's dismay, when the team had fled Lebanon, they had to leave the Ninja bikes behind. He'd joked about wanting one, never dreaming Ash would make it happen. If their relationship was cemented before, now it was forged in steel. Ash was like a brother to him, and they spent many a happy hour at the shooting range at the *Kidon* team's training facility at Kfar Saba and racing around on their motorcycles.

Inside Mossad HQ, a guard directed him to a conference room on the sixth floor. He smoothed back his wind-tossed black hair and entered. A quick scan of the room brought him eye-to-eye with the Ramsad, Noam Levi, who nodded to him. The wily leader of Mossad was also known as *Hashu'al, The Fox*. Levi's wiry gray hair stood on end, and his sharp eyes scanned everyone in the room. Cyrus, along with everyone else present, understood the Ramsad's unwavering purpose and dedication as protector of Israel. Cyrus, who had a knack for seeing beyond the stoic front of their leader, glimpsed a shadow of worry in the older man's flinty gray gaze. Israel faced a threat.

"I believe we're all accounted for now. Shall we begin?" Said the *menume. Menume* was the title by which the head of Mossad was known.

Cyrus grabbed a cup of coffee and took a seat at the oval table. He acknowledged the other government heads sitting at the table. The deputy of the Atomic desk with its focus on Iran and the Arab nations looked grim. Sitting next to him was the deputy director of the European desk. Uri Klein, the operations, planning, and coordination director, chewed the nub of his pencil. Cyrus found it noteworthy to see Metsada's special operations director, Dov Berman.

Iranian-born and a veteran of Iran's secret intelligence agency, MOIS, Cyrus decided he was here because the Ramsad and prime minister believed the new threat came from the IRI.

The Ramsad took a seat and nodded to his assistant. The large plasma screen on the wall came alive. The video showed a reporter standing in front of a smoldering townhouse with a caption in the upper left-hand corner that read: *Live from South Kensington, London.* Bundled in a trench coat, the journalist reported in an ominous tone. "Neighbors tell us that right before ten p.m., they heard an explosion that rocked the quiet neighborhood of South Kensington. A residence that is said to be the home of Saman Amin, an Iranian diplomat, and his family, exploded in a fiery blast. The London Fire Brigade has been battling the fire since arriving on the scene minutes after the explosion. There is no report yet as to the cause of the blast or who was inside the house when it took place. Authorities believe there are no survivors.

"The Islamic Republic of Iran, known by its acronym of IRI, wasted no time in accusing Israel and the U.S. of causing the deadly inferno, heightening tensions between Iran and the West," the reporter continued. "The Ayatollah issued an immediate condemnation and demanded a thorough investigation into what he called the West's attacks against the Islamic state. He also warned that the West can expect repercussions in kind. Tensions have been high since the U.S. pulled out of the JCPOA deal that began on January 16th of 2016. The current U.S. president had pulled out of the nuclear non-proliferation deal signed by the previous administration and its European allies in May of 2018, leaving the U.K. and the other signatory nations scrambling to preserve the only stop gate on Iran's nuclear aspirations. After the assassination of Iran's second in command, General Qasem Solatani, by a U.S. drone strike last month, one can only wonder what reaction might come out of Tehran after tonight's explosion."

The Ramsad paused the screen, and all eyes turned to him. "I've spoken with U.S. intelligence, and they claim they had nothing to do with this attack," he began. "I can tell you with certainty that we had nothing to do with it. Our best guestimate is that this was an inside job by Iran, an assassination to rid themselves of someone suspected of traitorous behavior. As you know, there has been a rising tide of dissatisfaction within Iran. Protestors have been marching in the streets daily, and the pressure is mounting against the regime. Without question, it would serve the regime to refocus the righteous anger of the people back on Israel and the U.S.

"Neither country can actively instigate war or take a direct hand in regime change. Our interests won't be served by war, and our citizens are not interested in a war. I can't blame them. Our most visible action has been to voice our support for the oppressed Iranian citizens and provide them with arms when possible. Our best hope for regime change is an internal revolution, but we all know how difficult that would be. What we do know is that Iran grows closer to becoming a nuclearized nation every day, and every day they affirm their threat of annihilating Israel."

The Ramsad paused as mutters of agreement echoed around the room.

"Recently, our deep-cover *katsas* inside Iran have contacted a small revolutionary group that operates covertly," he continued. "We're beginning to receive intel from the group. These informers are risking their lives, and if discovered by the Islamic Revolutionary Guard Corps. they would undoubtedly be arrested, tortured, and murdered. However, to date, they have managed to survive, and their resistance is growing."

Cyrus knew that the Islamic Revolutionary Guard Corps provided the foundation for the Ayatollah's power. Since its inception in the 1979 constitution as the protector of the Islamic political system, it had slowly gained control of Iran's economy, politics, and institutions. The IRGC had amassed extensive wealth and would fight to the death to keep the Ayatollah in power. Cyrus also understood, as did the Ramsad, they would launch nuclear missiles against their enemies as well as themselves if they believed their power was diminished.

"We need to disprove the allegations coming out of Iran. The people of Iran need to know their government is snowing them." His gaze swept the faces of each person sitting at the table. "The world community, and particularly the United Nations, cannot hang this assassination on Israel." The Ramsad turned to Cyrus. "Cyrus, did you have any prior contact with Saman Amin when you were in Iran?"

Cyrus stared at the frozen images of the burning house. He scrubbed his face as he remembered the man he'd known. He wondered how Saman factored into the unfolding events. "Yes, I knew him. He and his wife, Tara, had four children. Two boys and two girls. Lovely family, I hope they weren't all in the house during the explosion.

"He worked at MOIS before entering the diplomatic core, and that's where I met him. Of course, in Iran, it is difficult to determine anyone's actual beliefs or politics because of the oppression and the fear of repercussions. The man I knew was a hard-liner and strictly a party follower. He might have changed — some people do in the face of evil. He may have come to realize the writing on the wall, that Iran was suffocating its people and perpetrating unrest and destruction across the Middle East. I haven't seen him in years, so I'll have to brush up on what he was up to since I left Iran."

Noam nodded and then looked around the room. "That's what I want from all of you. Everything there is to know about Saman Amin. We're particularly interested in whether he worked with the counter-revolutionaries in Iran. We need to shed light on the lies coming out of Tehran and keep the flame of discontent alive in the streets. Only good can come from toppling this regime. But remember, to certain factions in this world, Israel is always considered the aggressor, always the culprit. So, we must step delicately. We will be issuing a denial to the allegation that Israel was responsible for the tragedy, but no one is going to believe us given the circumstances."

The Ramsad's attention shifted to the back of the room, and he nodded. One of his aides strode quickly to his side and whispered in his ear. The rest of the attendees at the table began to gather up their belongings, preparing to leave. The Ramsad held up his hand. "Hold on." Everyone froze in place, waiting for the aide to finish his message and for the Ramsad to address them again.

Noam patted the man on the back, nodding his satisfaction. "Good work. Put it up." The aide grabbed the remote and a video loaded. The video displayed a young woman clinging to the bars in front of the Israeli embassy. It was raining, and her hair was a straggly wet mess obscuring her features. She yelled and pounded on the gate. The girl turned several times to look behind her, and the cameras revealed a glimpse of her face. Cyrus had seen that look a thousand times. There was no mistaking what the young woman felt. She was terrified.

The Ramsad picked up the remote and froze the frame. "Minutes ago, this woman, claiming to be the daughter of Saman Amin, arrived at our embassy in London pleading for asylum. We've taken her into protective custody, and we have given her temporary refuge until we sort out who she is and why she came to us instead of the British authorities. She was too traumatized for us to interrogate her tonight, and our people have sedated her. Tomorrow one of our agents in

Germany will fly in to investigate the situation. Cyrus, do you recognize her from the footage?"

"She looks familiar, but I haven't seen any of the Amin children in years. The last time I saw the girls, they were in their teens. If it's Jazmin Amin, the eldest daughter, she'd be in her early twenties now. But I can't make an absolute identification from this footage."

"Tomorrow, we should have more information about her and better photos for your inspection. The girl showing up could be the breakthrough we seek. It seems our mystery girl may hold the key to what happened to Saman Amin and his family." He looked around the room. "In the morning, we will reconvene."

Cyrus studied the frozen face on the screen. Even in her hysterical expression, he could see she was beautiful. Jazmin's mother was a great beauty, and Jazmin, more than any of the other children, resembled her. Looking at the young woman's face triggered a memory.

It was right after Ramadan, and he'd been invited to the Amin home for the break the fast celebration called *Eid ul-Fitr.* The tradition passed down by Mohammad where the gathered guests break the month-long fast of Ramadan with dates. Once the traditional break the fast concludes, it is followed by a sumptuous feast. Most of what occurred on that day he'd forgotten, but one incident returned to him. He and Saman had been deep in conversation when a teenaged girl with thickly lashed hazel eyes interrupted their conversation. She was exquisite, with pouty lips as ripe and pink as a melon, a girl transitioning to womanhood. She'd whispered in her father's ear, her gaze locked on him, and he'd been unable to keep an amused grin off his face. When she finished her message to her father, she'd sauntered away but not without throwing Cyrus a flirtatious look over her shoulder. Saman had laughed dismissively. "Jazmin will be the death of me. The girl is irreverent and strong-willed. She thinks you are as handsome as a movie star and she asked me to arrange her marriage to you. Can you imagine? What am I to do with such a daughter?"

"If we were of another faith, you could confine her to a convent, but that would be a waste of such an irrepressible spirit. It is a shame I'm too old for her. I might have taken her off your hands."

"Frankly, I'd give her to you now if I could and save myself years of torment," said Saman, laughing.

"Tell her I'll wait for her to grow up, but I expect her to be pure as the driven snow. That should keep her in line."

The two men had shared a great deal of laughter over the teenage temptress, and Cyrus had commiserated with Saman on having to bear such a bold daughter. Could the terrified young woman in the video frame possibly be the teenage drama queen who'd singled him out for marriage? Would she remember him? If she did, would she trust him? Tomorrow he'd know more, and he'd confide his past association with the girl to the Ramsad. It might give them a leg up in figuring out why Saman was targeted. If the girl in the video was truly Jazmin, and she remembered him, perhaps she'd trust him enough to confide in him, and they could find out the truth about the explosion and what may have led up to it.

CHAPTER FOUR

Monday, February 3
London, England

The assassin, known to his clients as Gurga, "The Wolf," hopped out of the white van belonging to the Kensington Royal Flower Shop and grabbed his satchel. He glanced around the rooftop parking lot, making sure it was empty. Satisfied he was alone, he swung open the sliding side door of the van. The sickly sweet fragrance of flowers wafted toward him. He shook his head. *Disgusting.* The pungent odor reminded him of the stench of a battlefield and rotting corpses. Ignoring the overpowering smell, he focused on what he did like — killing.

He loved taking a clean shot and seeing the look of surprise or horror on the target's face. Oddly, he hated the sight of blood, was repulsed by most bodily functions and was a germophobe. He never thought about what happened after a kill because he didn't want to know. He thought of himself as a consummate professional and an expert in his field. The expression of any sentimentality was enough to make him gag. It was a skill set, in his opinion, that required a brilliance beyond that of any other job. His line of work allowed no room for error. An error could cost him his life or capture, and that didn't fit in with his plans. As far as footing the blame for murder, the formula was easy — he was merely the instrument of other men's misdeeds and desires.

Reluctantly he observed the dead flower delivery driver, satisfied that he looked peaceful in death. Having rolled down his window when Gurga approached, the helpful fool had sealed his fate. Before he could protest, Gurga grabbed the man's neck and punctured his skin with a tiny needle. The man's eyes bulged, and his mouth opened like a fish out of water, gulping for air. Paralysis. Asphyxiation. Death. All in less than a minute. The dead man slumped sideways, and Gurga had shoved him to the back of the van, climbed in, and drove away.

Job done, Gurga now scanned the interior of the van, making sure he'd left nothing that might identify him. He wore white gloves, a padded baggy white jumpsuit, a white baseball hat, a nose prosthesis, facial hair, and tinted glasses. His work attire varied depending on the hit and his exposure to cameras. London was inundated with cameras. He locked the van, taking the keys with him. No need to make things easy for law enforcement. If he was lucky, it might be days before anyone investigated the abandoned truck. A stickler for details, Gurga had chosen a parking garage miles away from central London. The building had few visitors, was rarely full, and no one parked their cars on the roof.

Working quickly, he removed the jumpsuit. Beneath the billowing folds of the garment, he wore black jeans and a black tee-shirt. He stuffed the jumpsuit, gloves, hat, and shoes into a duffel bag and removed a bottle of antibacterial cleanser to clean his hands. Doffing a black baseball cap, he pulled the brim low over his brow, meeting his mirrored sunglasses before he took the stairwell down to the street. He kept his head down and away from the view of any video cameras. He walked three blocks to another parking structure and got into a black BMW with dark tinted windows. He threw his bag into the backseat and pressed the ignition. The engine roared to life.

He pulled out of the underground parking and smoothly merged into traffic. As he drove, he evaluated his performance, going over each step. It wasn't like him to leave any loose ends, but he'd had no choice. For the most part, the job had gone without a glitch. He'd arrived at the door holding a massive floral arrangement. The maid welcomed him in, and he followed her to the dining room where he placed the flowers on the table. They exchanged inane conversation, and she turned her back to him, escorting him to the front door. By the time she'd taken three steps, he pulled his gun and killed her with a single, silenced bullet to the head. Then he followed the sound of voices and laughter into the kitchen. Easier than shooting fish in a barrel. Pop, pop, pop, one after another, they fell like dominoes. Nine people dead in the blink of an eye. Contract target and family dead. It should have been mission accomplished. But when he tallied up, he realized the older daughter wasn't there. In a matter of minutes, he swept the house but found no one. *Where was she?*

Ever deliberate, calm, and collected, Gurga checked his watch. Time was running out. The bomb he planted in the floral arrangement would detonate in a matter of minutes. He left in frustration, slamming the door to the house. Keeping his head down, he drove away. Two minutes later, the explosion rocked the neighborhood. A glance in the rearview mirror confirmed a tower of fire reaching upward as if clawing the night sky with flaming fingers. The blaze would consume everything, leaving no trace of what had occurred, his favorite way to finish a job.

The police would find no leads, but it angered him that he'd have to let the client know about the snag. It would mean delaying his flight. He was meticulous, and in the ten years he had worked as a contract killer, no law enforcement agency, including the CIA, had anything on him. Skilled in the art of traceless poisons, he was an expert in kills that appeared to be from natural causes. His kills were legendary, spoken about in hushed whispers in every intelligence agency in the world, but none had any clue as to the identity of the man who left a trail of death behind him.

For this reason, he was paid the big bucks — he got the job done. That's why he was irked by a sloppy misstep on his part. He'd surveyed the family for weeks and knew everyone's schedules to a tee.

It was odd that on the night before her wedding, at a celebratory family dinner with the groom's family, the girl had not been there. Something must have delayed her, but what? He wasn't worried, only annoyed that, in all likelihood, he'd have to spend a few extra days in a filthy city finishing the job.

Gurga took pride in his work. In the Arab world, they called him *Al dhiyb,* in Italian *Il Lupo,* in French *Le Loup,* in Spanish *El Lobo.* What they called him didn't matter. Whichever language used resulted in the same outcome — death. There was no way he would let this bitch get away. He'd find and eliminate her. He had the advantage — he knew her friends, her favorite places to eat, everything, while she knew nothing about him. *I'll find you yet, my little rabbit and then I will finish the job.* Nice and clean. The way he liked it.

What he needed now was to wash away the dirt and stench of death. He needed a hot meal and a whiskey. His vulpine features settled into a cruel smile. Then "the wolf" would hunt once more.

CHAPTER FIVE

Tuesday, February 4
London, United Kingdom

Aryeh Stern arrived at Heathrow dressed in business attire. After receiving the call from the Ramsad, he'd scheduled an early flight from Zürich to London. He traveled under one of his many passports, Franz Stark, a German-Swiss banker. After dropping off his bags at the Gore Hotel, walking distance to the Israeli embassy at 2 Palace Green, he grabbed a coffee and a croissant. Then he headed over to the institute, aka Mossad headquarters on a secured floor in the embassy. Once he cleared security, an attaché met him and escorted him upstairs to a door where an armed guard stood sentry.

The woman who opened the door was familiar to him. Beyond her, he saw a female with her back to him resting on a bed.

Softly, he said, "*Shalom* Golda. How are you?" Golda's hair was grayer than he remembered and the lines in her face deeper, but the twinkle in her blue eyes hadn't changed a bit. One other thing hadn't changed about the veteran agent, her black pantsuit always looked as if she'd slept in it.

She turned her cheek up to receive his obligatory kiss. "*Shalom Aryeh.* For an old soldier, I'm doing fine." Golda Sachs was a seasoned Mossad operations coordinator. Her well-earned nickname of Mother Teresa illuminated her saintly demeanor but it didn't begin to reflect her abilities. Golda brought the best out of people, or more important, she got the truth out of them. Her motherly ways could break the most recalcitrant of spies. She operated under the principle that no one wants to disappoint their mother.

The girl, Jazmin Amin, would need understanding and compassion. She'd just lost her fiancé and family. She needed gentle handling by a mother, and Golda was the paragon of motherly virtue.

Golda held her finger up to her lips. She led him outside, closing the door behind her.

"How is she?" Aryeh asked.

"She's in a state of shock, poor dear. Barely communicative. I haven't asked any questions. It's better she should think of me as a comforting ear, someone who asks nothing of her but is there if needed. I don't know if she'll open up to you, but it's imperative we know what she knows. I think the best approach is to tell her we want to help, but we must know why she chose the Israeli embassy to ask for asylum and not the British authorities or the Americans. Why not her own country, Iran? Start there."

"Thanks, Golda. We'll talk when I'm done."

"I'll be in the command center."

The gray-haired veteran of countless operations walked away. Aryeh rapped on the door once more. When there was no answer, he opened it and peeked inside. A petite figure lay curled on the bed, hugging her knees. Her body language told him everything — she was suffering. But the vulnerable way she'd positioned herself with her back to the door communicated she wasn't afraid of anyone at the embassy. It might also mean she'd given up and accepted whatever her fate might be. Aryeh hoped it was the first scenario and not the latter. The latter would mean she'd need psychological counseling, but then again, she probably would require that no matter what.

He spoke gently to her back. "Jazmin, I hope you don't mind my using your first name? My name is Aryeh, and I've been sent by the prime minister of Israel to ask you a few questions. I know how traumatic the last twelve hours have been, but to help you, we need to know what happened."

He waited, but there was no response. "I'm going to bring a chair over to the bed and sit. That way, you and I can get to know each other." He pulled the desk chair to the bed, sat, and studied Jazmin's face. Her eyes were open, and she stared out the window at a gloomy sky where low-hanging gray clouds predicted coming rain. From the blank look on her face, he doubted she saw anything other than what was in her mind. Her eyes were red-rimmed, and tears stained her face. Aryeh could see she was pretty. *Correction, beautiful.* Over her shoulder hung a thick black braid. Unconsciously she twirled the end repetitively around her index finger. Aryeh leaned back and placed his hands on his thighs non-aggressively. After a minute of silence, her hazel eyes turned to him with an impassive stare, seeming to size him up.

He took her eye contact as an invitation to speak. "I know you've been through a horrific ordeal. Of course, I have no idea what you saw or heard, but the fact that you turned to the Israeli government for help tells me you don't trust anyone else. I want to reassure you that you are safe here. We will do everything in our power to help you through this. But we know very little about what happened. Is there anything you can tell us so that we can figure out how best to help you?"

"Cyrus Hassani," she said barely above a whisper. "I will speak only to Cyrus Hassani."

"Cyrus? I know him very well. We've worked together, and I consider him a good friend. How do you know him?"

"My father told me if anything terrible happened, I was to trust no one but Cyrus." She swallowed visibly and nodded as if reassuring herself. "Cyrus will know what must be done."

"Okay, let me see what I can do. You understand this might take a few days?"

Her gaze returned to the window. "Time means nothing to me anymore. I have nothing. No one. There is nothing left to me." Tears flowed down her cheeks like rain.

"In the meantime, is there anything I can do for you? Anything that might bring you comfort?"

She turned her gaze back to him, her teary eyes glowing with fire. "Expose and bring death to whoever murdered my family."

CHAPTER SIX

Tuesday, February 4
Tehran, Islamic Republic of Iran
Azadi Square

Will we ever be free?

Ibrahim Nassiri held tight to Shira Darbandi's hand. The press of the crowd felt protective as they marched side-by-side with thousands of protestors down Azadi Avenue toward the giant square surrounded by vast gardens. The leafless trees that bloomed in a riot of colors from spring to autumn lay dormant in the winter cold. Standing sentry in the distance was the white marble monument once known as the Shahyad Tower. Built by the shah, who'd been ousted from power and fled Iran during the Islamic Revolution. Mohammad Reza Pahlavi's fall had ended a dynasty that had ruled over Persia for seventy-five years.

The original name and purpose of the monument had long ago been obfuscated by the Ayatollah when he seized power in 1979 and renamed it the Azadi Tower. The one hundred forty-eight-foot white marble sculpture had been built to pay homage and to express the bonds between the classical civilization of Persia and the future accomplishments of a modern Iran. To Ibrahim and many of Iran's oppressed, it represented the loss of freedom and the harsh reality of a tyrannical state.

Since the fall of the shah, the people of Iran had been ruled by the Ayatollahs and their revolutionary guards. For years, the resistance against the totalitarian regime had been growing. The recent protests had initially erupted in reaction to hikes in gasoline prices, but the people's discontent ran far deeper. Ibrahim, one of the organizers of the protest, walked among the shouting dissidents with their banners raised, calling for the end of the oppressive regime. Ibrahim knew simultaneous marches were taking place in Alborz, Kurdistan, Zanjan, and in more than thirty provinces where massive unrest had ignited protests across the country. In every instance, lethal force was used against the protestors, and everyone knew their lives were at risk. But out of tyranny, heroes are born. Normal people who under other circumstances would never step forward to resist and fight had begun to stand up to oppression. In every revolution, there are those who find their true calling and risk everything to bring light out of the darkness. Knowing they might die so that others may live a better life.

Ibrahim linked his arm with his girlfriend, Shira's. Looking around him, he could see the determination on the faces of the fellow protestors. The resistance against the regime was growing regardless of the regime's efforts to shut it down. Young and old alike stood fast in their demands for political freedom, but it was the women, like his beloved Shira, who were igniting the fires of change. Daring to dance in the streets and refusing to back down, even in the face of ruthless reprisals. Videos of Irani women dancing in the streets, expressing their personal freedom, had gone viral over the internet and had fired a storm of sympathy from around the world.

The Supreme Leader Ali Khamenei had issued statements condemning the protestors as "villains" and ordering his forces to crush the demonstrators by any means. The revolutionary guard had posted snipers on rooftops, randomly shooting into the crowds, but nothing could stop the surge of humanity as more and more citizens took to the streets.

Everything had shut down. Not a single business dared open its doors. Whether they marched in protest or sympathy didn't matter. It mattered that the peaceful demonstrations of Iran's citizens brought the country to a halt.

The marchers surged forward until they reached an area where two giant flags lay on the ground, the United States Stars and Stripes and the Israeli Shield of David. Ibrahim grabbed his phone and recorded the remarkable sight. In the past, the flags of the two countries, labeled the "Great Satans" and hated by the Islamic regime, would have conjured up anger, and the enemy flags would be burned or shredded, at the very least stomped underfoot. But with deference and respect, the throngs of marchers split in two and walked around the flags. This small action required no commentary — it spoke louder than the shouts of "death to the dictator," and "our enemy is right here — they lie when they say it's America." Ibrahim uploaded the extraordinary video to the secure link his new friend had given him.

Only moments before, Ibrahim had texted images of the immense crowds to the invisible eye in the sky. He wasn't sure whether it was an American or Israeli satellite that monitored from above. Ibrahim's contact also had given him a satellite phone and a pistol. When Ibrahim questioned him, the man had told him it was better if he did not ask. The only important thing was getting the truth out and encouraging peaceful demonstrations. Frankly, Ibrahim didn't care so long as the world could see how many of the people in Iran wanted their political and spiritual freedom and were ready to fight for it.

Shira punched in numbers on her cell phone and shook her head. "They've shut down the phones. Like last time."

"It's okay. We'll be fine. The satellite phone is working. I uploaded images." He looked around at the crowds. "There must be a hundred thousand people marching. The world will see we mean business."

"Believe me," she shouted above the din, "they're going to try and shut us down. It's going to get bloody." For too long, the people of Iran had been controlled by a fanatical religious theocracy that quashed individual rights and policed every aspect of their lives. The "Green Movement" of 2009 had been silenced and gone underground. Now because of economic grievances, environmental degradation, and the endless sanctions that crippled the economy, the people were rising again. What began as complaints of shortages were now being directed against the regime itself, but Ibrahim knew that if threatened, the regime would do whatever it took to stop them.

It was images like those uploaded by Ibrahim that the government did its best to censor. The regime used satellite jamming and web filters. They blocked any news from getting in or out, but citizens found ways to circumvent the controls and send out messages of resistance and a call for change.

The regime's most recent tactic was shutting down the phones and the internet. Naturally, the government denied their culpability, but the word spread and Amnesty International was holding the regime's feet to the fire for their atrocities. The world was watching every move made by the belligerent mullahs. The will of the people would not be denied, and regardless of the government's draconian efforts to suppress the truth, bits and pieces were finding their way out and onto social media.

Shira squeezed his arm and gestured at the arrival of the Basijis, the voluntary militia guards on their motorbikes, trying to divide the crowd. They swung batons as they drove through the marchers smashing heads, forcing the unarmed protestors into smaller groups so that they could better control them. Ibrahim and Shira couldn't see them from their vantage point, but Ibrahim knew they were surrounded by armed revolutionary guards who spurred the Basijis to further aggression. In response, the voices of the brave rose even louder, chanting "Death to the Dictator" and "We will die, we will die, we will take back Iran."

As the cries grew louder, grenades were thrown into the crowd, and billowing clouds of smoke engulfed them. Ibrahim pulled his scarf up around his nose and eyes, as did Shira. Around them, the cries and screams rose to a deafening pitch, but the crowd stood firm and pressed forward. Ibrahim held fast to Shira's arm as she buried her face in his coat. The Basijis would use any means to disperse protestors. They were violent and fanatical in their support for the regime. But a hundred thousand or more people weren't so easily bullied.

Ibrahim shouted above the roar. "We need to get out of here before they close in and start arresting. We can't afford to be caught and interrogated." He knew many of the stalwarts would remain into the evening, lighting trash cans on fire and chanting anti-government slogans. There would be arrests, beatings, and even deaths, but he and Shira needed to live to fight another day.

Shira nodded. He took her hand and pulled her against the tide of marchers. They needed to get back to the university. It was nearly time for Ibrahim's secure VPN call with his uncle in London, and he didn't want to miss it. Ibrahim and his uncle Saman, a diplomat in London, used a virtual private network for their weekly communications. Their phone conversations were securely encrypted through a private server.

Saman, a diplomat assigned to the London embassy, had confided in Ibrahim his fears for the future of Iran. He admitted his realization that the government he'd supported his entire life was corrupt and self-aggrandizing, putting its survival above the will of the people. The straw that broke the camel's back occurred when he'd seen the stockpiling of hundreds of solid-fuel rockets and ballistic missiles buried deep within tunnels in the mountains. These "missile cities" nearly two thousand feet below the earth could no longer be labeled a deterrent — they were the spearheads of an apocalypse. Saman had told Ibrahim that uranium gases were being enriched in the centrifuges at Fordow and other sites in direct violation of the ban and treaty signed in 2015 by Iran and the JCPA.

Fordow had resumed processing and began again to churn out enriched uranium. And Fordow was only one of several facilities. No longer able to look away, he'd begun working with Ibrahim to upend the regime and bring about what he hoped would be a peaceful change of power. Ibrahim appreciated his uncle's support, but he held no illusions. He believed the regime would rather destroy the world than relinquish its control. Ibrahim knew the ultimate battle was coming.

IT TOOK Shira and Ibrahim an hour to reach the outskirts of the crowds and the University of Isfahan. Ibrahim, a professor, taught graduate courses in nuclear physics and worked on government projects on the side. His apartment was but a few blocks from the university.

Ibrahim closed and locked the door and turned on the television. Shira shed her coat. "I'll make us some tea."

Ibrahim sat on the couch and laid his phone on the table as he waited for his uncle's call. Half-heartedly he watched the television. Only broadcasts permitted by the government came from state-run television, mostly propaganda. Still, sometimes he could glean something from what was said, or left unsaid, by the government-controlled commentators. Shira carried in a tray and joined him on the couch. She poured the tea and handed him a cup. Steam rose and clouded his glasses when he sipped. He took them off and pinched the bridge of his nose.

"What is it, *aziz-am?*" She leaned in and kissed his cheek.

"I'm tired, that's all." Drying the lenses with the coattail of his shirt, he slipped them back on and checked his watch. His uncle was always precise about calling, never a minute late. Something was wrong. He stared at the talking head on the screen. The image changed to a burning building. He grabbed the remote and turned up the sound. "It can't be true —" his words were halted by choking sobs. "Please say it's not true."

Shira grabbed his face, forcing him to look her in the eyes. "What is it, Ibrahim, tell me what can't be true?"

Ibrahim buried his face in her hair. "They've killed him, my uncle Saman, Tara, the whole family. They're blaming it on Israel and the U.S., but I know it's them. Saman must have been compromised."

"Are we in danger?"

"I don't know." He dragged his fingers through his dark hair and shook his head. "I don't know."

"We need to get out of here. I'm not going to sit here waiting for them to break through the door and murder us. If they know about your uncle, then they know about you, too. My parents have an apartment in Astara. It's quiet in the winter. We can go there and hide out until we have a better grasp of what's going on."

Panic brought on confusion — it was impossible to think. "That's nearly a seven-hour drive from here," Ibrahim rasped.

"You have any better ideas? I will not be raped and tortured by those bastards, Ibrahim."

Ibrahim stared at the screen, anguish coursing through his soul. "No. You're right. We must leave. We'll pack up and stop at your place and grab your passport. We need to take everything that ties us to the movement. The flash drives and computers. Leave nothing behind."

They decided Shira's car would be the least conspicuous. If the authorities searched for them, they'd be looking for him, and his license plate would be on the stop and detain list. They loaded up Shira's Samand LX and were buckling their seatbelts when they heard tires screeching and saw flashing lights coming toward them.

"Down!" Ibrahim shoved Shira's head down and dived over her, so they were invisible through the car's windows. Three cars flew past and made the turn into the apartment complex where Ibrahim lived. Ibrahim sat up and peeked behind him. "It's good you parked on the street."

Shira inched up and followed his gaze to the parking lot in time to see a group of men run into the building. "Do you think they're looking for you?"

"I can't imagine who else they'd be after. The sooner we're out of Tehran, the better. Come on, let's get going."

Shira pulled out from the row of cars on the street and drove away. "Ibrahim, I think it's time for us to leave Iran. I don't want to die here."

Ibrahim caressed the back of her head. "I know, *aziz-am*. We'll find a way. I won't let anything happen to you." The statement was meant to reassure Shira, but the truth was he had no idea how he could guarantee her safety. If the authorities were looking for him, she would be in immense danger as well. If the photos on the flash drives were discovered, he and Shira would be strung up by a crane as traitors in a public hanging. Their deaths would send a clear message to those who opposed the theocratic regime. The world needed to see the incontrovertible evidence tucked into his knapsack. "The flash drive is our ticket out of Iran. The Israelis and the Americans will help us." He began texting on the safe phone he'd received from Kaspar. *We are compromised. Leaving Tehran. Will connect when we're situated. Afraid to say more. We need your help!* Ibrahim stared at the lit screen, willing

Kaspar to respond. He expelled a sigh of relief when a reply appeared. *Get to safety & reach out. The phone I gave you is safe & encrypted. I will begin preparations. Do not, I repeat, do not use any other device other than this phone. Get rid of your cell phones & destroy the SIM cards. Speak to no one else. Trust no one. K*

CHAPTER SEVEN

Tuesday, February 4
London, United Kingdom

Gurga poured himself a tumbler of scotch and returned the bottle of Balvenie 30 to the table where it shared space with his bomb-making chemicals. He was haggard and dog-tired, but his efforts had paid off — he'd located his target. He rolled the glass between his hands and faced the windows, his gaze drawn across the river Thames to Westminster Bridge, the clock tower of Big Ben, and the buildings of Parliament. The loft apartment he'd rented was in an old factory converted to apartments in the area referred to as the South Bank. Besides its spectacular views, the apartment took up the whole upper floor of the building, making it both private and secure.

Gurga sipped his scotch and returned to his workstation, which comprised three large computer monitors, each dedicated to a different task. It had taken most of the night, but he'd hacked into London's CCTV system and accessed London's half-million cameras. London was the most surveilled city in Europe. After narrowing his search to those cameras covering the area around the Amin house, he'd begun the monotonous task of watching the footage. Using the new facial recognition system that the London police had installed, Gurga had hacked in and loaded a photo of Jazmin Amin. He'd picked up video footage of the girl a block from the house. He froze the frame, taking a break to pour another drink. Taking a deep sip, he hit play and set the speed to slow-motion. Frame by frame, the video inched forward, and he watched her run away from the back of the townhouse. The time-stamp indicated minutes after the fiery explosion rocked the neighborhood.

He tapped his fingers nervously on the keyboard as he watched her make her way down the street. She looked to be crying. Her hands were in constant motion, wiping at her eyes, and her body shook as if it were riddled with shudders. He played the video back and watched it again. There was no question in his mind. She must have seen what happened at the house. That would explain the emotional display playing out before the cameras.

As she crossed street after street, the CCTV lenses blurred from the rain that had begun to come down in sheets. The action switched from camera to camera, changing angles, first her front, then her back, and then seamlessly the image jumped to the next camera. Occasionally she passed someone on the sidewalk, but she turned away, seeming to avoid eye contact. Cabs whisked by, but she made no effort to hail one.

The possibilities rampaged through his mind. How had he missed her? Where in the house had she hidden? He replayed the scene over again in his mind. He'd walked quickly from the dining room into the kitchen and fired before anyone could react. The windows in the kitchen had no curtains. The kitchen was at the rear of the house and opened to the patio and backyard. It was cold out, but he knew the girl snuck an occasional cigarette. Had she been outside having a smoke at the exact moment he entered the kitchen and shot everyone? She would have seen everything. It would have been impossible to see her in the dark, but she would have seen him clear as day.

Gurga downed the rest of the scotch and banged the glass on the table. If Jazmin Amin had witnessed the killings and could ID him, she now posed a threat to his existence. What had been just another assignment now had become personal. Finding and killing her was no longer only a part of the job. He had to eliminate her to save his own skin.

He could feel his heart pound in his chest as the girl began to run. Where was she going? He'd hoped her destination would be the Iranian embassy, which would have wrapped things up tidily. Instead, his hopes sank when she grabbed hold of the black fence surrounding a Georgian-style brick residence formerly owned by the novelist William Makepeace Thackery. He knew the building — it was the Israeli embassy. Why the hell would an Iranian national seek safety with the Israelis? It didn't make sense.

He watched as the gates opened, and Jazmin collapsed into the arms of a security guard. Then he lost sight of her. The drenching rain made it impossible to see much beyond the gate. Gurga rubbed the dark stubble on his face. Killing her while under the protection of the Israelis would not be easy. But there was no question, killing her was what he was going to do. Tomorrow he'd arrange for surveillance on the embassy. The Israelis wouldn't be able to keep her under wraps for long. London police and British intelligence would figure out where she was, as he had. Since the attack happened on British soil, they'd be fevered up to solve the crime. No, they'd have to move her, and when they did, he would be ready to make his move.

He took one more perusal of the screen where the live feed from the security cameras he'd installed around his apartment building displayed. Everything appeared quiet. He needed to grab a few hours of sleep, and then he'd put everything in place. Gurga dreaded the call he had to make to the client, but he'd already decided to refund the client half the fee. He would take responsibility to fix his own error without charge. Such was business. Sometimes the unforeseen came into play, and adjustments were required. After he dispensed with the girl and completed the job, he'd take a break. His blunder demanded that he regroup, take some time away from the action, and lay low at his island retreat in Malta. But first, he would destroy Jazmin Amin for his own safety.

CHAPTER EIGHT

Tuesday, February 4
Tel Aviv, Israel

"Come, there's somewhere I need to go, and I want you with me." The Ramsad led Cyrus down a hallway of unmarked doors to the elevators. In front of Mossad HQ, an armored car idled. The two men got in, and the vehicle drove off.

The sun shone brightly on the Holy Land. It was the perfect day for a picnic or a day at the beach, but Cyrus didn't expect to experience either of those activities on this day. Over the last year, he'd learned to read the mind of Noam Levi better than most. The serious intent carved into the Ramsad's face meant a storm was brewing. Cyrus wondered if anything in London had changed that he wasn't aware of. Noam was pensive, which meant his boss needed to make some choices. Cyrus couldn't imagine the Ramsad seeking his advice. No, likely, this was a learning expedition meant for him. The Ramsad wanted to convey important information that would affect Cyrus's response to what the Ramsad had in mind. Cyrus shifted in his seat, preparing to be surprised, as was often the case when the wily old fox took an indirect approach.

"When I need to recharge my batteries, this is where I go." It was the only comment from the grizzled warrior. Noam settled into silence, his gaze fixed out the dark tinted window.

Cyrus had heard the whispers from those who'd lived through other *menumes*. The current leader of Israel's most secret intelligence agency was a serious student of military and intelligence history. Stored within his mind were the details of every past mission ever undertaken by Mossad. Mossad was his life. He lived, breathed, and dedicated himself to keeping his people and his country safe. The Fox was always a step ahead of his enemies. He was a chess master, a strategist who never tired of the game. The only thing the Ramsad understood was winning. What it cost him, Cyrus couldn't say, but he didn't envy the older man's position.

Cyrus was curious to know where they were going but felt no compunction about pressing the issue. Thirteen minutes later, they arrived at a group of innocuous buildings not far from the Mossad training center where Cyrus had learned to become an agent so many years ago. Cyrus was grateful to Noam and thankful that Mossad had orchestrated the phony deaths of his mother and sister to remove them from harm's way.

To the eyes of the Iranian regime, Cyrus's only remaining family members had been killed in a boating accident when their catamaran capsized during a holiday at the Caspian Sea. As Cyrus returned to Iran from Paris to attend the funerals of his mother and sister, Mossad had safely transported the women to a kibbutz in Israel.

For his part, Cyrus had returned to France after the funeral, where for the next two years, he'd commuted undercover from Paris to Israel for his training. Mossad had arranged a counterpart to take his place at the Sorbonne while he was away on training. The doppelganger attended classes for him and forwarded notes and assignments. Cyrus's workload had been immense. Besides his training with Mossad and learning Hebrew, he had to prepare his dissertation in nuclear physics for his doctorate. Fortunately, he'd been blessed with an eidetic memory, which explained his ability to absorb not only his doctorate workload in nuclear physics but the immense amount of information he would need to serve Mossad. It was also why he was fluent in five languages. This unique ability had helped him rise through the ranks at Mossad. It had also saved his neck on more than one occasion.

Cyrus's mother and sister had remained in the kibbutz until last year, when Ester married an artist in Tzfat. Cyrus's mother, Aster, now lived with Ester and Aaron in the ancient mystical city above Galilee. Aaron Goshen was a good man. Cyrus had him thoroughly vetted and was relieved that he was what he presented to be, a talented artist and a caring husband and son-in-law. Layla was thrilled to have an artist in the family, and Cyrus was happy that his mother and sister would live a relatively normal life and find peace once more. He looked forward to the day when he wouldn't have to see them in short, hurried spurts, and they could come to stay with him, Layla, and Cerise for a lengthy visit.

It seemed such a long time ago, yet only eleven years had passed. Everything he'd done since then remained focused on keeping Iran from becoming a nuclear power. Keeping weapons of mass destruction out of the hands of religious fanatics was his primary mission. He was a trained killer who prayed for the day when there would be no need for killers like him to exist. Unfortunately, the world he lived in held no hope for such dreams.

Their car made a turn, and Cyrus tucked his memories away and paid attention to where he was. Their driver cruised slowly up the road, passing the security check with a salute, and parked the car in a black-topped parking lot. The driver got out first and eagle-eyed the perimeter. Then he opened Noam's door, and the Ramsad exited. Cyrus got out on the other side and looked about. In an open area under the shade of eucalyptus trees, a group of old men played chess and sat together talking. Their laughter carried on the breeze to Noam and Cyrus as they walked toward one of the buildings.

One of the old men caught Cyrus's eye, and they exchanged a nod of greeting. Cyrus sensed the man was a retired agent. It crossed Cyrus's mind that someday he might be sitting in the shade of a tree reliving the escapades of his Mossad career. Then he remembered that everything about his career was top-secret. He'd be long dead before any of his exploits would ever become public knowledge.

By now, he'd figured out where he was — the Israel Intelligence Heritage and Commemoration Center. Oddly, he'd never been here before. For years, the families of agents had pressed for something to be built where they could visit and pay tribute to their fallen loved ones. After constant pressure and outcries from the families, the only memorial dedicated to those who'd fallen in the service of Israel's intelligence community opened in 1985. From what Cyrus could tell, Noam Levi was a regular visitor. Everyone they encountered greeted him as though he were another old friend and fellow agent.

The memorial was unlike any Cyrus had ever seen. Sunlight cascaded down through the skylights, illuminating the walls in a golden glow. Noam led him through the labyrinth of angularly cut sandstone blocks to the core, where five alcoves dedicated to each era in the nation's intelligence history were displayed. Inside the maze, Noam paused and placed his hand on a wall of incised names.

When he spoke, it was not the impatient, raspy, commanding voice of the man who expected his minions to jump when he asked something of them. Instead came a subdued, gentle tone of reverence, barely above a whisper. "These are the names, dates of birth, and dates of death of our unsung heroes — the men and women who gave their lives in service to our country. They are the shadows that have kept us safe. I knew many of them personally. I sent them on dangerous missions from which they never returned. Others were colleagues I worked with shoulder-to-shoulder many years ago. I come here to pray for guidance. These names remind me of the great responsibility that I have to the people of Israel and to the memories of those who fought so bravely. I thought it fitting that you should join me today before I ask you to tackle your next assignment."

"Sir, everyone under your command knows that you have our backs. You ask none of us to do what you would not do yourself. We place our faith and our lives in your capable hands," said Cyrus. "Whatever you have in mind, I will carefully consider." Cyrus placed his hands reverently on the wall beside Noam's. "Each of these men and women knew what was at stake, as I do."

"It grieves me," said the Ramsad, "that so many names are missing from these walls because their identities must be kept secret for national security reasons or to protect those agents still living and undercover. But we cannot forget them, Cyrus. Never."

Cyrus smiled. "I suppose if I were to die, I'd fit in the category of the unmentionable."

"Unfortunately, too many know who you are as it is. Including the Iranians. That is why I'm hesitant to send you on this mission."

Cyrus inclined his head and whispered. "Is it safe to talk here?"

"When I'm here, no one is allowed inside. The only ears that can hear us are the ghosts of the dead. They never betrayed us in life — they certainly will not in death."

Cyrus nodded. "I'm prepared and willing to accept whatever challenge you have for me."

"London. I'm sending you to London. I've been weighing this decision heavily, but I can find no other alternative."

"Is it Saman's daughter?"

"She has asked for you. Claims her father insisted if something ever happened to him, she could trust only you. We have reason to believe Saman had turned against the Iranian regime. We think he gathered inflammatory material and proof of Iran's ongoing nuclear and ballistic missile build-up. We hope he had proof of the locations of those missiles and nuclear centrifuges. We've suspected for some time that Iran is processing uranium at new facilities. It's possible the evidence burned in the fire but Saman may have stored it at a safe location. The daughter may know where."

"You want me to gain her trust and find the evidence?"

"Exactly. We have no clue as of yet on the assassin's identity. He is out there and will most assuredly be hunting her. If this is what we think it is, the assassin most likely already knows her location and will strike at the first opportunity to eliminate her and the threat she poses."

"Has she said anything so far?"

"She wants vengeance. She's already expressed that to Aryeh. She wants the killer and those that control him exposed and destroyed. We can help her with that. Aryeh is in London waiting to fill you in on everything we know to date."

"I don't see anything about this mission that we can't resolve. What are your concerns, sir?"

"Beside the fact that there is a *fatwa* on you and there would be nothing better than getting you in the open, there's a problem beyond what I've told you, Cyrus."

"Sir, whatever issues arise, we will overcome them."

"There's a professor in Tehran who's been a credible source for us and is one of the organizers of the underground freedom fighters in Iran." Noam's fingers traced a name on the wall. "The professor has gone missing, and his apartment was ransacked and raided. He managed to get away with his girlfriend, and they're on the run from the IRGC."

The past was never far away. Memories of being on the run in Iran flooded Cyrus. Six years had passed, and yet it still felt like yesterday when he and Layla were desperately trying to find a way out of Iran. Cyrus was a trained operative and a deadly spy trained by both the IRGC and Mossad, but this man was a professor, hardly capable of eluding his hunters. "What do you have in mind?"

"The young man's name is Ibrahim Nassiri, and he's the nephew of Saman Amin."

"He's a smoking gun. I'd say his ass is in a heap of trouble." Cyrus studied the Ramsad's face. "He factors into what happened to Saman doesn't he? They were working together."

Noam nodded. "We suspect so, but we must find out for certain. The regime may have been tailing Ibrahim and figured out the connection. Ibrahim may have unwittingly compromised Saman. Or perhaps Saman had compromised himself, and now Ibrahim and his girlfriend are in danger. Whatever is going on, we need to find out fast. Iran is blaming Israel and the U.S. for Saman's death. We must prove without a doubt that we were not involved. I believe Iran ordered the execution of Saman and his family. Ibrahim is a nuclear physicist and may have crucial evidence against the regime. I want to rescue him and his girlfriend and get them out of Iran. I certainly can't send you back there, so we need another option. Aryeh speaks Arabic but doesn't speak Farsi. We must find someone who can pass as an Iranian and send him or her into the hornet's nest. Put all of your resources on this — find me the man or woman for this mission."

"If I have to go, then I will. Disguised, I can pull this off. There is no one more suited than I."

"I knew you would say this, but you are my last resort. Now, what are you going to do about Layla? If we send you to London, Layla needs to go with you. It would be best for you to go as members of our diplomatic corps. Her presence will give the appearance of normalcy to your mission. Cerise must remain here. It would be too disruptive for her and too dangerous."

Cyrus rubbed the back of his neck. It was impossible to predict Layla's reaction to this change in their lives. Since her kidnapping and rescue, she'd been reluctant about leaving Cerise even for a few hours. However, her time at the IDF training facility had seemed to empower her with confidence and independence. Cerise would be safe with Dina and Morris, Layla's grandparents. "I'll talk to her tonight and test the waters. I think it would be good for her to travel to London. She's always expressing her desire for us to travel someday. Given Layla's own experiences in the past few years, she might be able to help Jazmin, too. I'll frame it to her as a working holiday."

"I leave it in your hands, Cyrus. I would also suggest that Cerise, Dina, and Morris move into the safehouse in Ramat Hasharon. Considering what happened last time when you were in Beirut, I'd rather not tempt fate."

"I think that will go a long way in convincing Layla."

"Excellent. Then we're all on the same page, but we need to move quickly. Let's get back to the Institute. There is much to do. I want you in London yesterday." They strode through the rest of the maze in silence. One alcove displayed no names on the walls. Instead, the words etched into the stone read, *Dedicated to the memory of those from whom the fog cannot yet be lifted and whose names cannot yet be revealed.*

Cyrus held no fear or foreboding of the future. He believed his abilities would keep him safe, but even the best of the best was capable of error, a wrong decision that might cost their lives. So, it was understandable that a fleeting thought breezed through his consciousness. *Will I become one of the unnamed?* In the equation of his work, Layla was his greatest vulnerability. London was a city crawling with terrorists, arms dealers, and criminal elements willing to ignite the powder keg and wreak death and mayhem. Keeping two women safe would be a test of his abilities.

Layla was always quick to remind him that he loved the danger, the pulse-driving thrill of dodging bullets. He never denied it. At his core, it was who he was, but he loved his wife and child more than anything in this world, and keeping them safe was the primary reason for what he did. The regime in Iran posed the greatest threat to Israel and the world, and he would do whatever it took to see their nuclear aspirations thwarted. The general who'd sought his destruction was dead, but others were ready to take his place. Tehran had not forgotten him.

CHAPTER NINE

Friday, February 7
London, United Kingdom,

As the town car navigated the crowded streets of London, Layla's thoughts returned to the last time she'd been in the U.K. It was during a trip overseas with her father, the summer after her mother died. Her father had decided to visit his family in Edinburgh. She was turning thirteen, and both she and her father were heartbroken and mourning the loss of Rebecca, who'd been ravaged by breast cancer. A shroud of sadness and despair had blanketed her world with the belief that she'd never be happy again. They'd been forced to lay over at Heathrow in a storm after a frightening flight from Boston, full of turbulence. After hours of waiting for the storm to pass, she and her father had finally boarded their connection to Edinburgh.

What should have been a memorable meeting with her paternal grandparents had turned into a nightmare. Her father's parents were strict in their Calvinist beliefs, and Layla had discovered that her father and his parents mixed no better than oil and water together. The elderly couple had meant well, but they'd been relentless in their efforts to convert her to their Protestant beliefs. Perhaps she should have realized the reason her father had moved across the world to study at Harvard, and in the ensuing years, never returned.

Aleck and his parents had grown apart until no common ground existed that could breach the gap and lead to any closeness. Like most scientists, Aleck was an agnostic, or rather he had been until he'd found comfort in prayer after Layla was kidnapped by Quds Force terrorists in New York. Aleck had no use for organized religion but found praying to God had helped him manage his fears of losing his child.

After the death of her mother, Layla needed a loving cocoon to lose herself in, but her grandparents were not demonstrative with their affections. Instead of finding a thread of love to sew into a garment that would carry her through the storm of loss, she found only her grandparents' resentment that their son was lost to them and that their granddaughter was doomed to end up in hell.

It was a difficult trip that failed to ease the grief both Layla and Aleck suffered. The elderly couple could not deal with a teenage girl outside their faith or a son who'd abandoned their religion. The best part of the trip occurred when she and Aleck left to spend a week traveling around Scotland. They'd visited Edinburgh Castle, and Layla had been swept away by the story of the *Lia Fail*, the Stone of Destiny, an ancient relic of sandstone used to crown Scottish Kings for more than a thousand years.

She knew little about her Scottish heritage as Aleck had adopted the traditions of his wife and her Jewish heritage. The trip through the Scottish Highlands did succeed in creating an unbreakable bond between father and daughter. By the time they arrived in London, the healing process had begun, and Layla and Aleck enjoyed the best of London, including numerous nights at West End theatres. Layla had fallen in love with Agatha Christie's *The Mousetrap*, the longest-running stage performance in history. She'd begged her father to take her three nights in a row. She'd come away from that trip with an inordinate fondness for theater and Indian cuisine. Father and daughter found a respect and love for each other that would forever be indivisible.

Now she was back in London, married and a mother, but working undercover for her Mossad agent husband's current mission. The town car pulled up to a mid-terraced Regency-style home north of Kensington High Street on tree-lined Campden Hill Road. Layla stared up at the curved bow windows and smiled. The Ramsad had made sure that she would be living in stylish comfort. "It's a charming street," she said as she got out of the car.

"Only the best for you, darling." Cyrus grabbed a suitcase and his briefcase and followed her up the steps. The door swung open, and the agent greeted them. "Mr. and Mrs. Benveniste, it's a pleasure to meet you. Tom Clancy at your service." Benveniste was the surname the Mossad travel department had assigned to the wealthy builder from Malaga, Spain, and his American-born wife, Serena. They'd rented a flat for a month in London to celebrate their first anniversary.

Cyrus's Spanish accent was spot on, "Call me, Alphonse, Tom, the pleasure is all mine. This is my wife, Serena."

Everyone shook hands, and Tom grabbed the suitcase out of Cyrus's hands and led them inside. "I've stocked the refrigerator and wine cellar so you can take your time settling in." The driver followed them in with the rest of the luggage, and Tom directed him to the upper floor and bedroom, then took them on a tour of the flat.

After the driver and agent had left, Cyrus went to the bar, opened a bottle of Bordeaux wine, and poured them each a glass. Layla sat in the living room in front of the green marble fireplace on a purple velvet sofa and put her feet up on the oak coffee table. "I love everything about this place. Especially the charming patio and garden. I'm so excited to finally get a chance to travel with my husband."

"Sí mi amor, es muy lindo." Cyrus winked, continuing with his sexy Spanish accent. He sat next to her, draping his arm around her shoulders and kissing her temple. "It's going to take me some time to get used to this new version of my wife, though."

She ran her fingers through the short strands of bleached blonde hair tipped with strawberry color on the upright spiked barbs. It was a striking but necessary change to her appearance. "You like it, don't you?"

"Yes, it reminds me of Cass, who is definitely one hot cookie." Layla pictured the FBI agent with whom Cyrus had worked to stop a nuclear threat at Three Mile Island and who helped rescue her from the Quds Force terrorist kidnappers nearly a year and a half ago. She shuddered, shaking off the shadow of shackles and pain at the hands of her kidnappers. Her PTSD could have overwhelmed her if she had not received months of therapy. Cass Saladino was an itty-bitty powerhouse and a martial arts expert. The FBI agent had inspired her to learn self-defense. After her rescue, Layla vowed to herself that she would never be a victim again.

"Not to mention, a tough cookie who can defend herself against any male adversary," Layla added. "She really is an inspiration. That woman doesn't take crap from anyone. It's no wonder David is so besotted with her."

"Yeah, Cass is something else, and David Weiss's adoration of her is no secret. But hey, don't I look like a doting husband?" He sipped his wine.

She patted his cheek and pursed her lips. "Yes, you are, and that's why I love you so much."

"And don't you forget it." He pulled her closer. "Okay, so tomorrow morning, I'll head out early to the embassy, and I'll be there most of the day. But tonight, *eshgham,* I'm all yours. What say you to ordering Indian food and making love to our heart's content? It's been so long since we were truly alone. I have this aching desire to show you how much you're worshipped."

She cupped his cheek with her hand. "Sounds like an offer I can't refuse. Besides, who could decline an invitation from such a handsome Spaniard? But aren't you in the least bit worried that I'll be cheating on my husband?" Layla couldn't help but tease the man who no longer resembled the man she'd married with his new look of a goatee, mustache, and dark brown eyes.

"While the cat's away, the mice will play. A little spice is good for a marriage."

She laughed. "So, you're in favor of a now-and-again affair outside of matrimonial bliss?"

"Only if you wish to be responsible for the death of another."

Layla snuggled closer into Cyrus's embrace. This teasing, sexy repartee that had marked their relationship from the beginning had been missing lately. It was understandable, considering all the tragic events they'd endured the past few months. Surviving a bus bombing that led to a miscarriage had torn her apart, but she was beginning to return to her usual self. Flirting with her husband was a sign that she was mending. Cyrus's being in the field in London didn't seem to her to be nearly as dangerous as Tehran or Beirut. It almost felt like a second honeymoon. Who knew, maybe she'd become pregnant again?

"That's the problem with being married to a deadly assassin. A girl can't have any fun," she said with a pout.

"Aah, but the advantages of having a tireless and creative lover can add such adventure and excitement to the doldrums of everyday life." Cyrus's warm breath tickled her ear.

She closed her eyes, enjoying the simmering heat that embraced her body. "Wasn't there a movie called *The Spy Who Loved me?"*

"As I recall, that's a James Bond flick."

"Yes, but it's also my life," she said.

"But your movie and life have a happy ending. Not every woman gets her very own Bond. James Bond," He said with a perfect Sean Connery Scots brogue. "If it's within my power, it's yours."

She giggled. "Mm," she craned her neck to give him better access. "Anything?"

"*Aye, anythin',*" he mimicked perfectly as he sucked on her earlobe. "So, what will you do tomorrow while I'm at the office, Mrs. Benveniste?"

"What any woman worth her salt would do. I'll go shopping. You do know London is a shopping paradise. And then maybe tea at Claridge's."

"Tea at Claridge's? Alone?"

"I don't mind — besides, you never know, someone interesting might join me."

He pulled away and studied her face. "Are you trying to make me jealous?"

"Moi? What's wrong with having tea by myself?"

"What time is tea? Maybe I can sneak away and meet you."

"Could you?" She tried to hide her pleasure at the thought of him doing something as ordinary as having lunch with her.

"I don't think it's a big deal for me to take an hour. Besides, it gives our story for being here more authenticity."

"Three o'clock. Claridge's. I'll meet you there."

"Deal. I'll text you if I'm running late or if anything goes awry."

"I'm excited."

Cyrus grinned sexily at her. "Are you? Well, I'm excited to lure you upstairs."

"You have a one-track mind. You're going to wine and dine me first," she laughed. "I'm starving."

"I'll order the food, and you open a bottle of champagne. It's five o'clock, and it's time to get this party started."

"I'm going to unpack first, take a bubble bath, and slip into something sexy."

"Perfect. Mind if I watch?"

"Watch me unpack?" she teased.

"No, I was thinking more the bubble bath part of the equation," he chuckled. "It's very erotic to watch a woman bathe. Ask all the artists throughout history who've been obsessed with painting women at their toilette. You know, like Cezanne, Gaugin, Seurat, Degas, I could name several more."

"I see your time at the Sorbonne didn't go entirely to waste."

"You know I love museums. Why do you think I married a curator?"

"Guaranteed free entry to the museums of the world?"

"Damn, you've discovered my secret."

"Touché, Mr. Benveniste." She leaned in until her lips were only an inch from his. "You can't fool me, though. The real reason you married me is to save water. I suppose you didn't notice that the tub upstairs can accommodate two."

"You bet I noticed. Now I know we have a supply of champagne and bubbles. The only thing missing is a scented candle."

"Oh, trust me, I packed them," she purred.

"Is it any wonder I fell madly in love with you?"

"It did take some time for you to come to your senses."

"Men are reticent beasts when it comes to love."

"Tell me more, my beast."

"Why waste words when I can show you?"

CHAPTER TEN

Saturday, February 8
London, United Kingdom

The wipers slapped rhythmically across the windshield of the town car. A foggy, wet haze and drizzle added to the dreariness of the day. But Cyrus was barely aware of the weather. His focus was on the girl he hadn't seen in eight years and what she knew. The town car rolled through the gates at 2 Palace Green and pulled up in front of the stately brick building. Cyrus slipped from the car with his umbrella open, which served to block him from view. He purposely avoided surveillance — the less known about him, the better.

Golda was waiting for him downstairs on the other side of the security station in the reception area. She watched as he emptied his pockets and passed through the walk-through metal detector. "*Shalom,* Cyrus, it's been a long time."

Cyrus hadn't seen Golda in more than ten years, not since he'd begun training with Mossad. Mossad had assigned Golda to assist during his transformation from college student to spy. In Cyrus's case, the need for mothering and encouragement had been a necessity. At the time, he'd recently lost his father to suicide, and Mossad had faked the deaths of his mother and sister to keep them safe. He had no idea how heavy the burden would be to have no family, no friends, and no one he could trust once he returned to Iran. As a deep-cover spy, he would have to survive in a cold, hostile environment with the threat of discovery and torture always looming over him. All he had were his wits and the skills he'd learned from Mossad. Golda had been a godsend through his transition.

"Golda." He wrapped his arms around the short, stout woman. "It's been too long." When he released her, she patted his cheek.

"*Boychik,* I see time hasn't diminished your appeal. Handsome as ever."

"Still sweet on me, aren't you?" Cyrus grinned, remembering Golda had thought him too good-looking to be a spy. If she told him once, she told him a thousand times that a spy needed to be invisible, and invisible Cyrus would never be.

"I've always thought you were too handsome for your own good. And those green eyes of yours. Too beautiful for a spy. But you proved me wrong, thank God, accomplishing the impossible. I understand you're married with a little girl."

"Yes. The woman who saved my soul. I thank God every day for my Layla. We have a daughter, Cerise, who inherited the green eyes. She recently turned five and is the light of our lives. Layla's here in London with me." He winked. "We're celebrating our anniversary."

"I hope I get to meet her. But for now, we have a difficult task ahead of us. I need to fill you in on where we stand with our guest before you meet her."

"Yes, ma'am."

Golda led the way down the hallway. A plain-clothes guard unhooked the velvet rope, giving them access to the upper floor. "Thank you, Aaron."

Cyrus followed Golda up the stairs to the second floor. They entered a large, open area with at least a hundred men and women, eyes glued to state-of-the-art monitors set atop sleek, modular desks. The agents sat in ergonomically correct chairs, and the lighting was adjusted to soothe the eyes. Cyrus had always been impressed by the care that Mossad had for their agents, both administrative and in the field.

Golda led him into a small office at the far end of the room and closed the door behind them. She offered him a chair and took her own seat on the other side of the desk.

"The girl has fallen into a deep depression and speaks little," Golda began. "Understandable, of course. We're certain she witnessed the murders of her family, fiancé, and his parents. The one statement she's made innumerable times is her desire for revenge. Aryeh has tried to make headway with her, but she refuses to speak to anyone other than you. We believe her father advised her to trust no one except you."

"It's possible. We worked together for a time and shared a reasonably good relationship. Saman, of course, knew of my compromise and that I escaped from Iran by the skin of my teeth. He must have known about the *fatwa* on my head. The Ayatollah would want to deter anyone from following in my footsteps. But the only real explanation is that Saman philosophically changed and no longer believed in the oppressive regime he'd supported his whole life. He must have decided that the only hope for his family, should his traitorous leanings be discovered, would be to reach out to someone he'd known who'd also switched sides. Someone he'd once considered a friend."

"That's what I think, which leads us to an important question. Had Saman prepared for such a day by accumulating evidence against his government, and if so, where is it?"

GOLDA RAPPED SOFTLY on the door. There was no reply. She inched the door open and poked her head in. "I have a surprise for you, my dear," she said in a gentle voice. "Someone has traveled a long way to see you." The girl lay on the bed with her back to the door. The drapes were open, but minimal light shone through. Dark clouds hung in the sky, and beads of raindrops slipped down the windowpane like tears down a cheek.

The bitter taste of sorrow hung in the air. Cyrus could taste it on his tongue. It brought back the worst moment of his life — opening the door to his father's office and finding him dead. The horrific tableau would forever be imprinted on his brain — the contorted position of his father's body, bits of bone and brain matter splattered on the wall like a macabre painting. And a blackened pool of blood seeping into the carpet. Cyrus had collapsed on the floor in anguish when he'd realized that his father had taken his own life.

He pushed the stark memory back to the dark corners of his mind. As terrible as that moment had been for him, nothing could compare to what Jazmin had witnessed. He approached slowly, aware of her fragility, not wanting to startle her.

"Jazmin, do you remember me?" he said in a soft voice.

As if the effort were almost too much for her, Jazmin turned her head in slow degrees toward him. Her eyes were vacant as if she'd just awoken and had no clue where she was. Cyrus inched closer and sat on the edge of the bed.

Then a flash of memory lit her gaze. Without a word, she crawled to him and laid her head on his thigh. Golda, who'd remained in the doorway, nodded. "I'll leave you so you can talk in private. Buzz if you need me."

Cyrus ran a comforting hand gently over Jazmin's arm. "I'm here because you asked for me," he whispered. "I want to help you. I know this is difficult, but you need to tell me everything."

Jazmin's voice cracked when she spoke. "I should have died with them. I don't understand why God let me live."

"I think sometimes God gives the most difficult burden to those he knows can shoulder it with courage and grace."

"I don't feel particularly courageous at the moment."

"But you are, Jazmin," he said. "Your courage and wits helped you get away to safety. You were wise to seek sanctuary here."

She sat up, and he helped her lean against the headboard, placing pillows behind her back.

"Can you tell me anything about that day?"

"I-I was so nervous about the wedding, you know? Hoping that everything would be perfect. Darien and I — we'd planned every detail together." She swiped away the tears that ran down her face. "He-he is so —" she swallowed, "was so wonderful that way."

"As it should be."

"Yes, b-but I was worried about all the little things. There was a mix-up with the flower arrangements, and I fretted that they wouldn't be changed in time. Darien tried to calm my fears, but I couldn't help it. Stupid. All that worry seems so stupid now," she croaked.

"You felt what every bride feels the day before her wedding. There is nothing stupid about feelings. They are what they are." Cyrus poured her a glass of water from the pitcher beside the bed and handed her the glass, holding onto it as she sipped. Then he placed the glass back on the side table.

Jazmin nodded her thanks. "I snuck out for a smoke. And then I was worried that Darien would find me. He hated that I smoked. Darien was in the final year of his internship at the hospital. He was such a brilliant and caring doctor. And, of course, anti-smoking. He'd seen far too many blackened lungs. He encouraged me and helped me quit. He was never judgmental. He reassured me that he understood how hard it was to quit. It *was* hard, but I did it. But then, with all pressure from the wedding, I started again. Only a cigarette or two when I was feeling too stressed. I hid it from him, but I promised myself that I would quit right after the wedding." She looked up at Cyrus, her eyes swimming with tears. "I'll never get to keep that promise to him."

"You *can* keep that promise. Do it in honor of his memory."

"But now it doesn't matter. Nothing matters."

"Nothing matters?"

She clenched her jaw. "Only justice matters. Revenge."

"Revenge can be a bitter pill. It might give you satisfaction for a while, but if you don't let go, eventually it will destroy you."

She grabbed a pillow and held it tight to her chest. "I have to tell you what happened. If I don't tell someone, I'll go mad."

"Then tell me. Unburden yourself."

"Papa told me you were the only one I could trust."

"You can trust me. You can trust Aryeh, Golda, all of us. We want to help you."

She nodded and took a deep, shaky breath. "We were having an informal dinner for our immediate families. I didn't want a fancy rehearsal dinner. Neither did Darien. The wedding would be fancy enough. We ordered a catered buffet — and it was set up in the kitchen so everyone could help themselves…" She paused and closed her eyes. "Darien made sure it included a dish that was a favorite of each person there." She opened her eyes and looked at Cyrus, quirking a half-smile. "Darien's idea. He was always so thoughtful."

Cyrus nodded in understanding. Years of working as a Mossad agent had honed his interrogation skills of criminals and terrorists, but since becoming a husband and father, he'd also become better at interviewing victims. Engaged listening encouraged most people to keep sharing.

"I was feeling a bit anxious, its being one day before the wedding, so I snuck outside for a smoke. I kept peeking in the window, watching the faces of everyone smiling and happy. Chatting and joking. Darien's parents and mine were thrilled about the union of our families. Everyone was. His mom treated me like the daughter she always wanted. And then…"

Jazmin's features twisted as though in pain, as though she were trying with all her might to stop herself from crying. Cyrus laid a gentle hand over her tight fists, still clenched around the pillow. She stiffened her jaw, and the rest of her story came out in a torrent. "He burst into the room so fast, it didn't register on anyone's face. I heard a muffled pop, pop, pop, and one by one, they dropped like rag dolls. I screamed, but nothing came out. And then his gaze looked out the window, and I dropped to the ground. I could have sworn he saw me, but it was bright inside and already dark outside. A few minutes must have passed, but it felt like hours. Then I heard the door slam, and I let instinct take over, I guess. We have a big tree at the far end of the backyard near the back hedgerow. I ran toward the tree and hid behind it, thinking he was coming after me. But he didn't. He didn't come after me. Instead — there was an explosion. It was m-massive, and it took me completely by surprise — the house completely consumed in flames. I don't remember much after that. I ran away."

"Why did you come here, Jazmin?"

"A week before — before it happened, my father told me that if I were ever in trouble, I should go to the Israeli embassy and ask for you. I asked him why I couldn't go to the Iranian embassy to seek help, and he grabbed me by the shoulders and shook me. I don't think I ever saw him so angry. He yelled at me not to question his wisdom. I should only listen like a dutiful daughter. And so, I did. I trusted that my father was looking out for me, but..." She turned to Cyrus with wide questioning eyes. "Why? Did he bring this horror upon our family?"

"If he did, he didn't mean to. Did you see the man who did this? Could you identify him if we showed you pictures?"

Her body shuddered, but she nodded. "I-I think I could. The monster wore a baseball cap and a white jumpsuit that was clearly too big for him. But I saw his eyes and I'll never forget them. They were distinct, pale like petrified amber. His features were sharp as if carved from stone. He didn't look human, no sign of remorse. His gaze was pure death."

Cyrus reached for her hand and held it between his palms. "Jazmin. You've been very brave. But this has only begun. The assassin most likely has realized that he didn't kill everyone at the house. He would have known who was there and who wasn't. You're in grave danger. We need to get you out of the country. Protecting you here is too difficult, not to mention the Brits are eventually going to figure out you're alive and where you are and will demand access to you for their own investigation."

Cyrus stood and walked to the window and looked out at the rain-drenched street. "Jazmin, did your father have any other places away from the house where he might keep things? Files or important documents?" He turned back and met her gaze.

He watched her pull a necklace chain up from beneath her shirt. From the end of the chain, a gold key dangled.

"Do you know what that key opens?" he asked.

She nodded. "It's for my father's humidor. A few years ago, he rented a locker at the Wellesley Hotel in Knightsbridge. Papa called it his sinful habit, but he loved to go after work and share a smoke and chat with people. I think he may have kept more than cigars in his humidor."

"Jazmin, would you mind if I take the key and inspect the locker?

I'd prefer to do it with you, but it's too dangerous. I promise to share whatever I find."

"Papa said I could trust you." Jazmin lifted the necklace over her head and walked to Cyrus. She took his hand and dropped the key and chain into his palm, then closed his fingers around it. "Cyrus, I want to expose and destroy the man who did this. Will you help me?"

"I think that's what Saman had in mind when he told you to seek my assistance."

Tears filled her eyes, and she wrapped her arms around him, resting her head on his chest. There was a knock on the door, and Aryeh walked in. The look of surprise on his face was unmistakable. Cyrus could imagine what he must be thinking. He pulled from Jazmin's embrace and took her hand, leading her back to the bed. "Aryeh, *achi,* how are you?"

"I'm good, brother." Aryeh looked at Jazmin. "It seems you two know each other."

"Jazmin, Aryeh is like a brother to me." Cyrus reminded her. "You can trust him as you trust me. Do you understand?"

Jazmin nodded.

"Good. You're safe here at the embassy for the time being, but we have to move you soon. I need to make arrangements." He smiled. "I'd like to introduce you to my wife, Layla. I think you're going to like each other very much."

"You're married?"

"Yes, and I have a five-year-old-daughter named Cerise. But you'll have to visit Israel to meet her."

Jazmin smiled for the first time since he'd walked into the room. "Do you remember when I was a teenager, I asked my father to arrange our marriage?" Jazmin blushed. "I thought you were the most handsome man I'd ever seen."

"Cyrus is the pretty boy of our team," Aryeh said in a dry tone.

Cyrus rolled his eyes. He was used to the jokes and comments from his fellow agents. When he was younger, before he met Layla, he certainly used his looks to his advantage. But everything changed after he married Layla. He was no longer the ladies' man, nor did he seduce women to get information. He left that to the unmarried and unattached spies. Cyrus smiled at Jazmin in a brotherly way. "I also remember the way you sashayed away, so sure that whatever you wanted, you could attain. Your father said he wished I'd take you away, claiming you'd be the death of him."

Her smile faded. "Maybe I was."

"No, he loved your spirit. He adored you. Never forget that. And he trusted you to be brave and clever. You did the right thing coming here. We'll protect you through this."

"Thank you. Right now, what I want most is vengeance."

"We're going to make that happen, but remember, you mustn't live your life filled with hatred. You'll need to find a way forward. Hatred will only bring you unhappiness. Trust me, I know."

She turned to Aryeh. "Are you married too?"

Aryeh laughed. "No, I haven't been blessed in that way. I'm a grumpy old bachelor."

"Yeah, he holds the record for youngest grump at thirty-six," Cyrus said with a smile.

"Will you help me find the man who murdered my family?"

Aryeh bowed. "I promise you that I will do everything in my power to find, expose, and destroy him. He will pay for his crimes."

CYRUS AND ARYEH sat in the safe room in front of a big screen. The walls of the room were lead-lined and secured by electronic jamming technology. They could speak freely with the Ramsad without fear that their conversation might be compromised.

"We need to extract the professor from Iran," the Ramsad said. "Although not confirmed yet, our contact there believes the physicist and his girlfriend have evidence regarding the IRI's stockpile of weapons and enriched uranium. Have you selected a team?"

Cyrus spoke first. "I've been combing through files of Mossad agents, and so far, I haven't found a team suitable to deploy. I'm beginning to think this mission is going to have to fall to me, but I can't be in two places at the same time."

The Ramsad shook his head. "No, Cyrus. It's too risky. I want you focused on Jazmin and finding the incriminating evidence her father may have stashed against the regime here or in Europe."

Aryeh interrupted. "I've been giving this some thought, and I have an idea. But my better judgment warns me that we'd be opening a pandora's box."

The Ramsad leaned forward and waved his hand impatiently. "Stop beating around the bush. Tell me."

"Zara could be the answer."

"Zara?" The Ramsad rubbed his chin. "Where is she?"

"I'm not sure, but I have an idea."

"Oy, Aryeh, you're such a pain in my *tuchus*. Explain."

"Zara disappeared in Argentina. The General Directorate of Eternal Security, France's intelligence service, had posted her to Buenos Aires for some out-to-pasture job, and then six months ago, she dropped off the radar."

"So, what makes you think you can find her if the French can't, and why do you think she'd be interested in such a mission? Zara speaks Arabic, but I don't recall her speaking Farsi."

"I think she's living with Mustafa Mughniyah, hiding under new identities somewhere in Argentina. I'm in contact with her parents in Marseilles. The French authorities returned her belongings to them, including her passport. Not that she couldn't get another one, but I've done some initial checking, and there is no record of her leaving the country. As you know, I've been hunting for Mustafa since the Lebanon mission. I had a suspicion from the beginning when Zara was working with him that there was more to their relationship than honeypot and target. My hypothesis is he reached out to her and convinced her he'd changed. I have some ideas of where they might be, and I'm going to find her."

"And how does finding two lovebirds help with the rescue in Iran?"

"Mustafa speaks fluent Farsi, and Zara is semi-fluent. Mustafa is on our hit list for what happened in Lebanon. He's wanted for war crimes. I say we offer him a chance to clear his name. We remove the threat over his life and make sure he and Zara can have their happily ever after if he helps us get the professor and his girlfriend out of Iran.

Even though my trust in Zara is diminished, I think she would agree if there's a chance to redeem herself and make sure her lover is in the clear. Prior to disappearing, she reached out to me several times, but I was angry. I cut off communications. I accused her of allowing her emotions to get in the way, and because of that, Mustafa was able to release that damn warhead."

"We stopped the missile in time, thank God," the Ramsad said.

"Yes, but then Zara let him escape when she could have stopped him."

"You are thinking like the wise man I know you to be," Cyrus said.

"Thank you. Sometimes, I do have an occasional clever thought. Besides, it's time I bury the hatchet."

"Are you saying we recruit an ex-Hezbollah terrorist to assist Mossad?" asked Noam.

"Why not? We've blackmailed or bribed untold numbers of terrorists to help us before."

The head of Mossad held his hands in prayer over his mouth. Cyrus knew the pose. Noam Levi was calculating the risk and the potential gain. "This is *mashugana.* You know that, don't you?"

Aryeh's lips curled in an almost smile. "You might be right. I am crazy. But this could also be our only chance."

"I'll allow it. But time is of the essence. Get your *tuchus* to Argentina and find them. You have forty-eight hours. I need to get the professor and his girlfriend out of Iran."

CHAPTER ELEVEN

Saturday, February 8
Astara, Islamic Republic of Iran

An icy wind whipped up large waves that crashed upon the sandy shoreline of the inky blue Caspian Sea. Seagulls bravely flew into the wind, hovering as they flapped their wings but making little headway. Shira and Ibrahim walked with their fingers entwined on the deserted beach. They'd been cooped up in Shira's parents' apartment for four days. The cold weather discouraged most people from venturing out, but Shira was going crazy, so they picked a particularly inhospitable day to take a walk, hoping they'd garner no attention. Astara, a popular beach resort in the summer months, was a virtual ghost town in winter.

The good news was no one from NAJA, the agency in charge of domestic Iranian law enforcement, or its special force YEGUP, a fearsome unit that had been created after the Green Movement to suppress and destroy the protests in the country, had shown up knocking at their door. But the more Ibrahim ruminated over the damaging information on the flash drives, the more he knew their lives were in danger. He was sure the regime had killed his uncle and family, and he was next on the list.

"Kaspar texted me on the satellite phone."

"When?" asked Shira.

"Last night."

"Why didn't you tell me sooner?"

"I don't know. I guess I didn't want to get you too excited."

"Are you crazy? What did he say? Can he get us out of Iran?"

"He said they're working on it and that we should sit tight and keep a low profile."

"Did you tell them where we are?"

"No. I didn't want to risk it. I told him we'd go to wherever the point of extraction would be."

"You should tell him we're in Astara. We're so close to the Azerbaijan border. With the proper papers, we could simply walk across."

"I will tell him, Shira." He didn't tell her he trusted no one, not even his contact.

Shira wore a wool scarf around her hair, and her face was hidden within the billowing folds. She turned her face up to him, and her eyes were liquid with tears. "Do you think they will harm our families?"

He'd tried not to consider the possibility of repercussions or blackmail. "I hope not. Even if they did, it wouldn't be your family they harm. It will be mine. You've done nothing wrong besides disappearing with me."

She squeezed his hand. The sea was turbulent, and large waves pounded so loudly against the shoreline that it was difficult to be heard above the roar of wind and water. On the horizon, black clouds gathered and the blustery wind drove them shoreward. Soon the rain would pummel them with the ferocity of bullets.

"We should go back before the downpour starts."

As a precaution, they took the stairs instead of the elevator to the second floor of the apartment building. Ibrahim was unlocking the door of Shira's parents' apartment when their neighbor's door opened. Shira and Ibrahim turned to see the man raise a finger to his lips, shushing them to silence. He motioned for them to come into his apartment. The look on his face bore lines of worry. He quietly closed the door behind them.

"Two men came looking for you. I'm sure the *haroomzādehs* are NAJA. I told them nobody has been in the apartment. They gave me a number to call if I see you. Whatever you've done to attract their attention, I don't want to know about. But I hate those bastards and will do whatever I can to help you."

Shira began to tremble, and Ibrahim grabbed her elbow before she collapsed. "Did they believe you?"

"I don't know, but I'm sure they'll be back."

Ibrahim did his best not to scare Shira, but he needed to find out everything he could about what happened. "Do you think they might have surreptitiously placed any cameras in the hallway or the elevator?"

"No, not in the hallway, but I don't know about the elevator. I watched them through the peephole. Their good neighbor rescuer had introduced himself as Izad. "I think the bastards will be back shortly and, my guess is, they'll insist on searching the apartment."

What are we going to do?" she asked, her voice laced with fear.

"I have to think," Ibrahim answered.

"I have an idea," said their neighbor. "My family has another apartment in the building. You can move in until we can find another situation for you."

"Why would you help us and put yourself at risk?" Ibrahim asked. He was so distraught, he trusted no one.

"My family has suffered greatly at the hands of this murderous regime. I will gladly take retribution in whatever way I can." He walked to the window and gazed down at the parking lot. "Come, there's no time to waste. Let's get you settled before the animals return."

"We need to get some things from the apartment," said Ibrahim.

"No!" Shira grabbed his arm. "Let Izad do it, it's too risky."

"Okay, but we'd better make a list for him and tell him what is necessary." His expression warned her of what he was thinking.

Izad patted his shoulder. "Do not worry, whatever you need I will bring to you. Make the list."

Ibrahim opened the door to the Izad's family's apartment and let Izad in with their suitcases. The first thing Ibrahim did was check his toiletry bag where the flash drives were in a box of Q-tips. "Thank you, Izad."

"Don't thank me, my wife Soraya packed everything, and she straightened up the apartment. Everything is in its proper place."

Shira hugged Izad, making his ruddy cheeks redden.

Recovering himself, Izad added. "I think it best for you to remain sequestered in this apartment for a day or two. Anything you need, I'll be happy to get for you."

"How can we thank you for your kindness?"

"No need. Someday this country of ours will belong to the people once more. That will be reward enough for all of us."

A short time later, Ibrahim and Shira heard raised voices in the hallway. Ibrahim watched through the peephole as two plain-clothed men argued with Izad. It was difficult to make out exactly what they were saying, but Izad returned with what must have been a master key and opened Shira's parents' apartment. The men pushed past Izad and waved him away and slammed the door in his face. Izad glanced to the end of the hall to the apartment where Ibrahim watched. He nodded and returned to his apartment, shutting the door.

After the men had finally left the building, Izad knocked on their door. Ibrahim and Shira followed Izad back to Shira's parents' apartment. When they opened the door, Shira cried out. It looked as if a tornado had worn a path through the entire place. The cushions on the sofa were slit and the stuffing pulled out, drawers pulled open and emptied, clothing torn and scattered throughout the rooms. Nothing was left untouched. Tears slipped down Shira's face as she looked at the damage.

"Everything is destroyed. My parents are going to be so angry."

"Don't worry," said Izad, "when this is all over and you are safe, we'll clean everything up. Be glad you weren't here. I'd hate to think of what they would have done to you."

Shira grabbed Izad's hand. "Thank you, Izad. I'm sure you saved our lives."

The older man patted her hand. "You are welcome, child. Tonight, you will dine with my wife, Soraya, and me, and we will discuss the future of our homeland and how to keep you safe."

CHAPTER TWELVE

Saturday, February 8
London, United Kingdom
Wellesley Hotel, Knightsbridge

A rainy afternoon made the cigar bar and lounge a perfect refuge from the inclement weather. The room echoed with laughter, boomeranging back and forth from table to table, heightening the show of masculine comradery. Accompanying the laughter, curling tendrils of cigar smoke filled the room with a heady bouquet before disappearing into the air filtration system. Well-dressed clientele occupied nearly every seat. These men of consequence were presided over by two portraits of the most improbable pairing of men, Winston Churchill wearing a hat and smoking a cigar, and a smiling Fidel Castro with stogie in hand. Britain's greatest leader, who led his people to victory over the Nazi oppressors, and the tyrant who presided over his nation with an iron fist. Churchill, of blessed memory, would have felt at home at the Wellesley Hotel, his rotund figure conforming to the contours of the elegant plush blue leather chairs and the bottles of aged cognac dating as far back as the 1800s.

Cyrus could imagine Saman holding court among the cognoscenti that gathered during the lunch and cocktail hours to discuss affairs of state and the salvation of the world by men such as he. Under different circumstances, Cyrus would have enjoyed lingering to watch the revelry, but since Jazmin had presented him with the key, he could think of nothing else but finding out the contents of her father's humidor. Saman's locker and what it might hold possessed his thoughts. It seemed far too easy. Iran's greatest secrets, their nuclear aspirations hidden amid a stash of cedar boxes and cigars.

The concierge greeted Cyrus and directed him to the humidor and private lockers. Only one other man was in the cigar locker room. The two men exchanged pleasantries. Jazmin's key opened a cedar-lined box much like a medicine cabinet. Inside the temperature and humidity-controlled vault were boxes of Cuban Montecristos and varying brands of other premium cigars.

Out of the blue, the other gentleman who'd closed and locked his humidor offered up. "Do you know how those fine cigars of yours got their name?"

Cyrus, who'd been lifting cigars and running them under his nose in order to delay things until the other man left, looked at him with curiosity. "No idea." The older man held up his cigar as if it were a baton, and he was about to conduct an orchestra with it. His posh accent gave away his years at boarding schools.

"In the cigar factories in Cuba, a gentleman known as a lector would read to the cigar rollers. I suppose it must have been difficult to keep the buggers awake, what with the unbearable heat and the drudgery of their work. Guess what their favorite book was?"

Cyrus smiled. *"The Count of Monte Cristo."*

"Exactly. You might say it was the original audiobook. I'm sure you will never light up again without remembering this conversation."

Cyrus chuckled. "I don't suppose I will. Thank you for the story."

"Pleasure is mine. Enjoy your book." The man raised his cigar in farewell as he left the locker room.

Alone at last, Cyrus began to search the contents of each box carefully. He found nothing except cigars. He took a deep breath and started over. *Something must be here. Why else would Saman give Jazmin a key?* He lifted each box out of the humidor and removed all the cigars, laying them out on a table. When he lifted the last box, he noticed something different about it. The box held fewer cigars than the others, yet it was the same size. *Of course.* He turned the box upside down and shook it. A sheet of cedar slipped out, landing in his hand. Beneath the separating sheet, he found a thin, enameled box with beautifully scrolled Farsi. He lifted the lid and was surprised to find another key and an envelope. Cyrus opened the envelope and read the handwritten missive.

Daughter of my heart,

First, I bless you and ask your forgiveness for the danger you now face. Know that if I could have spared you, I would have. If you are here, then I am no more. What I have sown I now reap. I have supported and upheld evil, sought war and destruction instead of peace. Propagated lies against my own people and oppressed them. But a man can change, and I pray with this final act, I may find redemption.

"May Allah the Almighty guide us, forgive all our sins, help us to stay firm on the right path, and unite all of us with our family and friends in His Jannatul Firdaus. Ameen."

I pray, my precious child, one day we will be together again in the eternal garden of Jannah.

For you, daughter, the duty remains to stop the Fourth Horseman of the Apocalypse. It is ordained the end of times is coming. It is prophesied by Islam, Judaism, and the Christian faiths. The apocalypse will arrive on the winds of the four horsemen astride white, red, black, and pale green horses. The Lamb of God, the Lion of Judah, will break the first four seals of God, releasing the horsemen who will rule the earth and bring quiet to the masses before the final outcome and the end of times.

The Day of Judgment, Yawm al-Qiyāmah may be upon us. No man knows when it began nor when it will end. There is still time to prevent the beginning of the end.

It is written that the Lamb of God broke the seal and from it emerged first the white horse and horseman. Crowned and brandishing a bow, he rode forth in conquest. White is the color of the Christian Church. It has reigned for two thousand years, wielding its power over the masses. Spreading like a plague across the earth, claiming to be the one and only true faith.

From the second seal came the second horse and horseman. For nearly two hundred years, communist tyrants have spilt the blood of more than one hundred million people. These men have masqueraded their evil philosophy for the betterment of mankind but brought only death and destruction. Red is the color of Russia and China — communism — red is the second horse of the apocalypse. He rides forward carrying a raised sword and rules authoritatively by denying freedom and shackling all who are conquered into complacency and subservience. He promises a proletariat paradise without the rule of God. His time will end.

The third horseman bears in hand the scales of justice and commerce. He is the democrat and capitalist, representative of man's unbridled lust for power and money. He is Western civilization. The consequences of his goodwill have spread famine and greed. In his lust to rule, he has forgotten the tenets of charity and strayed from the path of God. But it is possible that he will find his way and sing the praise of the Almighty.

The fourth horseman is Death, and he rides a pale green horse. Green is the color of the Islamic world that rules over nearly two billion people. Iran is the mightiest of Islamic nations and is building the arsenal that will bring forth the end of times. We must stop the prophecy from being fulfilled. You must stop Iran's nuclear ambitions and remove the evil regime from power through a peaceful revolution. You must expose them for who they are — the true oppressors who hunger to rule the world.

The key within is for a safety deposit box held at Julius Bär, Bahnhofstrasse. You are under no circumstances to go to the bank alone. The contents of the box are of great value and must not fall into the wrong hands, or all will be lost. Trust Cyrus, he will know best what to do with it, and he will protect you, with Allah's blessing. What you will find in Zürich is everything you need to expose the evildoers and light the fires of freedom. However, there is one more piece of the puzzle. "I" must be extracted from Iran. He holds the final key and the codes to prevent the destruction. Without him, there can be no resolution.

I pray for you, daughter, and I exact a promise from Cyrus that he will protect you.

With all my heart,

Saman

Cyrus re-read the letter. Had Saman lost his mind? All this talk of "end of times" and religious symbolism was so contrary to the man

Cyrus remembered. Saman had always been pragmatic, a man who saw the world for what it was. And who was the referenced "I"? Was he referring to Ibrahim Nassiri? Had Saman been compromised by his own nephew and murdered because of his betrayal? No, it couldn't be. Ibrahim was on the run trying to get out of Iran, but then again, the regime would consider him an unacceptable loose end. Maybe Ibrahim realized too late that by cooperating with the regime, he'd, unbeknownst to him, unleashed his own death sentence. "He that lieth down with dogs shall rise up with fleas."

Five years had come and gone since Cyrus had moved amidst the highest echelons of the Revolutionary Guards. How much further had Iran traveled on the road to nuclear armament? Had Saman managed to amass the whereabouts of all Iran's secret facilities, and did Ibrahim possess the codes to access and dismantle them? It seemed almost too hopeful to imagine.

Cyrus stuffed the letter and key in his briefcase. He'd promised to meet Layla for tea at Claridge's. He left the old-world haven of upper-crust male conviviality for the pretentious old-world sanctuary of tradition.

CYRUS ENTERED the soaring elegance of the foyer, which was crowned with Dale Chihuly's silvery-white, twisted glass Hydra appropriately called Gilded Dawn. Afternoon tea at this pantheon to the aesthete was formal and archaic, yet he was loath to admit, utterly charming. Finding his wife amid the splendidly attired guests was instantaneous. Layla was as dazzling as a pearl seeded within an oyster.

Cyrus bent to kiss her cheek. *"Hola, querida."* For practical purposes, he was once more lost in the guise of Alfonse Benveniste. "Have you ordered?" Cyrus sat, placing his briefcase on the floor so that it touched his calf.

Layla beamed. "I have. It should be here in a minute."

"Good. I'm sorry I can't stay long, still a few things to get done at the office. How'd the shopping go?" He eyed the bags on the floor surrounding Layla.

"I had so much fun. I can't wait to surprise you when you take me out for our big date."

Cyrus shifted in his seat uncomfortably. "About our date." He leaned in and whispered. "We're going to have to postpone that for a bit. It seems we may be leaving London. Probably tomorrow."

Layla couldn't hide her disappointment. "Where are we going?"

His voice was nearly indiscernible in the room that echoed with the conversations of others. "Zürich. As soon as I can arrange everything."

Layla's brows raised. Her mouth opened as if to speak but was interrupted by the arrival of the waiter bearing a tray. He placed a beautiful green and white striped platter filled with finger sandwiches on the table.

Cyrus eyed the presentation suspiciously, and Layla laughed at the dismay on his face. "You needn't look as if it were your last meal, and it won't be enough to see you into the next world." The sandwiches were the classic examples, including smoked salmon, egg and cress, chicken, cucumber, and ham, which she efficiently placed on his plate. "It's not like you to be judgmental about food, darling. Besides, wait until you see dessert."

The waiter poured their tea and left the pot on the three-tier-cake stand next to their table. He found the cake stand quite sensible, allowing for a clutter-free table. He bit into a sandwich and nodded his approval. "It's delicious. I guess I shouldn't be surprised."

"No, you shouldn't."

"Although it would probably take at least fifty of these tiny sandwiches to make a meal."

Layla chuckled as she sipped her tea. "Do you want to tell me a bit more about this sudden change of plans?"

"I'll tell you later when we're alone. Right now, I'd like to hear about your day. Did you make it over to the Tate?"

"Yes, and it was spectacular. The Turner collection was breathtaking. I told you the Tate has the largest holdings of William Turner's in the world. The paintings brought me to tears. Turner's brushwork was so free and ethereal. He's considered the father of modern art and really paved the way for the Impressionists. I wish you could have joined me. Maybe after our side trip?"

Cyrus kept one eye on his wife while she chatted about art and his other eye on the room and the entrance of the hotel. "Yes, I'd love that, *mi amor.*" Layla, who knew him so well, was sure to see his distraction, but his thoughts were not entirely on her. It worried him that he'd dragged Layla into a dangerous vortex. Although he didn't think he was being followed, his sixth sense had been alerted when he read Saman's letter warning that a force was gathering like a storm on the horizon. The sooner they got out of London with Jazmin, the better. In fact, he'd already planned their departure for tomorrow. But first, they needed to sneak Jazmin out of the embassy without any prying eyes on the outside knowing, then get her safely ensconced in their flat. By now, whoever had murdered the Amin family had likely discovered Jazmin's whereabouts and was monitoring the embassy. He needed to get her off the radar as quickly as possible.

The waiter arrived carrying what looked to Cyrus to be the *pièce de résistance* of the tea. He was suddenly pleased with Layla's coercing him into a bit of respite from his duties. The raisin and apple scones with jam and vanilla ice cream and the tray of sweets and pastries were right up his alley, and he happily dived in. The rest of his day and evening were not likely to be as enjoyable, so he might as well grasp the precious, carefree moments left to him. When he lifted a bite to his lips, Layla grabbed his wrist, and before he could pull away, she directed his bite to her own mouth. "Hm," she hummed. Her tongue sensuously swiped her lips, and he felt his body harden.

He shifted in his seat. "Hey, *mi amor.* You stole the first bite."

She leaned back and proceeded to do a perfect imitation of Meg Ryan's immortal performance in *When Harry Met Sally*. She shook her tousled blonde locks and moaned. It was a moan he'd only ever heard from her during their impassioned lovemaking. He felt his face flush red. Without looking, he knew every eye in the restaurant was on them. Through gritted teeth, he whispered, "Behave yourself, you're going to get us thrown out, and I'm going to be distraught if I don't get to eat this dessert." The chuckling from other tables made him realize that Layla's performance was beneficial. As a seasoned spy he understood that doing the opposite of what is expected is the perfect cover.

She giggled, her poise returning her to her naturally elegant self.

"Sorry, I couldn't resist. Your thoughts were elsewhere. I wish you could see the look on your face. As they say, priceless." She delicately lifted her fork and took a bite of cake, this time minus the orgasm. As much as he wished to keep his thoughts in the here and now, the danger ahead would not be forgotten.

It was a shame he wasn't a practiced magician or illusionist since it would have served his plans well if, by a cloak-and-dagger wave of his wand, he, Jazmin, and Layla could disappear. But he did understand the art of misdirection. Cyrus sipped his tea and smiled at his wife, hoping everything would go to plan.

CHAPTER THIRTEEN

Sunday, February 9
London, United Kingdom

Gurga studied the computer screen streaming a live feed from the CCTV camera monitoring the Israeli Embassy. The usual suspects had come and gone all day, but the one person who'd piqued his interest now pulled up and exited a Mercedes. The man reminded him of himself the way he adeptly avoided being seen by the cameras. This was not the man's first visit today.

Gurga's desk was clean and orderly. There was no sign of the meals he'd consumed while watching the screen. Even his fixation with rectifying the botched mission had no effect on his obsessive personality. He kept to his healthy diet and kept his work area spick-and-span. Six days had passed since the Amin girl had arrived at the gates of the embassy. She would have to be moved to another location soon, and he must be ready to strike.

He'd been vigilant in his monitoring, keeping detailed notes of the comings and goings of everyone at the embassy. The blonde man in the business suit hadn't made an appearance in two days. Gurga had downloaded photos of him and forwarded them to his employers to run through their systems. The results had revealed he was suspected to be Mossad. Of course, that wasn't unusual. Many of the people inhabiting embassies were usually part of their country's secret intelligence services, whether it be CIA or Mossad. Working at the embassy was their cover for being on foreign soil. It also provided diplomatic immunity.

Gurga picked up the buzzing burner satellite phone that connected solely to the client who'd hired him for the Amin assassination. "*Marhaba.*"

On the other end of the line, there was no greeting.

"What have you to report?" The client snapped across the phone line in Arabic.

Gurga couldn't blame him. The mission was a complete disaster. Clients weren't interested in excuses, only results. "The package is being held in the embassy. It needs to be moved, and when that happens, we will be ready to intercept. Don't worry, I've already told you the results will be the same, although a little delayed."

"So, you say, but we are concerned. We're not sure how much information was compromised. Your assurance that nothing usable could have survived the blast is insufficient. The target might have prepared for this possibility with an alternate plan and given the package, as you call her, access to a duplicate copy. Should this get into the wrong hands, the damage would be unacceptable."

"I understand —"

"I don't want your understanding. I want results. Have you brought in backup?"

"Yes, my operatives are in place. Airports and trains are being monitored. She won't escape our net."

"See to it, or you will find yourself the hunted instead of the hunter."

Gurga swallowed his anger and contained the temptation of a scornful reply. "I will keep you posted."

"See that you do."

The line clicked off. Gurga growled under his breath, "Bastard." If there was a God, one day, that smug prick would end up as the target of a contract. Now that would give him immense pleasure. Hell, he'd even do it pro-bono. The client had been hounding him with calls, which merely served to enrage him. He didn't need the distraction. How dare the man try to get into his head with threats? For what purpose? Did he think his jabs would affect the outcome? Gurga collected his anger and stored it for a future day. What he needed was to do his job and wind up this contract. He threw the phone on the desk and swore to himself. *No more jobs for religious assholes who need others to do their dirty work.*

Two hours later, he was still staring at the computer screen. Bored and fatigued, his fingers drummed rhythmically on the desk. He stretched and then twisted his head in his hands and heard the crack of his spinal cord aligning above the sound of sirens in the distance.

The back door of the Israeli embassy swung wide, and Gurga leaned forward, his face inches from the screen. Two burly men in blue overalls carried a rolled carpet into the embassy. Fifteen minutes later, they exited with what appeared to be the same carpet. They set it on the ground while they opened the back of a white van with black lettering on the side advertising The Persian Rug Cleaning Company. Gurga had seen the van come and go for two days. Yesterday the same van and workmen had picked up a rolled rug. There had been other arrivals too, a heating and air-conditioning company van, and a plumber. He kept a detailed list of the comings and goings of every visitor and employee at the embassy, time of arrival, length of stay, and time of departure. He knew what they carried in and what they carried out. Nothing about today appeared different than yesterday or the days before.

But Gurga's instincts were triggered, nonetheless. Something about the way the two men lifted the carpet and put it into the van made him zoom in. The two men seemed to be handling the carpet with undue care and attention. Gurga hit the computer keyboard and posted a side-by-side video of the carpet being delivered minutes before and zeroed in. There was no question. The circumference of the rug was greater than before. He recalled the story of how Cleopatra, desperate to get an audience with Caesar, cunningly had herself rolled in a carpet and was delivered to the Roman dictator as a gift. He smiled to himself, nodding. *Very clever.*

The van pulled out of the electric gates of the embassy. Gurga's fingers flew over his keyboard at lightning speed, and his computer began tracking the van through the CCTV system.

By the time the van pulled in front of a townhouse on Campden Hill Road in the posh neighborhood of Kensington, Gurga had pulled on his jacket and was on his way out the door.

CHAPTER FOURTEEN

Sunday, February 9
London, United Kingdom

Cyrus monitored the movement of the white van from the black Mercedes, tailing it through the dense London traffic. His driver dropped him down the street from their rented townhouse. He jogged up the street and met the two men who were opening the back of the white van. Cyrus unlocked the front door, and the two men carrying the rug from the embassy followed him into the house. The two men gently laid the rug on the entry's wood floor and cut the cords binding it. Cyrus and the two men unrolled the rug, revealing a figure wrapped in a sheet. Cyrus tore the sheet away, and Jazmin sat up gasping for breath. "Oh my God, I could hardly breathe in there. It was horrible."

"I'm sorry," Cyrus said as he opened the door and let the two agents out, "but it was necessary. We couldn't take any chances on your being seen leaving the embassy."

"Cyrus, what is going on down there?" Layla called from upstairs.

"Layla, honey, come downstairs. I have someone I want you to meet."

Layla trotted down the stairs dressed in gray wool slacks and a navy-blue sweater. "What is going on? Where did that rug come from?"

Cyrus chuckled. "Don't worry about the rug. Layla, *eshgham,* this is Jazmin Amin."

Jazmin shyly smiled, and the two women shook hands and exchanged greetings. Cyrus bent to kiss Layla's cheek. "Darling, Jazmin is coming with us to Zürich."

"I see," said Layla.

Layla's curt response had Jazmin looking down uncomfortably. Cyrus patted her arm reassuringly.

"Yes, well, there's no time to waste. We need to leave immediately. Honey, I need you to pack a suitcase for both of us, and clothing for Jazmin. Except for the difference in height, you look about the same size. We'll pick up whatever else we need along the way."

"How are we getting to Zürich?"

"We're driving. I've already booked us on the Eurotunnel. I'm going to leave you two to pack while I wait outside for the rental car."

"Cyrus, I don't understand. Why aren't we flying? That's a ridiculously long drive."

He smiled. "We need to keep a low profile. Trust me, it's better this way." The British authorities were already in a huff demanding that Jazmin be turned over to them, and the assassin was likely to be monitoring the airports. They would be sitting ducks at the airport with both sides coming for them. The sooner they opened Saman's security box in Zürich, the better. And the sooner they got Jazmin safely out of Europe, the better. She wouldn't be safe until they touched down in Tel Aviv, but first, they needed the contents of the safety deposit box.

Cyrus sensed Layla's annoyance. He knew this change of plans unbalanced her. They'd barely settled into London, and now they were leaving. Jazmin looked nervous, probably sensing Layla's discomfort. This was not what he needed right now. "Jazmin, would you like a cup of tea?"

"Yes, please."

"Have a seat on the couch and relax." He took Layla's hand and pulled her toward the kitchen. "Come help me, *aziz-am.*"

Layla waited for the butler's door to close. She pulled her hand from his and crossed her arms over her chest. "Why didn't you tell me about Jazmin or that she was coming with us to Zürich? Don't you trust me?"

"I'm sorry, *eshgham,* but the Ramsad forbade anyone to know. Please don't be angry over something that was out of my hands. You know I trust you with my life." There was no time to waste, and he made Jazmin's tea while he spoke.

"I'm not angry, just hurt."

"The entire embassy is on high-alert. While we were out yesterday, headquarters had a team in here and swept the place for bugs. This is about security and nothing else."

Cyrus looked at his watch. "*Aziz-am,* believe me, I need you with me. I can't do this without you." He kissed her cheek. "Come, I don't want to leave Jazmin alone for too long. She's been through hell. I promise I'll fill you in on everything later."

"Okay." Layla nodded. Cyrus carried Jazmin's tea, and Layla followed him back to the living room. He handed the cup and saucer to Jazmin.

"*Merci,*" Jazmin said.

Cyrus's phone buzzed with an incoming text. "Shit, I don't believe this."

"What?" Both women asked at the same time.

"The rental car was on its way, but it was in a collision. I have to get a cab over to the rental company and pick up another car. I'll put the alarm on and be back as quickly as possible. Let no one in the house."

"But —" Layla began to ask.

"Honey, you'll have plenty of time to ask me questions. We have an hour and a half drive to Folkestone, where we board the train, then it's thirty-five minutes through the Chunnel to Calais. We'll drive half of it tonight and should arrive in Metz, France, around midnight. In the morning, we'll drive the remaining four-plus hours to Zürich. Think of it as a lovely sightseeing excursion."

Layla huffed sarcastically. "I'll be sure to take lots of pictures for our family travel albums."

His lips twitched as he suppressed his smile. He never grew tired of

Layla's ribbing, but now was not the time to scuffle with her. "Be ready to leave by the time I return. I should be back in less than an hour."

GURGA HAD PARKED his BMW down the street from the house. The white van was parked on the street with its emergency lights blinking. His laptop rested on the seat beside him. It was a shame he couldn't get there before the van arrived and see them carry the carpet into the townhouse, but he did see the delivery guys leave empty-handed. Gurga had expected to be scouting the location for some time, and it surprised him when he saw the man he'd seen at the embassy leave the house a short time later and jump into a cab. In a few minutes, he hacked into the alarm system and disabled the alarm.

It doesn't get better than that. It seemed the fates were aligning to make this hit easier than he'd expected. As soon as the taxi disappeared, Gurga got out of the car, thinking he'd have this case wrapped up in a few minutes. In the pocket of his coat, he fingered his gun and silencer, then walked toward the front door of the house. This time his prey would not slip away from him. This time he would leave her in a pool of blood, and he'd be on his way to Malta by evening.

As always before a kill, everything shifted inside of him. His mind stilled whatever apprehension he'd been experiencing, and his head cleared of emotion and remorse, giving him predatorial insight. There was also the anticipation of his favorite part of a kill — the exquisite feeling of omnipotence at the look of disbelief that clouded the eyes of his victim before the final moment. He was fast, and he was efficient. And he never missed. At least not until now. But he would soon rectify that.

Gurga glanced around before taking the lock-picking tool from his pocket. Twenty seconds later, he slipped into the house and pulled out his gun. Silence greeted him. His gaze scanned the carpet lying on the floor and the cut cord that remained. He took in the décor, searching for a human presence. He checked the downstairs. The kitchen was spotless, with no crumbs of food or unwashed dishes. He returned to the entry and climbed the staircase, as quiet as a panther stalking its prey. At the top of the stairs, he paused to listen. He heard movement to the left and silently made his way toward the partially open door of a bedroom. He peeked in and saw a woman packing a suitcase. Her back was to him, and he turned away and headed down the hallway in the opposite direction. The Amin girl didn't have short strawberry blonde hair, and she was several inches shorter than this woman. He opened the door to the next bedroom and found it empty. At the end of the hallway, he came to the last room on the floor. He turned the knob. This was it — he knew it — he sensed it.

Gurga opened the door and felt his pulse ratchet upward. She stood at the window, her back to him. She'd chopped off her long black hair, her slender neck exposed, but he'd know her anywhere. He held his breath, enjoying the seconds of anonymity and invisibility.

She turned and faced him, her gaze serene. Fear should live in her eyes, her heart pounding in her chest so loudly that his ears would echo the reverberation. Instead, she offered him a slip of a smile.

"Have you come to finish the job?" Her eyebrow lifted in a provocative mocking manner as if his answer carried no import.

It disconcerted him, this lack of dread. She should beg to be spared, plead for her life, try to dash past him. He scrutinized her as if she were a strange species of insect pinned beneath the microscope of his eye. Yet her gaze never dropped even once to the gun in his hand with its muzzle and silencer. She showed no acknowledgment of the threat to her life, only a curious gaze probing his.

"You knew I would," he said, his own voice sounding strange to his ears. This was something new for him, exchanging words with his victim. He paused, waiting for her bravado to shift to whining and begging. But none was forthcoming. She showed no sign of prostrating herself before him. He was intrigued and curious as to what she would say next.

"I'm not afraid of you anymore. That night I was, but no more. I saw what you did. I should hate you, but for some reason, I don't."

"And why is that?" Was he really conversing with someone already dead?

"Because you're nothing. You have nothing. You love no one. You're empty, soulless, and I feel sorry for you."

"Brave words for someone who will die in a moment."

She chuckled then. "I am already dead."

His breath caught at the echo of his own thoughts.

"You made certain of that," the girl continued. "But I do feel sorry for you. Because while I am young, I have lived a life of love. And I will die knowing that. Whereas you have never loved anyone, least of all yourself."

Adrenaline surged through his veins, goading him to pull the trigger, yet he delayed. Her eyes were luminous, heavily veiled with thick dark lashes. He'd never acknowledged her beauty because he knew not to humanize a target. This was not a killing sparked by passion. It was calculated and cold-blooded. He'd long ago perfected his impassive business plan — pay to slay.

Yes, she was a beauty, but her words chilled him as much as her sultry voice heated his skin. "Do you think you can stir my pity by pointing out my deficiencies? This is my profession. I do not seek forgiveness."

"I'm not offering any. You are nothing to me. When you die, no one will mourn you, for you have left no mark of humanity. You are but a speck of dust to be trampled beneath the feet. What a loathsome way to earn a dollar."

She aroused him. Why had he allowed her to disrupt his pattern, his routine? Gurga's fingers closed firmly around the pistol grip, and his finger quivered, then squeezed the trigger.

His head jerked forward, and his body started to fall. A curtain of blackness plunged him into darkness. He never felt the pain of the blow.

LAYLA'S BREATH bellowed in and out as she stood over the sprawled assassin, her arms still holding the heavy brass fireplace spade. She could have grabbed the poker, which would have surely impaled his brain, leaving her soaked with blood and shattered bone. She'd felt his presence, and when he'd crept down the hall toward the bedrooms, she'd spied him. Choosing the hefty spade over the poker, she'd gathered her nerve. If she killed him from behind with a poker penetrating his skull, there would be an investigation and inquiry by the authorities. Both she and Cyrus were in the country on fake passports sent by Israel. This could blow up into a huge international disaster, a quagmire that would compromise everything they were here for.

It was difficult enough to find the wherewithal to do him harm. She wasn't a killer. Uninvited visions of being kidnapped twice and assaulted flooded her. The brutal guard at Evin Prison who'd nearly raped her. But even worse were her memories of Ali, who'd coerced her into sex and raped her, forcing her to act as if she enjoyed it so he would spare Cerise's life.

Mentally pushing away the feelings of dread that threatened to overwhelm her, she breathed deeply through her nose. Her monsters were dead. The therapy and her training with the IDF kicked in. And she regained her equilibrium. For some reason, the intruder hadn't killed Jazmin on sight. Layla heard snippets of their conversation as she'd crept down the hall with the spade. On silent feet, she came up behind him and walloped him over the head, swinging the spade like a baseball bat. She'd hit him so hard, she'd felt the force travel from her hands to her shoulder. *Good enough.*

"Is he dead?" Jazmin's face shone pallid as the moon. From where she stood, Jazmin couldn't see what Layla could, the minute expansion of his body with each breath. He wasn't dead. Sooner than later, though, he would gain consciousness.

"No. I wish he was, but he isn't. We need to get out of here, now." Layla lowered the spade and bent to pick up the gun. She studied the puzzlement on Jazmin's face. "Do you want to finish him?" she asked. In the short time they'd been together, Layla knew Jazmin wouldn't kill the monster regardless of what he'd done.

Jazmin shook her head no. "I can't. If I kill him, I'll be no better than he is. Besides, Cyrus found a letter from my father. My father died for something he believed in, and he begged me to finish what he began. I can't let anything get in the way. We can't afford to be questioned or detained. We need to get to Zürich." She stared at the assassin's prone body. "At least we should tie him up."

"Hold the gun on him, and I'll be back in a second."

She returned, holding an array of colorful neckties. "It's all I could find."

"It'll work." Jazmin held the attacker's hands, and Layla bound them.

When they finished, Layla pulled her cell phone from her pocket. She took a few pictures of the man's face. "It would be better if it was a straight-on view, but it will have to do. I'm not about to rearrange the scene. Now let's get out of here before he wakes." Taking Jazmin's hand, she pulled her to the master bedroom. The younger woman looked dazed. Layla had been impressed by her courage in standing up to the assassin and keeping him talking. It had given her the time to do what she had to do. She'd been angry when Cyrus had brought Jazmin home without giving her a heads up. Cyrus apologized for it, and she knew he meant it, but she was still finding her feet when it came to being married to a spy. Her experiences over the past few years had been rocky, but her training at IDF and her therapy had done more than help her cope with her PTSD. It had helped her understand Cyrus better. His calling. His love for her and Cerise was infinite, but his sense of duty to the greater good was embedded in his DNA. She wondered if her superhero husband would ever retire. She almost chuckled as she thought of what it would be like having him prowling around the house full time. Her foodie husband would probably spend his days cooking and baking. Perhaps a restaurant lay in their future. But only if they could add an art gallery featuring up-and-coming artists as well. Now that would be a great family business if only she could convince him. One day, perhaps.

She handed Jazmin a royal blue coat made of cashmere. Good thing she'd brought more than one coat with her, she thought as she slipped on a cherry red coat of the same wool. She tossed the gun into her satchel with her purse and slung it over her shoulder. Layla handed the suitcase with their clothes to Jazmin and hefted the matching suitcase that belonged to Cyrus. She led the way downstairs with Jazmin on her heels, their suitcases thumping on each step behind them. Spying Cyrus's briefcase on the kitchen counter, Layla grabbed that too, along with the thermos of coffee she'd prepared and the bag of sandwiches. She was nothing if not practical. "I'll call Cyrus as soon as we're clear of this place. Right now, the important thing is to put distance between *him* and us."

"He could have killed me, but he hesitated. We shared an eerie conversation. You know how they say when you save someone, they belong to you forever. What do you think it means when you spare someone you could have killed?"

"I don't know what it means. But we can ponder that later — we need to get out of here."

They fled through the backdoor in the kitchen, out the garden gate into the alleyway. When they reached the intersection of Campden Hill Road and Kensington High Street, they slowed their walking to a more relaxed pace down the busy thoroughfare of the shopping district. Layla kept looking behind them as they wove through the crowded street filled with late afternoon pedestrian traffic. Her senses were on high alert. Regardless of their success in escaping the hunter, she knew they were ill-equipped to elude him for long. They ducked into Waterstones Bookstore and made their way to the back. The high bookshelves offered cover from the street. Layla sat on a bench, pulled out her cell phone, and punched a button.

"Cyrus —" Her voice sounded like a triggered alarm, carrying a fearful ominous tone.

"What is it, *eshgham?*"

Her eyes flooded with tears at the sound of his voice. She'd been operating on automatic pilot, with her emotions shut down, but hearing Cyrus's voice sparked an electrical charge that jolted her to awareness of how close she and Jazmin had come to death. Layla gave Cyrus a rundown of what happened, keeping her voice to a whisper.

"I'll be there in five minutes. Four-door gray Mercedes. I'll pick you up out front on Kensington High Street. Come out only when you see the car."

"We'll be there."

"Be careful *aziz-am*. I'll be there soon."

"I love you."

"I love you more."

Layla hung up and took a deep breath. And glanced at Jazmin. The girl was operating in shut-down mode. She knew the signs. Jazmin sat quietly, staring straight ahead. Her terror-filled days had triggered a self-protective armor of emotional deadness. And then there was the mission she'd referenced. Layla could imagine that Jazmin had grabbed onto it as if it were a lifeline being thrown to her. It would keep her mind occupied and not dwelling on her tremendous loss. Regardless, Layla was grateful for the younger woman's calm demeanor. It helped her navigate her own fears. She peered around the bookcase, watchful of the street.

A few minutes later, the car screeched to a halt in front of the bookstore. Layla grabbed Jazmin's hand, and they ran out, dragging their suitcases, and jumped into the car. By the time the doors slammed, the car was speeding down the road.

GURGA STUMBLED DOWN THE STREET, ignoring the curious glances of the people he passed. He'd come to not long after the women had fled. He'd checked his watch and knew it to be true. They couldn't be that far ahead of him. He managed to slip his knife from its leg holster, and it only took a couple of minutes for him to cut through the neckties. If anyone on the street had questioned him or spoken to him — he probably would have gone berserk.

He should have shot that blonde banshee in the bedroom before he found Jazmin.

"The Wolf" had never left loose ends before. Loose ends led to mistakes, and mistakes would lead to his own downfall.

It should have been over in a heartbeat — she should have been lying in a pool of blood. Finished. Done.

But the dark-haired beauty had surprised him with her taunting words.

Her hatred and defiance flashed in her hazel eyes.

And he'd hesitated.

He winced, rubbing the egg-sized swelling on the back of his head. Fortunately, he'd only been hit with the flat end of a spade. He'd seen it lying on the floor beside him when he came to. The skin was unbroken, and it had only rendered him unconscious for a short period of time. When he'd awoken, they were gone, and so was his gun. It was clear they weren't coming back anytime soon, as the suitcases the blonde had been packing were also gone. Encumbered with bags, they wouldn't have gotten far.

He figured they'd head toward the busy main street, and that's how he'd come to be hobbling down Kensington High Street peering through every storefront window. All he needed was a clue, any clue as to where they were headed. And then he heard a screech of tires, and he saw them dash out of the bookstore and jump into a gray Mercedes. His gaze zeroed in on the license plate, indelibly imprinting it in his mind. They drove right past him, and for a split second, he caught sight of the dark-haired girl. Her face was also indelibly imprinted in his mind. Anger flooded his senses. And something else. Desire? Yearning? Such a strange and dangerous dichotomy to feel these powerful emotions about the same person. What acts would satisfy this peculiar compulsion he was feeling? The only way to know was to capture her. Take her somewhere. He needed to hold her fate in his hands. Then and only then would he be able to exorcise this craving that had taken root.

I'll find you. That's a promise.

CHAPTER FIFTEEN

Saturday, February 8
Mendoza, Argentina

Twenty hours, that's how long Aryeh had been traveling, and it showed. He stared in the mirror of the hotel bathroom. The hot shower had helped, but the dark circles under his eyes were a dead giveaway. At times like this, he wondered if he was getting too old for the job. He took heart that the old, grizzled spymaster in Tel Aviv, "The Fox," still had faith in him.

Since her disappearance a few months back, finding Zara Zayani had become somewhat of an obsession for Aryeh. He'd called in favors at the DGSE and implored Zara's parents to help him find her. They were only too happy to comply. They hadn't heard from her since she disappeared and feared for her life. He rubbed his unruly beard absentmindedly as he pondered his friendship and partnership with Zara. They'd been through so much together over many years. Yes, sex had complicated matters. But she'd always been a free spirit. They had never tied each other down. They loved hard and then moved on. Their relationship had never gone down a romantic road. Did he regret it? If he were honest with himself, he'd have to say no. Zara was a unique woman — brave, beautiful, and intelligent. Still, he could not see himself connected to her in any way other than as a friend, a comrade in arms, and an occasional lover. But marriage and children? They were beyond that. Which was why he was completely dumbfounded about her falling for Mustafa. Zara had never been interested in marriage or children. She wasn't built that way. Neither was he. He thought he'd understood her.

An image of Jazmin flashed in his mind and he shook it off. Yeah, Jazmin was a beauty, but her soul had been shattered. Far too vulnerable. She was also far too attached to Cyrus. Aryeh was surprised to find Cyrus's arms wrapped around Jazmin that day at the Embassy. But he realized the girl was unconsciously seeking comfort with someone from her past. Someone her father had trusted, and therefore, someone she could trust as well.

Besides, Cyrus was head over heels in love with Layla and would never stray. Never in a million years. *Now there's a woman worth risking everything for.* And Cyrus had risked everything. He'd blown his cover in Iran, a cover that had taken him more than a decade to build. And he'd almost lost his life getting Layla out of Iran. Hell, then he'd done the stupidest thing he could have done and disappeared from Layla's life after their return to Israel. Aryeh shook his head. He'd probably have done the same. Cyrus had believed Layla would be better off without him. But in truth, his life was a misery without her. Aryeh had never believed in the concept of soul mates. He'd always been cynical when it came to love and relationships. But when he saw Cyrus and Layla together, that theory flew out the window. But he also knew Cyrus's marriage was not without conflict. The life of a spy was volatile and uncertain. You stared down death every single day. Layla was a strong woman, indeed, to balance everything.

He thought again of Jazmin and how broken and fragile she'd looked to him. But also how angry and desperate for revenge. He shook his head. He'd been a spy for so long. On his own for so long. No love and no complications, that was his motto.

Did he have the ability to change for the right woman? "Don't even go there, man," he said aloud as he grabbed his shaving kit. "What I need is a *different* kind of change." He would shave off his beard. Maybe that would help.

His thoughts turned back to Zara. In Lebanon, Aryeh had suspected Zara had fallen for the Hezbollah terrorist, her target. She believed he was the mastermind of a planned EMP attack against Israel. She'd been right. Then things got messy. Zara had denied she had feelings for him, but when she allowed Mustafa to escape after the launch of the EMP rocket, Aryeh was convinced she'd betrayed the team. For years he and Zara had partnered on missions — and in bed.

But after Lebanon, Aryeh lost his trust in her. So did the French government. The DGSE recalled her. Zara's career as a spy was over. They re-assigned her to a desk job in Buenos Aires. For Zara, this must have been on par with being sent to Siberia. Aryeh could well understand how upset she must have been to be discarded without recognition for her years of service. His own abandonment of her and refusal to answer her communications to him must have been like pouring salt on a wound. He'd allowed his pride to get the better of him and destroy a life-long friendship that had meant so much to both of them.

His guilt was immeasurable. Zara had no doubt been emotionally distraught and vulnerable to Mustafa's romantic shenanigans. If only Aryeh hadn't cut her off. Could he have prevented her from hooking up with the terrorist? Over and over again, he'd asked himself that question.

Mustafa Mughniyeh had launched the rocket in Lebanon and nearly delivered Armageddon. Then he disappeared. Thankfully, his desired destruction of Israel had been thwarted. Aryeh was certain Mustafa had searched for Zara and found her in Buenos Aires. It was hard for Aryeh to imagine that this woman he'd known so well had abandoned all contact with everyone she knew — both friends and family alike — and vanished. Months had passed since she'd last reached out to him, but the passage of months had given Aryeh time to deal with his anger and place it in a proper perspective. Now, he needed her, and God help him, he needed Mustafa. What Aryeh offered in return was the possibility of rewriting the pages of history. It was a proposition of redemption and forgiveness, and he hoped Zara and Mustafa would take it for their own good and also for his.

CHAPTER SIXTEEN

Saturday, February 8
Mendoza, Argentina,

Aryeh leaned against the car he'd rented. He squinted through field glasses. In the distance, a snow-capped Mount Aconcagua, the highest peak in the Americas, rose above the clouds. After grabbing a quick breakfast, Aryeh had rented a car and driven to the Malbec wine region of the Uco Valley. The valley lay about sixty miles from the city center and the tree-lined streets of Mendoza.

Aryeh wiped his brow as the eighty-degree January heat sent rivulets of perspiration down the back of his shirt. As far as the eye could see, vineyards stretched in endless rows, seemingly to the base of the Andes that rose above the coastal plain dividing Argentina from Chile. Leafy green vines, their stems drooping with the weight of thick-skinned, dark purple Malbec grapes, ripened in the sun. The harvest was almost ready for the Vendimia celebration that took place during the last week of February. But Aryeh's focus had nothing to do with the riot of colors that filled his vision. No, his focus zeroed in on the hacienda with the red-tiled roof.

She'd exited from a side door to a blooming vegetable and herb garden. Carrying a basket, she made her way to a row of ripe tomatoes. Behind her trotted a fluffy silver ball of fur. The woman's straw hat protected her from the sun, but also made it impossible to make out her features. Something about the way she walked was familiar, the gentle sway of her slim hips. He knew every inch of her face and form. A pang of sadness overcame him at the loss of their physical closeness. Their sensual encounters were memories now. But even more sad was the other loss. The greater loss. Her friendship.

Memories came to him in a rush. Running for their lives from a burning Berber camp near Casablanca, nearly dying of exposure in the desert. Bleeding and bruised, clearing the debris from a train in Belgium that a terrorist's bomb had derailed as they frantically searched for survivors. Working together, afraid to even breathe as they defused a bomb destined for the Israeli embassy only seconds before it would have exploded in a banlieue tenement slum in Paris.

Aryeh's senses flooded with images as he watched the woman in the garden. Their sexual encounters seemed like burnished leaves in autumn swept from the trees, each leaf a memory that returned to him as fragments of their conversation filtered through his head. Their courtship had played out amid death and devastation, but it had created a lasting bond. Or so he'd thought.

The last time they'd been together as lovers was in Beirut, they'd been lounging in bed afterward, and he'd burst into sudden laughter.

"What's so funny, *mon cher?*" she'd whispered in her husky French accent. "I insist you share. It's not fair for you to joke at my expense."

"Most lovers share memories of romantic assignations — a beach, a cabin in the mountains, a cruise in the Caribbean. We share the pleasure of heart-pounding near-death experiences, of bloodbaths and bruises, of ticking bombs, and narrow escapes."

Aryeh remembered the way the light had faded from her eyes. "It's who we've become. *Mon Dieu,* It is who they've made us."

"Do you ever think about who you'd be if Jacob hadn't been murdered?" he'd asked. Jacob was the reason Zara had become a spy. Her brother had died when an IED exploded at the train station in Saint-Michel. It must be ten years since the tragedy had devastated her parents, and she'd set aside her academic endeavors. Her memories of Jacob always produced a river of tears. His death changed her and completely derailed her course. Swearing her revenge, she'd enlisted in the DGSE and hardened into a killer. The most dangerous kind of killer, a killer without fear or remorse.

"What if his train had pulled away safely and he'd lived? Would Zara be living an ordinary life, married with children a linguistics professor at the Sorbonne instead of risking her life as a spy and in between grabbing a few stolen moments of pleasure?"

She got up from the bed then and poured them each a glass of cognac. "When I lost my brother, my life changed forever. All I cared about was revenge. I can never live a normal life as long as those monsters wage war on the innocent." Sighing, she'd drunk deeply from her glass. "No use dwelling on what might have been, Aryeh. The woman who taught at the Sorbonne died a long time ago with Jacob. The woman who emerged from the ashes bears no resemblance to her." Her gaze had penetrated his, and for a moment, he wondered if that idealistic young woman was still there, somewhere, buried deep. But the moment passed.

"You need to focus on the here and now, not on what might have been," she'd said to him. She set down her glass and stood before him, dropping her robe. "Before you is a woman who needs you. Make me forget everything, Aryeh."

And he had, or at least he'd tried.

The evidence appeared incontrovertible to him now that somehow the hardened spy had emerged from the ashes once more and found another life. She'd managed to shed her skin and peel away the layers of the duplicitous life she'd led as an undercover agent to start afresh. He imagined her in love, married, and content. He told himself he was not upset that she made her start without him. After all, he never asked her for more. In fact, if anything, he'd praised the fact that their relationship had required no commitments or promises that could be broken.

What they'd shared was complicated, yes, but given without strings attached. No, what truly pricked at him was the sharp knife of disappointment that she found her happily ever after with a terrorist.

In his mind, Aryeh couldn't comprehend how the woman who lost a twin brother to a terrorist's bomb and dedicated her life to stopping acts of terror could fall in love with a man who perpetrated acts of violence. A man who'd been raised to head Hezbollah, the sworn enemy of Israel whose sole purpose was to kill Jews. A man who did, in fact, unleash a nuclear warhead against Israel. And if it hadn't been for Mossad intercepting the bomb, that man would have caused the death and destruction of all they held dear.

"And she forgave that arsehole."

He sighed. If he lived a million years, he would never understand the mind and heart of a woman. He stowed those bittersweet memories away and walked toward Zara and the dog that danced at her heels. He had no idea how she would receive his sudden appearance, but more uncertain was Mustafa's reaction. Mustafa carried a price on his head — wanted by Mossad — dead or alive. Aryeh checked his shoulder harness and the pistol beneath his loose-fitting linen shirt.

Zara bent over a hoe with her back to him. The ball of fluff growled.

"Have you a drink for an old friend?" he asked. Her back stiffened, and for a moment, neither of them moved or spoke. Only the buzz of bees flitting among the flowerbeds and the singsong of birds in the trees filled the air.

She straightened and turned slowly as if collecting herself in the process. By the look on her face, he could tell his appearance wasn't a complete surprise to her. Was it a woman's sixth sense, or had she known that to disappear off the face of the earth was impossible? Her calm reaction revealed that she'd prepared for this day. She did, after all, know him so well.

She tilted her head and smiled. It was the same irresistible smile that had launched a thousand ships, or at the very least, had lured a thousand men to the rocks. In the depths of his heart, maybe he'd hoped to be the recipient of that smile forever. But that dream was long gone. "Did you travel halfway around the world, *mon ami,* for a glass of wine?" she asked.

"What do you think?"

"I'd like to think that in honor of our years of friendship and all that we've been through together, you've come here with good intentions."

"I mean you no harm, Zara. I come in peace. But I'm also here to make you an offer."

Her smile vanished. "You're here to blackmail me." It was a statement, not a question.

"An opportunity for redemption."

She arched a dark brow at him but said nothing. Instead, she picked up the small dog and kissed the top of its head.

"Look, can we get out of this blasted heat and talk?"

She shrugged. "Come, I'll pour us a glass of wine."

The house was one level, built in a U-shape surrounding a stone courtyard. Through the glass sliders, he saw a long wood table and seating, and beyond that, a firepit, swimming pool, and barbeque. Rose bushes abounded, and Aryeh imagined the pleasure of relaxing in such an inviting space, surrounded by their perfume. He couldn't help but feel a spark of envy. Zara had carved out a little paradise here with her true love.

Aryeh followed her into a chef's kitchen of stainless steel and granite counters. He inhaled the scent of spices and fresh herbs. From a temperature-controlled wine storage unit, she pulled out a bottle of deep purple-red wine.

There was pride in her voice when she spoke. "This is the wine we produce from our vineyard, Viñedo de la Montaña." She poured the wine into two goblets and handed him one. "Tell me what you think."

Holding the stem, he swirled the rich dark liquid. Burying his nose in the glass, he inhaled. The aroma was infused with the perfume of red cherry, pomegranate, blackberry, and a hint of chocolate. Sipping, he found the flavor as rich as the aroma. "It's excellent." He nodded and took another sip, watching the dog she called Lulu dance around his feet, vying for his attention.

Zara beamed. "I think so too, and you know what a wine snob I am." He bent and scratched the head of the begging ballerina at his feet.

"Yes, *mon amour,* you are, if nothing else, a true Frenchwoman when it comes to your tastes."

She sipped and contemplated the burgundy liquid in her glass. "Why did you never answer my texts?"

"Because I'm an idiot."

She chuckled at that.

"I was angry, and if I admit the truth, I was jealous too. It was wrong of me, and I'm sorry. Can you forgive me?"

She nodded, accepting his apology. "I have already done so. Besides, true friends don't stand on ceremony. Life is too short."

"Thank you."

She lifted her glass to his, and they toasted like old times.

He gestured to the surroundings. "You have a beautiful home here. Your life is good?"

"Very good. It's more than I could ever hope for."

He nodded. "I'm happy you've found contentment." But even as he said it, understanding eluded him.

Zara read his mind. "He's not the man he was. He — I think he had already begun to change back there, but his father's grip had been so absolute. He cannot change the past, but he is making up for it. I've forgiven him."

The kitchen door burst open. "Habibti, how —" his words ceased when he caught sight of Aryeh.

"*Mon amor,* we have a visitor, an old friend of mine. Mustafa, this is Aryeh, whom I've told you so much about."

Mustafa hesitated for a moment, his gaze observant. Then he stepped closer and offered his hand. "Welcome to our home. What brings you to Mendoza?"

Zara poured another glass of wine and brought it to him. She kissed his cheek, and he hugged her, encircling her waist and holding her possessively against him. Aryeh was impressed that Mustafa seemed genuine in welcoming him and that his face hinted at no jealousy.

It takes self-possession to welcome your woman's former lover into your home.

"I bring a proposal from the prime minister of Israel."

"I see. And what might that be?"

"Can we sit down? There's much I need to tell you."

"Yes, of course," said Mustafa. "Bring the wine bottle, Zara. It seems we will be in need of it. And, please, some snacks. I'm starving."

"Of course, give me a few minutes." She shot Aryeh a sharp-eyed look. "Aryeh, please wait before you begin. I want to hear everything."

Aryeh sat facing the view. He kept the conversation light, inquiring about the vineyard, the harvest, and the wine. His interest sparked an enthusiastic response from Mustafa. It took little encouragement to get Mustafa to expound on his favorite subject. It was as if a dam had opened its floodgates, and he effused about viticulture and the forthcoming picking of the grapes and the crush that would follow. It puzzled Aryeh how this love of farming had developed. But even more mystifying was the transformation of Mustafa from terrorist to vintner. It was unprecedented and impossible to imagine. Two occupations could not be more diametrically opposed.

Zara entered carrying a large silver tray laden with a tempting array of cheeses and crackers, figs, nuts, and Bakoula, a Moroccan feta and pine nut hand pie. "Perfect, my treasure," Mustafa said. He stuffed a pie into his mouth. "You must try one, Aryeh. I'm a lucky man. Zara is an amazing chef."

Aryeh smiled and nodded agreeably. "Thank you." Had he somehow landed in a parallax world? He was having difficulty reconciling Zara, the journalist and spy, with this picture of domesticity. As for the new-and-improved Mustafa, this he found even more confusing. How could this be the son and nephew of two of the deadliest terrorists who'd ever lived? A man born to rule a dynasty built on terrorism. Mustafa's place had been at the top echelon of Hezbollah. He was raised with one purpose, to rule Hezbollah, an organization dedicated to the destruction of Israel.

Aryeh had never believed that love could have such a transformative effect. True, Cyrus had changed after he'd fallen in love with Layla. But Cyrus had been a hardened spy with a string of mistresses, not a deadly terrorist. Could a leopard change its spots? Aryeh was having difficulty comprehending it, let alone believing this miraculous transformation could be true.

Zara sat on the couch, shoulder to shoulder with Mustafa. The poodle cozied into her lap as her fingers caressed the dog's silken ears.

Aryeh put aside his awe at the love that clearly emanated from the couple seated across from him. Time to get down to business. "You've seen the news, I presume, out of London. The blowing up and murder of the Iranian diplomat Saman Amin and his family."

"Yes, it's a tragedy. May their memory be blessed." Mustafa shook his head dolefully. "Does Mossad have any ideas as to who might have done such a thing?" A degree of accusation lay beneath his query.

Aryeh took the bull by the horns and addressed the question head-on. "Iran, of course, has blamed this on Israel and to a lesser degree on the United States. I can tell you with certainty neither Israel nor the U.S. did this. Israel doesn't assassinate innocent wives and children. If it was us, the only person dead would be the target."

"I accept your explanation. Admittedly, this doesn't fit Mossad's playbook."

"You might have heard that simultaneously all over Iran, protests and marches are going on against the regime."

"People protest, but nothing ever changes," Zara noted ruefully.

"This time may be different," said Aryeh. "The authoritarian regime is under extreme pressure because of their incompetence, tyranny, and degradation of the environment. The people are tired of sacrificing for endless sorties and wars in the Middle East. They pay the price with shortages and embargoes that cripple the economy.

"We have evidence that Saman Amin had prepared to defect and compiled proof of sites and locations where uranium for nuclear warheads is being processed, and where underground cities of stockpiled ballistic missiles are stored. It's the kind of proof that indicates the regime is preparing for war. There are experts who believe that if pushed to the wall and forced to hand over power, they will opt for self-destruction. That instead of going quietly, they might commit regime suicide and bomb the hell out of Iran and surrounding countries, maybe even beyond the Middle East."

"That would be tragic, but Zara and I are no longer part of this world. As you can see, we live a peaceful life here. We have foresworn the worlds we came from. Besides, what could we possibly do to stop such an attack?"

Aryeh's lips stretched into a thin line. He spoke softly, but the underlying intensity sounded loud and clear. "You may have forgotten your past deeds, Mustafa, but we have not."

"Are you here to assassinate me?"

"No. As I said, I'm here to make you an offer."

"An offer I can't refuse, to paraphrase Don Corleone from the cinematic masterpiece 'The Godfather.'"

"Spit it out, Aryeh." Zara held back none of her indignance. Their years of closeness and shared history meant she was entitled to say whatever she wanted to him without a filter. They'd never played games before, so why start now?

"What we are offering is simple. Israel will forgive your terrorist acts and leave you to enjoy the fruits of your labors and this idyllic life you've built here if you and Zara help us."

Aryeh saw the flash of anger in Zara's eyes. She was about to lash into him, but Mustafa put his hand up, silencing her. "Help you in what way?" Mustafa asked.

"We need you to go to Iran and rescue Saman's nephew and his girlfriend. They were working with Saman — they have the proof we need on this deadly regime and their plans. We will —"

"No!" Zara thundered at him before he could finish his sentence. "Is this your way of destroying my newfound peace? You blackmail us into a deadly mission that will likely get us killed —?"

"Sh, Zara, let him speak."

"I will not be shushed. This is a suicide mission. If discovered and captured by the Iranians, they will torture us and hang us as spies." Her eyes narrowed, and daggers flew at Aryeh. "Is this your revenge?"

"This is not about revenge. This is about protecting the innocent and bringing down an evil regime that terrorizes the world, including their own people. This is about preventing a future nuclear holocaust and saving a brave man and his girlfriend. The man is a college professor who's been organizing peaceful protests, and he is the nephew of Saman Amin. He and his girlfriend are in danger and unprepared for what is to come. You and Mustafa are the only ones who can pull this off, save their lives, and bring to the attention of the world the information they possess. Both of you have been to Iran, both of you speak Farsi and Arabic. Both of you are warriors trained in the art of subterfuge. It's a chance for Mustafa to clear his name and for both of you to return to Mendoza without fear of being hunted. You used to care about the innocent, Zara, about making the world a safer place."

Zara threw Aryeh a furious glare. He fired back with an equally angry stare-down.

"Such a display of anger could only be shared by two people who care for each other very much ...or at least used to. We all need to think clearly and rise above our emotions." Mustafa took Zara's hand and kissed it. "Regardless of the danger, my darling, we must consider this offer your old friend presents to us today."

Zara caressed his cheek. "We don't have to do this."

Mustafa smiled. "I didn't have to press the button and launch the missile either, but I did. I cannot free myself from my guilt for my past sins. But doing this will help me atone for them." He paused and his eyes met Aryeh's. "More important, it will ensure that I will no longer be hunted — at least by Mossad."

Aryeh nodded in affirmation.

Mustafa's gaze reclaimed Zara's. He lifted her hands and placed a delicate kiss on both palms. "But most of all, we can heal this rancor between you and your friend. We can start anew, my love. Live our lives without the specter of the past looming over us."

Zara sighed. "As always, you surprise me, Mustafa."

"Hopefully, we will live long enough for me to surprise you a thousand times more." He turned back to Aryeh, and his face settled into hard lines of serious intent. "Now, tell us this plan of yours."

CHAPTER SEVENTEEN

Sunday, February 9
Folkestone, United Kingdom

Cyrus drove to the A2 just short of a reckless speed. It would take them an hour and a half to reach the tunnel in Folkestone. He'd memorized the London grid, but there was a huge difference between committing it to memory and actually navigating the tangle of streets, especially when he was worried about getting Layla and Jazmin out of the city safely. After the gazillionth gasp from the women as he took yet another sharp turn, he decelerated and maneuvered the labyrinthine streets with less gusto until they were out of London. Once on the highway, he took a breath.

"I'm sorry I wasn't there to protect you. I shouldn't have left you alone." He stole a worried glance at Layla. Her cheeks were pale. "Is it my driving, or are you angry with me?"

"You couldn't have known you were being watched, and I'm used to your driving by now. I think." She twisted her wedding ring. "Maybe I should have killed him."

It pained him to hear Layla ponder such thoughts. He reached over and covered her hand with his. "No, you did the right thing. You were brave, *aziz-am*. When the time is right, I'll kill him. Besides, we left him in our dust. We can focus on the next step — getting to Zürich and the safety deposit box."

His gaze darted to the rearview. "Jazmin, tell me in detail everything that happened and what he said to you. Everything is important. Something he said might be a clue to his identity."

Jazmin repeated the odd conversation and her even odder reaction when she turned and came face-to-face with the killer. "I-I don't know why, but my hatred dissolved when I saw him. The look on his face… those cold dead eyes. And the way he looked at me as if I were a bug under a microscope. It was so strange. Like he didn't understand what I said to him. I must have shocked him. I didn't understand it myself. I never thought of myself as a courageous person, but I think standing up to him made him fear me in some way. Does that make sense?"

"Yes, it does," Layla said. Her eyes met Cyrus's. He nodded his encouragement for her to continue.

"It's like standing up to a bully in a schoolyard. Surprising as it may seem, it can throw them off guard. You were very brave, Jazmin." Layla gave the younger woman a smile.

Cyrus nodded, pleased that Layla had taken the girl under her wing. "And because you stood up to him, it gave Layla time to hit him over the head. You both did well under terrifying circumstances."

"Thank you, my love," Layla said.

Cyrus winked at his wife. "And you both got a good look at him?"

"Wait —" Layla grabbed her phone out of her purse. "I forgot that I took a picture of him lying on the floor. He's unconscious, but you can see his face."

"Smart thinking, *eshgham*. We need to send it to headquarters. They'll be able to run the photo through Interpol, CODIS, and every other terrorist and criminal database. It's possible we could get a hit."

"His eyes are light brown, the color of petrified amber," Jazmin whispered. "Barren. Like what you expect from a sociopath. I will never forget what he looks like."

Cyrus studied the photo that Layla held up in front of him, his eyes darting from her cell phone to the road. "Okay. Layla, text me his photo." He handed her his phone. "My phone connects through a satellite, then we can send it on to Tel Aviv. I want them on this immediately."

"Do you think they'll figure out who he is?" asked Jazmin, leaning forward.

"With luck. Few assassins operate outside the grid, and they are almost impossible to trace and rarely show up in databases. One thing is for sure, this guy is good. A pro through and through. He managed to figure out where you were hiding, Jazmin, and he laid in wait for you to leave the embassy. He most certainly compromised London's CCTV cameras. He's not only an assassin but an accomplished hacker. He's a threat on many levels. We'll ditch this car when we get to France and rent another one. He must have seen me leave the house, and that's when he made his move. If he could do that, he may have seen the license plate, and tracking us will be easy."

"But why do they want to kill me," Jazmin said, her voice cracking. "And why did they kill m-my family? Why is this happening?"

"They're afraid of what your father may have found and squirreled away. They want you dead, but it's really about what you may know or what you may have access to. And they feared you would reach out to their enemies. Which you did. The assassin's client wants you dead because you're the last link. I'm convinced it's the threat you pose to them, which means the client is probably someone in the IRI. They hired an outside entity to do their bidding because they can't afford to be linked to what happened. It would only bring more condemnation on the regime, and they've got plenty of that already. So they hired an assassin." Cyrus swerved out of the lane to pass a truck. As he spoke, he eyed the rearview, searching for tails. "You both heard him speak. Did either of you place an accent?"

"Yes, but I'm not sure from where," Jazmin replied. She shook her head. "I'm sorry. I was too caught up in what he was saying that it didn't register how he said it."

"It's all right, Jazmin," Layla said. "You did great. As I made my way down the hall, I could hear him fairly well. His English was precise, as if he'd taught himself how to hide his origins."

"Yes, you're right, Layla," Jazmin agreed. "His English was very good. Very practiced."

"Hired gun, no question about it. They wouldn't have sent an Iranian." Cyrus didn't give voice to the rest of his thoughts. Both Layla and Jazmin now had targets on their backs. Dammit. If he'd been there, he could have finished off that bastard. Cyrus was not going to put Layla's life in danger again. No matter what Mossad had initially intended. Once they were in Zürich, he would arrange for her safe return back home to Israel. She would fight him, of course. But he would insist on it. He glanced at Layla, her beauty never failing to take the breath from his lungs, and gave her a reassuring smile. "All will be well, *aziz-am*. I promise."

She smiled back. "As long as I'm with you, my superhero, all will be well."

CHAPTER EIGHTEEN

Sunday, February 9
Folkestone, United Kingdom
Euro Train

While Jazmin and Layla bought coffee and sandwiches at the rest stop, Cyrus broke down the Glock 27 Layla had taken off the assassin along with his Sig Sauer P226 and stored the pieces in the false bottom of his suitcase in a lead-lined bag. Before boarding the train, they passed through both British and French passport control without additional questioning, and he sighed with relief that Jazmin's newly minted passport raised no eyebrows.

Cyrus drove down the narrow lane and queued up for the Euro Train. The passage held one car at a time. Although he didn't voice his discomfort, beads of sweat coated his forehead and gave testament to what he was feeling. He'd always been claustrophobic, and the space allotted between the cars on the train was nil. The fluorescent lighting and the walls closing in on him sent his pulse racing. He didn't dare think about the fact that the chunnel was seventy-five meters at its deepest point below the English Channel. Confined spaces were the only thing he feared. It was an anxiety that even Dahlia, his shrink at

Mossad headquarters, hadn't been able to cure. Fortunately, even though it raised all of his levels — pulse, heartbeat, breathing — it also intensified his acuity. His senses sharpened, and that heightened keenness had never failed him.

Layla reached over and massaged his neck. There was nothing about him she didn't know, and this chink in his superman armor wasn't new to her. "It's only thirty-five minutes, and we'll be in Calais."

"Yeah," he breathed. "I'm fine. I hate confined spaces."

"I know. Here, eat something. It will take your mind off the train."

"I need my gun."

"Let me get it," Layla said. "Less conspicuous."

He gave her a jerky nod, and she got the bag out of the trunk, pulling out two blankets as well.

She got back into the back seat and made a show of folding one of the blankets into a pillow and slipping it behind Jazmin's head. Then she took out the gun pieces from the false bottom and passed them to Cyrus. Jazmin shifted and mumbled in her sleep. Layla covered the girl with the other blanket. In a minute, Cyrus reassembled the Sig Sauer and Glock and stuffed both into his trench coat pockets while Layla slipped in beside him in the front seat.

Layla gave him a reassuring wink this time. A quick glance told him that neither the people in the car behind or in front had paid any attention. Layla handed him a sandwich, and he took a bite and scrolled through his cell phone. He was worried that the assassin who'd tracked Jazmin to the flat in London would track them to Metz. They needed to ditch the Mercedes and rent another car.

He sighed with relief when they exited the chunnel. It wasn't nearly as bad as he'd feared. The vibrations were minimal, and he kept his claustrophobia at bay. Before he knew it, they were in France and on their way east.

Cyrus picked up the A26, the quickest route to Metz. Glancing in the rearview, when they drove through a lit overpass, he noticed a black BMW not far behind them. Varying his speed to confirm they were being tailed, he could see the BMW adjust its speed, keeping a safe distance. Enough not to be obvious but enough to keep them in sight. It was dark, and Cyrus weighed his options. They'd barely made the train, being one of the last cars to load, so he knew the BMW wasn't on the train. But it was plausible the assassin had cohorts at his beck and call. Cyrus didn't believe the assassin would leave the actual kill in the hands of anyone but himself, but dead was dead, and Cyrus wasn't about to take any chances.

They were outside Reims when Cyrus put the pedal to the metal, and with a powerful roar, the Mercedes shot forward. The speedometer pushed past 170 kilometers per hour. In the rearview, he could see the tailing BMW speed up.

"Cyrus, you're driving over a hundred miles per hour." Layla had been dozing on and off, but the increased speed must have woken her.

He nodded toward the back and stole another glance in the rearview. "We've got company."

Layla swiveled to look out the rear window. "Oh, God, what are you going to do?"

"I'm going to draw them out and then lose them." He hissed, his jaw clenching.

"Jazmin, get down," Layla ordered.

The BMW shot out of the lane and came up beside them. *I guess the cat and mouse game is over.* The passenger window came down, and from the corner of his eye, Cyrus spied the muzzle of a suppressor.

"Get down," he yelled, swerving. The BMW made its move. Cyrus slammed on the brakes, and the sound of screeching tires pierced the silence. A bullet shattered the passenger side window, sending glass flying.

Jazmin screamed from the back seat.

"Shit!" Cyrus gritted his teeth and hit the gas again. "You want to play chicken," he growled. "I'll play."

The few other cars on the highway were pulling over left and right, trying to stay out of the way of both vehicles as they raced dangerously close to one another. Another bullet hitting the car sounded like the bang of cymbals.

"Are you okay, Jazmin?" Cyrus shouted.

"Yes, I'm on the floor, but there's glass everywhere."

"Damnit! Stay down and brace yourselves, ladies."

The BMW slowed and again positioned to take a shot. The muzzle of the gun pointed right at Cyrus. He turned the steering wheel sharply and slammed into the BMW. The scraping of metal on metal was deafening, a clanking, screeching sound of two objects tearing against each other. Again, Cyrus smashed against the BMW, and this time the BMW bounced off the Mercedes and swerved away, trying to avoid contact.

The separation was enough to give Cyrus the chance he'd been waiting for. "Honey, grab the wheel and keep your eyes on the road ahead."

Layla grabbed the steering wheel as he aimed his gun, held his breath, and shot out the front and rear tires of the other vehicle. It was a nearly impossible shot to make, but he managed it, and the speed and imbalance of weight sent the other car into a tailspin. The driver of the BMW had no other choice but to hit the brakes and screech to a halt, a plume of burning rubber rising from the tires.

Cyrus grabbed the wheel again and gave Layla a quick kiss on the lips. "Baby, we would have made one hell of a Bonnie and Clyde team."

"You watch too many movies." Layla's hands shook and she clasped them together. Cyrus rubbed her shoulder. "You did great, *eshgham.*"

"You were both amazing!" Jazmin excitedly echoed. Cyrus peered in the rearview mirror and saw Jazmin had managed to put the blanket up to cover the broken window and now sat on the other side of the back seat, behind Layla.

"Thanks," Layla and Cyrus said at the same time. They drove on, putting miles between them and the BMW. The sign ahead read Reims, and Cyrus veered off the exit, tires squealing. He saw flashing lights in the rearview mirror, and he wasn't about to be stopped, searched, and questioned. Hopefully, the thugs would be arrested and at least spend the night in jail. He slowed to the legal speed limit and drove through a roundabout toward Reims.

"I can't believe they shot at us right out in the open," Jazmin said.

He smiled. "Criminals don't follow the rules. That's why they're called criminals."

"Well, I, for one, have had enough excitement for the day," Layla said. "Everything will be better tomorrow after we've gotten some sleep." She smiled at Jazmin over her shoulder.

"I just want a hot shower and then a hot chocolate."

"Tomorrow, we'll rent another car and head to Zürich," Cyrus said. "Right now, I need to apprise headquarters of what's happening, and I want to find out if they've identified the assassin. We need to know what we're up against. I also need to touch base with Aryeh. I want him to meet us in Zürich."

The traffic was light at ten p.m. as they drove through the streets of Reims. Cyrus had been here before while attending the University Paris Sud, an adjunct of the Sorbonne, where he studied nuclear physics. Before he joined Mossad and began his training in Israel, he enjoyed taking weekend trips to different parts of France. Being the son of an architect, he was fascinated to see the architecture that had influenced his father when he attended university in Paris. Reims was only an hour and a half drive from Paris. Soon after he arrived in Paris for his first year of graduate school, he went to see one of the masterpieces of the Gothic period, Reims Cathedral, and its glorious rose stained-glass window. Both Layla and Jazmin were wide-eyed as the towering cathedral came into view.

The cathedral provided a perfect opportunity to get their minds on something other than that damn assassin. "I visited Reims when I was at the Sorbonne," Cyrus said. "Reims Cathedral is over eight hundred years old. Twenty-five of France's kings were coronated here." As he spoke, he recalled a story he'd heard all those years ago. "Legend tells that the Holy Ampulla, a glass vial containing the chrism, the oil used to anoint the kings of France, arrived on the wings of a white dove for the anointing of Clovis I in 496. The ampule was destroyed during the French Revolution, but purportedly a few pieces and some of the oil were saved and hidden."

"Considering that I'm an art history major and a curator, how is it you've never told me about your visit here?" Layla asked.

He studied the twin bell towers. "If I told you everything, then there'd be nothing left to tell. I wouldn't want you to become bored with me," he teased.

Layla chuckled. "That, my love, could never happen."

Cyrus also recalled that Joan of Arc liberated the cathedral from the English in 1429. "I think it's a good sign that we're here. This is where Joan of Arc won her greatest battle. As I recall, two statues of The Maid of Orléans still exist. One where she sits astride a horse in full armor riding into battle with her sword held high above her head, and one of her standing demurely with her sword in full battle dress. A brave woman like the two of you." He winked.

"What a remarkable woman she must have been," Jazmin said, her voice filled with awe. "It is truly inspiring — makes me feel a little stronger about myself, imagining all the other women throughout history who stood up for something they believed in."

"Yes, it is inspiring when you think about all the atrocities endured by women and children — and the innocent — over the centuries. Yet they still fought bravely or walked into the lion's den with their heads held high."

Cyrus shook his head. He'd sought to get their minds off what was going on, and now they were even more embedded. "Yes, you are both right, but we have might on our side. Mossad. So please don't worry."

"My superhero, you forget, we're like warriors now," Layla quipped. "I wish we could stay and take a tour. I've always wanted to see the stained-glass rose window and the Gallery of Kings sculptures above the window." She gave him a gentle shove. "You're not the only one who knows their art history. It's fortunate the window survived both the bombing and burning of the cathedral during World War I."

Cyrus heaved a mental sigh. Back on art history stuff. His wife could talk for hours about it, which was what they needed now. It would provide a mental break from their fear and anxiety. Despite their bravado, he knew they were scared. He needed to be calm so he could stay focused on keeping them safe. It was much better for Jazmin and Layla not to spend every minute thinking about being hunted and on the run from a deadly killer. He looked forward to meeting up with Aryeh. He could use his help. Cyrus sensed a coming confrontation with the assassin. Considering the threat the killer posed to Layla and Jazmin, he would have to kill him. He found a degree of satisfaction in the thought.

"It's beautiful, isn't it, Jazmin?" whispered Layla. "It's hard to fathom all the history that's taken place here. I wish we could visit it."

"It is incredibly beautiful. In my country, we have beautiful mosques that are decorated with intricate mosaics of colored tiles and crowned with golden domes. We have our fables and legends of greatness too. In Khorasan Province, in northeastern Iran, lies the village Neyshabur. My father took me there as a child to see a twenty-five-meter-high statue of the mythological phoenix called Simorgh. The poet Ferdowsi writes in his epic poem *The Shahnameh* about an albino baby named Zâl, who was rejected by his parents and mothered by the phoenix. When Zâl's father returns for him, Simorgh gives the boy some of her feathers and tells him if he ever needs help, he should burn one of the feathers, and she will come to him in the form of a black cloud. The day comes when the boy's wife, Rudâbeh, is dying while giving birth. Desperate to save his wife and child, Zâl burns a feather, and the phoenix appears. She tells Zâl to cut the baby from Rudâbeh's belly. The mother and baby are saved. The baby grows up to be the legendary holy-warrior Rostam." Jazmin's eyes grew misty. "Have you been to Iran, Layla?"

Layla stole a glance at Cyrus, and he nodded his encouragement to her. "I have been to Iran, but I'm afraid I didn't get to visit any of the mosques or see many of the magical wonders of your country. But one day, I'll tell you about my adventure to Tehran and how I met my husband."

Jazmin's voice fell with sadness. "I don't think I will ever see my country again."

"I know you love Iran as much as I do," Cyrus said, swallowing a lump in his throat. "Never say never. One day the people of Iran will rise up like the phoenix and take back their country. Then we can all visit together. How does that sound?"

Jazmin gave them a wobbly smile. "I would like that very much."

"Layla put both Reims Cathedral and Iran on our bucket list."

"I don't understand. What is this bucket list?" asked Jazmin.

Layla's eyes glowed. "It's a list of all the places you want to visit before you die. It's an American colloquialism."

"You're American, aren't you?"

"I am born and raised, but now I live in Israel." Layla tapped on her mobile. "This is a picture of our daughter, Cerise. She's five years old."

Jazmin stared at the phone and smiled. "Oh, she's beautiful. A perfect combination of both of you."

"Yes, she is. But truthfully, she's a clone of her father. Same brilliant mind, same stubbornness." Layla laughed.

"Hey, our daughter is a new and improved version, and she's all you when it comes to getting what she wants," he teased back. "Okay, ladies, we need to find a hotel. Use my phone and pull up some options."

After discussing availabilities, Cyrus picked the Hôtel Mercure because of its location on the Vesle River. He liked the idea of an additional avenue for escape should they need one. It also offered underground parking and a French restaurant. They had one suite available. The living room held a sofa bed. He could sleep on the fold-out, and the women could sleep in the king bed in the bedroom. There was no chance he'd allow Jazmin to sleep in a separate room. Not when he knew a killer was on the hunt for her.

They checked in and dropped their stuff in the room before heading to the restaurant. Cyrus ordered a skewered steak au poivre with pommes frites and a bottle of red wine. He was ravenous and needed to refuel. The ladies opted for omelets and salads.

Layla pushed her food around the plate. "What is it, *eshgham?*"

Jazmin's eyes were on her plate, but he noted the smile that crept across her face whenever he used a Farsi endearment of love with Layla.

"I'm thinking about how fast everything happened. We've only been in Europe for two days, and we've nearly been assassinated, shot at from a moving vehicle, and nearly run off a highway. I can't imagine what will come next." She raised her gaze to his. "And then I remember that you face this all of the time. Every time you're called away on a mission, it must be like this for you."

He took her hand and kissed her palm, smiling. "It's not always about avoiding bullets. Sometimes it's more about leading a team and planning. You know logistics. The boring stuff. That's what I'm trained to do."

"Don't sugarcoat it. You walk a tightwire without a net."

"You and Cerise are my net. Knowing that when I come home, you'll be there. But in this business, you're only as good as your last mission. Right now, keeping you and Jazmin safe is all I care about." He leaned in and whispered. "And finding out what Saman left in that box. It may be the key to saving millions of lives, and that's why I do what I do."

His phone beeped, reminding him he needed to call the Ramsad. "Let's finish up and head upstairs. I need to text Aryeh to meet us in Zürich." And then Cyrus remembered the letter Saman had left in the humidor for Jazmin. "Jazmin, with all of the excitement, I forgot to let you read the letter Saman left you."

Jazmin, who'd sat quietly listening to Cyrus and Layla's exchange, snapped to attention. "The letter. Did you read it?"

"Of course. It was instructive and important as to the safety deposit key."

"What did it say?"

"I'd prefer you read it upstairs. There's a lot in it that is cryptic and cries out for explanation. References that possibly you'd have an insight into."

"My father sometimes spoke in riddles. It was a game we often played with each other. I will try to shed light on his words."

CHAPTER NINETEEN

Monday, February 10
Lufthansa Flight Buenos Aires to Zürich Flight

Aryeh had gained a day flying to Argentina, but now he was losing a day on the flight back. It reminded him of his life, a gain here, a setback there. He nursed a glass of scotch on the rocks and stared out the window. He was at the airport when he received the text from Cyrus. His initial booking had been to London, but Cyrus needed him, and Aryeh rebooked and caught a flight to Zürich. Zara and Mustafa would leave tomorrow for Tehran. Mossad was creating new identities and passports for them that would be overnighted to Buenos Aires. Their newly minted identities had them married and off to celebrate their honeymoon in Iran, where Arman Shirvani and Mustafa's fabricated parents were from. His new wife Francoise was French Algerian. Both Arman and Francoise worked in the wine industry, Arman in sales, and Francoise as a vintner. Once in Tehran, Zara and Mustafa would meet with a deep-cover Mossad agent and receive whatever support necessary for their success in extracting Ibrahim Nassiri and Shira Darbandi and getting them out of Iran to safety.

Predictably, seeing Zara again had opened a can of worms. He'd always considered her his alter-ego, his female counterpart. He swirled the ice cubes in his glass as he contemplated his feelings for her. How had he been so wrong about her? He'd always believed they were on the same page when it came to relationships. Both dedicated to their work with no room for personal entanglements — an Achilles heel that might compromise them. He'd convinced himself that to survive in their business, a man or woman needed to be free of weakness. A weakness, if discovered by the enemy, could mean death.

It had never occurred to him that she might have been holding a dream of marriage and children. Now he realized he'd been blind. She'd hidden it well beneath a façade of indifference. Sex was a delight to be shared when the opportunity presented itself, but commitment never factored into the equation. She'd been careful to present herself as an agent first and a woman second. He knew now it was a safety measure. Could what they'd shared become more if he'd only showed his own feelings? Could they have built a life together if he'd been more open and told her how he'd really felt about her? Now it was too late, and it seemed as if the roof had caved in on him. He'd lost his chance, and Mustafa had claimed what might have been his. Another swig of scotch wouldn't eliminate the truth no matter how much it burned as it went down.

Zara had agreed reluctantly to the assignment, but he had seen in her eyes that she blamed him for convincing Mustafa to take on what might turn out to be a suicide mission. He could tell she'd convinced herself it was his revenge upon her. In her mind, he'd suggested her to the Ramsad as the perfect candidate for the rescue and then tracked her down to punish her for choosing Mustafa over him. Was it true? Had Zara, who knew him better than anyone, hit the nail on the head? Had he purposely sent her into harm's way to exact revenge? He owed it to her to ask himself the question and answer it truthfully. And then he owed her an apology, again, for what he'd put her through.

He took another swig of whiskey to loosen his thoughts. Aryeh knew he would never do anything that wasn't in the best interests of Israel. The present situation was tenuous, and a firestorm would erupt that could set the world ablaze if it weren't disarmed. Iran's threat to

Israel and the world was exponential. If the rogue regime opted to release Armageddon, everyone would be affected, but Israel would not survive. There would be no havens, no future for anyone. Mustafa and Zara were uniquely qualified for this mission. The professor and his girlfriend had information that could ignite change, a revolution that could bring down the corrupt regime. The "what if" that the Iran regime would destroy itself and take as many of their enemies as possible out with them before relinquishing power was a scenario that had to be prevented at all costs. If Aryeh could have gone instead of Zara and Mustafa, he would have gone gladly. In any case, Cyrus had texted, requesting his help with Saman's daughter Jazmin and the safety deposit box in Zürich. It was too dangerous for Cyrus to protect the two women on his own and get to the box while fending off an assassin.

Jazmin was another question burning in his mind. His gut churned with anger when he thought of what she'd been through. To see her family and her fiancé murdered in cold blood on the night before her wedding. And then, to add insult to injury, the bombing of their home so that her loved ones could not even be mourned over. The brutality represented to Aryeh everything wrong with the world. And now, like an animal, she was being hunted. Aryeh was, at heart, a simple man who fought for justice. He viewed the world through a black-and-white lens, good on one side, and evil on the other. There was no in-between, no reason that could explain away acts of savagery. It was one of the reasons he was a successful agent. Aryeh operated under the premise that life was precious, and each person deserved to live without the threat of anyone taking what was rightfully theirs. The Americans had voiced it perfectly in their Declaration of Independence, the unalienable right of "Life, Liberty and the pursuit of Happiness." He lived by that motto. If someone threatened to take that away, they were fair game, and Aryeh would be happy to deliver the sentence.

He finished the last sip of scotch. Sleeping the rest of the flight would prepare him for the day ahead. He thought of the Biblical Ecclesiastes passage that he turned to when embarking on a mission: There is a time and a season for everything:

A time to be born and a time to die,
A time to plant and a time to uproot,
A time to kill and a time to heal…
A time to love and a time to hate,
A time for war and a time for peace.

As Aryeh put his seat back and closed his eyes, he knew exactly what time was coming.

CHAPTER TWENTY

Sunday, February 9
Reims, France

Cyrus watched the nuances of emotion play over Jazmin's face as she read her father's final letter to her.

She wiped away the tears that slid down her cheeks. When she spoke, she didn't try to conceal the resentment. "I have cried an endless stream of tears, but never enough to dull the pain."

Layla put her arm around Jazmin's shoulder and hugged her. "I think it is clear your father had experienced a change of heart and feared what the regime planned. It's also clear that he loved you very much."

"It is strange now when I think of all the bits and pieces of conversations that I've listened to over the years. I never paid attention and didn't realize how much he'd changed over time."

"All of this is important, Jazmin," Cyrus said. "Knowledge is power, especially when it comes to understanding this regime. There are clues you may not have been aware of at the time."

"I think my father was very happy to move to London," Jazmin said. "As you know, the present Ayatollah Khamenei is the placeholder for the Twelfth Imam, Muhammad al-Mahdi, who is in occultation. Shiites believe he will soon return to bring justice to the world. This is why the Ayatollah is called The Supreme Leader. However, Khamenei started humbly and was not respected due to his lack of religious credentials by the clerics, and in order to consolidate his rule, he built up the Revolutionary Guards, the Quds Force, and Basij into the most powerful forces in Iran. In a sense, they are a private army with millions of warriors dedicated to preserving one life, the Ayatollah, and to enriching themselves."

Cyrus thought about the importance of Jazmin's words. "Yes, and through the Quds Force, the IRGC built and control Hezbollah, Hamas, the Houthis, and others. Through these surrogates, terror spreads all over the Middle East. Not to mention their ultimate goal of destroying Israel and subjecting the Sunnis to their dominance." Cyrus leaned forward on the sofa, clasping his hands in front of him. "Without the IRGC, Khamenei wouldn't last a week."

"It's true, I heard my father say this. Khamenei is old and not well. He's survived prostate cancer, but his days are numbered. It was of the greatest concern to my father who would succeed him."

Cyrus nodded. "I've heard whispers that nepotism might be in play. It seems the Ayatollah would like to keep the throne in the family. His son Mojtaba is a candidate to succeed him. Fitting, since he runs the Basij militia. Another tyrant in the making."

"When you feed a lion, you must be wary. He may eat you in the end," Jazmin said in a bitter tone. "My father believed the IRGC might steal complete power for themselves. Perhaps put up a proxy Ayatollah to do their bidding. The IRGC is untouchable. Their highest-ranking live like princes in a world apart from the rest of the people. They live in posh neighborhoods with their own schools and markets, and they control everything from the oil and gas industry to agriculture." Jazmin sighed and ran her fingers over her father's writing. Her gaze fixed on Cyrus. "What would you do to retain power and keep this immense wealth?"

He gave no answer, so Layla asked, "So why does Saman suggest, at least cryptically, that Iran might unleash Armageddon? It would seem the IRGC will do nothing to upset their gravy train."

"The riots and the sanctions are taking a toll," Cyrus said. "Iran is a joyless place. The people are oppressed. The last time this was true, it sparked a revolution. Who's to say it won't again?"

Jazmin took Layla's hand. Cyrus had noticed that surviving the assassin had brought the two women close. "My mother and father argued, not really argued, but discussed the fact that if anything could bring down the regime, it would be women. Women have returned to the universities and are a majority there. Educated women." She smiled at Layla. "Women like us will bring down this regime. Women are the catalyst. Iranian women cry out for equality. The mullahs would have us live under the thumb of Sharia law and breed like cattle. The IRGC has stolen what belongs to the people, but in some ways, they are preferable. The people might be thrilled to be free from the clerics."

Cyrus pondered the possibility. "A theocracy ruled by the elite of science and industry is an interesting concept. I wonder what it means to their nuclear ambitions or their desire to control the Middle East?"

Jazmin shook her head. "I do not know."

"Is 'I' Ibrahim Nassiri?" Cyrus asked.

"Yes, he's my cousin. Have you heard anything about him? Is he okay?"

"As far as I know, he's fine, at least for the moment." He studied Jazmin before asking the question that had been plaguing him. "Is it possible that Ibrahim compromised your father?"

"Never! Not in a million years. They were like this —" She held up two fingers together as one. "Inseparable, both of the same temperament and intellectual curiosity. My cousin is a nuclear physicist. He knows what's at stake. He's a patriot who wants freedom for his people."

Cyrus knew every effort was being made to get Ibrahim and Shira out of Iran before the authorities arrested them. Aryeh had texted him that Zara and Mustafa were leaving soon for Tehran to lead the mission to extract the dissidents. For the time being, it was best not to get Jazmin's hopes up. "Do you have any way to get in contact with Ibrahim?"

"No. My father spoke to him regularly, but I can't imagine what he must be thinking now. I wish I could let him know that I'm okay."

"We'll work on that. But for now, I think we should get some rest. We have to rent another car, and we have a long drive tomorrow. You and Layla take the bedroom and I'll take the couch."

Cyrus kissed Layla on the cheek and watched the two women disappear into the bedroom. Switching the lights off, he stood at the window. The moon's reflection fractured off the river, intermittently playing hide-and-seek with the clouds that sought to devour its light. Snowflakes fell silently, dusting the branches of trees and shrubs, and Cyrus wondered whether the world would be blanketed in snow by morning. The unearthly quiet made him aware that this moment of uninterrupted reflection might be his last for some time. He'd managed to elude their pursuers, but the assassin couldn't be far behind. For all Cyrus knew, the assassin might be in Reims already. Cyrus needed to get them safely to Zürich and then lay low until Aryeh joined them. He retreated to the sofa, his Glock pistol by his side. In the morning, he'd rent another car, and they'd be on their way. With any luck, they'd be in Zürich by late afternoon.

CHAPTER TWENTY-ONE

January 9, midnight
Reims, France

Idiots! Gurga stood at the window, his anger in complete contrast to the serenity beyond the pane of glass. Snow had begun to fall, and like a day without the sun, the world transmuted into the limited color spectrum of varying shades of black and white. Gurga's voice, modified by the software on his cell phone, sounded low and gravelly to his ears. On the other end of the line, a Serbian mafia chief received Gurga's venomous attack with a sharp intake of breath. He received his flagellation the way a warrior tied to a post received lashes from a cat-o'-nine-tails — seething but silent.

In most instances, Gurga worked alone, but when the need arose, he sometimes turned to a select group of criminal organizations to do his bidding. Arrangements were made using code names, and payments were made through untraceable offshore phantom corporations and trust accounts. In the underworld, names were better left unknown. But this time, the fools had gotten themselves arrested, and Gurga's quarry was now alerted that he was hot on their trail.

"You let me down, and I don't like being let down."

"Unforeseen problems arose."

Gurga could imagine the disdainful shrug that accompanied the man's pathetic excuse. "I'm in agreement with that. Of course, there will be no transfers due to unforeseen problems." The thug needed to understand the consequences of failure.

"Freeing my birds is going to cost me."

"Not my problem. Let them rot for all I care. They're not an endangered species. Plenty more to take their place. Next time see that they get the job done." He hung up, feeling only slightly better. It was the phone call before that ate away at him. After the unfortunately failed confrontation with the Serbian mercenaries, Gurga had tracked the Mercedes to Reims, where he'd intended to end the cat and mouse game with three well-aimed slugs. But he'd been told to stand down. He was an assassin who prided himself on no political affiliations, but the client had turned this into a recovery operation of sorts, and he wasn't pleased. Gurga hit the play button on his phone to listen a second time to the conversation he'd recorded with the client in Tehran. He'd expected a chastisement from the moneyman. What he hadn't expected was to be thrown off his purpose.

"We've hit a snag in our plans. The targets have a reason for this change of direction, a reason for this impromptu decision to flee London with the girl across Europe by car. It means we must hold off on termination."

"What do you want me to do?"

"They're after something detrimental to us. I want you to let them reach their destination. Once you are sure they are in possession of the merchandise, you're to gain control of it and then annihilate them."

"What is this something? You must have some idea of where they're headed. The body count on this job is beginning to pile up, which raises the potential for error."

"They're headed to a banking institution in a haven where names aren't important. Since they're driving, the destination can't be too far. You're looking for stolen information in the form of flash drives, photos stored on a cell phone, blueprints, possibly all of the above.

This information must never see the light of day. Intercept and deliver the goods to us, and your fees will be doubled."

"This will require considerable risk. Your enemies are accomplished, and obviously, they will do whatever it takes to retrieve the merchandise and hold on to it. I want triple our agreed-to compensation."

"You drive a hard bargain, my friend. As you wish, as per the terms of our agreement, half the funds will be transferred immediately and the rest as soon as the goods are delivered to us. But heed this warning. This information cannot fall into the wrong hands. I shouldn't have to remind you that if you foolishly think of blackmailing us, your death warrant will be signed. There is no place on Earth safe from our vengeance if you fail. The defenders of the true faith will not be appeased if you double-cross us."

"I do not respond to threats, General." It was the first time that Gurga let on that he knew the identity of the client. It was important for the man to know his own life was at risk. A few beats of silence followed in which Gurga could almost hear the client's pulse accelerate.

"It is not so long ago that we served *Hajj Qasem,* together in the desert," said the client referencing the martyred Quds Force general. "Did you think, my friend, that I would be foolish enough not to keep leverage over you? Deliver the goods, and your identity is safe."

Gurga ended the recording of the call. His brain fired on all cylinders as he slipped into the vortex that submerged the present with the past. Lightning struck — his throat burned from diesel fuel, his tongue peppered by grains of sand that lodged in his mouth, an assault of knives tearing his throat raw. He hit the dirt, expecting to be blown to pieces by an IED or shot by a sniper. In that second, he bonded with death and knew with certainty there was nothing beyond it. No virgins, no paradise, no gardens of Allah. Everything that had been drummed into him in the training camps was fool's gold. He was merely an instrument of another man's power struggle. He burrowed deeper into the burning sand as if dead. The AK-47 still hot from its deadly burst. He couldn't feel his limbs, he couldn't swallow, he couldn't breathe. Maybe he was dead already.

Gathering his strength, he rose from his shallow grave and ran forward with the curse of religious ferocity on his lips. "*Allahu Akbar*!" The shout that nonsensically forgave all acts committed in His name and sent terror into the hearts of the enemy was a warrior's blind devotional that paved the way to heaven. Around him, the dull thump-thump-thump of bullets permeating flesh. Splattered blood and bone splashed against his face in a sticky warmth. Rage is a powerful aphrodisiac that alters all perspective. A solo fighter reborn as a mythical warrior. It's not so different than the all-consuming desire of penetrating a woman. Once unleashed, nothing can stop it. Rage is primal, exclusive to man. Beasts do not rage. Only man is beleaguered with emotion. Rage is what got him through that battle and the battles that followed.

Gurga hailed from the Alawite Shia community, as did Bashar al-Assad, and the ancient city of Aleppo was the battleground where Gurga cut his teeth. He was but a teenager when he'd become a hardened warrior trained by the Quds Force Training Directorate, code-named "12,000" at their headquarters at the Imam Ali military base off the Tehran-Karaj highway in Iran. The Quds Force's Imam Ali Garrison training facility was run by the same brigadier general who, by chance, had hired Gurga for this job.

Gurga's Quds Force training and deployment in Syria had made him immune to the dead and dismembered, but when his unit marched through the streets of Aleppo on a November morning wearing gas masks, what he saw shredded his psyche. Women and children with white foam dripping from their lips. Without exception, their mouths open, gasping for breath. It was as if a school of fish had fallen from the heavens onto dry land to die. Their mouths opened and closed, desperate to breathe. He couldn't smell their death or the pulmonary failure inflicting their lungs. But it was as if his eyes were metal and the women and children's eyes were magnets. He was unable to look away. For some reason, he pictured them laughing, playing among the rubble of neighborhoods leveled by war. His own mother's face emerged from the face of a mother holding a dead baby to her breast. What God would allow this? The death in their eyes accused them all.

He hated what they had done. But he could do nothing to stop it. To alter the evil that burned in their hearts. Where was Allah in all of this? How did they dare claim this was all for the greater good? Women and children slaughtered for naught but a piece of desert. He would not be party to it. Nor could he do anything other than be a soldier.

He could not change the world, but he could escape the hell he found himself in. If he stayed, he would have turned to dust on the battlefield. He chose to leave and embrace a different kind of life, one that could give him the freedom he craved and the financial means to live it.

The world needed killers. Assassins for hire. Whether he worked for governments or crime syndicates, it didn't matter. He would apply all he'd learned and make as much money as he could, and then he would be free.

When the chance came, he arranged his own demise. He traded his military uniform with that of a dead man whose face was ripped away by a bomb. He switched dog tags with him and disappeared into the night, leaving behind a smoldering battlefield. Hiding by day and traveling by night, he made his way north to the border of Syria and Turkey, where a bribe bought him safe passage to join the thousands of refugees in Gaziantep. He cleverly devised a disguise by modifying a shirt and taping his arm to his side, pretending to be an amputee. The beginning had been difficult, but Gurga's training propelled him upward among the crime syndicates in Turkey. It didn't take long for him to make up his mind he would not be subjugated or hold allegiance to any one boss. One day he fell off the radar, emerging with yet another identity on the dark web where his skills could be bought and paid for and where he would decide which clients to take on. His business boomed, and he never looked back. It seemed there was an enormous demand for a hired killer that had proven himself to be reliable and effective. He shook his head, clearing it of past struggles. There was no sense dwelling in the past.

Now this same leader he'd worshipped long ago had threatened him. Even more offensive, he dared to use religious jargon as a weapon to enforce his intimidation. Gurga vowed to deliver his own justice to the hypocrite who hid behind platitudes of moral superiority. But for now, the client's threat resonated with authoritative finality. Gurga was on his own, and he saw no escape from what was demanded of him. Death waited in the wings, and he needed to make sure it wasn't his own life that was forfeited.

CHAPTER TWENTY-TWO

Monday, February 10
Tehran, Islamic Republic of Iran

Zara pressed her lips tightly together to keep them from trembling. After several minutes of studying their passports, the Disciplinary Forces Officer pulled them out of the line and asked them to follow him. A feeling of dread settled in her stomach as the NAJA agent led them to a cubicle where they were told to sit. The man held their passports open before him and typed commands into the computer keyboard, pausing to study the information on the monitor. Zara couldn't see what his searches revealed, but it made her nervous. This was the most dangerous part of entry, the test of whether their fake passports would hold up to scrutiny. Her stomach clenched, thinking of the repercussions if they didn't.

The official had a droopy mustache flecked with gray and a gaze of permanent suspicion. Deep grooves were etched into features that gave him the appearance of a walrus. He peered through wire-rimmed glasses, his eyes darting from their passports to their faces. He began questioning Mustafa, asking him about his family and profession and whether this visit to Iran was for business or pleasure.

They were both well prepared for this interrogation, and Mustafa's answers came easily and without hesitation. Mustafa was a consummate actor, but then Zara realized much of what he said wasn't too far from the truth.

"My wife and I are in the wine business in Argentina. We met a year ago. Francoise moved here from France, and I moved two years ago to Argentina from Canada. My wife is a vintner, and I'm in sales. I believe," he smiled, turning an adoring gaze to her, "we're a match made in heaven." Zara blushed at Mustafa's description that wasn't part of their disguise. Mustafa had expressed these very same words to her nearly every day since the day they had first met in Beirut.

He reached for her hand and squeezed it. She glanced at the officer's face only to find him intensely observing her. She averted her eyes, staring at her hands. When had she pulled out her prayer beads? They were part of her disguise, and she found herself rubbing them gently against one another. Breathing deeply from her nose, she tried to set her features into one of innocence and submission, the way a dutiful Muslim wife would. When she raised her eyes, the officer smiled at her, his eyes alight with approval.

In Arabic, the man asked, "Mrs. Shirvani, your parents live in France?"

"They did before they were killed in an automobile accident." The tears came easily to Zara's eyes. "When they were killed, I took the job in Mendoza. I needed to change my life." She smiled shyly at Mustafa. "Then, my life changed when I met Arman. My parents must have been looking after me."

"I'm very sorry about your parents." He cleared his throat. "*Inna Lillahi wa inna ilayhi raji'un.*" He offered the traditional Qur'an condolence, "Verily we belong to God, and verily to Him do we return. I'm sorry they aren't alive to see you happily married, but I'm sure they see to your welfare from the gardens of paradise."

"*Shukran.*" Zara nodded her thanks, pulling her green scarf more securely over her hair and around her neck and shoulders.

"*Afwan.*" The man then directed his attention to Mustafa. "Mr. Shirvani, you did not obtain a visa? It is required when you travel to the IRI. You understand I could deny you entry?"

They had rehearsed the answer to this question, but Zara was impressed with the cool authenticity of Mustafa's delivery.

"Forgive us, please, our visit was a last-minute decision. It can take months to get a visa, and our honeymoon leave from work is now. I got it in my head that I wanted to share with my wife the beautiful country of my parents. I've never been to my homeland, but I was raised with an abiding love for it. I hope you will allow us our honeymoon visit."

The officer studied Mustafa for several seconds after he finished with his plea. When he spoke, his tone softened. "It would seem you took a considerable risk with your decision. I have the ability to grant you a two-week visa." He opened a drawer of the desk and pulled out a stamp. "Enjoy your honeymoon Mr. and Mrs. Shirvani. *Narju 'an yakun zawajik mbarkaan."* The sound of the stamp striking their passports made Zara smile, as did the officer's blessing, may your marriage be blessed. *We've done it, or Mustafa did.* Zara sighed with relief.

As they returned to the final part of passport control, they waited for their luggage to be searched. What came next was a complete surprise. The officer who'd interrogated them stepped to the luggage checker and whispered in his ear. The two men shared a laugh, and without the nerve-wracking obligatory search, Mustafa and Zara were whisked on their way. As they rolled their luggage through the sliding doors, Zara was grateful that they didn't know what was sewn into the lining of their bags and their real reason for visiting.

They grabbed a taxi, and Zara's gaze fixed out the window, taking in the winter landscape. Mustafa jovially conversed with the driver in Farsi. Fatigue washed over her, and she sank into her own thoughts. Something bothered her, something she couldn't get past. She was a seasoned agent who'd faced death a thousand times, yet she'd always remained cool and unafraid. Nothing had ever pierced the armor she wore. She'd killed without remorse when needed and never lost an ounce of sleep over taking a life. But from the moment Aryeh had proposed this suicide mission, she'd been operating under an umbrella of absolute terror.

Why? There was only one explanation she could think of. It had to do with Mustafa. Before him, she'd been fearless — never caring if she lived or died. That's not to say she didn't enjoy being alive or sought her own death, but one way or the other, it really didn't matter. *When you have nothing to lose, you operate differently.* You calculate without emotion, never deviating from the plan, but now her life mattered to someone else. Mustafa's love had shattered her protective armor, and she felt exposed. The thought of him being harmed eviscerated her composure and her ability to think clearly. Mustafa had awakened her soul with his love.

He demanded nothing of her. When he made love to her, it was as if he squeezed the blood from his heart and offered it to her. He composed poetry to her, and she had to admit his words were beautiful. She lacked nothing, especially when it came to love. The truth was she loved him completely, but she always held a piece of herself out of his reach. And now she was hiding a secret from him. If she told him, it would weaken him, and she needed him to stay strong through the mission.

Zara had missed her last cycle three days ago. It was the last thing on her mind when Aryeh showed up. If she'd spoken up, she knew Mustafa would have refused the mission, but then she'd be manipulating him, and the thought of it sickened her. He was ecstatic with the idea of clearing his name, of closing the book on the past and what he'd done and been. The temptation of redemption was deeply seeded in his psyche, and she couldn't bear the thought of denying him this dream. He'd given up everything in his life for her. How could she rob him of a lifetime of peace?

She would not let the pregnancy and her fears get the better of her. She needed to focus on the mission. The pregnancy was in its infancy, and she was in tip-top physical shape. *Stay alive and get the nuclear physicist and his girlfriend, you, and Mustafa out of Iran. Then when we're all safe, I can tell you, mi amor.*

"Look, Francoise, it's the Azadi square and the monument."

Zara had been focused on her thoughts, hardly registering what she saw out the window. "Wow, it's striking. I'd love to take a walk, Arman."

"Great idea, *habibti.* Let's get settled and then explore." Zara could feel the excitement vibrate through Mustafa's fingertips as he held her hand. While they were exploring, they would locate the drop-box and pick up whatever had been left for them. Mossad was arranging for weapons and a vehicle, and they'd leave to find the couple when they received their orders. The sooner they began, the better. The sooner they began, the sooner they'd be able to escape, and their life could really begin. She tried not to think of the life growing inside her. She smiled to herself. If it was a boy, she'd name him Jacob for her beloved brother.

CHAPTER TWENTY-THREE

February 10
Reims, France

"Cyrus!"

Cyrus ran through the door, his heart banging in his chest and ready to burst. He was so afraid that he might be too late. He gripped his pistol so tight that his hand would likely carry an imprint of ridges on his palm. The vein in his temple throbbed, keeping rhythm with the rush of adrenaline that pulsed through his veins. Layla was in danger. How many times had she been threatened because of him? No, don't think of that. She loves you — you love her. You swore to protect her.

Turning in a circle with his gun ready, he scanned the room. How could it be empty? Literally four walls. Out of nowhere, another door seemed to materialize. "Cyrus!" Her cry undid him. He had to get to her before that monster hurt her. He ran.

He sucked in a slow breath, calming his vibrating nerve endings. His breathing evened, and his vision narrowed, focusing like a laser. "Eshgham, I'm coming," he breathed, willing her to hear him, afraid to alert the monster. "I'll destroy him, I promise."

He opened the door and rushed into the room but was blinded by a flash of lightning. Was there a freak storm that had smashed the windows? Or more likely a bomb attack? In the moment it took his vision to adjust, his mind reeled with a million possibilities of what could have happened. And then, as his vision cleared, he found himself standing outside a cabin nestled in a grove beside a mountain lake.

"Cyrus!"

He took off at a run. Careful not to be seen, he peeked through a cabin window. He saw a man hovering above her, tormenting her, dangling a set of cufflinks in front of her. Her mouth was gagged. The monster was threatening to force himself on her. Layla fought back as best she could, but the monster would overpower her and then.... After they'd shared the most beautiful night of love in his life, his mind now was filled with cold, deadly rage, an overwhelming fury that blackened out all else except the desire to kill Layla's tormentor. With lightning speed, a plan formed in his mind, and he ran to the other door on the side of the house that led into the kitchen. He slammed it, drawing the killers' attention.

Cyrus was once more a cold, calculating killing machine. One of the assassins holding an AK-47 stumbled into the kitchen, his eye pressed to the sight. Cyrus hid behind the door, and when the man got close enough, Cyrus pulled the killer toward him. In mere seconds, Cyrus covered the man's mouth and slashed the Glauca B1 seven-inch blade across his throat, slicing his windpipe and carotid arteries. The killer's life ended in a gush of blood and a silent gurgle.

Cyrus lowered the dead man to the floor, then opened the swinging door to the great room. The other assassin straddled Layla and readied himself to rape her. The rapist called over his shoulder for his friend to hurry and join him. No answer. Dead men don't speak. When he turned, his eyes bulged. Cyrus threw the knife, and it found its target — crunching bone — instant death. The knife had impaled the man, nearly splitting his head in half. The dead man fell forward and toppled onto a screaming Layla. Cyrus freed her and wrapped his arms around her. She buried her face in his shoulder and sobbed. "That's it, my angel, let your tears fall. I'll always be there to catch them." Killer to lover in less than an instant. He'd saved her then, and he'd save her now.

It was happening again, and he ran, opening door after door. "Layla!" He roared.

A cool hand caressed his cheek. He woke with a start, his breath heaving, his body damp with sweat. He stared into turquoise blue eyes filled with empathy, love, strength. "It's okay, my love. You had a bad dream." She smiled and kissed him. He wrapped his arms around her, pulling her in, burying his face in her hair. The fierceness of his love so great it strangled his ability to speak.

"*Eshgham,*" he whispered hoarsely.

"I'm here. I'll always be here."

He looked around the room to get his bearings. The dream of the lake in Varian, Iran, had faded. He was in France. Everything returned to him. The fear of losing her thundered in his mind. "This is turning out to be one hell of a honeymoon." His jest was edged with sarcasm. He was angry with himself. He was angry with his display of weakness. Layla needed to feel secure. She needed to know her Superman was strong for her and that he'd never let anything, or anyone, harm her.

Her fingers cupped his face, drawing his gaze to her. "You've never let me down. It was a nightmare, nothing more. Plus, the sleeping arrangements aren't ideal."

He brushed a stray hair from her face. "I had no choice about that, and I thought it better for Jazmin not to be alone. She's been through a lot in these past few weeks. It'll be easier when Aryeh gets here."

"What are you going to do, arrange for Aryeh to sleep with her? Or are you going to sleep with Aryeh?" A giggle escaped. Only Layla could find humor in their situation.

"How about two rooms, smartypants? Then I can sleep with my wife, and Aryeh can sleep on a couch."

"I knew I married you for a good reason. Clever man."

Layla, as usual, had managed to smooth his jagged edges with humor. Worry was replaced by playful banter that never ceased to arouse him. "You married me because you thought I was the hottest man you'd ever met. You couldn't resist my charms," he said with a smirk.

"Hm. Charm can only get you so far." She egged him on. His hand slid down her back and under her tee-shirt, his fingers lightly trailing along her smooth skin. Her eyes fluttered closed, and a sigh of pleasure escaped. The way she reacted to his touch made him feel alive. He was the luckiest man in the world to be loved by her.

Cyrus brushed his lips against hers. "You're right. At some point, a more direct response is warranted." His hand slipped lower, his fingers splayed around her ass, holding her in place as he pressed hard against her.

Her eyes opened. "This sofa, it's a pretty small space. Maybe we should wait?"

He growled, "I'm not waiting."

She thrust out her chin. "Have you forgotten it takes two to tango?"

"Have you forgotten the first time we made love was in a sleeping bag? Now that was a small space, but we managed. It was unforgettable for me, and I don't recall any complaints." He nuzzled her neck, inhaling the scent of vanilla and almonds and Layla. She arrested his senses and kindled his desire. It was a feeling he couldn't put aside even if he tried.

She lifted her chin, giving him better access. Her eyes closed and the smile teasing her lips was a green light to him. "It was unforgettable, but a lot of time has passed since then. People change," she whispered.

He paused mid-kiss and pulled back enough to see her face. When she opened her eyes, he saw laughter in them. "Nothing has changed. Nothing will ever change," he growled. He lowered his lips to hers, determined to love her until she shattered in his arms. *Small space be damned.* "You did close the door to the bedroom, right?"

"What do you think?"

CHAPTER TWENTY-FOUR

February 10
Reims, France

A subdued winter light poured through the drapery sheers. Gurga had left the heavy damask drapes open as he preferred to awaken each morning from natural light, a reminder that he was still alive. He rose and peered out the window. The banks of the Vesle River were blanketed in white. The storm had delivered at least half a foot of snow, and in its aftermath, the last of the clouds chased the creeping light of dawn across the sky to the east.

Before showering, Gurga did two-hundred pushups and two-hundred sit-ups, which was nothing compared to his normal routine when he wasn't working. Once this job was in the history books and he returned to Malta, he'd return to his body-building regimen. He turned before the mirror and assessed himself. After all, his livelihood depended on his physical strength and mental acuity, so it was important for him to judge the way he looked. His arms and chest were decorated with a dozen tatts that moved with a life of their own as he clenched and unclenched his muscles. He should never have allowed himself to be tattooed. They were dangerous identifiers to a man whose life depended on invisibility, but in a drunken stupor, he'd indulged in the first one — a samurai wielding a sword. A tattoo to celebrate his first paid kill. He'd learned not to drink after that night, but he'd returned time and again to add to his collection of body art. Every tattoo on his body marked a fresh kill. Every one a reminder that he was still alive. After that, body art had become an obsession. No one except the occasional one-night stand had ever seen them. He was also mindful of keeping his bedroom darkened. One time, a target had glimpsed his samurai tattoo, but Gurga snuffed out the chap's life before any damage could be done. He grinned with satisfaction as he flexed his muscles, watching his tattoos transform and stretch.

Gurga's confidence had returned. He was no longer flustered by yesterday's setbacks or by his conversations with gangsters and generals. What mattered was he'd located the two women, and as long as they were in his sights, he wasn't worried. Last night after he'd checked into the same hotel as his prey, he'd grabbed a hot shower and ordered room service. After fortifying himself, he opened his bag of tricks and carefully selected a prosthetic nose, blue contacts, and a pair of heavy framed glasses. Then he lightened his black hair to ash brown and straightened the tight crown of curls. Satisfied that the man staring into the mirror bore no resemblance to the man Jazmin and the other woman had seen, he went to bed and slept like a log.

He would tail them to wherever they were going, and when the time was right, he'd eliminate them. There would be plenty of time later to determine what was to be done with the gangster and the general. The gangster he'd punish with a dirty job in the near future. That was how the mafia did it. And wasn't he as powerful as a Don? With so many criminals hopping to do his bidding. On the other hand, the general had become a liability. The general had signed his death warrant the moment he'd uttered the veiled threat of revealing Gurga's true identity. How and where his end would come was yet to be determined, but there was no doubt in Gurga's mind that it would come down to that.

Gurga sat at a table in the hotel's dining room, coffee and croissant before him, his new prosthetic nose buried in a newspaper as he kept an eye out. There were quite a few people up early enjoying a French breakfast, so he didn't feel in the least bit conspicuous. Before too long, his patience was rewarded when the Mossad agent, Jazmin, and the woman with the short strawberry blonde hair arrived. Had they not shown up to the restaurant, he would have been alerted with a text by one of the clerks at the desk, whom he'd bribed lavishly to keep him posted in the event they checked out. From the corner of his eye, he watched as the threesome was seated on the other side of the room. It was a shame he wouldn't be able to eavesdrop, but it was better that none of them had any cause to look at him. As it was, the Spanish-accented Mossad agent took a hard look at everyone in the restaurant before sitting down. Gurga carefully avoided looking their way. When the waitress came to take his order, he ordered a hearty breakfast of Muesli with plain yogurt, fresh fruit, and a basket of chocolate croissants.

By the time his prey had finally emerged from the hotel restaurant, Gurga had already paid and was browsing in the gift shop where he had a clear view of the lobby. He almost gasped aloud as the two women made a beeline for the shop and came straight toward him. He was cornered. There was nothing to be done but to appear as casual as possible. He flipped through the pages of a magazine, seemingly absorbed, his back to Jazmin and the blonde.

He recognized Jazmin's voice. "It's going to be a long drive. I want to grab something I can escape into."

The strawberry-blonde chuckled. When she spoke, Gurga recognized an American accent. "That's a great idea," she said. "But I'm sure all the magazines and books are in French."

"My French is exceptionally good. My mother was fluent —" Jazmin's voice broke.

They were standing only a few feet away from Gurga, and from the corner of his eye, he saw a tear slip down Jazmin's face. The American put her arm around Jazmin's shoulder. "My French is only basic, not good enough to read a novel. Are you okay?"

"Every time I think of my family…the pain is unbearable," she said in a fragile whisper. He had to strain his ears to hear their hushed conversation.

"I can't imagine how hard this is for you," the blonde whispered back. "You should be somewhere safe, mourning and taking time to heal instead of being hunted by some animal."

"It will all be worth it once I fulfill my promise to my father and destroy his murderer." Jazmin picked up a thick paperback and turned it around to read the description on the back.

"I read that one," the blonde said in a louder voice, "you'll enjoy it."

"Great, then let's go." As the two women passed behind Gurga, Jazmin accidentally bumped into him.

"Je m'excuse," she apologized.

"Ce n'est pas grave," he answered without turning around. The close encounter was uncomfortable. Jazmin's tears had elicited a strange reaction in him, something he'd never experienced before — regret. Followed by an even more implausible emotion — guilt. The very fact that he kept thinking of her as Jazmin and not his target began to worry him. *I need this done and over with before things get out of hand.*

He sensed the threat that Jazmin posed. Her beauty and the courage he heard in her voice made a physical attraction to her unavoidable. This blossoming emotional connection, however, spelled danger. She was a temptation that could only weaken him. He needed to keep his distance. Being in her proximity only strengthened her appeal.

The moment he saw targets as human beings with hopes and dreams, his career, perhaps even his life, was over. His mind traveled back to Syria and the woman holding her baby in a frozen tableau of death. The agony in her face was enough to give him nightmares for the rest of his life. It had taken years to leave those memories behind in the red dust of the desert. He refused to go back there. Refused to feel anything other than satisfaction in getting paid for a job well done.

CHAPTER TWENTY-FIVE

February 10
Zürich, Switzerland

Aryeh glanced through the peephole first and then opened the door to the room. Jazmin stood beside Cyrus, chatting amiably about the décor of the hotel.

Aryeh had checked in earlier and managed to snag the last two junior suites available at the Widder Hotel. The Widder was a little too charming and romantic for their needs, but it provided excellent defensibility. The hotel had been converted from nine medieval houses where gentry, artisans, merchants, and the heads of guilds had once lived. The original historical buildings of stone and wood had been renovated and woven together with chrome, steel, and glass passageways that connected them in an esthetic blending of modern and timeworn architecture and décor. Fronting the turquoise waters of the Limmat River, the charming retreat was a tourist destination with all the amenities they would need. For their purposes, the hotel stood within walking distance to the Julius Bär Banking institution on Zürich's main street the Bahnhofstrasse.

Aryeh knew Zürich well. One of the identities that Mossad had created for him was a German banker with offices in Zürich. In fact, he operated out of a secured private banking office with a vault where an arsenal was stored. It was the first place he'd gone when his flight got in from Argentina. By the time Cyrus, Jazmin, and Layla arrived, he'd returned with a stash of weapons that were now stored in the hotel suite.

Aryeh had texted Cyrus the coordinates and told him not to bother checking in at the front desk because he'd arranged everything. When Aryeh opened the door, Jazmin stopped talking. Aryeh grunted for them to come in, noting the look of displeasure on her face.

Cyrus gave the hallway a once over. "Layla's in the room," he nodded toward the room next door. "I'd rather not leave her alone. Why don't we meet you downstairs in an hour and grab some dinner?"

"Sounds good. I haven't eaten since this morning. We can talk later."

Aryeh shut the door and turned to Jazmin, who had taken two steps into the room but had not said a word. "Why don't you put your things away?"

"I don't have much." She seemed nervous and uncomfortable and clutched a small bag to her chest.

"I'm not going to eat you. I'm here to protect you, Jazmin. I know this feels crazy, sharing a room with a strange man, but I can't do my job unless I remain close by."

She nodded but didn't move.

Did he need to explain to Jazmin that Layla suffered from anxiety too? That she suffered from PTSD from her own run-ins with terrorists in the last few years and losing the pregnancy. It had almost cost Layla and Cyrus their marriage. It was a lot to contend with, even for a strong and devoted couple like Cyrus and Layla.

Because of all Layla had been through, Aryeh hadn't approved of her accompanying Cyrus on this mission. In the end, it turned out to be a good idea because from what Cyrus had told him, Layla had been helpful with Jazmin, had even saved her life. Aryeh knew Layla would deny it, but he was sure the stress of coming up against the assassin had taken a toll. He was also sure that now that he was here, it took some of the pressure off. It gave Cyrus a chance to focus on Layla and any issues she might be dealing with.

Perhaps he and Jazmin needed that time, too. She needed to get used to being in close quarters with him. Hell, he did as well. *Spare me from another dark-haired beauty.*

Aryeh wasn't sure what it was about Jazmin that made him tongue-tied. For sure, it would be easier if she wasn't so damn beautiful. Something about those doe eyes that had seen too much drew him in. Even as cold and detached as he was, a vulnerable woman got to him. Even more so if she was brave, and Jazmin had proven her courage.

He wanted to kill that bastard with his bare hands.

He forced himself not to smile. He could only imagine what her reaction would be if she knew his volatile thoughts. A man couldn't be too careful about his behavior around women these days. If things kept up the way they were going, the human species might cease to exist. It was no wonder that Zara's independence and sexual nature to take what she wanted had appealed to him. Zara had always been upfront and honest when it came to sex. If she wanted a man's attention, she would seek it. If she didn't, she wouldn't. If a man gave her unwanted attention, she kicked his ass. Simple as that.

The more he thought about Zara, the more he realized that they would never have worked out in a relationship. Too much alike. Somehow with Mustafa, she'd discovered her chance for happiness. It wasn't something he could understand, but truth was a harsh mistress, and he needed to accept it. His friendship with Zara would last a lifetime, and he didn't want to sacrifice that because of petty jealousy.

Right now, as he stared at the woman who looked about as lost as a person could be, he wanted to comfort her and let her know she was safe. But the chance of that being misinterpreted was a roadblock. He tried to see himself from Jazmin's point of view. He was her traditional enemy, an Israeli. She'd been raised to fear him, to trust no one from the infidel nation of Zionists. He was a Jew, and she was a Muslim. He understood he must be a tough pill to swallow. With Cyrus, it was different. He was an Iranian and a friend to her father. She trusted him, and being an obedient daughter, she had no choice but to believe her father wouldn't have placed her in the hands of anyone who would hurt or misguide her.

Maybe she doesn't like me? That real possibility stung him. He wasn't immune to ego as a man or as a spy. Confidence played a big role in tackling the impossible. Whatever the case, he needed her cooperation, and dammit if he wasn't going to get it. "Jazmin, see that sofa there?"

Her gaze drifted to the sleek lines of the white leather sofa across from two chartreuse armchairs.

"That's where I'll be sleeping, while you, princess, will be sleeping in the very big king-sized bed in that equally big bedroom through that doorway."

A smile crept across her face.

Maybe I'm getting through.

"Now why don't you get cleaned up and relax a bit before dinner? You'll find some clean new clothes in the armoire and toiletries in the bathroom." Aryeh rubbed the back of his neck, trying not to sound as awkward as he felt. "Cyrus asked me to pick up some things for you and Layla. I hope everything fits, and I hope you like what I got." Folding his arms across his chest. "I don't know much about shopping for a woman, so don't shoot me if the clothes aren't to your liking."

"I appreciate your efforts in getting us those things." She held her bag to her like a shield, her eyes focused on her feet. "I — I would like to make amends and apologize for not thanking you properly back at the embassy in London." She straightened her shoulders and finally lifted her gaze. She looked him directly in the eyes. "I behaved like a silly schoolgirl. My father trusted Cyrus, and Cyrus trusts you. And so do I." She took a step closer to him and nodded. "I trust you, and I thank you for risking your life to protect me."

"Good. I'm glad. I hope you'll trust me enough to confide in me whatever troubles you. I'll do my best to get you through this."

"Thank you, but the only way I will get through this is if that monster is dead." A fire lit her gaze. He'd seen that look many times from those who sought vengeance.

"Jazmin, you need to remember, revenge won't necessarily bring you peace."

The steely determination in her eyes glistened with tears. "Cyrus said the same thing. Have you ever lost someone you love to violence?" It was as much a challenge as a question.

The query formed a lump in his throat. He hadn't expected her to ask something so direct, and before he could think it through, he answered with candor. "Yes, I have."

Her head tilted. "Will you tell me about it?"

He took her bag that she'd been clutching and placed it by the door to the bedroom. He gently took her hand and led her to the sofa. "Come sit with me for a minute."

He sat next to her on the sofa and ran his hands over his face. Composing himself, he stared ahead, letting memories flood his mind. He cleared his throat, but the hoarseness of his voice betrayed his emotional pain. "Years ago, I was a young agent leading my first operation. I had a team composed of both seasoned operatives and two fledgling agents. One of those first-timers was a young woman named Sarah. She was beautiful and fearless. She believed wholeheartedly in protecting Israel and its people.

"It shouldn't have happened, but sometimes when people work closely together, sparks fly, and passions are ignited. I was crazy in love with Sarah, and I did my best to keep our relationship professional, but one night after too much wine and too much pent-up desire, we gave in to temptation. After that night, we agreed that we needed to stop things before they got out of hand. We agreed to cool things off, but the opposite happened, and our feelings grew even more intense."

He sighed and shook his head. The raw pain that never went away returned. "I should have removed her from the team. I pretended that she and I could work together objectively. I thought I could keep everything balanced and watch over everyone as I should as team leader.

"But I allowed my personal feelings to blind my judgment. We were in Beirut on an operation. The target was an arms dealer who supplied a Hezbollah terrorist splinter group. The terrorists had slipped across the border into Israel and killed a family — mother, father, and twin babies all murdered by depraved cowards. It was comparable only to Nazi cruelty and brutality, the parents made to watch their infants held by their feet, and their heads smashed against a wall. Then the parents were summarily executed. We knew this because the terrorists filmed it and sent the video to us — "

A gasp escaped Jazmin, and he looked at her, taking in her trembling lips, the tears in her eyes at such shocking brutality. "I'm sorry." He tried to swallow his own grief.

"It's all right, please continue," she whispered.

"Well, you know the saying, an eye for an eye, and a tooth for a tooth."

She nodded.

"We were given the execution operation to go after those bastards and make them pay. Our plan was to conscript this arms dealer willingly or unwillingly to work for us. Every one of the terrorist murderers was targeted for assassination. The dealer, a real whoremaster, was into kinky BDSM sex. Sarah was the perfect bait, but I kept delaying because I was afraid for her. The bastard was dirty and dangerous, and Sarah might find herself alone with the monster. She was determined to bring the terrorists to justice. We tracked the target so well that we basically knew what time of day he took a shit."

Jazmin's brows went up at that.

Aryeh felt the heat creep up his neck. "Pardon my language." Genteel conversation flew out the window when he conversed with a fellow agent, but Jazmin was a civilian, not an agent. He rubbed the back of his neck again. "We planned this mission down to the second. The guy frequented a private sex club, and we arranged for Sarah to get inside. Sarah's innocence and beauty were bound to attract him. We installed cameras everywhere, and although she wore a wire, she had to go in unarmed. It seemed like we had everything under control, and we were across the street in case of trouble." Aryeh's breath grew more ragged as the panic of what happened took over. "To this day, I'm not sure what went wrong."

Jazmin reached out and laid her hand over his. "Go on," she whispered.

"One of my team picked up texts between our target and the terrorists. Sarah had been made. It was a trap. I broke protocol, tried to warn her, but she didn't answer. I was frantic, and we raided the club, but we were too late. We found her in a garbage bin in the alley behind the club. She was naked, beaten, bruised, and cut — unconscious." Aryeh choked, barely able to continue. "Raped," he hissed. "She died an hour later. She never regained consciousness. It was my fault. I quit the agency, disappeared, and drowned my sorrow in whiskey."

"Did you ever get the people who did this?"

"We got some of them, but not the leader." Aryeh clenched his fists. His hatred and anger pulsed through his veins like a ticking bomb. He took a deep breath and sighed, releasing the burden he'd carried for so many years. "Six months later, going through a pile of mail I'd ignored, I found a letter from Sarah. It was eerie and bizarre and opened everything up again. She confessed to having been pregnant by me. She said she was sorry, but she'd had an abortion and didn't tell me. I was livid with rage, furious that she didn't tell me. How could she do that, to wait and then send me a letter instead of telling me before the mission?"

He looked at Jazmin, unable to hide the pain and anguish. "If she'd told me the truth, I never would have let her risk her life that day. She'd be alive. Maybe we'd be together. I don't know." He ran his fingers through his hair. "Ultimately, it was my own fault. I should have seen what was happening — her thirst to prove herself to me, to the team. I failed to see that her bravado was masking her naivete. My blindness led her to take such a risk without considering the consequences."

"It wasn't your fault — you see that now, don't you? Sarah was an agent like you. She knew what she was getting into. She'd had the same training —"

"Some agents are born to do this work. Sarah thought because she knew how to throw a good kick, she was invincible. But the physicality of our work is only part of it. The mind has to be as strong as the body." His voice trailed off into a raspy whisper. It was so unlike him to reveal himself this way. He'd never told anyone about Sarah, not even Zara. The Ramsad knew, of course. His friendship had helped him recover. The Ramsad had also made sure he'd received the therapy he needed and then made sure Aryeh returned to Mossad. The man was like a father to him.

"Have you been able to forgive yourself?" she asked in a soft voice.

"It's not that easy to forgive yourself." A bitter laugh escaped him.

"I know. Ever since that night, I've hated myself for surviving." She averted her gaze when he looked at her.

"It's not your fault either. Surviving is not a crime. It's a blessing from God." He took her hand between his and gently held it.

Jazmin nodded, "I know that, too." She rested her head on his shoulder. Their shared tragedies must have broken the ice. For a few moments, they sat in silence.

Jazmin stood, breaking the connection. "Thank you for sharing your sorrow with me. I'd like to shower before we leave."

"Don't rush. I'll text Cyrus if you need more time." She returned his smile. Before closing the door to the bedroom, she said, "I can't wait to see what clothes you bought me."

I can't wait either, Aryeh admitted to himself.

CHAPTER TWENTY-SIX

Tuesday, February 11
Tehran, Islamic Republic of Iran

The meeting was on. Zara and Mustafa took a taxi to the largest shopping mall on earth, the Grand Bazaar of Tehran. It was after 2 p.m. With over six miles of corridors filled with purveyors of every product imaginable, it would take a tourist days to see everything worth seeing. Their taxi driver had said the bazaar was more than a thousand years old, but the oldest of the existing buildings was a mere four hundred years old. With over two-million visitors per day, the marketplace bustled with shoppers and tourists. The maze of corridors was a perfect place to lose oneself, and Zara and Mustafa had no trouble blending in and disappearing among the crowds.

Zara glanced up at the dappled light that filtered through soaring, intricately carved ceilings. Some of the passageways were beautifully maintained, while others needed repair. Everywhere she looked, a mishmash of old and new butted up against each other. The scent of fruit and spices lingered in the air, and Zara found the artistically tiled domes and stained-glass windows safer to look at than the ever-watchful green-shirted security officers who were everywhere.

Mustafa, as cool as a cucumber, ignored their presence, parting the throngs of shoppers who clogged the passageways shopping for spices, nuts, dried fruit, meats, electronics, fabrics, and everything imaginable under the sun.

Zara and Mustafa made their way through the teeming corridors to the carpet alley. As previously arranged, Zara wore her green cashmere scarf to identify them to their Mossad contact. Although compulsory for women to wear a headscarf and loose-fitting clothing in Iran, Zara had heard of instances where young Iranian women dared to be seen in public without the required covering, dared to dance in the streets, another forbidden act that could result in arrest. Sometimes the authorities looked the other way, while other times, the women and students were dragged away to prison. Wanting to remain inconspicuous, Zara's hair and shoulders were draped modestly.

Mustafa's hand rested lightly on the small of her back. She glanced at the resolute expression on his face. Sometimes when she looked at him, she was taken aback and amazed at the transformation. After Mustafa had launched the electromagnetic-pulse attack against Israel, Zara had refused to flee with him. Unable to convince her to come with him, he fled, and she expected never to see him again. The EMP attack, fortunately, was stopped by an Israeli drone that destroyed the missile. But even with the best outcome possible, Zara came away devastated. Hezbollah had discovered she was a DGSE agent, and because of her suspected involvement with Mossad, her friend and colleague, Faiz Khoury, had been murdered in retaliation. With her cover blown, the DGSE had banished her to a desk job in Argentina.

Months later, from out of nowhere, she'd received a strange missive from an unidentified person requesting she meet him at a local fishermen's pier on the Rio de la Plata. The man claimed she would save a life if she met with him. She spotted him at the end of the pier, but she'd been unable to identify him from that distance. It could have been a setup, and she approached him with caution. Even when she was but a few feet away, she couldn't be sure of his identity. But when he spoke, the world fell away. Although plastic surgery had completely altered his appearance, she knew it was Mustafa. The surgeries may have changed his face, perhaps made him even more attractive, but when she looked at him, she saw the man she had fallen in love with. The man who'd stolen her heart with his persistence and his unassailable belief that they were meant for each other.

He'd begged her for forgiveness and proclaimed his love for her. Though she was skeptical, she could not deny the way she felt about him. Since then, they'd been inseparable. Mustafa was a changed man who'd forsaken everything in his prior life to be with her. And she with him.

After her twin brother, Jacob, was killed in a terrorist attack in Paris, her life had been dedicated to stopping terrorism. She'd given up her professorship at the Sorbonne and any chance of a normal life when she joined the DGSE. Love, marriage, children, and any hopes of happiness were sacrificed for the good and safety of others. To have fallen in love with a terrorist seemed an impossibility, but it had happened. Now to free Mustafa from the chains of his past deeds, she was embarking on what could only be considered a suicide mission. It was understandable that she was angry and filled with anxiety. It was easy to be brave when you didn't have so very much to live for.

She would not forgive Aryeh so easily for putting them in this dangerous situation. Not that she didn't feel sympathy for the physicist and his girlfriend, but having found a modicum of peace and happiness with Mustafa she'd never believed possible, she was loath to lose it, and now there was the life growing inside her. The motherly instinct to protect was more than her changing hormones. It was her chance to start over and find the woman she once had been.

Her senses were on high alert as she perused the people they passed. The neatly stacked piles of carpets lining the storefronts meant they were nearing their destination. Jewel-toned carpets lay upon marble floors reflective of the pointed-arch tiled ceilings overhead. Through the windows she saw illuminated rugs hanging on walls displayed like paintings.

The showroom Mustafa led her into was a grand space the size of a ballroom, filled with hundreds of rugs. Inside he slowed, and they walked about examining the selections. With all the salesmen dressed in suits, hopping about for a chance to make a sale, it wasn't long before a bearded man with a formidable belly approached. His jovial countenance contrasted with piercing eyes that examined them beneath bushy eyebrows that reminded Zara of a tufted, wise old owl.

Mustafa answered the salesman in Farsi and asked if they would speak in Arabic so that his new wife could understand as well.

"How can I be of service to you?" asked the man.

Zara pointed at an unusual antique green carpet hanging on the wall. "Tell us about this carpet?"

"Your wife is not only blessed by Allah with great beauty, but she is blessed with a discerning eye."

Zara cast her eyes downward, blushing demurely. "As you can see by my scarf, I favor the color green."

"Which coincidently matches the lovely hue of your eyes, *sayidati.*" He respectfully addressed her as "madam."

"This rug from Tabriz is more than a hundred years old and rare. It hearkens to a time when the first Pahlavi Shah Reza Kahn seized power. It was a time of great hope in our nation. Would you care to join me in my office for some tea, and we can discuss your interest more thoroughly in a relaxed environment?"

"That would be most agreeable." Mustafa nodded.

The office was a small cubicle set off to one side of a warehouse and loading dock where more carpets were rolled and wrapped in brown paper. After seating them, the salesman who had introduced himself as Kaspar Rostam left them to get the tea. Zara scanned the ceiling for cameras. She imagined the salesman was at this very moment confirming their identities. She and Mustafa made small talk about the carpet, with Mustafa requesting she leave the negotiations to him. "The carpet will look beautiful in our home, *habibata.*" He took her hand and squeezed it. Leaning over, he whispered, "We will make love a thousand times in front of the fireplace on that lovely rug."

Zara knew it was Mustafa's way of assuring her that their lives would not end here, and they would survive and return home to their beautiful Viñedo de la Montaña in Argentina.

Kaspar returned carrying a tray with glass teacups that steamed enticingly. Zara inhaled the delicious aroma of cardamom and pistachios that scented the chai Kashmiri tea. "Excellent," she pronounced, "thank you." She was grateful for the refreshment, hoping it would settle the butterflies in her stomach.

Kaspar must have confirmed their identities because he wasted no time with further pleasantries. "This evening, a model C3 Pars Khodro black SUV will be delivered to your hotel. In the tire compartment, you will find a duffel containing armaments, ammunition, and satellite phones. The car is also equipped with a GPS tracking system that will monitor you by satellite. Tomorrow you will drive to Astara, a city that borders the Azerbaijan Republic on the Caspian Sea. In the summer, it's a major tourist destination, but in the winter, it's about as sleepy as a place can be. You'll find the route is already mapped out for you on the navigation system. We're sending you over an out-of-the-way route not normally taken during the winter months because of its icy terrain. The less your whereabouts are exposed, the better for all of us. However, I will tell you the views and scenery should prove quite pleasing. It's a mountainous paradise that cuts through the Alborz Mountains to the sea. Under the best of circumstances, it's a five-hour drive, but I suspect it will take you seven to eight hours, so plan on leaving early tomorrow. Rooms are booked for you at the Astara Shahriar Dolat Parast Hotel Apartments. It's not fancy, but the apartments offer more privacy than most of the other hotels, and they're open in the winter. The rooms are booked under Mr. and Mrs. Arman Shirvani.

"We're in touch with the couple, although the young man has been hesitant to reveal his exact location. He's understandably afraid of trusting anyone. I'll be in contact with him and arrange a meeting between you at some neutral location. It is important for you to gain his trust. Any questions?"

Mustafa glanced at Zara, encouraging her to speak. "What is the plan for getting us all out of Iran?" she asked."

"The office hasn't confided it to me yet, but I've been assured plans are in motion. I will tell you that the border crossing is open twenty-four hours a day and is considered stress free, especially in the winter when it isn't busy."

"See, *habibata,*" said Mustafa, "there is nothing to worry about. We will be out of Iran in a matter of days."

"*Mon amour,* it is better to be prepared for the worst than be fooled into complacency. We don't know what measures the government has put in place to apprehend these two. Their faces may be on hold-and-detain lists. Crossing the border at a passport control may be more difficult than you think." Zara returned her gaze to Kasper. "Speaking of passports, the couple needs fake passports. What are you planning in that regard?"

"That is a problem we must address. We have the ability here in Tehran, but not in Astara or anywhere in the Gilan Province. The secure phones in the duffel are already loaded up with a passport photo app. You can take pictures of Ibrahim and Shira and send them to me from those phones. Within two days, we should have their passports back to you. Just to lessen the scrutiny by the passport police as to their traveling together, we'll give them a married status.

"However, to provide them with more safety," he nodded at Zara, "Francoise, you will be married to the professor, and you, Arman, will be married to the young woman. We've also provided different contact lens colors, hair dye, beards, mustaches, and prosthetic wax to alter their appearances, which you should figure out before taking the passport photos. The more you can change their appearances, the better."

"I see you are well prepared," Mustafa grinned and nodded. "It sounds like this will be a piece of cake, don't you think, Francoise?"

"Yes, *c'est de la tarte." A piece of cake. Too easy, I'm afraid.* Zara was not lulled into believing the road ahead would be easy.

"The sat phones are pre-programmed to my number. Get a good night's sleep, and we'll speak in the morning."

CHAPTER TWENTY-SEVEN

Tuesday, February 11
Zürich, Switzerland

Cyrus heard the shower running when he returned to the room. Layla had lit the wood in the fireplace, and the warm glow comforted his weary mind. He kicked off his shoes, sat on the sofa, and took a deep breath. Having Aryeh in Zürich took some of the pressure off him. It gave him a chance to pay more attention to Layla, and it afforded them some much-needed privacy. Things hadn't gone exactly the way he'd hoped they would. Having Layla become the target of an assassin shook him to his core. It didn't take much for Cyrus to blame himself. Because of him, Layla found herself too often in danger. She constantly reassured him that he was her Superman, but for him, it was a reminder of why men like Aryeh kept their distance when it came to commitment and love. *It's a horrifying thing to live with, knowing that what you do puts your wife and family at risk.*

He dealt with that reality every day, but right now, he needed to distance himself and focus on the positive aspects of having a family. It was four days since they'd left Tel Aviv, and they'd only spoken to Cerise once. If he knew his rambunctious daughter, she'd be driving her great-grandparents, Dina and Morris, crazy by now with relentless questions about when her *aba* and *ima* were coming home. Layla's grandparents were Holocaust survivors and in good health, but a five-year-old and a puppy was still a lot to take on. Layla's father, Aleck, would stop by regularly, but Aleck, a nuclear physicist and professor, was busy with his doctoral students and his lab. His work was crucial to the State of Israel, and it demanded his full attention.

Aleck adored Cerise, but the only day that he could set aside his work and spend time with the family was Sunday. Normally, Layla or Dina made a Sunday dinner, and Aleck usually joined them. Occasionally Cyrus's sister and mother, Ester and Aster, would visit. Cyrus's sister had recently married and moved with their mother from the kibbutz where they'd been settled to a beautiful new home in the mountains. Ester's husband was an artist and deeply religious. He owned an art gallery in the hills of Galilee in the ancient Holy City of Tzfat. They were a small family, but Cyrus hoped that one day his sister would have a child and Cerise would have a cousin. He loved his sister, and so much had been denied her. He wanted her to enjoy the fulfillment of motherhood, which he knew would please his mother. Tzfat was only a two-hour drive from Tel Aviv, but with busy schedules, they did not see each other enough.

After Layla got out of the shower, they needed to call the safe house. If they didn't, Dina would pull no punches in her reprimand of their negligence, and she'd be right. Reconciling his married life and fatherhood with being an intelligence agent was puzzling to him. Having spent years undercover as a spy in Iran and now as an active Mossad agent heading missions around the world, answering to a five-year-old continued to perplex him. He was always in a struggle with himself, and surrendering himself to God's plan was a daily difficulty. Still, it never ceased to amaze him how a curly-haired, redheaded, green-eyed, dimpled child could perfectly disarm him with a bat of her eyelashes. He chuckled to himself. Thank goodness Layla wasn't so easily beguiled. Pouty lips or puppy dog eyes did not deceive Layla. She'd turned out to be the strict disciplinarian and took her parenting seriously. Cyrus tried but was often at a loss, especially when his prodigious child persisted in asking questions about topics he didn't want to discuss with her. Her inquisitiveness about making babies was one of those subjects that made him want to run for the hills.

The bedroom door opened, and the other half of his soul walked in with wet hair and her body wrapped in a thick white terry robe. The sight of her was enough to take his breath away. He wondered if, when he was ninety, he would feel the same way. He couldn't imagine it not being so. *Chemistry is chemistry, and loving Layla was what he was born to do. He'd fought it, but it was love at first sight.*

"Eshgham." He strode to her, taking her in his arms and burying his nose in the curve of her neck. "You smell delicious." Layla's scent enveloped him, and a yearning to make love to her heated his blood. The thought of sweeping her up in his arms and carrying her into the bedroom enticed, and he had to fight hard to tamp it down.

Layla melted against him, snuggling into his chest. "I've missed this. Not that I don't care about Jazmin, but I need to feel the man who is my foundation against me."

"I echo your thoughts, my love."

"How did the hand-off of Jazmin to Aryeh go?"

He kissed the tip of her freckled nose. "Wordlessly. She was shy and hesitant, but I'm sure Aryeh will gain her trust."

"If anyone can, it will be Aryeh. She's very fragile, poor thing. My heart breaks for her."

"We'll keep her safe, and better days are ahead. Speaking of better days, what do you say we call home and talk to our magnificent creation?"

"That would be wonderful. I miss her so much, and Dina is going to kill me if we don't."

"Tell me about it. Your grandmother is a force of nature and one I don't want to get on the wrong side of. Sometimes she reminds me of that cartoon Cerise loves, the Tasmanian Devil, a whirling tornado."

Layla giggled. "She is one powerful lady, that's for sure. *Saba* is a cupcake in comparison."

"Oh, Morris has learned how to manage Hurricane Dina. He could write a book on husbandry."

She playfully poked her finger into his chest. "Be sure you pay close attention and take notes. The apple doesn't fall far from the tree, you know."

"Believe me, I do." He laughed. "He's always reminding me that you and Dina are two peas in a pod."

"My mother was the third pea," she said wistfully.

"I wish I could have met her and told her how much I love her daughter."

Layla caressed his cheek. "I know she would have loved you."

"Let's call our prodigy." They sat on the sofa, and Cyrus entered the code that routed the call through the satellite. The phone rang, and he put it on speaker and set it on the coffee table.

"*Shalom,*" the familiar Polish-accented voice of Dina Freiberg Rose answered.

"Hi *Savta,* how are you?"

"Better now that I hear your voice, my darling. Are you having a nice vacation?"

"Well, it's been interesting," Layla said with a giggle.

"How's that handsome husband of yours?"

"He's here *Savta,* we're on speaker."

"*Boychik,* are you taking good care of my granddaughter?"

"I'm doing my best, Dina, and thanks for the compliment." In the background, he could hear Cerise squealing and Norit's squeaky barks. "Is that my *motek* causing all of that ruckus?"

"Daddy!" The sound of the phone changing hands and their breathless daughter's excitement crackled through the line.

"Hi baby, how's my girl?"

"*Aba,* is *Ima* there too?"

"I'm right here, love. Tell us everything."

"Here we go. That should only take about a week." Cyrus laughed, and Layla elbowed him in the ribs.

Cerise ignored Cyrus's aside, plunging in with excitement. "I taught Norit to sit! Daddy, she's so smart, and wait until you see how big she's gotten. Daddy, she's growing—huge!"

Cyrus couldn't help but wonder how much the ball of yellow fluff could have grown in four days. He didn't have long to contemplate before Cerise continued. "Have you been kissing Mommy? Did you make a baby? Is it a boy or a girl?" Cyrus could hear Dina cackling in the background. Cerise's thoughts were fluid and moved from one subject to the next without a breath.

"Yes, *motek,* we're kissing a lot, but I don't know if there's a baby yet."

"Kiss more! You promised."

"Enough, Cerise. A baby will come when God wills it," Layla interjected.

"Do you have to kiss God too, Mommy, to get a baby? Is that how it works? Do you want me to talk with God?"

What an imagination this kid has. Cyrus bit his tongue before he said something, and Layla gave him the stink eye.

"If you want to talk to God, there's nothing wrong with that, sweetie. So, what have you been doing?" Layla deftly changed the subject.

"Swimming, *Ima,* I love the swimming pool. Can we get a swimming pool?"

"Maybe someday, pumpkin." If he could, he'd make her every wish come true. "It's cold where Mommy and I are. How's the weather there?"

"Are you making snow angels? Oh, I forgot *Aba,* guess what Norit did today?"

"I'm afraid to ask," said Cyrus. He let the snow angel question drop while he focused on Norit's accomplishments. Ever since they stayed at the safe house in Switzerland, Cerise had been relentless in her desire to go back to the mountains and make snow angels. When Cerise fixated on something, she used all the tools in her toolbox to coax them — from logical arguments like her nuclear physicist grandfather to mock threats like her great-grandmother.

"Norit jumped in the swimming pool. She likes it, Daddy. At first, I was afraid she would drown. I screamed so loud, *Savta* came running out of the house in her underwear and her hair all in curlers, but Norit knew how to swim. She's so smart. I think we need to get a swimming pool for Norit."

Cyrus's chest rumbled with laughter as he listened to his daughter cajole with what she thought might be her winning ploy. "Okay, we'll work on it. Heaven forbid Norit shouldn't have everything she wants. And try not to scare the living daylights out of your great-grandmother."

"Oh, don't worry, *Saba* was outside with us. He told *Savta* to get dressed before she scared the nice men who are watching over us." Cerise lowered her voice to a whisper. "I think *Saba* was a little upset at *Savta* for coming outside half-naked, only thank goodness he didn't mention her hair all in curlers."

"Well, that's understandable. You know how great-grandmother is about her hairdos," Layla said.

"Yes, heaven forbid you don't compliment her!" Cerise exclaimed. "I always tell her how nice her hair looks." Her whisper was muffled by her hand. "That way she can't say no if I ask her for an extra piece of cake."

Layla and Cyrus exchanged amused glances. Layla bit her lip to keep from laughing. Cyrus shook his head at their outrageous child.

"But *Aba,* Norit really needs a swimming pool so she can become a better swimmer." Cerise stretched the "needs" out part to emphasize the life-and-death importance.

"Cerise, we'll discuss it when we get home," Layla said in her no-nonsense tone.

This time Cyrus changed the subject. "*Motek,* have you been taking good care of *Saba and Savta?"*

"Oh, yes, Daddy. I make sure they get their exercise every day. *Saba* swims laps, which he says will make him live forever. See, we really need a swimming pool for *Saba,* too!"

"Okay, Cerise, you'll make a fine attorney one day."

"Mommy, why do you always say that? I'm going to be an artist, I already told you."

"Yes, sweetie," she said with a giggle. "Sorry, I forgot."

"It's okay. I forgive you."

"Honey, we need to get ready for dinner. Take good care of Norit, *Savta,* and *Saba."*

"Oh, don't worry, Mommy, I will. I keep *Savta* very busy baking cakes. Norit loves cake, and so do the nice men who stand outside."

Cyrus squinted, pinching the bridge of his nose. "I told you cake isn't good for Norit, baby."

Cerise's voice dropped to a whisper. "Don't worry, *Aba,* I *tell Savta* the cake is for Norit. But I eat her piece and mine, but don't tell her."

"Okay, I won't," Cyrus whispered back. "I love you, love of my life."

"Love you too, but you know Mommy is the love of your life. Mommy, I love you. Oh, don't forget to kiss a lot so we can get another baby. Oh, I have to take Norit outside to make potty. *Shalom.*" Before either Layla or he could reply, Cerise hung up.

Cyrus wiped eyes that had teared up from laughing. "What a character. God help us when she's a teenager."

Layla rested her head on his shoulder. "She's one of a kind, that's for sure. But it sounds like she doesn't miss us too much."

"Yeah, that child is a free spirit. She may not miss us, but I sure do miss her. Maybe we can join a club with a pool."

"We'll figure it out." Layla combed her fingers through his hair and kissed him on the cheek. "I better get dressed for dinner. It's nearly eight, and I'm famished."

"Me too, *eshgham*. It's been a long day." As Layla walked into the bedroom, he thought about the call with Cerise. Hearing her irrepressible spirit reminded him of the reason he remained in the spy game and why this mission was so important. Israel would never be safe as long as the regime in Tehran vowed her destruction. Protecting Israel safeguarded his daughter's future, and he would do anything to keep her safe. When they returned to Tel Aviv, he'd figure out the pool situation. If they were blessed with another child, they would need more space. He wasn't surprised his daughter-attorney in the making had won her argument. It was time they moved to a bigger house with a backyard, and if he could afford it, a pool.

CHAPTER TWENTY-EIGHT

Tuesday, February 11
Zürich, Switzerland

The Widder Restaurant was over the top, but the only other restaurant, had little in the way of vegetarian selections for Jazmin. The Widder's dining room was country chic in shades of creamy gold and teal with coffered ceilings, frescoed walls, and white linen tablecloths. The walls were lined with banquettes on one side, the other side flanked by square tables that bordered the room. Richly upholstered striped barrel chairs in varying shades of blue and cream and solid red provided additional seating. The generous spacing of the tables allowed for privacy but afforded an open plan for people watching. Cyrus had scoped things out before texting Aryeh and Jazmin to come down from their room.

With his hand on Jazmin's back, Aryeh escorted her into the restaurant. After a quick scan of the room, he nodded, acknowledging Cyrus's hand wave from the table.

"Franz," Layla grinned, "you'd make an excellent personal shopper. The coral cashmere sweater you chose for Esfir and the blue one for me are perfect." Esfir was the name on Jazmin's passport that the

Mossad "passport factory" had created for her. They were using each other's fake names in public.

Aryeh's face reddened, and he scrubbed his dark blond stubble with his hand. "Tease me all you want, Serena, but I did nail the color of your eyes. So, no complaints."

"It's a compliment, Franz. I'm thinking of hiring you as a personal shopper. Alphonse is worthless when it comes to shopping. He thinks everything I put on is perfect. Frankly, he's more interested in me without clothes," she teased.

Both Cyrus and Layla could barely contain their surprise when they saw Jazmin take Aryeh's hand and squeeze it. Smiling up at him, she added. "I love the things you bought me. I can't figure out how you knew my favorite color is coral."

"It's how I see you." Aryeh returned her gaze with an unmistakable intensity that made Jazmin's cheeks pinken.

Cyrus sat back and crossed his arms over his chest. "I'm happy to see you two getting along so well. I was a little worried when I dropped you off at the room, Esfir."

"I was a little nervous, but now I'm fine. Franz and I had a lovely talk. We have a lot in common."

Cyrus glanced at Layla, and they exchanged a knowing look. "Well, shall we order some wine and food? I'm starving."

"Let's do it," said Aryeh.

The meal passed with amiable conversation. Nothing about tomorrow's plan was discussed. When it was time for dessert and after-dinner drinks, Cyrus suggested they order up in his and Layla's room.

WHILE THE LADIES were conversing on the sofa in front of the crackling fire in the hearth, Cyrus and Aryeh stepped onto the terrace to talk. The crisp air felt good after being in a heated dining room. Cyrus sipped his cognac, eyeing Aryeh. "I can't get over the change in Jazmin. What did you do, hypnotize her?"

Aryeh laughed. "What? Do you think you're the only guy who has a way with the ladies? We found some common ground, that's all."

"No, I'm not buying it. Both of you couldn't take your eyes off each other during dinner. I'd say there's more to it than that."

Aryeh shrugged. "The important thing is she's beginning to trust me. Which is what matters because I have every intention of keeping her safe. Now about tomorrow, what's your plan?"

"Okay, I'll leave the matchmaking to Layla. I believe the assassin is here in Zürich."

"Agreed."

"We're going to be exposed tomorrow no matter what we do. Jazmin needs to open the box, and we need what's inside."

"We'll both be packing, or don't you think that's enough?"

"The assassin won't be satisfied unless he kills both Jazmin and Layla. Both can identify him."

"Speaking of that, did you hear from the office as to who he might be?"

"I spoke to them today. They've got nothing. He's managed to cover his trail well. The quintessential ghost. I suspect he's a hired gun with ties to the Middle East. There's no question in my mind that the Amin family murder and the attempted arrest of Ibrahim and his girlfriend are linked. Have you spoken to Zara?"

"They arrived in Tehran and checked in. They should be contacting the nephew soon. Then comes the tough part, getting them all out safely. I have faith in Zara, but she was not a willing participant in this mission. Fortunately, Mustafa saw things differently. This operation gives him a chance to clear his name."

"It seems to me that would provide reason enough for them to succeed."

"I'm still worried. If anything happens to Zara, I'll never forgive myself."

"Have you come to an acceptance about her relationship with Mustafa?"

"To an extent. I still don't understand it, but when it comes to a woman's emotional needs, I've been wrong more times than I can count."

"You're not alone on that front, my friend." Cyrus raised his glass and clinked it against Aryeh's." Cyrus remembered what the Ramsad had said about Aryeh blaming himself for the death of a female agent a few years back. This wasn't the time to delve into Aryeh's insecurities, but one day he might. Aryeh was too good a man, too good a friend, and too good an agent to carry that kind of burden for the rest of his life.

Cyrus knew from experience that sometimes you had to let go. Things didn't always go exactly as you planned, and even the most carefully thought-out operations could go wrong. He'd nearly lost Layla when they were on the run in Iran. He'd been careless and taken their safety for granted on a tiny lake in the mountains. He'd left her sleeping, and when he returned, two IRGC brutes had captured her. They made the wrong choice, thinking they could rape her, and it had cost them their lives. He'd enjoyed every second of putting them out of their misery, but nothing would ever wipe away the image of Layla being at their mercy. He shook his head, trying to banish the horrific imagery from his thoughts that continued to linger after his recent nightmare.

Aryeh sighed and stared up at the sky where a few twinkling stars could be seen through the thin cloud cover. "How do you want to handle tomorrow?"

"I've been giving it some thought. I don't think we should all go into the bank together. I believe it was Julius Caesar, who said, 'divide and conquer,' and that's what I have in mind."

JAZMIN GLANCED out the sliding glass door at Aryeh and Cyrus, who were deep in conversation. "I'm nervous about tomorrow — afraid of what I might find in my father's safety deposit box."

"I know it's hard to imagine now, but everything is going to be fine."

"I hope so, but I have a bad feeling."

"Aryeh will keep you safe."

Jazmin smiled. "When I first met him in London at the embassy, I didn't like him. He made me nervous. He looks like a big mountain lion, very intimidating."

"I'm sure as you get to know him, you'll see what a pussycat he truly is," Layla said with a grin.

Jazmin giggled. "Yes. You know, it's strange. Even though I was educated abroad and moved in cosmopolitan circles, I still carried my own deep-seated prejudices. Both you and Cyrus are part Jewish, but Aryeh is Israeli born and bred. And I am Iranian born and bred. We have been taught by birth to distrust each other, hate each other. But I have learned that is not the case. My father had come to believe this, as well. And my own feelings over the years changed through my interactions with people outside of Iran," She plucked at the fine silk threads of the pillow in her lap. "The Middle East is so culturally diverse, each country so unique and even within each country, so many more unique ethnic groups. I wish we could all celebrate that uniqueness. Embrace it and enjoy it as we are enjoying this baklava here." Jazmin gestured to the platter on the coffee table filled with an array of small bites of pastries, including the delectable lemony pastry made with butter, honey, pistachios, and walnuts.

Layla nodded as she took a bite of the tasty dessert. "As far as I'm concerned, if only we could build bridges with food, culture, and sport, we'd be a far happier world. But tell me, how did you get over your nerves about Aryeh?"

"I asked him a question. I asked him if he'd ever lost a loved one to violence, and he took my hand and sat me down beside him and told me." She blinked back the tears that sprung to her eyes.

"Sometimes the fractures in each of us, once healed, make us stronger and wiser. I suspect the more time you spend with Aryeh, the more you will see what a good man he is. Truly one of the good ones. Like Cyrus."

Jazmin nodded. "I already do. But is it wrong of me to feel this connection? Especially so soon after…"

Layla reached for Jazmin's hand and gave it a squeeze. "It's all right. You can still grieve for the loss of your fiancé and find yourself with feelings for someone new."

"Darien, my fiancé, grew up very sheltered, like me. He was from a wealthy family, but he would have been a wonderful doctor. He wanted to help people. Truly make a difference. Which is why he studied emergency medicine. He didn't want to work in an ivory tower or cater only to the wealthy." Her hand covered her mouth as a sob escaped her. "I blame myself for his death. If he hadn't been engaged to me, he'd still be alive today and saving other people. And his lovely parents would be alive too. They treated me like their own d-daughter." She wiped the back of her hand along her wet cheeks.

Layla handed her a napkin to dry her tears. "You would have died along with them had fate not intervened. You stepped out for a cigarette and then a minute later, your world came crashing down. I know what you're going through." Layla shared her own experiences of being kidnapped and imprisoned in Iran and how she met Cyrus.

"Thank you for telling me your story. I don't know where you found the strength to get through everything, but I can only try to be as brave as you."

"You are brave. And clever and resourceful. You did the right thing going to the embassy in London. You can rebuild your life and go on, knowing that you achieved what your father had set out to do, and knowing you made a difference.

"I hope one day I can have the kind of relationship that you and Cyrus have," Jazmin said with a quirk of a smile.

"I have a feeling you will."

CHAPTER TWENTY-NINE

Tuesday, February 11
Zürich, Switzerland

Gurga had the targets in sight. He knew where their rooms were and had seen them enter the Widder Hotel restaurant. His preparations for the next day were planned. Palms had been smeared with baksheesh, and he'd brought in mercenary support. He was ready to pounce when the four made their appearance the next day.

What he wasn't prepared for was the reaction in his gut when he saw the Amin girl. He couldn't expel the feeling of desire that took hold of him when he looked at her. Yes, she was beautiful, but there were beautiful women everywhere, and while he did allow for the occasional tryst, his line of work didn't exactly encourage romantic liaisons. If anything, his existence had become almost monk-like in the past couple of years. He knew it was ridiculous, but it was as if she'd cast a spell on him. He wanted her. But it was more than that. He'd been seized with jealousy when he'd seen the protective way the blond giant caressed her back as he accompanied her into the restaurant. Like a bull charging a red cape held by a toreador, he'd wanted to impale the bastard and kill him.

After the two disappeared inside, it took him several minutes to calm his racing pulse and think clearly. He was like a teenager gripped by raging hormones. Lust and a thirst to kill warred within him. He gulped down the tumbler of scotch he'd been nursing, hoping the fire that burned his gullet would extinguish the fire that blazed in his mind.

Gurga had never allowed politics, religion, or ethnicity to influence his work. He'd even worked for Jews, knocking off a couple of blackmailers that threatened them. He'd been born a Muslim and would forever be one, but a professional assassin needed to separate himself from taking sides. Having a stake in the game was dangerous and led to mistakes. The famous assassin Carlos the Jackal had learned that the hard way. Now he was serving a life sentence rotting in a French prison for terrorism. But seeing this Israeli behave in an intimate manner with Jazmin, a Muslim woman — a blistering rage swept his emotions into chaos. That, coupled with his mystifying attraction to her, intensified the fiery response building in his veins. Yes, he was going to take a great deal of pleasure in killing this man. The question was how to do it and how to inflict the most pain possible.

CHAPTER THIRTY

Wednesday, February 12
Alborz, Islamic Republic of Iran
Chalus Road

The Chalus Road was open and Mustafa took it as a good sign. His research found that avalanches and road closures were normal occurrences in the winter. If the road was closed, they'd be forced to take a route that would expose them to more road inspections and interactions with the authorities. Mustafa drove the slick road slowly, but Zara had been suffering from a stomach ailment, and the sharp switchbacks and winding curves were making her sick.

He snuck a glance at her. "Do you think it was something you ate, *habibata?*"

Zara had her eyes closed and breathed deeply through her nose. "I don't know, it's unfortunate timing. And this road isn't helping."

"Closing your eyes is only going to make it worse. Crack your window and breathe some fresh air. I'm sorry, but we have another eighty miles to go. Try to focus on the incredible scenery, my love. This is probably one of the most beautiful landscapes in the world."

Zara rolled down her window and stuck her head out. "It's freezing, but maybe you're right. A little fresh air won't hurt."

"There are a lot of tearooms along the way. Maybe we should stop. A little tea and cake might do the trick."

"I think we'll have to stop. Of all the times and places to feel unwell, this is the worst."

"It doesn't matter how slowly we go, as long as we get out of the mountains before nightfall. Once we're in Astara, we'll touch base with Kaspar and arrange the rendezvous with the professor."

"Find that rest stop, *mon amour,* I need to throw up."

Zara sat at a table in the teahouse with her head in her hands. A young woman approached the table, holding a tray with steaming glasses of tea and a plate of pastries. Mustafa thanked the young woman, and with her hands together in a thanking pose, she nodded before walking away.

"Drink some tea, *habibata.* It will help."

Zara lifted her face from her hands and smiled thinly at him. *"Shukran,"* she thanked him. Outside the window, she noticed a deck covered in snow. She imagined it would be lovely to eat lunch there in the spring and summer. The deck suspended over a stream was fed by a natural waterfall that cascaded down a stone-faced wall. "It's really pretty, isn't it?" She brought the steaming glass to her lips and sipped.

"Yes, incredible."

The door to the teahouse opened, and two officers in green uniforms entered and took a table nearby. Zara visibly stiffened and averted her gaze.

Mustafa diverted her attention. "Eat, Francoise. It will make you feel better." He licked the sticky honey from the baklava off his fingers. "The baklava is delicious."

"I know that I need something for the stomachache, but the thought of eating makes me sick."

They finished and Mustafa left cash on the table. Neither he nor Zara could feel comfortable with the gendarmes observing them.

ROUTE 59 WOUND through the Alborz Mountains, and had Zara felt more herself, she would have enjoyed the spectacular views. When they'd stopped for tea, it dawned on her that the nausea wasn't from food, it was from the pregnancy. With determination, she ignored the telltale signs and forced herself to smile and converse with Mustafa. When he suggested they stop for a few minutes and take some pictures, she agreed more to please him than anything else.

In all of her life, she'd never seen water as clear and blue as the pristine turquoise waters of the reservoir formed by the Amir Kabir Dam, where the tiny hamlet of Varian could be seen nestled in trees. The map said it was reachable only by boat, and she had to admit she would love to see it in the summer with the sun's rays shimmering down on it. She could picture bright blue skies, green leafy trees, and pale aqua water. She sighed. *A visual paradise in a country wracked with division.*

"If questioned by the authorities, we have some documentation of our trip," Mustafa said, seemingly unperturbed over the paradox that was Iran. "It gives us authenticity and looks more like a vacation." He clicked away with his camera.

She posed next to him as he took selfies of them. "Yes, you're probably right. Sightseeing in the dead of winter, they may think we're insane, but they won't question our motives. At least, there's no traffic on this godforsaken highway. It seems we're the only tourists foolish enough to take this road in the winter." She shivered, hugging herself, and walked toward the SUV. "Let's go before we freeze to death. It must be zero degrees Celsius."

They drove for another hour until they reached the Kandovan Tunnel. On the other side of the tunnel, the road iced up, and Mustafa was forced to slow down. Zara cracked the window for some fresh air and heard the roar of the Karaj River below, the rush of water so loud it drowned out conversation. Zara felt her stomach lurch when they took a curve, and the tires momentarily slipped their grip on the road. She caught a glimpse of the raging river below, and nausea gripped her. The guardrails were non-existent, and one wrong move could find them plummeting down the steep incline and disappearing into the frigid water. Their bodies would not be found until spring. She almost chuckled to herself as she realized the most dangerous part of this mission was not the threat of being shot and killed by the authorities but crashing along the deadly road.

"Alquarf," Mustafa hissed under his breath, his eyes darting to the rearview mirror. Mustafa didn't normally curse, and hearing him say shit in Arabic took her by surprise. "We've got trouble."

Zara glanced over her shoulder. Tailing them was an SUV with flashing lights. It rode up on their bumper and indicated they wanted Mustafa to pull over. Zara's heart pounded in her chest. Visions of being arrested and taken to some hellhole prison pervaded her thoughts. Rumors abounded about the treatment of women in Iran's prisons — rape and torture were guaranteed, followed by a kangaroo court and jury with a verdict of death by hanging. Zara clutched her abdomen, protective of the life growing inside her.

"This isn't good." Mustafa grimaced.

"Take your time and pull over." Zara reached under her seat and grabbed her P365 Sig Sauer. Skillfully she screwed on the separate barrels of the Odessa silencer and loaded it with a subsonic magazine. The powerful gun was light, compact, and one of the most efficient weapons in the world. The suppressor would muffle the sound of gunshots, preventing an echo through the mountains. She hoped. They didn't need more cops after them. She hid the gun in her coat and draped her scarf over her hair and around her shoulders. "You get out and deal with them. Leave the window down so I can listen. If I don't like what I hear, I'll get out."

"Zara, don't use the gun unless it's absolutely necessary." Mustafa stopped and pulled out their passports and the new Argentinian driver's license Mossad had created to match his passport identity. He rolled down the window.

"Don't worry, I know what I'm doing." She smiled reassuringly, but her pulse throbbed in her temples. Mustering her courage, she did her best to project a calmness she didn't feel. Her skills might have been rusty, but when push came to shove, her muscle memory from years of working in the field would kick in. Their lives depended on her performing under stress, but more important, the life she carried inside of her demanded it.

The two men approached the car, one on either side, their hands on the guns tucked into their holsters.

Mustafa greeted them with a smile, speaking Arabic so that Zara would understand the conversation. "Is everything all right, officers?"

The man who peered in the driver's side window wore aviator glasses and chewed gum. Zara almost laughed at the visual stereotype of the highway cop that existed the world over. The officer took off his sunglasses and surveyed the interior of their SUV. He didn't return Mustafa's smile. The graying at his temples suggested he was older and the senior of the two men. "Papers *raja'*." His fake smile didn't reach his eyes, and his saying "please" came across as more disconcerting than politeness.

Mustafa handed them the passports. The policemen were probably NAJA and known for their strict enforcement of the law. Their reputation was every bit as frightening as the organization that preceded their formation, the secret police force SAVAK, the henchmen of the Pahlavi Shah who'd ruled Iran before the revolution. The demeanor of the regime's thugs was anything but friendly.

"My wife and I are traveling to Astara to visit the sea. We live in Argentina, as you can see from our passports. My parents were from Astara, and I've never been there. We decided to take the scenic route. It probably was a mistake as the driving conditions aren't all that great. Was I driving too slow?"

The policeman said nothing, glancing back and forth from their passports to their faces. Zara had kept her gaze modestly down, but she glanced up and recognized the officer from the tearoom. These were the men who'd entered before she and Mustafa left. *Why did they follow us? Boredom.* Her inner voice replied. *To get their kicks lording it over complete strangers.* Whatever the reason, it didn't matter now. She shifted uncomfortably in her seat. It was all she could do to keep still.

The other officer peered into the back window. Their suitcases were in the cargo hold. What worried Zara was what was hidden in the tire and tools compartment. The green satchel with their illegal cache of weapons would spell disaster if discovered.

"Get out of the car. We'd like to check the cargo hold."

"Of course." Mustafa exited the car. "Francoise, you might want to get some fresh air." He turned to the officer. "You don't mind, do you? My wife sometimes gets car sick, and this is a chance for her to inhale the fresh mountain air."

"Your wife does not concern us."

Mustafa walked to the rear of the SUV sandwiched between the two officers, one in front and one behind. Zara opened the car door and got out. Not for the first time, she felt grateful for the misogyny of Middle Eastern men, who always made the mistake of underestimating women and what they were capable of doing.

She intentionally stumbled from the car, taking deep breaths as if to calm her delicate stomach and feminine nature. Below the embankment beside the road, she could hear the thunderous roar of the Karaj River, which matched the pounding in her head. She walked around the car and joined the men at the rear. Mustafa pressed the button on the key, and the liftgate opened. Then Zara saw something that made her heart skip. A piece of the green duffel's handle could be seen. It had gotten stuck in a crack when they'd closed the compartment. She hoped the officers wouldn't notice it.

The older policeman seemed to be more interested in their luggage. He popped open first one suitcase and then the other. He set piles of clothing and small toiletry bags to the side, searching everything thoroughly. When the bags were empty and he seemed satisfied, he ordered Mustafa to reload the bags. He appeared to enjoy wielding power over them. Zara had known men like this all her life, and she knew there was always a reckoning for them. Every few minutes, the officer glanced back at her. She'd walked several feet down the road and pretended to be interested in the landscape. Only occasionally did she glance with frightened eyes at the harassment of her husband. Mustafa played his part beautifully as a somewhat befuddled and slightly obsequious man of no consequence.

When Mustafa finished repacking the suitcases, the officer lifted the cases and set them on the ground. "What's this?" he asked. Zara knew immediately what he was pointing at. It was the green strap poking out from the duffel bag. A chill skittered up her spine, and adrenaline flooded her veins.

"Uh..." Mustafa hesitated. I-I don't know."

"Let's find out. Open it!" The unfriendly voice had turned harsh and authoritarian.

"No!" Zara's scream reverberated throughout the canyon bouncing from one mountain top to the next. Mustafa's hand froze, and the officers turned in unison, their brows raised in question. By their expressions, Zara could see this was not what they expected. Zara stood, feet braced apart, pointing the gun at the officers. "Step away from the car and put your hands up in the air," she ordered in a knife-edged tone. She meant business, and the officers knew it. She motioned with the pistol which direction they should move. They shifted sideways away from the rear of the car.

"What are you doing?" the older of the men asked with a trembling voice. "Have you any idea what your punishment will be for pulling a weapon on law enforcement?"

"I'm sorry, but you should have left well enough alone." With a deep breath and exhalation, she steadied her hands.

The younger man made a grab for his gun, but before he'd lifted it out of his holster Zara fired off a round straight through his heart, and he stumbled backward and fell to the ground. The man who'd displayed a love of power blanched white, realizing what had happened. The look on his face was of complete disbelief. In the blink of an eye, he reached for his gun, but Zara shot a single bullet through his heart. He dropped like a stone before his face could register a reaction. The retort of the pistol with a suppressor was quieter, but the pfft was still loud enough to cause a flock of birds to take wing.

Zara lowered the gun, her chest heaving as she bent forward and vomited.

Mustafa ran to her and held her shoulders until she finished. "*Habibata,* are you all right?"

"I killed them." She felt vanquished by the act.

"You had no choice. it was them or us." He held her in his arms. "Come, get in the car. You're shivering."

"No." She shook her head. "We have to finish this and get out of here. Help me." Gathering her strength, she broke free of his embrace and walked to the police vehicle. "Position their car so that it's pointed toward the edge of the embankment."

"What do you have in mind?"

"We're going to put them in the car, release the brake, and put it in neutral. Then we'll push it over the ledge. Help me put their bodies inside. Quick, there's no time to waste. We must hurry, Mustafa. If someone drives up the road, we're sitting ducks. I've killed enough people for one day."

It wasn't easy to drag and lift the bodies into the vehicle. Their dead weight made them unwieldy and cumbersome. Zara wiped her forehead, sweaty from the exertion. With the bodies inside and the vehicle perched over the edge of the cliff, Zara released the brake and put the gear shift in neutral.

"Help me." Together they stood behind the vehicle and pushed. The car rocked back and forth a few times before finally hurtling over the cliff. They watched from the ledge as it bounced over the rocky terrain, the force of gravity driving its weight downward. The car hit a boulder and took wing, flipping upside down into the river with a splash. For a few moments, the rushing water carried it downriver. Then from the onslaught of water pouring in, the vehicle sank and disappeared.

Zara shivered, and Mustafa took her hand. She continued to stare down at the raging river, worried at what she would see in his eyes. Despite the necessity of what they'd done — what she'd done — would his romantic view of her dim?

"Look at me, Zara," he said softly.

She did, and the glowing love and admiration in his gaze was her undoing. She burst into tears.

Mustafa gathered her into his arms and held her close. "You've told me much of what you've done in your life," he said, his voice thick with emotion. "But to see you in action is another thing altogether. You are a remarkable woman, my love. I now know it wasn't me Aryeh trusted with this mission. It was you. He knows what you're capable of, and he knows you will not fail."

She sniffed and leaned back in his embrace so she could look at him. "Thank you, *mon amour*. But right now, all I want to do is ring Aryeh's neck. Damn him for placing us in this position. For forcing me into a situation where I have to kill again. I thought I'd left all of that behind me. This isn't the way I want you to see me. I pray we survive so that I can give him a piece of my mind."

"And how do you think I see you?"

"Like a cold-blooded killer."

"Ah...well, you are wrong there. You are a hot-blooded woman protecting the man you love." He kissed the tip of her nose. "Now, my hot-blooded beauty, I think we should get the hell out of here. We have an appointment to keep with destiny."

CHAPTER THIRTY-ONE

Wednesday, February 12
Zürich, Switzerland

Cyrus scanned the street in front of the Widder Hotel. The sky was as clear and blue as an alpine stream, and the newly shoveled sidewalks and snowplowed streets were already busy with the morning rush hour. When an Audi with black-tinted windows pulled up, he signaled Layla to join him. She exited through the glass doors, and he positioned his body as a shield to protect her until she was seated in the front passenger seat. Closing the door a half-second later, he rounded the car, threw his attaché in the back seat, got in and pulled away from the curb.

The streets were crowded with pedestrians and vehicles carrying people to work. He searched the rearview mirror for anything that might reveal they were being tailed. There was nothing suspicious or obvious. Beside him, Layla drummed her fingers on the handbag in her lap in a nervous rhythm.

He reached over and covered her hand with his. "Don't worry, everything's going to be fine. You're safe with me, and Jazmin's safe with Aryeh." He hid his own worries. There was no sense in exacerbating Layla's fears. The divide and conquer strategy he and Aryeh had settled on last night was in motion. Aryeh and Jazmin had left from a side entrance to the hotel. They were at this moment walking to Julius Bär at their main headquarters at 36 Bahnhofstrasse, a three-minute walk from the Widder Hotel. The plan was for Aryeh and Jazmin to open Saman's security box and retrieve what they found. When they exited Julius Bär, Cyrus would pick them up, and they'd drive directly to a Mossad-owned investment bank where the flash drives and information would be downloaded and sent to Tel Aviv. There was one glitch, one weakness in the plan, that neither Aryeh nor Cyrus were comfortable with. Aryeh was unarmed. He could not get through the metal detectors at the bank with a weapon. Cyrus, however, was armed and prepared to intervene in case anything went wrong. His focus was elsewhere, but the jitteriness in Layla's body was telltale. His wife was having a difficult time.

"I hope you're right, but I can't imagine the assassin is going to sit idly by and not make a move. We both know at some point he's coming for Jazmin and —" she couldn't finish the sentence. Cyrus looked over at her with concern. A glance at her face told him she was having a PTSD memory. That's the way PTSD worked. Any stress or fear could become a trigger. Layla was strong, but even the most seasoned warrior wasn't immune to the effects of past psychological trauma.

Layla covered her face with her hands. "I'm sorry. It feels like it was yesterday, as if it's happening again. In Pennsylvania, I felt so alone, so helpless cufflinked to that bed for days and worrying I'd never see you and Cerise again. You were operating under the belief that she was safe in that chalet. I can't tell you how many times I imagined her being shot and killed, her life snuffed out by an assassin. It tortured me."

Cyrus maneuvered the Audi into a parking place on the street a half-block from the bank. He kept his eye on the entrance but held Layla's hand in his to reassure her. "*Eshgham,* I know how hard it is to get past something like that, but Cerise is fine and safe. Take a few deep breaths."

She breathed in deeply through her nose and out through her mouth.

"Good girl. Right now, I need you to focus on the here and now. I need your help, your clarity of thought. Jazmin needs you."

"You're right. It's selfish of me, I know. Jazmin's the one who is in real danger right now. I'm sorry."

"It's all right, *aziz-am*. Everything is progressing as planned. Look, there they are," he kissed her hand, then reached into the backseat and grabbed the attaché case. Opening it, he took out a pair of binoculars and surveyed the entrance to the bank and the street. Jazmin and Aryeh disappeared inside the bank. "They're in and no sign of trouble."

"That's a relief. Now we wait. How long do you think it will take?"

"I don't know. I'm sure there's paperwork to be done, but Jazmin has everything necessary to make the legal transfer simple. Aryeh will text me before they exit."

"And from here, we go to the Mossad offices in the bank where Aryeh works?"

"Yes, and once everything has been sent to the head office, we'll drive to the airport where a private jet is waiting to take us to Tel Aviv." He looked at his watch. "Mossad is picking our luggage up and will have it delivered to the plane. We'll be home in a matter of hours, maybe in time to take a swim with Cerise."

"That would be nice, but you owe me a vacation because this one was not relaxing," she said with a giggle. "But what about Jazmin? Where will she go? Do you think she can stay at the safehouse with us for a few days and get acclimated? We can't abandon her once we get home. It's not right."

"I'll talk to the Ramsad. I'm sure he'll agree that the girl deserves what's best for her mental and physical health. If the contents in that safety deposit box are what we think, she will have delivered to Israel a precious gift."

Layla made her case for keeping Jazmin with them and it reminded him of Cerise. Both mother and daughter were expert and convincing when they campaigned for something they wanted. He knew the Ramsad would be hard-pressed to refuse Layla.

"It will be good for Jazmin after what she's been through to be with a family. "And," Layla's eyes twinkled with mischief, "maybe we can have Aryeh come for dinner and a pool party. I definitely think there's something brewing between him and Jazmin that needs to be encouraged."

"Okay, Madam Matchmaker, let's not forget that she's mourning a fiancé and her family. I think it's a little early to be planning their wedding."

"I know, but the best thing for her would be to start a new life as soon as possible. She needs to believe she has a future, or she will fall into despair. She certainly won't be able to return to Iran, and for her safety, she's best off in Israel. With our friendship and Aryeh's, she will have a chance to adjust and rebuild."

"I don't disagree, but I'm not sure Aryeh is marriage material. His whole life is Mossad."

"Don't be ridiculous. You didn't think you were marriage material either, and now look at you, husband extraordinaire, and father of the year."

Cyrus rolled his eyes at that. "I'll remind you of that during our next argument."

"*Next* argument? You assume we'll fight again?"

"I look forward to it. I'd rather fight with you than anyone else in the world. As long as there is always make-up sex afterward." He shot her a lascivious wink.

"Oh, you!" she swatted him on the shoulder.

"Ow."

She laughed and settled back in her seat. "Thank you, by the way."

"For what?" He flashed her a quick grin.

"You know for what. For helping me get through my PTSD memories. I lost myself for a moment and forgot my vow. I swore to myself when I trained with the IDF that I would never be cowered by anyone again. And I'm trying not to let my fears for your safety get the better of me."

"You know you're amazing. What a sorry soul I would be without you. You took my black-and-white world and filled it with color, *eshgham. Ani ohev otakh.*"

"I love you too, Superman."

Cyrus's phone pinged, and he glanced down. His smile was replaced with a frown. "They're coming out."

Both Cyrus and Layla sat at attention, keeping their eyes peeled on their surroundings. Around them, people walked about their day, absorbed in their own preoccupations. Cars drove by. Nothing was out of the ordinary. An elderly man exited a luxury Mercedes, barely standing upright as he leaned heavily upon a metal cane. Layered in a cumbersome winter coat that hid his bulk and a fedora that cast shadow on his face, his straggly gray hair hung loose over his collar, giving him the look of a wealthy eccentric.

"I don't like this." Cyrus put the car in drive and screeched out of the parking spot.

"What? What is it?" Layla shouted.

A van pulled in front of them and stopped and he had to slam on the brakes. He hit the horn, but nothing happened the van didn't move.

"Shit!" Cyrus pulled his pistol, tucked it into his waistband, and ran from the car.

"Be careful!" Layla screamed.

Two men jumped out of the van pistols drawn and Cyrus was forced to duck behind the van. He couldn't see the front door of the bank. He yelled to Aryeh, "Fauda! Fauda!" and peeked around the white van. Aryeh and Jazmin had exited the doors of Julius Bär. Aryeh's head turned toward Cyrus's shouts of "chaos." The elderly man moved as if in a marathon, running at Aryeh and grabbed his neck. The prick on Aryeh's neck must have stung like a bee, but the result was unfathomable. Aryeh stumbled.

The two men from the white van jumped back in and took off with a screech of burning rubber.

Layla pulled up next to him, screaming, "Get in!" She hit the gas and the Audi raced down the street.

"Go! Go!" Cyrus's heart stampeded like a herd of cattle, and his blood boiled with anger.

ARYEH'S HAND flew to his neck. Realizing his mistake, the color drained from his face, and he tried to grab hold of the old man imposter, but it was too late. The man wore a ring with a tiny needle that caught the sunlight, its tip now red with a drop of Aryeh's blood. Aryeh stumbled, his fists flying, but the poison rendered him useless and he pitched forward. He reached for Jazmin as his knees hit the ground. Jazmin screamed while bystanders watched in shock and bewilderment.

A glint of metal revealed the steel barrel of a handgun. The old man, who obviously wasn't old, pressed the muzzle to Jazmin's head. She'd dropped to the pavement to help Aryeh, but the assassin hoisted her up like a rag doll. "Get up! Move!" The man bent to search Aryeh's pockets. Glancing up he saw the Audi making a beeline toward them. He jumped up, grabbing Jazmin's arm. Jazmin writhed in his grasp but was no match, and he dragged her to the Mercedes, threw her in the backseat, and slid in beside her.

CYRUS CURSED and made a split-second decision. "Stop the car!" Rather than follow the Mercedes, he leaped out of the Audi and ran to Aryeh. The Mercedes drove away—tires screaming.

"W-why didn't you go a-after them," Aryeh managed, his voice barely above a whisper.

"It'll be okay," Cyrus said as he knelt beside his friend. "Can you walk?"

Aryeh managed a nod.

His breath was shallow, and his voice barely above a whisper. "G-get me o-out of here before the police arrive."

"That's my intention." With Aryeh's arm around his shoulders, he lifted and supported him. Once Aryeh was safely in the backseat, Cyrus opened his mouth to ask his wife if she'd tracked down the closest hospital, but she cut him off before he could even ask.

"University Hospital of Zürich," she said. "I added the coordinates to your GPS." Take a right, then another right. We have to cross the river."

Cyrus nodded and merged onto the road as the security guards rushed out of the bank, and the sirens sounded close by.

Layla whipped around to look at Aryeh. "Will he be okay?"

Aryeh looked in the rearview at his friend, whose head rested against the seat with his eyes closed. Sweat beaded on his forehead. The rise and fall of his chest looked infinitesimal with his shallow breaths. "Scientists in Israel have been working on an antidote to a spectrum of poisons. I wasn't allowed to tell you, but Aryeh and I volunteered to be guinea pigs. Most poisons would have killed him instantly, but he's hanging in there, so maybe the preventive antidote is working. How far is the hospital?"

"It says seven minutes."

"Seven minutes too long." He floored the gas pedal, racing around the corner, leaving burning rubber.

"I can't believe what happened. Dear God, what will that monster do to Jazmin?"

"I don't think he'll do anything when he figures out she's worth more alive than dead. We'll deal with finding Jazmin as soon as we know Aryeh's out of danger."

CHAPTER THIRTY-TWO

Wednesday, February 12
Zürich, Switzerland

When Gurga slammed the door of the Mercedes, he expected screams from Jazmin, a physical struggle, even tears. For this reason, he was prepared with a hypodermic needle filled with a drug that would make her compliant. Instead, she stared at her hands with a look of resignation on her face and said nothing. He'd never seen a victim act that way, and it perplexed him. He'd injected the Mossad agent who guarded her with a lethal poison and kidnapped her, and now she sat quietly beside him as though he were her husband driving her to the grocery store. Hysteria he knew how to deal with. But her calm demeanor was disconcerting.

She was an enigma, and he could not help the intense attraction that even now burned hotly in him. Jazmin was a calm port in a storm, and he was besieged by an urge to possess her. Once he had his fill of her, he'd kill her. He had no other choice.

"Aren't you afraid?" he asked.

"Should I be?"

"I injected the man protecting you with a deadly poison. I murdered your family, your fiancé. I would think you'd be afraid, but more so, I'd think you would be consumed with hatred that would make you fight back, make you strike out at me."

"What would I gain from such a reaction? Would it bring my family back? Or would I be giving you more power over me?" She turned to him, and he stared into the depths of her hazel eyes. He found himself unable to look away. How did this woman make him feel things he'd hadn't felt in years? He never cared what any of his victims felt. His goal was singular, kill them, and move on as quickly as possible. Who they were or who they had been was of no importance. Why did he desire to know what she was thinking? Why did it matter?

"Where are you taking me?"

"To my home."

She nodded. "I see."

"Don't you want to know where it is?"

"I'll know soon enough. Besides, what difference does it make? Wherever you take me is the same as wherever I've been. I belong everywhere and nowhere."

It was a cryptic answer, and he contemplated her words, wondering how pertinent they were to who she was or, rather, who she'd become. Although he was curious as to what she found in the safety deposit box, he didn't ask. *Plenty of time for that.* In fact, he'd begun to imagine keeping her alive for much longer than he'd initially thought. Call it his fascination, but he thought it would be amusing to spend time with her and find out what made her tick. His fortress above the Mediterranean Sea would provide a secure location, and he could observe her much as a scientist would study a rat in a lab.

Gurga removed his hat and the gray wig he'd been wearing. Call it vanity, but he was unable to look unkempt in front of her, and he ran his fingers through his thick hair that he'd lightened, smoothing and tidying it until it lay flat. "Since you're cooperating, there's no need for me to restrain you."

Jazmin said nothing, her expression unreadable.

"We should be at the airport in a few minutes."

"We're flying?"

"Yes, it's a two-hour flight." He knew it was because she offered no resistance, but it felt almost as if he was bringing her to his home for a lover's tryst. He shook his head to dispel the image. Instead, he wondered what her reaction would be to the grandeur of his fortress nestled in the rocky crags above the Port of Valletta.

He'd begun his life nearly illiterate, but in the ensuing years, he'd educated himself and considered himself a Renaissance man. When he wasn't traveling the world and administering the lucrative contracts that ended lives, he spent his downtime immersing himself in study. The volumes of books in his library were impressive by any standard, and Gurga prided himself on having read all of them. A smile crept across his face as he considered the look of surprise on Jazmin's face when she saw the splendor of the world he'd built. He knew she was an artist and held a degree in art history, and the thought of whiling away the hours discussing various topics with her appealed greatly to him. In fact, he'd never felt a compunction to do anything like that until now.

He felt her eyes on him.

"Is there something you find amusing?" she asked.

The smile that had softened his features withered away. "I was thinking that you might, for all of its oddity, find this to be an adventure of sorts — both informative and illuminating."

Her laughter filled the air like a musical tune, reminding him of a glockenspiel with its bell-like tonality. It was the first time he'd heard it, and a tantalizing warmth enveloped him. He looked away, not wanting her to see the effect she had on him. "You are an unusual specimen. First, you murder everyone dear to me, then you set out to find me and kill me. Instead, you kidnap me. And now you act as though I'm your invited guest."

He didn't dare say where his thoughts had strayed and what he was contemplating. "In a way, you are my guest, albeit unwilling," he shrugged, "but welcome all the same." He looked out the window. "We've arrived. Don't try anything. Everyone here has been well paid not to see you. You're invisible as far as they are concerned." The Mercedes entered Zürich International and stopped at the gate. Gurga had gotten a pre-clearance, and they drove directly onto the runway where a Learjet 75 Liberty awaited their arrival. They were barely strapped into their seatbelts before the jet took off.

A minute later, the flight attendant asked, "Would you like champagne?" Before Jazmin could refuse, Gurga answered, "Yes, bring us each a glass, please." There was no reason for him not to relax. He was in possession of the girl and most likely the flash drive, and he'd left the Mossad agents out in the cold. It was true he hadn't eliminated the other woman who could possibly ID him, but he'd deal with that later. For the moment, the only thing he was interested in was Jazmin and unlocking her secrets.

CHAPTER THIRTY-THREE

Wednesday, February 12
Zürich, Switzerland

"Honey, why don't you go down to the cafeteria and grab a coffee," Cyrus said as he dropped a kiss on Layla's head.

"I don't want to leave in case something happens," she said, turning to look at him and wincing.

Cyrus's hands went to her shoulders and began to knead her knotted muscles. Layla sighed and dropped her head forward so he could rub the back of her neck.

"It's okay *aziz-am*, he's stable. I'll text you if anything changes. Go get yourself a coffee and relax a bit."

"Okay, I do need a jolt of caffeine, or I'm liable to nod off in this chair any second. I'll bring you back a treat." Layla blew him a kiss on her way out.

Cyrus grinned and marveled at how lucky he was to be married to her. He would never take their marriage for granted. Life was too precious. He rubbed the kinks out of his own neck and did a few deep stretches. Finally, he did a quick fifty pushups to wake himself up.

They'd sat vigil for more than four hours, waiting and hoping for

Aryeh to wake up. When Layla and Cyrus had rushed Aryeh to the hospital, the man had been at death's door. Any thoughts about Jazmin's kidnapping had been sidelined by their concern for their friend. His condition upon arrival appeared hopeless. But after a blood transfusion and the administration of a series of antidotes, including atropine, he seemed to improve. The IV alleviated the dehydration, which was a side effect of the poison that the assassin had injected him with.

The doctors hadn't expected Aryeh to live, but they didn't know what Cyrus knew, and he wasn't offering up the information to them. But Layla had been another matter. After Aryeh had stabilized and the medical team had left, Layla had given Cyrus one of her "looks," coincidentally the same expression Dina had used on him many times. Cerise was fast learning the very same look.

Cyrus relented and filled Layla in on what he'd mentioned briefly in the car as they drove Aryeh to the hospital — both he and Aryeh were guinea pigs in a new protocol that Mossad was piloting. They were among a handful of agents being tested in the ongoing study. The goal was to create a preventive drug that could save a person's life if poisoned. The science was groundbreaking and under wraps. Because injecting them with poisons to test the serum was out of the question, the researchers could not determine the effectiveness of the serum if or until one of the agents was poisoned in the field. Given the dangerous work of Mossad agents, it was more than likely to happen at some point.

Now that the protocol had been truly put to the test, the research team in Israel was anxious to know everything about Aryeh's symptoms and the progress of his recovery. Cyrus was keeping them apprised and feeding them updates directly from the doctors' reports.

Cyrus had also contacted the Ramsad, who'd been relieved the "Lion of Judah" would survive and that they'd planted a tracking device on Jazmin. A plan for rescuing Jazmin was already under way. The mission would go forward with or without Aryeh. The Ramsad had also updated Cyrus on the progress of Zara and Mustafa, including the narrow escape they'd survived in the mountains. They'd made it to Astara, and the meetup with the professor was imminent.

The Ramsad wanted to be notified immediately when Aryeh gained consciousness. They needed to know what the safety deposit box had contained and whether the assassin had gained possession of it. The Ramsad worried that the flash drive might have been lost during the altercation.

Cyrus and Layla had been so preoccupied about getting Aryeh to the hospital and then rushing him into emergency, they hadn't had a chance to search his clothing or his belongings.

Aryeh was a master at hiding things and could have even strapped the damn thing to his balls. It wouldn't have been the first time he'd done something outrageous. When Aryeh had been taken to a Hezbollah secret prison to see his nephew before arranging a prisoner exchange, he'd worn an ingenious tracking device in the shape of a mole. As the team argued about where to place the mole, Aryeh broke the stalemate and suggested they tack it onto his ass.

No bigger than a mole, it was new technology the Israelis had developed. Aryeh had stuck it to Jazmin's head beneath her hair at the nape of her neck. Virtually undetectable, it emitted a steady signal, and both Cyrus and Mossad headquarters had been tracking the assassin and where he was taking Jazmin.

As Cyrus was stretching once more after his pushups, he heard a groan come from the bed. He whipped his head around and noted Aryeh's eyes were open. A hint of color had returned to Aryeh's ashen face. Cyrus went to his bedside and laid a hand on the older man's shoulder. It took but a minute for awareness to snap into his gaze. and before Cyrus could stop him, Aryeh sat up with a jerk. "Where's Jazmin?" he rasped.

"Whoa, *achi,* take it easy and lie back down. You've just returned from the dead, and you need to take it easy."

"I'm fine now. Where is she?"

Cyrus crossed his arms over his chest. "If you settle down, I'll fill you in on everything."

"Fine." Aryeh's head hit the pillow. He groaned and closed his eyes. "Tell me."

"The assassin got Jazmin."

"Fuck!" He cracked his eyes open again. "But the tracking device is working, right? We know where she is, right?"

Cyrus nodded. "She's in Malta."

"Malta?"

"He must have a safe house there. I don't think he's going to kill her. She's his insurance. Besides, she doesn't have the flash drive. I hope?"

"You haven't checked my things, yet have you?"

"Excuse me, I was too busy saving your arse."

"Get me my left shoe."

"You're not putting on your shoes, and we're not going anywhere yet."

"Bring the shoe, *boychik*."

Cyrus shook his head all the way to the closet where Aryeh's clothes hung. The shoes were on the floor, and he brought the left one to the bed. Aryeh took the shoe and turned the heel to pop it off, revealing a hollowed-out compartment. He pulled out a black and red flash drive and handed it to Cyrus.

"You're better than Maxwell Smart."

Aryeh rolled his eyes. "Load it into the laptop and send it to the Ramsad and then call the nurse and get me unhooked from these bags. We need to get to Malta."

"The Ramsad is sending the team to Malta to assist us. We fly in the morning and plan an assault tomorrow night. But you're not going until they give you a clean bill of health."

"My health is fine. Find out what we need to do to get me released ASAP. I don't want Jazmin in the hands of that monster a minute longer than need be."

Cyrus glanced at the IV bag, which he could see was nearly empty. "The nurse should be here in a minute to change out your IV. She can call the doctor, and we can discuss your release."

Layla pushed open the door, balancing a tray with coffee and an assortment of sandwiches and snacks. Cyrus jumped up and took the tray from her.

"Aryeh! It's good to see you awake." Running to him, she gave him a huge bear hug.

"*Shalom,* Layla. It's good to see you, too."

"How do you feel? We were so frightened we were going to lose you."

"It'll take more than a little poison to slay this dragon. Are you ready to get out of here?"

"Oh, no, you need to relax and recover."

"Sorry, sweetheart, but no can do. Jazmin needs us."

Layla's smile took an about-face and headed south. "I'm so worried about her, but what are we going to do?"

"We're going to Malta. Have you ever been?"

"No —"

The nurse entered, and three pairs of eyes turned to her.

"Can you please call the doctor," Aryeh said with a charming smile. "I'm ready to check out."

She gaped at him as if he'd lost a screw. "But, sir, you survived a harrowing ordeal. You need to stay right where you are."

Layla and Cyrus exchanged glances. *Oh, boy, here we go. Wrong answer.*

Aryeh's look was apoplectic. "I don't think you're hearing me correctly. With or without your help, I'm checking out. So please get the doctor before I rip these tubes out."

While Layla stepped in to smooth things over between the irate nurse and the equally irate patient, Cyrus inserted the flash drive into his laptop and began downloading its contents for analysis and transmission to Mossad headquarters. Then he called Mossad and arranged for a private jet to fly them to Malta first thing in the morning.

That would give Aryeh one night to rest and recoup. Cyrus hoped it would be enough. He sensed that Jazmin held a fascination for the assassin. Otherwise, he would have eliminated her already. The tracking device not only transmitted her location, it also transmitted her vitals. She was alive. The assassin was operating outside his usual modus operandi of kill and disappear. He might even be considering her as blackmail potential with his employer, but for some reason, Cyrus didn't think that was it. His instincts told him this had become personal for the assassin.

Maybe he feels remorse, or he's attracted to her.

She would be helpless against the bastard if he chose to attack her. Cyrus knew Aryeh had concluded the same, which most likely furthered Aryeh's anxiety to get to Malta. He knew the secretive Mossad agent harbored his own magnetic attraction to Jazmin and would not rest until she was safe. But Jazmin was smart. Cyrus hoped she would sense the assassin's weakness and use it to her own advantage.

Having made all the necessary arrangements, Cyrus ended the call as the mollified nurse left to fetch the doctor. Layla sat on the bed and held Aryeh's hand, doing her best to reassure him that Jazmin would be okay. She was a level-headed and courageous girl and had proven so time and again.

Cyrus checked the tracking device again and saw that it was stationary and holding in place somewhere on the island of Malta. The office was working on pinpointing the exact location. The team had left Tel Aviv and was already on its way to Malta. Their passage on a cabin cruiser motor yacht had them arriving about the same time as Cyrus and Aryeh. Once the full team was in place, they would plan their assault and rescue of Jazmin. He prayed they'd be in time.

CHAPTER THIRTY-FOUR

Wednesday, February 12
Astara, Islamic Republic of Iran

Ibrahim pulled his hoodie up over his head, casting his face in shadow. The key he'd been given by Izad opened a door in the underground parking garage that led to an alleyway behind the building. He slipped through the door, shoved the key and his hands in his pockets, and took a circuitous route that kept him off the main thoroughfares. Shira had protested his going alone to the arranged meeting, but he'd insisted she was safer in the apartment than on the streets. It agonized him to put her in more danger than she was already in. They lived in constant apprehension since the NAJA agents had begun searching for them. If it wasn't for Izad's help, Ibrahim knew he and Shira would have been arrested already. Since their first visit, a rotating duo had shown up randomly to ask Izad if he'd seen hide or tail of the professor and the student. Every time they showed up, Izad told them the same thing. No one had been to the apartment or the building for that matter since the cold weather had set in. He'd explained to the agents that the owners of the other apartments only came in the summer, but as the manager of the building, he and his wife remained throughout the year. The agents seemed to believe him, mentioning there had been a sighting of Ibrahim and Shira in Bazargan, near the Turkish border, which was where the authorities were focused. But because of the persistence of the authority's inquiry, Ibrahim and Shira remained under lockdown, hiding in the apartment. It had become difficult to keep their spirits up.

By the time the agent in Tehran had contacted them, they'd nearly given up hope. Izad's wife shopped for them and many an evening invited them for supper. The friendship with the older couple had proven to be a godsend. Izad did his best to distract Ibrahim, inviting him over at every opportunity to play chess. The game reminded Ibrahim of what was at play in Iran.

Ibrahim and Shira would never be able to repay Izad and his wife for their kindness and aid. The older couple shrugged off their thanks. They considered their actions a small act of resistance to the murderous regime that had siphoned off and destroyed the wealth and freedom of its people. The more they learned of Ibrahim's role as an organizer of the marches, the more devoted Izad and his wife became to them.

An icy wind cut through the empty streets of Astara, and Ibrahim had to lock his teeth together to keep them from chattering. In conversation with their contact in Tehran, Ibrahim had learned that the couple meeting him was from Argentina and that the woman would be wearing a green scarf that matched her eye color. Ibrahim was cautiously hopeful that this meeting might be the first step in securing his and Shira's escape from Iran. Where they would go from here, he had no idea. But Shira had cousins in Los Angeles, and maybe they would welcome them there. They even considered Israel and its sunny climate, but as far as Ibrahim was concerned, it wasn't far enough away from Iran. In the end, it would be Ibrahim's ability to secure work that would factor in the most.

Right now, he had more important things to worry about as he hunched his shoulders down into his coat to fend off the icy wind. Ibrahim had been told to go to the Parkway Café and Fast-Food restaurant at 9 a.m. It was a little over a mile from the apartment, and he picked up his pace, not wanting to be late. By the time he pulled open the door of the restaurant, his brisk pace had warmed him. A man greeted him, and Ibrahim explained he was meeting a client and his wife for breakfast.

"Yes, yes, they arrived a few minutes ago. They are seated at a booth in the back. You can't miss them."

Ibrahim thanked the man and took his time walking to the back so as not to look suspicious. He glanced at the few other customers, pleased that no one looked like law enforcement. He spotted the green scarf and made his way to the booth. The couple sat facing the entrance. He was glad because it was easy to spot them. His back would be to the door, but the man and woman were seasoned agents, so they could keep their eyes peeled if anyone approached. He slipped into the booth across from the duo, relieved no one was sitting nearby. Their conversation would be private and unobserved.

He held out his hand to the man. "Ibrahim Nassiri. It is a pleasure to make your acquaintance."

"Arman Shirvani and this is my wife, Francoise. The pleasure is all ours. We're sorry your wife couldn't join us."

"My wife —" he was taken aback for a moment. "Yes, of course, my wife…she wasn't feeling well."

"Perhaps another time."

Francoise Shirvani said nothing, but she studied him intently, her steady gaze seeming to dissect his every movement. Arman kept up a stream of banter about their flight from Argentina and, much ado about nothing, about their trip so far. Ibrahim went along with the charade, while all the time wondering how these two were going to get him and Shira out of Iran.

After they'd ordered breakfast and had their coffees refilled, out of nowhere, the woman cut in and brought the conversation to the true intent of the meeting. "Explain how you've been living these last days since you got to Astara. Who else knows you are here? Any visitors, friends, outsiders?"

Ibrahim was taken aback at the abrupt change in conversation but figured their initial discussion was necessary while they'd ordered and waited for their meals. And then he realized why Arman chatted about nothing for the first few minutes. It was so Francoise could observe him and look for any tell-tale signs of ill intent. He would tell Shira about it. She would be fascinated by the methods the agents used in their work.

Ibrahim told the couple about the NAJA officers who'd shown up a few days after their arrival and had torn Shira's parents' apartment to pieces. And who'd continued to show up numerous times after to "check up on things." Ibrahim told them about Izad and his wife and how they'd helped them and given them one of their cousins' apartments to stay in. Ibrahim insisted, "They are good people who hate the regime."

"That is fortunate," added Arman, "to find friends."

"I don't know what would have happened to us without them."

"A blessing from Allah for sure, is it not *habibata?*"

"Yes, I believe that is a good sign. However, it means we'll need additional precautions."

"How are you going to get us out?" Ibrahim whispered.

"That hasn't been decided yet, but it's being worked on as we speak," Francoise said. "Ibrahim, we need to take photos of you and Shira to prepare passports for you. I will come to your apartment for this. I will wear a disguise. I think a cleaning woman would not draw too much attention. You can arrange that with Izad, can you not, for tomorrow morning?"

"Yes, yes, that would work fine. He will be at work, but his wife will be home."

"Good, then it's settled. Do I need a code to enter? It's best if it looks like I'm a regular visitor to the building."

Ibrahim grabbed a napkin and wrote everything down for Francoise. She glanced at the paper and stuffed it into her pocket.

"And Ibrahim, be prepared to give me the flash drives when I come. The sooner they are out of your hands, the safer you will be."

Ibrahim wrinkled his brow. Would it be safe to give up their insurance policy before they got out of Iran? It frightened him to think that once the agents were in possession of the damning materials, they might abandon them.

Francoise seemed to read his thoughts. "Ibrahim, you have to trust Arman and me. Remember that our lives are also in peril should anything go wrong." Her voice dropped to a whisper. "Both Arman and I are veteran agents. We will do everything in our power to see you to safety. The people we work for always keep their promises. Trust me, I know."

Ibrahim's throat closed down, and the best he could manage was a nod. He hadn't expected their escape to be managed by a woman. It wasn't that he didn't think a woman capable of being in charge. He'd been taught since childhood about a woman's place, and despite his rejection of those twisted beliefs imposed by the regime, he realized he still had some internalized biases to work through. After all, wasn't that part of what the demonstrations and marches were about? Change and empowerment for the people? Especially women. Thank goodness for Shira. Since she'd come into his life, he saw first-hand how indomitable a woman could be. Yes, Shira had qualities similar to Francoise.

With a shaky voice, he asked. "Do you know if anyone survived the bombing in London that killed my uncle and his family?"

"Yes. Your cousin Jazmin survived."

Ibrahim swiped away at the tears that came unbidden to his eyes. "Allah be blessed. Where is she?"

"Don't worry, you'll see her soon," said Arman.

Ibrahim's heart filled with joy. To know that a family member had survived that awful blast. "Do we know who did this?"

Francoise held his gaze. "We believe it was a targeted hit by an assassin. The regime is accusing Israel and the U.S., but we know neither country was involved. This assassination was ordered by Tehran, or we suspect by some high-ranking official in the regime."

Ibrahim felt the heat of rage ride up his neck. "I will have everything ready for you tomorrow. How long will it take to get the passports?"

"We've been told two days," said Arman. Francoise had returned to observing him silently.

"How are things in Tehran?" Ibrahim asked.

"From what we could see, it seemed quiet. But we heard about massive unrest recently. We felt tension in the air."

"The people are on the verge of revolution. If it weren't for Shira, I'd remain here in a leadership position, but I fear for her life."

"You're doing the right thing. You may be more effective outside of Iran than inside."

"There is nothing I wish for more than to bring down this government. We are young, educated people who deserve better."

"I couldn't agree more," said Arman.

"We have to make sure that the fall of the regime doesn't result in Armageddon," Francoise interjected suddenly.

"What do you mean?"

"What if those in power decided to unleash a nuclear holocaust rather than relinquish their control?"

Ibrahim's face could not disguise his troubled thoughts. "I have asked myself that question a thousand times. We must bring down the regime before they are fully nuclearized."

Arman nodded. "The mix of religion and politics is never a good thing."

Zara asked. "Tell me, Ibrahim, what information is on your flash drive?"

Ibrahim glanced around and dropped his voice to a whisper. "It holds the access codes to nuclear enrichment facilities around the country and to the computers that regulate gas storage and other industrial manufacturing sites, including the ports."

"But how —?"

"I was working on a project at Fordo. I stumbled onto the entryways at Fordo. I applied the same methodology to Arak, Natanz, and Isfahan, the known processing sites, but also others that are unknown outside a very small circle in the regime and implanted my own access code."

"Is your uncle's flash drive a backup?"

"No. I have the codes; he has the locations. One without the other is useless. They have to be integrated and matched, which can only be done by one of us." He swallowed the lump in his throat. "Since he is no more, that leaves me."

"All the more reason to get you safely out of Iran."

"I was hoping you'd say that."

CHAPTER THIRTY-FIVE

Wednesday, February 12
Valletta, Malta

The views to the Grand Harbor of Valletta were breathtaking — blue sky, aquamarine waters, luxury yachts at anchor, and an ancient city whose walls turned to a dozen shades of ochre, yellow, and gold in the glow of the setting sun. Had she not been abducted and brought here by the assassin against her will, Jazmin might have gloried in the splendor.

After landing at a private airport, the assassin ushered her into a Range Rover. Twenty minutes later, they were driving a winding road that wove through rolling hills and terraced vineyards. Finally, they arrived at a fenced property with a security gate manned by armed guards. After passing through the gate, they drove down a long, winding road that curved around groves of lemon and orange trees. The view opened, and Jazmin spied a castle-like fortress perched on a bluff. They drove under an archway into a graveled circular courtyard in front of a manor with an imposing edifice of stone and sculpture.

The assassin jumped out of the vehicle and opened her door. "I welcome you to *Il Castello a Picco Sul Mare,* the castle overlooking the sea. Since you and I share a love of art and history, you might like to know the founding stones of the castle date back to 1589. Legend has it she was built for a knight of the order of the Knights of St. John. And now she is mine." The pride in his voice was unmistakable. He didn't wait for her reply but strode to the front door, which opened as if by magic. "Come, there will be plenty of time for you to look around."

His reference to plenty of time made her insides knot, but she hid it as she grabbed glimpses of the grotesque heads and creeping vines and leaves carved onto stone consoles, doors, pediments, and lintels that decorated the double doors and windows. Lush greenery and flowers filled dozens of stone planters that flanked the entrance of the house. A pretty, dark-eyed woman in a white starched apron and pink uniform greeted the assassin in Italian. Jazmin's gaze was drawn across the entry floor of earth-toned pavers to the view of stone balustrades surrounding the terrace at the back of the property. She could see a green lawn, flower gardens, and an inground swimming pool. "Anna, please prepare the blue room for our guest, Jazmin. And please bring tea and refreshments to the library."

"Si, Signore."

The assassin removed his coat, then he slipped Jazmin's coat from her shoulders and handed them both to the girl, who scurried away.

The assassin walked away, and Jazmin followed him. She'd accepted she was his prisoner, and there was nowhere for her to go and no escape from his fortress. Still, her curiosity was far greater than her fear. They passed through what must be the main salon of the house, a lavishly decorated room filled with antiques, old-world paintings, and cut-velvet upholstered sofas and chairs. The paintings looked original, and she wondered if the assassin was also a thief. Arrangements of towering white orchid sculptures decorated every flat surface.

Jazmin felt overwhelmed by the opulence and sickened by the thought of how many had been murdered to pay for this decadent display of wealth. She was also surprised that a man who was nothing more than a thug and a murderer had developed such cultured tastes. The more she learned of him, the more off-putting he became to her.

Perhaps it was a way for evil people to explain away their depravity. If an individual perceived himself to be intellectually superior, it would entitle him to wield power and take from those he considered inferior. Wasn't that the philosophy of the Nazis?

Jazmin had only recently, since living in England, learned the truth about the Holocaust. As a child in Iran, the worst genocide in the history of the world had not only been denied, but any reference to it ignored. The Nazis, like the assassin, were culture vultures who'd stolen great works of art from the Jews and others and reclaimed it for themselves, as though only they could appreciate it. They possessed a love for art, music, and rare books, which they believed elevated them to a superiority that only made them more loathsome. They'd stolen so much from others. Even now, paintings that had been stolen were still being found.

Her kidnapper pulled open the doors to the library. He crossed the room and sat behind a heavily carved desk. Donning a pair of reading glasses, he turned his attention to a stack of papers as though he didn't have a care or a worry that she might suddenly make a run for it. *He's placed me in a gilded cage.* She observed him as he sorted through his paperwork. *He must feel quite smug knowing the house staff would never help me escape…and even if I did escape, I'm still marooned on an island isolated from the world."*

Jazmin's gaze drifted around the room. Mahogany bookshelves filled with leather-bound books lined two of the walls. French doors facing the back of the house admitted the last of the day's sunlight and opened onto a rose garden surrounding a patio, a small table, and chairs. Heavy silk taffeta drapery pooled on the floor on either side of the doors. The room was crowned by a coffered ceiling centered by a brass chandelier with wax candles. The finishing touch comprised a pair of reading chairs that faced a carved stone fireplace, cozily contained and surrounded by books.

The room held a dream-like quality.

His voice startled her. "Sit down, Jazmin." He indicated the chair across from him at the desk. "You must be tired." He scribbled some notes on a pad and ripped the sheet free, setting it aside.

His seeming concern for her wellbeing surprised her, and she wondered what game he was playing. Sitting, she played along as if their relationship and her presence was the most natural thing in the world. "This place is..." she hesitated, not knowing how to describe it. "Surreal. Murder must be a well-paying job."

He leaned back in his chair with his hands together and his fingertips pressed to his lips. Pleasure played across his face as he appraised her. It was uncanny, but if she didn't know who and what he was, she'd think him an aristocrat or a wealthy businessman who dabbled in art and academia. It was as if she'd entered a parallel universe.

"Considering that you are my guest, and since I call you Jazmin, please call me Khalid."

"I think 'guest' is a misnomer. A guest would have been offered an invitation, at least. They're not abducted at gunpoint and whisked away against their will." She thrust her chin out in full defiance.

"Ah, yes. There is that. However, since you are now here, I think it best we treat each other with civility. Tell me what you found in your father's safety deposit box?"

She bit her lip. Even if she behaved civilly, she had no intention of aiding the monster. For a moment too long, he focused on her lips. "A flash drive," she answered as much to distract his attention as to inform him of what they'd found.

His gaze shifted, and he drew his brows together. "Do you have it?"

She shook her head.

"I checked your friend's pockets, and he didn't have it."

"He hid it. I didn't pay attention to where. It's probably gone forever since you murdered him."

"Perhaps," the assassin said, intruding on her thoughts. "But then again, perhaps not."

Jazmin had tried not to think of Aryeh these past few hours. Had it only been that morning? It seemed like months ago that he had escorted her to the bank in Zürich. The short walk from the hotel had been so much fun.

Fun. Yes. That was a good word to describe it. Aryeh had made her laugh with stories from his childhood. He held her hand and smiled at her as though he were a besotted boyfriend on vacation. Nothing about his behavior seemed false or contrived. She'd wondered if he did truly have feelings for her. Then she'd chased those thoughts away. After all, Aryeh was an intelligence agent, adept at seducing women to get what he wanted...and yet she had been fully cooperating with Mossad, had put her trust in them and in Aryeh, and he was Cyrus's and Layla's friend.

She missed Aryeh and Cyrus and Layla. They had formed a close bond of friendship. It was not based on a lie or because they were after the flash drive. Jazmin felt right down to her bones that Aryeh, Cyrus, and Layla cared about her. Layla had become like a sister to her, even in such a short time, or perhaps because of it. Layla had confided in Jazmin about her own past turmoil and how she'd met Cyrus. How they'd fallen in love so fast and how rocky things became after they escaped Iran. Was something similar happening between her and Aryeh? Could she mourn the loss of her family and heal? Could she grieve Darien, the love she'd lost, and still be able to find love again? Layla had given her hope that she could forge a new life, make a new family.

Jazmin closed her eyes and remembered how Aryeh had looked that morning. Yes, it was that very morning. Only a few hours ago. His blue eyes and dark gold hair. The graceful swagger with which he carried himself. It was odd, but she'd never been attracted to fair-haired men. She supposed the blond hair made them seem less rugged to her, but there was nothing delicate about Aryeh. He truly did remind her of a lion. Did? She hoped he'd survived. Prayed for it. *I'm so sorry, Aryeh, for having dragged you into this mess.*

A gentle rap on the door interrupted. "Come in."

Anna entered, pushing a teacart. She unloaded a tray laden with figs, dates, and nuts, along with a variety of cheeses and slices of crisp French bread. She poured two cups of tea from a samovar and handed Jazmin a cup. The maid snuck a curious glance at Jazmin, who murmured, "Thank you."

"Anna," the assassin said. "Ahmed will drive you into town. I've given him a list of things for you to pick up. Jazmin and I will be dining in. Give this to Chef so he can prepare my request." He handed her the paper torn from the pad. "Thank you, you are excused."

Anna nodded, *"Si, signore."*

"Oh, Anna."

She turned. "Ask Maria to come and take Jazmin up to her room. I'm sure she'd like to bathe and rest before dinner. I have work to do."

After Anna had gone, the assassin's gaze returned to Jazmin. "I'm sending Anna into town to pick up some things for you. Size four, am I correct?"

"How long are you planning on keeping me here?"

"I have no idea. In all honesty, the answer lies with you."

"Me? What use am I to you? I don't have the flash drive, nor do I know what was on it."

"Does it really matter what my reasons are? For now, you intrigue me."

"I'm not sure if that's a compliment."

"Take it however you wish. The only thing I require of you is your time." He smiled. "And having dinner with me. It is a long time since I dined with anyone."

Was he flirting with her? An acidic burn rose in her throat. "Given these surroundings, you could find plenty of women who …" she spread her hands to indicate the opulence, "would give you whatever you wanted."

"I don't bring women here. I trust no one. This is my place of refuge, my retreat from the ugliness of the world. And," he added, "no other woman interests me as you do."

Jazmin couldn't begin to process the import of his words or what they implied. The possibilities were too frightening. She countered with, "Do you not realize that you're a perfect example of what you call the ugliness?"

He stood and threw her a glare. She feared he was going to strike her, but instead, he strode to a bar cart filled with crystal decanters and cut crystal glasses. He poured a glass of amber liquid and took a deep swig. "Would you like a drink? It might relax you and curb that acid tongue of yours."

"No, thank you. I only drink wine."

His penetrating gaze made her shudder. "White or red?"

"Red, but I'd rather not —"

He cut her off. "I'll see that we share an excellent vintage with our dinner."

A knock on the door ended their conversation. "Ah, Maria, please show our guest to her bedroom." Turning to Jazmin, he said, "I'll expect you at eight for dinner." He turned to Maria. "Maria, please show Jazmin where the dining room is on your way upstairs."

He returned to his desk, adjusted his glasses, and addressed his paperwork, seeming to dismiss her.

He didn't look up until the door closed. With her gone, the room felt empty. The words on the page blurred before his eyes. Gurga took another sip as he pondered their conversation. Why was he indulging such a dangerous impulse? He knew this attraction he felt, which was increasing every moment he was around her, was not reciprocated.

How can she feel anything but hatred for the man who killed her family and the man she was going to marry?

Yet, for some reason, his desire persisted, grew. Did he detect a trace of humanity lurking in his ruthless heart? Was this the woman of his dreams, or was she the Delilah that would be his undoing?

The temptation of seducing her enlivened his spirits. He enjoyed their banter and reveled in the power he had over her. He even relished the power she held over him. Not physical, of course, but beguiling and bewitching. Perhaps the notion of Stockholm syndrome was working in reverse? In time, would her feelings change? Would being in such beautiful surroundings enable him to break through her wall of defiance and rage and get to the remarkable woman inside?

If he wanted to, he could force her to submit to his desire, but where was the sport in that? No, he found it more exciting to discover what made her tick. Finding the flash drive paled in comparison to finding the way to Jazmin's heart. He would discover the key to unlocking Jazmin's desire, and perhaps, her love.

She was alone in this world now, and her God invoked his followers to practice forgiveness. Could even a monster like him be forgiven? It made him laugh to consider it. Perhaps he needed to dangle the possibility of redemption before her. Wouldn't it be a service to mankind if she could change him, save him? He hadn't realized up until now how tired he'd become of the contract-for-hire game.

His years of hard work had paid off. His financial means were more than enough for two lifetimes. He could retire and live off the interest alone from all his wise investments. Perhaps have children, a family of his own. Yes, he could give it all up for the right reason, the right woman.

But first, he had to deal with the bastard general in Iran who'd proven to be a thorn in his side. Him, he would kill, but no money need be exchanged. That would be a death for his own personal satisfaction. Jazmin might even be pleased with that bit of revenge. After all, her family's death had been ordered by that sanctimonious butcher in Iran. Gurga had merely been the instrument of delivery. He'd only been doing a job. There had been no feelings involved. No, that had come after. After seeing her. Meeting her. Getting to know her. Yes, he had begun to change, and Jazmin was the catalyst for that.

Would it not be a fitting wedding gift to her?

He caught himself at such a thought. Marriage to Jazmin would be the embodiment of a dream he dared not dream. And yet, he'd read about such things in history. Daughters of vanquished lords were given in wedlock to the victor, were they not? Why, even in the grand English society, who consider themselves to be the purveyors of Western civilization, they'd embraced such practices in the past. Perhaps he could convince Jazmin as well. After all, was she not a student of history? His mind drifted to visions of Jazmin in a resplendent white gown awaiting him beneath a canopy of roses. He shook his head at his own foolishness. Too soon?

But once thought, the idea implanted itself in his mind. Why not? They were both alone in the world, without family or friends. Outcasts. Maybe there was a way for them to join forces, to heal each other, and create a new life together. He pictured her lips and what it would feel like to part them with his tongue. The thrill of killing was replaced by the thrill of seduction.

It rushed through his veins, and he felt himself harden. He shifted in his seat. *Yes, possessing her would be the greatest thrill of my life.* He was sure of it, and now he knew he would stop at nothing to claim her for his. Their dinner tonight would be the first step to conquering her heart. *Jazmin has ruined all other women for me.* The idea of one-night stands with women for hire would never satisfy him again. He wanted more. He wanted intelligent conversation, laughter, mystery, and blinding beauty. Jazmin was all of that and more. Yes, tonight would be the beginning.

He'd spent his entire life overcoming obstacles. Surely, he could conquer the heart of one woman.

CHAPTER THIRTY-SIX

Wednesday, February 12
Valletta, Malta

Jazmin sat at a vanity in the blue bedroom while Anna put the finishing touches to her hair, twisting it into an updo. Fastening it with a pearl-encrusted brooch, she pulled a few wisps loose to trail down her neck. Anna had informed her that the assassin had requested she should be formally attired for their dinner. Anna had called him *Signore* Khalid.

Signore indeed! Jazmin refused to call him by his name. Refused to think of him as other than "the assassin." Doing so would humanize him. She could never accept him as a fellow human being, not after what he'd done to her family, to her. In any case, she was sure Khalid wasn't his real name.

An entire wardrobe hung in the closet, beautiful clothes, including the burgundy velvet gown he'd requested she wear. Along with delicate lingerie and underthings that sickened her, knowing that he'd purchased them for her to wear.

She looked at her transformation in the full-length mirror. The low cut of the heart-shaped bodice scarcely contained her ample breasts, and the back of the gown with its plunging vee made her feel naked. A single teardrop jewel suspended from a silver chain hung down her back. The gown was something a temptress would wear. What did the bastard think would happen? Did he think she'd fall for him? Did he think his opulent wealth and fancy house could transform her loathing to loving? *He must be mad.*

She felt like a mouse being toyed with by a cat. Her body went rigid at the mere contemplation of the moment when the cat would pounce.

Desperate for a distraction, her gaze looked past her reflection in the mirror and took in the room. Having seen the lavish décor throughout the house, she wasn't surprised that the blue room was as sumptuous as the rest of the castle. The walls were covered in royal blue and gold striped satin, and a palatial four-poster canopied bed centered the room across from a fireplace that Anna had lit. The plush midnight blue carpet, patterned with a gold fleur-de-lis, was regal by any measure. A room fit for a queen.

Jazmin wasn't comfortable with any of it. She'd begun to feel like she'd been cast in a movie, and this was a movie set. Everything had been constructed to perfection, but it was all a façade. The room was beautiful, but even without bars on the windows, it was still a prison. And she was its prisoner.

Jazmin had succumbed to tears earlier when Anna had given her privacy for her bath. Her thoughts had strayed to Aryeh, and the tears she'd held back flowed freely. She felt certain in her heart that if he was alive, he'd move heaven and earth to free her. But he was dead, and it was too late to tell him how she felt. That she'd begun to care for him as more than a bodyguard or a friend. He'd given her hope for a future, and now that hope was dead. It broke her heart that his life had been sacrificed protecting her.

She wanted revenge, but how to achieve it? Tonight, she needed to plan. She needed to figure out a way to destroy the assassin. He'd given her the tools. The sexy dress was no mistake. It was meant to lure him. She might have to swallow her disgust if he touched her, but somehow, she'd find a way to bring him down. The tracking device was still embedded beneath her hair, and she knew in her heart that

Cyrus and Layla would keep their promise and rescue her. The head of Israel's Mossad had promised her they would help her with or without her father's flash drive. She hoped that by now, they would have discovered it in Aryeh's shoe. She'd fulfilled her father's wishes in the letter, and that filled her with satisfaction. She prayed her father was in Jannah, his soul at peace in paradise.

Her thoughts were interrupted. "There," Anna smoothed her hair, "you look beautiful. *Molto bella.*"

Jazmin smiled weakly. "Thank you." She'd already figured out that the staff was loyal to the assassin, and she sensed both Maria and Anna were smitten with him. They thought he was a wealthy businessman with a love of art and culture and the polite manners of a courtier. These women would do nothing to help her. She was sure of it.

"Is there anything else you need?"

"No, thank you. You may go. I'll be down in a minute." The door closed and Jazmin rose. She opened the bottle of perfume and dabbed a few drops behind her ears and between her cleavage. *You can do this. You can play his game as well as or better than he can. He may be a killer, but he's also a man with the same desires as any other man.*

He watched her descend the staircase, fascinated as much by her transformation as he was by his own reaction to her. Gurga wasn't sure what he'd expected but seeing her stole his breath away. She carried herself like a queen, and not for the first time, he found himself speechless in her presence. But the slight tremor in her hand as it lightly skimmed the wrought-iron banister assured him he wasn't the only one who was nervous. It reassured him, reminding him he was in control. She stopped on the last step, bringing her face even with his, which he found daring and provocative. One more reason he was taken with her. Her bravery mesmerized him. He'd rarely seen this kind of composure in men, let alone a woman. This is the way he envisioned her as a consort. Not a slave to his whims, but an equal.

"You look stunning, Jazmin. I hope you're pleased with everything Anna brought you."

"Everything is lovely, but I can't imagine why I would need so many outfits. I don't expect I will be staying long enough to wear them all."

Her eyes smiled at him, but he could see the fear in their depths and knew her bravado was a pose. Still, she was gutsy. He'd give her that. She was also his prisoner. No one knew where she was and freeing her was a near impossibility. A veritable army protected his fortress. "I wanted you to have enough variety to suit your tastes."

"Why would you presume to know my taste? You don't know me, and we haven't really anything in common, do we?"

It amused him the way she managed to insult him, yet not insult him. She stepped down and looked up at him, her eyes glimmering with guile. "But then maybe we share the same taste in food. I'm famished."

She swept past him, heading in the direction of the dining room, the scent of her perfume floating around him. *She is a worthy adversary.* She'd put him in his place, but it only steeled his determination. He followed her, his gaze locked on her swaying hips and the beautiful contours of her back. It was hypnotic the way the jewel that dangled down her back swung in rhythm with the gentle sway of her hips. The dress was made for her, clinging in all of the right places.

Drawing in his breath, he imagined what it would be like to inhale that heady fragrance up close, kiss the delicate skin of her neck and trail his fingers down her slender back. *Patience. Nothing worth having ever comes easy.* But he couldn't drive away the vision of him unhooking the clasp that held the dress in place and seeing it slowly slip to the floor.

Lit only by candlelight, the dining room emanated intimacy with only a small table for two that glistened with cut crystal and sterling. It was the way he preferred to dine since he rarely entertained. He pulled out her chair and she sat. Unable to resist, he caressed her shoulders and felt the smallest of trembles. Leaning in, his lips brushed her ear. "I know you hate me, but I hope you might find forgiveness in your heart."

She turned and locked eyes with him. Her lips were inches away, and an irrepressible urge to kiss her burned inside of him. He ached and struggled to contain it before he stepped over the line.

"Why are you doing this? What do you want from me?" Fire and tears did battle in her eyes.

He took his seat across from her. "I'm lonely, I suppose." Admitting his weakness didn't come easy. It was a new experience for him, and it made him feel human and vulnerable.

"I don't understand. You meant to kill me with my family. When you realized I was still alive, you came after me and tracked me to that townhouse to shoot me in cold blood. You hesitated, and I escaped again. Then you tracked me down and kidnapped me and brought me here to your impenetrable fortress. There is no way for me to escape. I am well and truly your prisoner. So, why don't you kill me now?" She flung the words at him, as though taunting him.

Gurga knew that the other side of the coin of hatred was love. Passionate hate could be transformed into passion of another kind. There was chemistry between them, and it ricocheted back and forth like an electrical current. Could she feel it too? Was that why she was so defiant? Because she felt the same pull of attraction and was trying to suppress it, even deny it?

Gurga was also a student of human nature. He had to be since his line of work depended on his survival. And so, he'd learned to read people. Despite Jazmin's mercurial behavior, or perhaps because of it, he could see something that she was loath to admit. The possibility that *she* was also attracted to him. Also, she was right. He had several opportunities to kill her, and yet he hadn't. Did that not tell her something? Did that not prove to her his feelings? And if she could sense that he was drawn to her in such an inexplicable way — if she could sense the magnetic attraction that he felt for her, would it not be possible for her to feel the same toward him?

He decided that honesty would be the best approach here. He steepled his fingers together on the table and leaned forward. "In my line of work, I learned not to delve into the hearts of those I was hired to erase. Purely transactional, nothing personal. A man such as I had no skills to offer the world except one, my ability to kill. The truth is, I did not know you until I knew you if that makes any sense. But now that I know you, everything has changed." He filled their glasses with burgundy wine. "I think you'll like this wine. For you, I'm pouring the finest in my cellar, a Petrus. I am interested to know what you think."

She brought the goblet to her lips.

"Wait," he blurted. "We need to make a toast."

A laugh escaped her, which was music to his ears. He longed to hear her laugh again and again. But though it pleased him to hear her laugh, this laughter bore the sting of distaste.

"And what are we toasting?"

"Let's begin with friendship and see where that takes us."

"*À votre santé.*" Jazmin sipped. She leaned closer. "Are you sure all you want is forgiveness and friendship? Perhaps what you need is a priest."

She was teasing him, and that gave him hope. He leaned back and took a deep breath. His heart beat against his chest with fists. She generated an excitement he'd thought dead in him. If this was what real conquest felt like, then he was hooked. His interactions with women were, for the most part, transactional. He purchased and took what he wanted. There were few words exchanged, and what was said meaningless. But every look and word from Jazmin challenged him. As much as he loved the thought of kissing those luscious lips, he equally loved hearing what she'd say next.

"I will admit I want more." His gaze swept from her eyes to her décolletage. It thrilled him when he saw the blush rise from the curve of her breasts to her cheeks. *She knows she's playing with fire. She's trying to figure out how not to get burned.* But that was the furthest thing from his mind. He wanted to set her on fire, yes, but only with the same passionate fire she lit in him.

"I see."

He watched her gulp down her wine. She was searching for courage in the glass. He hid a smile and refilled her glass. "You should slow down, or you won't make it through dinner, and I'll end up carrying you upstairs to your bed." The thought of doing just that sizzled through him.

"Do not tell me what to do." She glared at him. "I know you are trying to seduce me."

She was daring him, he knew, using her own blunt honesty as a weapon as he'd done. *She's no fool. She knows her self-control is fragile, and perhaps by getting herself drunk, she can take away any responsibility for what might happen if I did carry her to bed.*

But what she didn't know, he thought, was that with every taunt, he was becoming more enslaved to *her.* He knew she presented a danger to him. An emotional quagmire. But instead of retreating, he forged ahead. With eyes wide open. He wanted the same from her. He didn't want her to submit to his advances drunkenly. He wanted her sober and hungering for him as much he hungered for her.

The knock on the door was a welcome intrusion. "Come in," he called over his shoulder, relieved that their meal had arrived.

Her back shot up straight, and she grabbed her napkin, unfurling it onto her lap.

"Just in time." He chuckled, knowing she walked as much of a tightrope as he.

CHAPTER THIRTY-SEVEN

Wednesday, February 12
Valletta, Malta

Jazmin rose from her chair, her fingertips touching the table to steady herself. She'd drunk enough wine to feel tipsy. The dinner was delicious, and Khalid proved to be an attentive dinner partner. When had she started thinking of him as Khalid? It had happened at some point during dinner, as he told her about his favorite artist, Caravaggio, whom he believed to have been greatly misunderstood. She agreed, having studied the artist and written a paper on him. Had she not been his prisoner, and he not been a murderer, the man who killed her family, she might have enjoyed herself. But those truths were never far from her mind.

After this day without end, all she really wanted was to collapse in the bed upstairs. But Khalid suggested they step out to the terrace for fresh air. Perhaps that would help to clear her mind and regain focus. She needed to find a way out of here. Or at least figure out a way to contact Cyrus and Layla.

She'd removed the mole-shaped tracking device from the back of her head before her bath and tucked it into her shoe to keep it safe.

When she retrieved the device from her shoe and hid it again beneath her hair, she was reminded of Aryeh and his caution that if anything went wrong the tracking device was her safety net. Thinking about Aryeh brought a fresh wave of grief. In a matter of days, she'd lost her entire family and fiancé and then miraculously found herself embedded with an agent assigned to protect her. But not just any agent. A giant of a man with dark golden hair and a smile that made her laugh and eyes that delved into her soul. *I'm sorry, Aryeh. I'm so sorry you had to die trying to protect me.* Another death to add to her grief and splinter her conscience. *If I make it out of here alive, I will never forget you.*

Khalid took her hand, drawing Jazmin out of her thoughts. He tucked her arm through his in a gentlemanly fashion. She didn't resist since she was unsteady on her feet. Stupid! She'd been foolish to have imbibed so much. But a part of her had wanted to let go. Needed to lose herself for a few moments. But now, in the coolness of the night, with a bracing breeze to refresh her, she regretted her indulgence. Khalid walked closely beside her, his thigh brushing against hers. His closeness made her skin crawl.

The moon floated above the Mediterranean, slipping in and out of the silvery cloud cover. Moonlight fragmented into a thousand silvery stars that danced upon the sea. It was cold, and when she shivered, he removed his burgundy smoking jacket and draped it over her shoulders. His scent enveloped her, and she struggled not to gag. The silence of the night and his closeness reminded her that he was in complete control of her life. *If only I had a dagger.*

It must have been the alcohol that loosened her tongue when she asked, "How does someone become a killer? I mean, do you wake up one day and say to yourself, here is something I'd like to do. This is a profession where I can make my mark." She covered her mouth to suppress the giggle that erupted.

A smile softened his features, displaying amusement. "That's exactly what happened. It was my calling."

Her mouth fell open — she was aghast. "No, seriously. Why?"

He shrugged. "I came from a place where to survive, I was taught to kill. So, I fought on many battlefields for the cause I was born into. It wasn't my choice, and I controlled nothing of my destiny. I was fine killing soldiers, but the death of innocents sickened me. Killing women and children was not what I signed up for."

"My family and my fiancé were innocents." It was as if fire burned within her veins.

"Your father, I'm afraid, brought this on your family." He shrugged. "It's not the same as seeing babies and mothers gassed."

Jazmin stared at him. *How do you reason with madness?*

"Anyway, one day, I stopped believing, and I fled. The only options open to me because of my skills were among criminals. After a time, I realized I was smarter than they were. Instead of working for a middleman, I could work for myself."

"Are you implying there's a code of ethics for murder? That murder is acceptable if contained within certain parameters?"

He shrugged. "It sounds like a foolish notion, but in truth, killing certain targets is quite rational."

"And that rationality of selective killing gave you all of this?" She looked around.

"No, not all of it. It was the seed money. I educated myself and invested in other businesses."

"I see. So now you don't need the money from…I'm not sure what to call it, your day job. So why not stop — killing?" She hiccupped and covered her mouth. Again, she couldn't suppress a giggle.

"I never found a reason."

"But you *could* stop, couldn't you?"

He took her chin and forced her to meet his gaze. "I could."

She trembled when his lips met hers. It wasn't horrifying, but it frightened her, nonetheless. His moan came from his depths.

She pulled back and stared into his eyes and thought she could see right into his soul. And she knew. The wisdom of countless women who came before her — the power was in her hands, and she knew she could manipulate him. He was already in love with her. She could see it in his eyes. When the time was right, his love for her would be the instrument of her revenge.

She closed her eyes, hoping he could not see what resided in her own soul. And pressed her softness into his hardness. She deepened the kiss and began to weave a silken web around him as her fingers wove through his hair. She would relish his destruction. The man who destroyed her entire world.

Yes, it was true, murder *was* acceptable if contained within certain parameters.

She broke from the kiss, but not from his embrace. "I-I'm confused and probably a little drunk. I-I'm not sure of myself right now. May I go to my room? I'm very tired."

He rested his forehead against hers. She could feel his heart beating against her breast and the shallowness of his breath. His eyes were closed as if he battled a great internal struggle. "Of course, I'll see you to your room."

"Thank you."

She held his arm as he escorted her upstairs. When she opened her door and turned to say goodnight. He pulled her against him and kissed her again, this time with a fiery passion. When he let her go, it was he who exuded control. He cleared his throat. "Goodnight, Jazmin."

"Goodnight, Khalid." She closed the door and leaned against it, trying to catch her breath and calm her racing heart. Then she heard a key turn in the lock. She tried the door, but it was locked. Whatever inroads she'd made with him they were not enough.

She was still his prisoner.

CHAPTER THIRTY-EIGHT

Thursday, February 13
Birżebbuġa, Malta

O*ne second! I should have seen through that old man's disguise!*

Aryeh was pissed off with himself and frustrated that his brush with death left him weak as a kitten. Even so, he couldn't stop monitoring the signal from the tracking device he'd hidden in Jazmin's hair. The nanotechnology emitted a continuous signal and an approximate location of where she was being held. Yes, they knew it was Malta, but that wasn't good enough. They needed to know her exact location. They needed surveillance and a plan.

Aryeh's patience had worn thin. He'd failed Jazmin, and it ate away at him. Everything was coming together far too slowly for his comfort. And his mind kept drifting back to Sarah. Because of his emotional attachment to her, he'd lost sight of the big picture and the possible dangers that had ultimately led to her death. He still carried the emotional scars from that botched mission, and he couldn't bear the thought of anything happening to Jazmin on his watch.

Tensions were running high. Zvi, their computer Einstein, was busily getting the control center operational. The state-of-the-art hub featured multiple computers and monitors, a communications system that shared information live with Tel Aviv, a satellite interface, and drone command capabilities.

After arriving on the fishing yacht, the team had converged on a farmhouse and begun transforming it into a base of operations. Mossad had rented the three-bedroom farmhouse in Birżebbuġa to serve as their headquarters for the mission. The same team that had deployed to Beirut to stop Hezbollah's EMP attack had re-assembled. Only Nira and Daniel were missing. Both had been injured in the assault on the Hezbollah compound in the Beqaa valley a year ago and were still in physical therapy, recovering.

Levi, a twenty-two-year-old gaming genius, had been added to the lineup. Levi was the star of the IDF's drone division. He was the geek who'd been in control of the drone that had taken out the EMP rocket launched by Hezbollah from the Beqaa valley. The twenty-two-year-old, curly-haired, beardless wunderkind was the unsung hero that had saved Israel from nuclear disaster.

Aryeh, couldn't help but chuckle as he watched the overgrown teenager's jaws work a wad of pink bubble gum. The young man slouched on a chair with his feet up on a desk, immersed in a video game on his phone. Aryeh nearly jumped out of his skin after the nerdy kid burst a giant bubble and covered his face in a transparent layer of pink goo.

"Hey, schmuck, quit smacking that gum before I smack your head off. It's driving me crazy."

Levi picked the sticky pieces of gum from his face, gathering them back into his mouth. "Sorry. It helps me concentrate." The kid worshipped Aryeh, and any criticism from his hero was hard to swallow.

"Well, it sure as hell isn't helping *me* concentrate." The kid made him twitch, but Aryeh understood how important his skills were for the team. "Tell me something, why don't you get that drone of yours up in the sky and begin surveillance? We can start accumulating aerial photographs. Who knows? Maybe you can catch a sighting of Jazmin or the assassin. That would be useful. When can you launch?"

Levi took the gum out of his mouth and tossed it in a trashcan. "I'm waiting for Zvi to get everything up and running. We need to narrow the location down to about a mile, and then I'll go to work. The drone will work in a square grid, moving inward until we lock in on the exact target."

Zvi looked up from behind the desk where he was working on unraveling and connecting what looked like a pound of spaghetti. The mess of wires and cords were scrambled together, and Aryeh wondered how Zvi could make heads or tails of the mess.

"Aryeh, stop scaring the young recruit," he laughed, "you'll have him pissing his pants."

Aryeh had forgotten what it felt like to be a novice member of a team. "Sorry, kid. I'm a little out of sorts."

"It's okay. Don't worry, if she makes an appearance outside, I'll find her."

Aryeh nodded. "I need to get some air. Let me know when you're ready to launch."

"Sure thing, man." Aryeh couldn't fail to see the relief wash over Levi's face. He needed to go easier on the kid.

Aryeh joined the rest of the rescue team in the living room. Ash, their ballistics expert, and Ben were inspecting and cleaning weapons. They'd draped a tarp and towels over the dining room table, and Ash busily performed a detailed inspection of his preferred weapon, the MacMillan Tac 50 long-range sniper rifle. Aryeh remembered Ash saying he was determined to break the record of the Canadian Joint Task Force sniper who held the longest-range sniper kill in history. The kill of an ISIL militant was recorded in 2017 in Iraq. Maybe this would be his lucky mission. Yitzak and Cyrus were huddled over a map. When Aryeh walked in, everyone looked up.

"How's Zvi doing? Is he up yet?" asked Cyrus.

Aryeh growled impatiently. "Not yet, but soon."

He'd been the focus of everyone's attention since the poisoning, and it made him testy. He knew they were all concerned for his wellbeing, but he wasn't the one in danger. Jazmin was.

Layla entered carrying a tray with a large pitcher of lemonade and glasses filled with ice.

Cyrus took the tray from her hands and put it on the coffee table. "Thanks, baby."

Layla poured a tall glass of lemonade and gave it to Aryeh. "The doctor's orders said you needed to drink a lot of liquids, so drink up."

He took the glass with a nod. Layla was the one person he couldn't be testy with no matter what. He'd grown so fond of her that she could do no wrong. Rescuing her from the Hezbollah terrorist in Pennsylvania was one of the things he felt most proud of.

The door opened from the control room, and Levi poked his head out. "We just received intel from the office. I think we may have an exact location for where Jazmin's being held."

Everyone raced into the control room behind Aryeh, who'd been first through the door. "What have we got, Zvi?" Aryeh barked.

"Since the Solatani hit last year, the CIA and NSA have been monitoring a few of the IRGC biggies. One of those generals, Davood Choudhury, has been outspoken about crushing the protests around the country, so he's on a watch list. Lo and behold, Choudhury was in communication with Saman Amin prior to Amin's assassination, and the two men were quite friendly. Choudhury has also spoken regularly over what he considers a secure line to someone based in Europe. Then Interpol corroborated that they were closing in on a professional assassin known as Gurga, who perchance lives on the island of Malta. Now for the coincidence. Gurga happened to fly to Malta by private jet from Zürich yesterday. I should have the coordinates for Gurga's Malta residence in minutes."

Cyrus took over. "Levi, I want live surveillance from the drone. Zvi, I want construction blueprints from the planning commission here in Malta, anything we can learn about the inside of the structure. Once we have the data, we'll plan our assault for tomorrow night —"

"Why not tonight?" Aryeh cut in.

Cyrus looked at him as if he might have lost his mind. *"Achi,* you better than any of us know that an assault needs to be planned. The target is fortified and defended, and he probably has guard shifts and routine defense mechanisms that need to be studied. I understand your frustration because Jazmin is in a precarious situation, but I can't risk the team's safety by not preparing adequately."

"We're adaptable and trained to react under changing circumstances. Every minute we delay is a minute too long. Jazmin's life hangs in the balance. Right now, we hold the element of surprise, but he lives here. He could have armies of civilians paid to alert him to unusual activity. Like us showing up. How long do you think before he's informed of our presence?" Aryeh pounded his fist into his other fist to emphasize his argument. "We strike tonight!"

Cyrus looked around the room as if seeking consensus. The team nodded in agreement. "You make a strong point, my friend. All right. Listen up, we prepare for an assault tonight, but I will call it off if the risk outweighs the benefit of immediate action."

"Agreed." Aryeh was satisfied with the decision.

"Get that bird in the sky, Levi."

"Yes, sir."

CHAPTER THIRTY-NINE

Thursday, February 13
Valletta, Malta

Gurga's face reddened as he listened to the tirade emanating from the general on the other end of the phone line. "Your incompetence endangers us all," the man shouted. "You were given a simple task. Get us whatever is in that security box and eliminate the girl. The only thing you managed to do was kill some nobody Mossad bodyguard. The girl is worthless to us, yet she lives."

Gurga yelled back. "I'm done taking orders from you. This whole operation was compromised from the beginning. Saman Amin was on to you. I'd say you underestimated his abilities. He knew who he was dealing with and planned accordingly. Killing the girl doesn't gain us a thing. She knows nothing about what was inside the box. I'll terminate her in my own good time. In the meantime, General, I'd prepare for the worst. I have a sneaky suspicion you've been acting outside of official channels for your own reasons. I would be covering my ass if I were you.

"Oh, and be wary of threatening me. You may know my identity, but I also know yours." Gurga tossed his cell on his desk. He'd made up his mind. His last targeted killing would be this pompous-ass general. Choudhury was obviously a loose cannon. It would be no problem to pin it on Mossad. They took the blame for most of the hits in Iran anyway, one more wouldn't make a difference. He chuckled. The Israeli government might even give him a medal. He glanced at his watch. It would make a fine gift to Jazmin to take out the man who ordered the deaths of her father and family. More and more, he embraced the notion of a new life with her. A leisurely breakfast by the pool with his lovely guest. That's what he needed, not some asshole general demeaning him as if he were a lesser minion.

He rapped lightly on the door to Jazmin's room and then unlocked it. She was asleep, but he needed to see her, to talk to her, to feel her energy. He sat down on the edge of the bed, yearning to crawl in beside her and take her into his arms. "Jazmin." Even saying her name aloud filled an emptiness he'd never given voice to or acknowledged. "Please wake up."

She stirred, her lashes fluttering, and then she bolted up, startled. "Where am I? What are you doing here?"

He couldn't resist the impulse to brush her hair back gently from her forehead. "I'm sorry if I scared you."

She recoiled from his touch, and he refrained from pushing her beyond her limits. Being woken up so suddenly was bound to elicit a reaction. He gave her a minute to put things in perspective.

As her awareness returned to her, she calmed. "Is something wrong?" she asked.

"No, I thought you might like to join me for breakfast by the pool. I would enjoy your company very much." He stood. "I'll leave the door open and will wait for you outside on the patio. I'll send Anna up to get you. It's a lovely day. You might like to take a swim. The shop sent a bathing suit and coverup, didn't they?" Seeing Jazmin in a swimsuit would improve his day immensely.

She looked at him quizzically as if questioning his sanity. He could only imagine her confusion. None of this made any sense. It was as if his world had narrowed to one burning desire. He wanted only to gain her forgiveness and find a way into her heart.

Her answer surprised him. "After all I've been through, it would be nice to be outside. It feels like years, yet it's only been a matter of days since everything..." she left the sentence dangling and dropped her eyes, avoiding his gaze. Gurga studied her face. Did he sense a change, a mellowing in her reaction to him? He felt a weight lift from his shoulders. It was almost too good to be true, and yet perhaps he had reason to nurture the hope in his heart. "I will wait for you by the pool." He smiled at Jazmin and nodded. Then he turned and left, feeling as if all things were possible.

Anna escorted her downstairs, through the living room, and out the glass sliders. At a table under an umbrella, Khalid read a newspaper. The front page in Arabic bore the name *Al-Ahram*, a print newspaper published in Egypt. She wondered if there were any updates about her family's murder. When Khalid caught sight of her, he tossed the paper aside and stood.

The way he looked at her revealed more to her than any words he might say. His gaze touched her from head to toe, and a vulpecular smile spread across his face. She wore the one-piece swimsuit and coverup he'd suggested, which allowed him a glimpse of her body beneath the see-through lace. Why was this man, a murderer and assassin, so obsessed with her? She couldn't understand what drove his compulsion.

It wasn't that she was unaware of her attractiveness. It had been one of the banes of her father's existence, how to keep a daughter pure when she was coveted by most men who saw her. No one was more relieved than her father when she became engaged. But there were plenty of women in the world far more beautiful and accomplished than she.

Khalid had been hired to kill her, and yet she lived. He had murdered her family, and yet he kidnapped her and treated her like a beloved. She found his attraction to her both bizarre and frightening. Did he think by treating her like a treasured lover and showering her with gifts that he could gain her forgiveness and atone for his sins?

Jazmin was determined to dig deeper into this flaw in his makeup and capitalize on it. When she realized that her survival had become secondary to his destruction, she felt empowered. Keeping her wits about her might be her only chance of escape. Cyrus and Layla had promised her they would rescue her, but what if they had to deal with the aftermath of Aryeh's death? *Aryeh.* She'd cried herself to sleep the night before, thinking of Aryeh. Of his sacrifice. Of her blossoming feelings for him, snuffed out by this snake who was now showering her with beautiful clothes, luscious food, and shiny trinkets.

She held out a ray of hope that Mossad would send a team. But she could not sit by idly and wait to be rescued by a knight in shining armor. She swallowed the lump in her throat as she pictured Aryeh's crooked grin. Yes, he had seemed to be a knight in shining armor — a golden-haired knight with the heart of a lion.

When she sat down across from Khalid, she glanced into the azure sky where she spied what looked to be a gull hovering stationary on the wind currents. The bird flew high above, merely a black speck, but for some reason, she took note. The bird was free and unshackled. She yearned to take flight as that bird had done and escape this gilded cage.

"I'm so glad you joined me for breakfast. I have things I wish to share with you." Khalid's voice arrested her fanciful daydream, returning her to the reality of her predicament.

She lifted the pitcher of orange juice and filled her glass. "I'm listening." She sipped the juice as Khalid droned on, her gaze once more drawn to the bird in the sky. *Why isn't it moving?* Even though the sun's rays were warm on her skin, she felt goosebumps rise. She looked away from the bird that wasn't a bird and found Khalid staring at her.

"What is it?" He followed the direction of her eyes.

"Nothing," she reached across the table and placed her hand on his, intent on distracting him. Her touch must have surprised him because his gaze bolted back to her. She forced a smile. "What do you want to share with me?" Her jaw ached from the effort to hide her real feelings, which was what she was forced to do every second she spent in his presence.

"I have decided to give up contract killing. It's long been in the back of my mind but meeting you has inspired me to make this change."

"Me? What have I to do with your decision?" The strain of showing no facial expression caused her jaw to tighten and tick.

But Khalid's cunning gaze missed nothing. He reached across the table and caressed her jawline with the back of his knuckles. "You have everything to do with my change of heart."

She shook her head, and his hand fell away. "Whether I'm the reason or not makes no difference. What matters is that you've made the right choice."

She laughed derisively at how ludicrous this conversation had become. It was as if they were discussing his giving up cigarettes or alcohol, or some other vice and not the murdering of human beings.

"Why do you laugh?"

"Don't you hear yourself? We're talking about you giving up killing the way people talk about quitting smoking. It makes me wonder if you'll have withdrawal or difficulties giving up what has been such a part of your life for so many years."

He shrugged. "I suppose in your mind it is a bizarre proposition. In actuality, I have one more job before I retire — and this one is for you." His mouth quirked in a knowing smile.

Her eyes flashed fire. "Are you going to kill yourself?"

He should have taken offense, but instead, he roared with laughter. "No. I'm not contemplating suicide. Maybe I should clarify that this hit will satisfy both you *and* me."

She gaped. Her hand flew to her breast, where her heart galloped. He'd murdered Aryeh already. Was he thinking about Layla and Cyrus? The photo Layla had shown her of the beautiful red-haired child blazed across her mind, and it terrified her that they might be his targets. "Who are you planning to kill?" She fought to keep fear out of her voice.

Khalid's eyes had darkened to black and flashed with vengeance. The venom contained in his gaze frightened her, and she was grateful that she wasn't the recipient of his hostility. "The man who paid for your family's death. He will never rest until you're dead, and I won't let that happen. He must die so that you may live."

She was dumbfounded. In a total reverse of direction, what she now prayed for changed. What he planned on giving her was more important than his immediate destruction. He was right. She would have paid him for this if he asked.

Without looking in the sky, she sensed the bird's presence, and she knew it watched. Her rescuers were coming. If Khalid died, his unexpected gift would be lost. The irony of the real perpetrator escaping justice was enough to make her howl aloud like a wolf. Now Khalid must live, and that prospect bore its own consequence. Vengeance was within her grasp, and she realized that Khalid was the only man who could deliver it to her. Mossad did not know who'd ordered her family's destruction, and if they were able to ferret out that information, would they destroy him? She could not rely on that, especially considering how spy agencies worked. Sometimes they allowed the worst of humanity to continue to exist if it meant achieving a greater cause. It seemed the only sure way to avenge her family's death was for Khalid to kill the monster who paid him to kill her family. "You would do this for me?" she asked.

"I would do anything for you."

The irony of his statement almost made her laugh. A bitter laugh indeed.

CHAPTER FORTY

Thursday, February 13
Astara, Islamic Republic of Iran

Zara dragged a shopping basket cart behind her. She was about to press the intercom buzzer for the manager's apartment when two large men appeared at her side. She hesitated, glancing at each of them and allowing modest concern to show on her wrinkled visage. One of the men smiled and told her that it was all right to press the buzzer. They were here to see the manager, too. Zara's Farsi was adequate for a simple conversation, but not much more beyond that. The less she said, the better. With her eyes cast modestly downward, she thanked them.

In the window, she saw the reflection of her gray wig and headscarf. Thank goodness the two men, who obviously were NAJA, couldn't hear her heart pounding beneath her heavy winter coat. She pressed the buzzer, and a woman's voice asked who is there. "It's me, Samara," Zara answered in an old-sounding voice, "and two gentlemen who wish to see you."

There was a slight pause before Soraya answered. "Come in." The door clicked, releasing the lock, and Zara entered. She took the elevator to the third floor and turned right with the two men close on her heels. A woman answered the door and welcomed her with warm familiarity as though they'd known each other for years. She asked Zara to start in the bedroom. Zara nodded to the men and dragged her cart inside, then made her way down the hall to a door at the end. The men had remained outside the apartment, and once she was out of sight, she stopped and listened to the conversation. Soraya explained her husband was at work and that nothing had changed since the last time they were here. The couple in question hadn't made an appearance and neither had anyone else. She answered a few more questions and then shut the door. Leaning against it, she sighed with relief.

Zara returned to the entrance and pressed her eye to the peephole as the two men got into the elevator. "You can relax. They're gone."

"Praise be to Allah," she breathed.

Zara congratulated her and told her she did a fine job. The woman beamed and said she was honored to help in any way she could. Zara waited a few minutes before exiting the apartment. She rolled the cart down the hallway to the opposite end.

Before she reached the door, Ibrahim opened it and ushered her inside. "That was a close call."

"We were lucky, but they'll be back." She removed her scarf and pulled off the annoying wig, scratching her scalp.

"Your disguise is very good. You look thirty years older."

She laughed. "By the time this is over, I will have aged thirty years." She continued to scratch her head. "The wig is really itchy." A young woman came out of the kitchen, carrying a tray with a teapot and tea glasses.

"Shira Darbandi, please meet Francoise Shirvani," said Ibrahim.

Shira put the tray down, and Zara extended her hand. "Pleased to meet you, Shira."

Shira nodded. "Likewise." She indicated the sofa. "Please sit. I've prepared tea."

Once they were situated and past the benign exchange of pleasantries, Shira asked. "Have you a plan for getting us out?"

"First things first." Zara stood and began unloading the shopping cart. "We need to transform your appearance." Shira leaned in as

Zara unwrapped the items. "Hopefully, after the photos are done, we'll have the passports in a couple of days. Then we will finalize our escape plan. But for now, we plan to cross the bridge at the border on foot. From what I understand, it may be a slow process but it's fairly cut and dried if you have the proper papers. A few hours at most."

Shira's eyes widened. "Isn't walking in plain sight of the military dangerous?"

"Not really, so long as our disguises and our papers are good. But I must warn you, things change day by day. What works today might not work tomorrow. Nothing is written in stone." Zara snapped open a box, and both Shira and Ibrahim peered over her shoulder.

"What's this?" Shira asked.

"We need to change the way you look for your passport photo." She studied Shira's face. "We'll dye your hair black Shira, darken your skin color and give you dark brown contacts and perhaps make those lovely eyebrows of yours look overgrown. That and a hijab should be enough." Zara looked at Ibrahim. "As for you, Ibrahim, a full beard, gray hair, and wire-rimmed spectacles and an overbite should do the trick."

Two hours later, they were ready for their passport photos. "I need to complete your disguises with a few extra bells and whistles." Zara pulled out the clothes they would be wearing. While the young couple retreated into the bedroom to change their clothes, Zara thumb-tacked a white sheet against the wall, exactly the same as the ones used by Iranian authorities. She'd also been warned to make sure there were no shadows.

A few minutes later, Zara stood back to observe both Shira and Ibrahim. She smiled at their transformation. "Even your mothers wouldn't know you. Shira, those bushy eyebrows did the trick, and with the plain headscarf, your beauty is well and truly hidden." Zara turned to Ibrahim and nodded her satisfaction at the marked change in his appearance. "And Ibrahim, you bear no resemblance to the young and handsome academic that you are."

The young couple stared at each other and burst out laughing.

"Well, this is certainly a change," Ibrahim said.

"It will be a lively story to tell our grandchildren, God willing," Shira added.

It's good for them to experience a moment of levity, thought Zara. The reality of danger would set in soon enough. "As soon as the passports come through, we'll need to meet again and go through our stories. In the meantime." She handed them each a notebook. "These are your new identities. Memorize them, then burn the notebooks. I expect you to know these false histories backward and forward."

Both Ibrahim and Shira flipped through the pages, their eyes focused in concentration, their foreheads lined with concern at the details written on the pages. "Don't worry, you have plenty of time to prepare yourselves. A good way of doing this is to test each other. Approach it like studying for one of your term exams. I am certain that memorizing these notes is a piece of cake compared to writing an exam on nuclear fusion."

The couple smiled at Zara. She sighed, pleased at least that she had made them feel more comfortable in completing this important task.

An hour later, the photos were done, and Zara began packing up. "You should know that to keep things safer — Shira, you will be married to Arman, who'll have a different name, of course, and Ibrahim, you will be married to me. It's important that we separate the two of you from each other. In case they are looking for you and have photographs and are smart enough to see beyond our clever disguises." She winked. "Besides, both Arman and I are experienced and prepared for any problems. We will be better able to protect you this way. We'll have to pass through metal detectors, so carrying arms won't be possible."

Zara didn't need to tell them about the polymer pistols that she and Mustafa would hide in their clothing. The new technology Kaspar had supplied them with would make it through whatever metal detecting system was used at the border. The only worry was that plastic guns were notorious for misfiring and inaccuracy, not to mention they were capable of firing only one bullet. However, Kaspar had informed them that these were new and highly improved models developed in Israel that were far more dependable. But it was better for Ibrahim and Shira to be kept in the dark about this. As long as they had their false identities memorized, they would be fine. The fewer details they knew about the rest of the operation, the better off they would be.

"Ibrahim, may I have the flash drive, please?" Zara empathized with the fear and nervousness she saw in their eyes, but she needed to exert control and kept her replies confident, concise, and unquestioned.

"Oh, I forgot. Excuse me a minute." He left the room.

Shira's voice trembled. "Are you going to upload it to the Israelis now?"

"No. I'll do it when I get back to the hotel. Don't worry, I have a secure satellite connection, and there's no possibility of it falling into the hands of NAJA or anyone else."

Ibrahim returned and handed the drive to her. "Excuse me while I hide this." She turned her back to them and stuffed it into a slit she'd cut out in the padding of her bra. "As soon as it's been received securely, I'll destroy it," she said over her shoulder. She turned to face them once more and smiled. "And now I must go. She pulled the gray wig back on, tucking her escaping wisps of dark hair out of sight. She wrapped the hijab securely around her hair and shoulders and put on her coat. "Don't worry, everything is going to be fine. A few days from now, we'll be out of here."

CHAPTER FORTY-ONE

Thursday, February 13
Birżebbuġa, Malta

Aryeh couldn't take his eyes off the live footage coming from the drone playing on the control room monitor. A part of him celebrated that Jazmin was alive, but he was sick seeing her in the hands of that killer.

Her beauty shone brightly in the sun. She looked stunning in a bathing suit and wrap. Aryeh could clearly see how besotted Gurga was with her, how he touched her and drew her close. It made his insides crawl.

But what shook him to the core, though, was the expression on her face when she looked up at the sky. It seemed as though she knew they were watching her. Her eyes looked right at him, begging him to save her. He felt helpless. Powerless. His hands tied behind his back. He'd let her down, and that guilt gnawed at his reasoning to the point where he was ready to throw caution to the wind and go in with guns blazing.

Cyrus squeezed his shoulder. "You're eating yourself up, friend.

You must let this guilt go. She's alive and unharmed, and that's what matters. We're going in to get her, but we have to do it smart."

Aryeh growled. "The way he behaved with her tells me this is different. The reason she is alive is this bastard wants something from her that has nothing to do with the contract on her family or the safety deposit box. He wants her for himself."

"I don't disagree with you, but I don't think he'll force her. It looks to me like he's trying to win her affections. She's smart, and she knows how to string him along."

"Yes, but she also wants revenge. I think she'll do whatever it takes to achieve it. I've been there, Cyrus. If she follows through with what I think she's contemplating, it will ultimately destroy her soul. We need to rescue her before that happens."

JAZMIN SWAM the length of the pool. Each time she turned her head to take a breath, she could see Khalid matching her stroke for stroke. The water felt delightful, and it was a relief to burn off some of her anxiety. They swam to the steps, and Khalid helped her out of the pool. She slicked her hair off her face, grabbed an oversized towel, wrapped it around her body, and tucked a corner over her breast. Then she wrapped a smaller towel around her hair, turban style. Khalid wrapped his towel around his waist and dried his hair with a smaller towel.

Jazmin sat on the chaise lounge and drew up her knees. She found it difficult to stop herself from glancing up at the sky to see if the bird still hovered. She'd agreed to take a swim in the hopes that whoever watched could see her and know that she was there.

The way Khalid's eyes had devoured her when she'd removed her coverup had been unsettling, and she'd nearly changed her mind about the swim. But then she realized it would be better for her to stay outside for as long as possible so the eye in the sky could see her. If it was a Mossad drone, as she hoped, she wanted them to know she was okay.

But it wasn't easy to accept the hunger in Khalid's eyes and pretend that she was beginning to welcome it. She wasn't stupid. It was clear he was fixated on her. His eyes watched her like a hungry wolf eyeing a lamb.

She didn't like the exposed feeling. For her own peace of mind and safety, she needed to turn the tables once again. Khalid had removed his towel and draped it over the back of his chaise. She allowed her gaze to wander over his myriad tattoos.

"Do you like body art?" he said in a velvety voice. He stood and flexed his muscles for her and turned in a slow circle, like a professional bodybuilder on stage.

"It's become something of a passion for me," he went on. "Wearing the story of your life on your skin. What do you think?"

His confession struck her as strange. "I-I don't know...I haven't seen many tattoos up close."

He grinned and sat beside her on the lounger. "Don't be afraid. You can touch me if you'd like," he whispered.

She stared at the tattoo emblazoned across his hairless chest. Khalid was indeed preoccupied with appearances and must have had his chest hair lasered in order to show off his body art. The tattoo was large and completely covered his pectorals. A recreation of the Garden of Eden. Between his muscled pecs was the tree of life bearing one apple. On one side, a half-coiled serpent flickered a red tongue. On the other side stood a naked Adam and Eve. Adam embraced Eve, restraining her, but her foot was poised as if already in motion toward her fate, the apple tantalizing and drawing her to its tempting sweetness. Eve's hand was extended, ready to pluck the fruit from the tree that would bring about their fall from grace. The tattoo was expertly rendered and as colorful as a painting. Whoever had created it was a true artist.

And like Eve, Jazmin reached out and touched his chest. Her fingers lightly grazed his skin along the lines of the image.

Khalid flexed his pec muscle, and the snake came to life, causing her to jump back and gasp. His eruption of laughter made her flush with embarrassment. She used it to her advantage and looked down in shyness. "That was silly of me."

"Not at all. I shouldn't have frightened you like that."

"I'm not frightened. I was surprised."

"Are you wondering why I chose this scene from Genesis?"

"Perhaps."

"It is a reminder to me to beware of temptation. To be cautious of whom I trust." His dark gaze probed hers. "Do you think I will ever be able to trust you, Jazmin? Or are you my Eve, the woman who will bring my fall from grace?"

"Why *should* you trust me? I don't trust you. We would make a very odd couple, indeed. To fathom it is insane."

"Why? We're both alone in the world. Maybe I'm the only man you can ever trust. There are no secrets between us. You know exactly who I am and what I did. I would give up my past and my way of life for you. I would make a new life here with you. Or anywhere else you would like to live. The world is your oyster, and I have the means and the desire to make your every dream come true — "

She stood abruptly and pulled the towel from her hair, using it to dry the still damp ends. She'd felt too vulnerable with him seated so close to her on the lounger.

He sighed and stood as well. "I'd like to thank you," he said.

"For what?" She unhooked the towel wrapped around her body and draped it over the back of the lounger to dry. Then she slipped back into the wrap. Hoping she'd given him enough of a show for one day.

"I don't think I've ever spent a nicer day."

"I'm glad you're enjoying it." She couldn't keep the sarcasm from her voice. *Damn!* So much for her acting ability. She should have been more careful with her words.

He stepped closer to her and grabbed her arms in a steely grip. His neck and face burned red, and the amber color of his eyes flashed with anger. "Are you intent on torturing me?" he hissed.

I should back down. But she refused to be cowed. She thrust her chin out with defiance and held his gaze fearlessly. "Will you kill me now?"

His hands relaxed on her arms, and before she could push him away, one of his hands slipped behind her neck and the other caressed her face. He bent slowly, watching her reaction as he claimed her lips in a demanding kiss.

It sickened her. But a small part of her found their exchange exhilarating. *Power does that. But whose power is it, his or mine?*

He pulled back and stared into her eyes.

She gazed back at him as her instincts took over. *I can do this! I can fool him into thinking I can't help myself, that I am physically attracted to him. That I desire him in spite of how we got here. I need him to think he can conquer me with that desire.*

She leaned into him a hair's breadth, opened her lips enough to tempt him, and closed her eyes. Slowly, languorously, as though she couldn't help herself. As though *he* were having a hypnotic effect on *her.*

He growled low in his throat, and the kiss burned her with its intensity. His hands roamed up and down her back. His lips grazed down her neck to the top of her damp swimsuit.

Her fingers trailed through his hair, and she hoped her light gasping moans were convincing.

When he groaned in reply, she knew she was winning. She moved closer to him and molded her body against his. She could feel his hardness pressing into her softness.

His hands reached for her face. Cupping her cheeks, he pulled back and stared at her. Looked deeply into her eyes. Searching. Seeking. She knew he was trying to figure out if this was an act or if she really was falling for him. She feared that she wasn't a good enough actress to convince him. So she closed her eyes and parted her lips once more. And he growled again and pulled her in for another kiss.

His arms tightened, crushing her against him. When he released her lips, she felt his heart pounding, echoing against hers. His lips swept her neck to her earlobe, his gasping breath filling her ear. "I want you, Jazmin. More than I've ever wanted anyone or anything in my life. You pretend to hate me, but I sense a yearning in you that is as great as mine. Are you curious to know the great pleasure I can give you?"

Her eyes were closed, and she was glad he couldn't read the terror inside her. Maybe she should give him what he wanted. Maybe once he had her, he would be rid of this passion of his. Would he kill her then?

Is that what she wanted? To die and end this life that had stolen everything from her? The thought shocked her but would it not be easier that way? How could she live with herself knowing what she was doing, what she was contemplating? Allowing him into her bed.

A betrayer, that's what she was. Her family was dead, and her reward from the devil was his promise of everything the world had to offer. If she accepted, she'd be lost, exposed for what she was. Khalid had no idea how prescient he was. She *was* Eve, and his paradise was already lost.

She pulled out of his arms and directed her gaze at him. "What do they call you in this world of contract killers and paid assassins?"

His eyes narrowed. "Why do you ask?"

"Curiosity. It seems to me that people in your field would have a sobriquet that describes them in place of their identities."

"The wolf. They call me the wolf."

"How fitting. Am I the lamb?"

At first, he looked as if he might laugh, but instead, his face grew serious. "Are you the she-wolf?"

What did Khalid imply when calling her a she-wolf? Was she a predator who would do whatever it took to get what she wanted? Maybe she was. "It's an interesting notion that I'm the predator. If so, shouldn't you be running as fast as possible away from me?"

"Do I look like a man who runs from danger? Especially when the prize is so extraordinary."

No matter how hard she tried to project calm, her shortness of breath and the rapid rise and fall of her chest couldn't hide the truth. His face was inches from hers, and she couldn't breathe. "Allow me some time to consider your offer."

Khalid's gaze dropped to her lips as he ran his hand from her cheek down the length of her body, eliciting a shudder from her. "Take your time but allow me one more kiss."

He claimed her lips, and she bought some time.

His physical power over her was taking a toll. She'd started out thinking she could turn the tables and make him think she was falling for him and, in turn, make him fall for her.

But everything was becoming topsy turvy. Was she Delilah, who held sway over Sampson? Or was she Eve, who succumbed to temptation? Perhaps she was both. It didn't matter because she was still a prisoner. He wouldn't let her go. Only death would release her. The drone was flying overhead, ever watchful, but could she be sure it was Mossad? Or could it be the general's minions doing his bidding? In that case, what chance did she have?

She was well and truly trapped. In her quest to wear him down, she was, in truth, the one who was weakening. Her physical ability to resist him was fading. Would her mental ability soon follow? Was she suffering from Stockholm syndrome and beginning to fall for her captor?

She was grateful they were outside in broad daylight and not in her bedroom. For she didn't know how much longer she could fend him off.

How long had she been here? It had scarcely been twenty-four hours, yet it felt like twenty-four days or years. It hadn't taken him long at all to break down her defenses, what little she had left. She was already broken. Watching her family disintegrate had done that. Her fiancé being obliterated had done that. The hopes and dreams she had of a happy marriage and children of her own were like dust in the desert. And then she'd met Aryeh, and she'd begun to feel something, a spark of hope for her future. But Khalid had destroyed that too.

And now? He was succeeding because she was getting tired. Tired of fighting him, tired of matching wits with him, and tired of being held prisoner. When would her prayers be answered? She thought about the strange bird-like drone in the sky. *I pray it's an eagle that will fly me to safety and not a hawk that will drop me to my doom.*

CHAPTER FORTY-TWO

Friday, February 14
Valletta, Malta

Aryeh crouched behind a stone retaining wall surrounding the villa. Beside him, the techno-geek Levi chewed a wad of bubble gum, his eyes riveted to a small screen. Levi held a joystick in his hand with which he maneuvered the drone.

Resting on Levi's crossed legs, the computer broadcast the live feed from the drone in night-vision green. The drone's camera focused on the guardhouse of the assassin's villa. A thousand feet away, Ash lay on the ground lining up the MacMillan Tac-50 sniper rifle. Cyrus, Ben, and Yitzak were hiding, waiting for Ash to take out the guards and give the go-ahead for the team to begin the assault. Zvi coordinated the action from a van parked half a mile down the road. From their best guestimates, they'd counted about twenty enemy combatants guarding the fortress, although they suspected only half of them were on duty at any given time.

Because of Aryeh's concerns about Jazmin's safety, they'd moved up the operation and decided to go in just before dawn. He couldn't take another day of watching Gurga maul Jazmin by the pool. He knew what she was doing, of course. He knew it down to his bones. It was a dangerous game she was playing. At least Sarah had been a trained agent, if an inexperienced one. But Jazmin? She was a lamb going up against a wolf. She'd had no training and no experience to undertake such a bold plan. Seducing Gurga and then killing him. If something happened to her, Aryeh's guilt would sear his soul.

No. They had to go in without delay and rescue her before it was too late. Their plan was simple. While the team neutralized the opposition, Aryeh would infiltrate the house to find Jazmin. Their goal was to free Jazmin and eliminate the assassin and then make their escape in the van. Earlier in the day, the drone had caught a glimpse of Jazmin standing on a balcony on the second floor of the villa. They'd pinpointed the bedroom and assessed it to be the room where they'd most likely find her. Cyrus had tried to assign Ben to scale the house and find Jazmin, but Aryeh had insisted pain or no pain he was going in. He bore no argument from Cyrus or anyone else. He would scale the house and enter through Jazmin's bedroom terrace while the rest of the team concentrated on taking out the security team and the assassin. Levi would direct the drone from his position on the ground.

Normally Levi controlled the drone from an operations room, either on base or at HQ, but Cyrus had insisted the fledgling team member operate on the ground hand-in-hand with them. It was important for him to become a fluid member of the team and for him to be able to adapt to any changes on the ground. Even if he was a skinny geek, he'd had the same physical training they'd all had with IDF and had experienced combat conditions.

Aryeh glanced up at the waxing crescent moon and the brilliant star nearby that wasn't a star but the planet Venus. The sliver of moonlight provided a stunning backdrop. The first hint of dawn glowed on the horizon. Everyone on the team wore black tactical gear. They jokingly called it their ninja gear, but whatever they called it, they appreciated that it made them nearly invisible.

An owl hooted, and Aryeh could make out the swoosh of wings flapping overhead. He peered over the wall — he saw no movement from his vantage point, and everything appeared to be quiet.

"What's happening, Ash?" Aryeh whispered.

"Waiting for a clear shot. Two buffoons to take out."

"Okay, we go on your direction."

"Roger that."

Waiting for the action to begin was never a good thing. All kinds of negative scenarios bombarded Aryeh's psyche as he waited. What would he do if he found Jazmin in bed with the assassin? That imagery was eviscerating, which only made him consider his feelings toward her. Since Zürich, he couldn't get Jazmin out of his mind. They'd shared their darkest secrets and found comfort in each other's presence. The possibility had taken root that together they might be able to heal what was broken inside of them and build something worth having, but he couldn't cast off the feeling that Gurga was experiencing his own catharsis and had fallen for Jazmin too. And if she were planning seduction, then she would be in even greater danger.

You are one messed up hombre. Better not let your imagination get ahead of you.

He glanced down at Levi's screen at the exact moment when a series of flashes burst from Ash's rifle muzzle. He could see the gases and bullets explode from the muzzle, but he couldn't hear them, thanks to the suppressor.

Levi's computer screen resembled one of those video games he played when he wasn't managing the drone. Aryeh watched as an enemy combatant toppled outside the guardhouse. The other was nowhere to be seen. The heat sensor on the drone registered no life inside or outside, which meant they were no longer of this world. "Let's go, Levi." Aryeh jumped the wall and wolfed in a breath to combat the fatigue in his limbs. Adrenaline would kick in soon, he hoped. He ran before Ash signaled the-all clear to proceed. Levi jumped, struggling to keep up with Aryeh, who rushed toward the house.

In his bedroom, Khalid woke to the silent alarm indicating the perimeter of his home had been breached. He hit the number on his watch that connected him with the guardhouse. While the phone rang, he dressed and grabbed the pistol from under his mattress before heading out the door and down the hallway to the blue room where Jazmin slept. He had no time for niceties.

"Jazmin, get up!" He moved to the side of the window and peered through the drapery. Gunfire had erupted, and he made out movement on the ground. His security team had spread and now ran, exchanging gunfire. He had to assume this was an effort by Mossad to rescue Jazmin and in retaliation for killing one of their own.

Jazmin sat up. "What's happening?" she said in a groggy voice.

"Get dressed now. We're under attack. It's time to get out of here." Khalid strode to the bed and yanked her up. "You have one minute."

"I don't understand. Where are we going?"

"I have an emergency escape route. Don't make me ask twice."

He pointed the gun at her. "Move!"

Khalid followed her into the closet and watched as she slipped on a pair of jeans and a sweater. "Let's go!" He dragged her by the arm down the hallway toward his bedroom and shut the door. Placing his hand on a touchpad, the sound of bolts sliding into place sealed the door. Khalid flung open the slider to the terrace. A spiral staircase led upward. He motioned with his pistol, "Quick. Up the stairs."

"Where are we going?"

"You'll see."

GUNFIRE CRACKLED as Aryeh ran toward the house. In his ear, he heard Cyrus, Ben, Yitzak, and Ash engaging the enemy. The team worked like synchronized watches, each man in step with the other. Within minutes Aryeh heard Cyrus radio. "All clear outside. Ben and I are blowing the front door."

Aryeh assessed the patio area. "Levi, take cover and keep the drone above the house and listen for my commands." He threw a miniature grappling hook to the ledge of the room where Jazmin had been sighted, and hand over hand, with his legs braced against the wall of the house he climbed. His chest heaved and he gasped with each breath. But Aryeh ignored the burn in his arms and legs and continued upward. He knew he wasn't fully recovered from the poison, but he fought against the debilitating weakness of his body and made it to the second story and swung his body over the balustrade. Catching his breath, he tried the sliding glass door and found it unlocked. Cautiously, he slid it open and slipped through the sheer drapery. A quick scan of the room told him it was empty. The sheets were thrown back on the bed, and the closet light glowed. He found Jazmin's nightgown discarded on the floor. Aryeh looked around, frustrated. "Levi," he whispered, "I want eyes on every possible exit of the house."

Levi answered, "There's a heli on the roof. The rotor is spinning."

"Shit!" Aryeh ran down the hallway, the muzzle of his rifle aimed and ready. An explosion downstairs and the chatter in his ear told him that the team had blown the front door. "I'm upstairs in the hallway," he barked into his mouthpiece. "Whirlybird on the roof. Target escaping with Jazmin."

"On our way. Roger."

They converged in the hallway. Aryeh tried to break through the last door in the hallway, but it didn't budge.

Yitzak opened his tactical backpack. "I'll blow it. Stand by!" He molded Semtex around the door. Everyone backed down the hallway into one of the other bedrooms.

"Five…four…three…" the team braced themselves. "Two…one…."

A deafening explosion followed. As a unit, the team raced down the hall, rifles ready. They plowed through plumes of smoke and debris and entered the bedroom. The slider to the terrace was open and Aryeh ran for it. He was desperate to get to Jazmin before she was whisked away. "Spiral staircase to the roof." He climbed before anyone answered. As he reached the roof, the helicopter lifted. "Levi, is she in the heli?" He roared into his earpiece.

"No, I don't think so. I'm not sure what happened. One second they were on the roof, and the next second they were gone. Check for some outcropping that might have hidden them from the drone's view."

"What the hell! Are you saying they vanished into thin air?"

"I don't know."

Aryeh fumed. By now, the entire team was on the roof, searching.

Aryeh combed every inch looking for an escape hatch, a door, anything that might provide an escape venue. He was ready to explode when he studied the side of the building and noticed a flat panel in one side of the structure. The panel looked out of place. He pressed it and it popped open. He yelled, "I've got something." He climbed over the balustrade and stepped onto a ledge, balancing on the rim of the opening. Grabbing his flashlight, he directed it into a hole at least forty feet deep.

"Where does it go?" asked Cyrus.

"Looks like a shaft that drops below the foundation. It's like those tunnels Hamas builds to infiltrate Israel. I bet there's a tunnel at the bottom that leads to somewhere off the property."

"Who's got a zipline and grappling hook?"

Ben was already digging in his backpack. "I've got one." He found it and hooked it around the balustrade and gave it a good tug. "It's secure. Be easier with gloves."

Aryeh grabbed hold with gloved hands and began descending. When he reached the bottom, he yelled up. "I'm going ahead."

With his pistol in one hand and flashlight in the other, he moved forward. Behind him, he heard the rest of the team descend quickly, following as he plunged ahead through the tunnel.

"This guy had his shit together. He probably was afraid whoever attacked might blow the whirlybird out of the sky, and it was safer for him to have another avenue. Ten to one the chopper is on its way to pick them up." Cyrus's voice came through his earpiece.

"Yeah, that's what I'm afraid of," Aryeh growled back. His heart pounded in his chest. What if the assassin got away with Jazmin? Where would he take her and how would the team find her? Hopefully, the tracking device was still functioning. He quickened his pace. The tunnel seemed to go on forever. He'd run only about a quarter of a mile when the taste and scent of shrubbery and grass hit him. A spiral metal stairway loomed ahead. Aryeh climbed up to ground level. The wind from the spinning rotors of the helicopter hit him in the face. He pumped his legs as fast as they could go toward the helicopter.

It didn't occur to him that he might be in danger. He yelled above the roar of the chopper, but his words disappeared into the wind.

Jazmin must have sensed his presence because she looked down through the glass window of the copter. The light of impending dawn glimmered.

Aryeh saw the surprise on her face. Her eyes widened, her mouth formed an O. A split second later, a smile lit her features. Aryeh watched in disbelief as she turned to speak to the assassin who sat behind her. An argument erupted between them. Everything happened so fast. Aryeh kept yelling as he ran toward the helicopter. He had no way to stop it from taking off, and if he fired, he might hurt Jazmin. When the whirly began to rise, the door swung open. Five feet, ten feet, fifteen feet. Aryeh threw his weapon to the ground and rushed forward.

Dear God, she's going to jump!

CHAPTER FORTY-THREE

Friday, February 14
Valletta, Malta

Cyrus gaped. *What the hell?* He couldn't believe what he was seeing, yet there it was.

Aryeh ran toward the helicopter like a madman with arms outstretched, clearly ready to brace the fall of Jazmin, who looked like she was going to jump from the helicopter twenty feet in the air.

Everything seemed to shift into slow motion.

Above the whirling wind from the rotors, Cyrus heard a voice from the copter yell, "No!"

Gurga grabbed frantically for Jazmin, but he could no more stop her than stop a tornado from its destructive path.

Gravity was her friend.

Cyrus doubted he would ever forget the look on Jazmin's face.

Pure joy mingled with complete trust. Of course, she must have believed Aryeh was dead, and to see him alive and running toward the helicopter must have propelled her to risk life and limb to get to him.

She stepped onto the landing gear rail, crouched, and grabbing on she dangled for less than a second and released. It was too high off the ground. She'd break every bone in her body, and if Aryeh broke her fall, he could be injured or killed. The team stood frozen on the ground, unable to stop the momentum of events.

With outstretched arms, Aryeh caught the plunging Jazmine, his knees bent to absorb the impact. He grunted, his breath whooshing out as he caught her, and the two of them smacked against the ground and rolled one on top of the other, arms and legs flailing until they came to rest in a patch of dirt.

Overhead the helicopter hovered. Cyrus looked up, locked eyes with the assassin who leaned out with his face contorted in anger. Neither Jazmin nor Aryeh moved. Forgetting about the assassin, he ran to the prone figures on the ground and felt the pulses of his friends. They were both alive but unconscious.

The helicopter took off, but Cyrus paid it no mind. He was focused on reviving Aryeh and Jazmin. He dug in his tactical backpack and found an ammonia inhalant. Opening it, he placed it under Aryeh's nose.

Mossad's "Lion of Judah" growled and shook his head, swearing a litany of curses at him.

Yitzak joined Cyrus on the ground and held a bottle of water to Aryeh's lips while Ash administered to Jazmin.

A massive explosion knocked everyone off balance. Cyrus's gaze snapped toward the sky. The disintegrating helicopter rained down smoke and bits of burning metal. "What the hell happened?" Cyrus shouted.

"I don't know." Ben's face filled with confusion. "But no one in that bird will ever see another sunrise."

The blast must have stunned Aryeh back to awareness. He croaked, "Is Jazmin okay?"

Levi ran toward them. "Are they all right? Is Aryeh alive? Did you see what I did?"

Cyrus stared at the youngest member of the team. "Yes, he's alive, but what are you talking about? What did you do?"

"I took out the copter." Levi's face was a mix of pride and worry.

"What? How?" Cyrus looked at Levi like he'd lost a screw. The kid stopped chewing the wad of bubble gum in his mouth.

Aryeh sat up, pushing Yitzak away, choking and coughing. "You're going to drown me." Suddenly aware of his surroundings, he sat up. Jazmin was pale and hadn't moved. Aryeh gently brushed a strand of hair off her face. "Wake up, sweetheart. Come back to me," he whispered.

Jazmin's eyelashes fluttered on her cheek.

"Don't try to move too quickly," he said. Can you wiggle your toes and fingers?

A slow smile spread across her face. "You're alive," she croaked.

"You bet I am, and so are you."

She opened her eyes. "I prayed, but I didn't think anyone was listening."

Aryeh gently lifted her into his arms and held her close. He buried his face in her hair. "You crazy woman. How could you even think of jumping out of that helicopter?"

She laughed and then groaned in pain. "I — I acted on instinct. I was so happy to see you alive, all I wanted was to get to you."

He threw back his head and laughed. "You got me, and it looks like you got your revenge too."

"What are you talking about?" Her gaze swept left and right.

"Didn't you see what happened to the helicopter?"

"No. Tell me."

Aryeh directed her question to Levi. "Tell us all what happened. Levi."

Levi's face reddened with everyone's attention on him. "When I saw Jazmin jump and land on Aryeh, I kind of went crazy. There was no way I was going to let that bastard get away, especially if anything happened to Aryeh."

Aryeh couldn't contain his laughter. "Okay, kid, I get the fact that you love me. Now tell us what you did."

Levi's face turned beet red. "I was tracking the device in Jazmin's hair, and the drone picked up when she and the assassin exited the tunnel. I may have failed to mention that the drone carries a self-destruct device. Basically, it's a bomb. Because of the technology, we can't allow it to fall into enemy hands. After Jazmin jumped, I snapped. I guess I went a little crazy. Anyway, when the helicopter hovered, I got the idea. I flew the drone to the helicopter and attached the drone to the bottom. When the bird started moving again, I detonated the self-destruction mechanism and blew him to kingdom come, although in his case it won't be heaven, more likely hell." Levi cast his gaze downward and shrugged his shoulders. "I'm sorry if I acted without permission, sir."

All eyes bore into Levi, with their mouths gaping open. "Shit, Levi, remind me never to get on your bad side," Ben joked.

"Yeah," said Ash, "I thought *I* was cold-blooded. That was fricking awesome, dude."

Levi looked up and beamed, and Cyrus slapped the young man on his shoulder. "Nice work, *achi.*"

Jazmin whispered, "No." She covered her face, and sobs escaped her.

A rash of red rose up Aryeh's neck. And he pulled back, giving her space to breathe as she wept.

"Don't let your thoughts get ahead of your sense," Cyrus whispered in his ear as he watched the mixed emotions fly across Aryeh's features. "She's been through hell and is probably in shock."

"You're right. It's not her fault." His words were weighted with resignation. Slowly, he dragged himself to his feet. "Let's get her to a hospital. Ash, I'm a little unsteady. Why don't you carry her."

Cyrus could tell the last thing Aryeh wanted to do was let Jazmin go, but her reaction to the assassin's death had clearly blindsided him. Cyrus would do his best to get Aryeh through this. He understood better than anyone what being a hostage could do to a person's psyche. Layla had suffered from Stockholm syndrome and PTSD after being kidnapped and held captive. Jazmine was probably suffering from the same thing. He prayed the monster assassin hadn't forced himself on her. If he *had* violated her, the bastard's death would never be enough to satisfy Aryeh's anger.

Cyrus had his work cut out for him. Strange how it worked. Aryeh was a man of wisdom when it came to helping Cyrus through his struggles. Now it was Cyrus's turn to return the favor for his friend.

He was anxious to get back to Layla. Anxious for this ordeal to be over. Anxious to get back home to Cerise and Norit. Layla was probably sick with worry. But she was made of strong stuff, his beloved. And Layla, more than anyone, could help Jazmin get through this. He was sure of it. It would take time.

Let's move," Cyrus ordered. "We're done here."

CHAPTER FORTY-FOUR

Astara, Islamic Republic of Iran
Friday, February 14

Zara's nerves were taut as a high wire strung above the ground for a circus act.

Zara and Ibrahim stood in line at passport control a few people behind Shira and Mustafa. She scanned the room, her gaze flitting away from the guard who carried an assault rifle. She knew if the mission was going to fall apart, it would happen now. She prayed Mossad's *katsa* in Tehran hadn't slipped up. She'd checked everyone's papers a dozen times, and everything seemed to be in order. The passports looked good, and the visa stamps looked authentic.

She was worried if Shira and Ibrahim could hold up under possible interrogation. She and Mustafa had grilled Ibrahim and Shira for hours to make sure they had their fake histories memorized backward and forward. During mock questioning, the young couple did fine, but a pretend grilling wasn't the same as a real one by the enemy.

Zara tried not to stare or appear too curious when Mustafa and Shira reached the head of the line. The passport control officer perused their papers. The phone on his desk rang. He answered and frowned. Zara felt the bitter taste of bile in her mouth. Was this it? Would they be arrested? Maybe the NAJA officers had returned to the apartment house and threatened Izad and Soraya, and they'd folded under pressure. Every worst possible scenario raced through her mind. Zara hoped it wouldn't come to a shoot-out. She couldn't bear the thought of everything ending here, not with the fragile life growing inside her. Not when she'd been so happy in her new life with Mustafa.

She held her breath, waiting for the worst to unfold.

The officer continued to listen to the speaker on the telephone line, and after a minute, he absentmindedly handed the passports back to Mustafa and Shira and waved them on.

Zara began to breathe again. Then as the couple was about to exit the building, he called, "Stop! Come back." He waved his hands, and all eyes darted to the unfortunate couple. Zara's breath froze in her chest, her lungs refusing to expand. Shira and Mustafa stopped and turned. For a nanosecond, she and Mustafa locked eyes. He smiled, and cool as a cucumber, took Shira's elbow and led her back to the officer. "Your passports, I forgot to stamp them. I'm sorry, the phone distracted me." He took their passports, and with a fair amount of flourish, he pounded the stamp on them. *"Rooze khoobi dashteh bashid."*

Zara was a second away from throwing up. She swallowed and willed herself to calm down. Mustafa threw her a brief glance, but she read in his eyes everything she needed to know.

I love you, too.

Zara adjusted her scarf, cast her eyes down, and resumed the demeanor of a submissive wife. Ibrahim moved forward to the officer, and she trailed him. Ibrahim handed the official their passports, and the interrogation began. "The reason for your visit?"

"My wife and I were visiting family in Tabriz." The official nodded and continued to look at their passports, his gaze shifting several times to Zara. "Your wife has a very distinctive eye color."

During one of her throw up sessions she must have lost one of her brown contacts. She'd searched everywhere this morning and came up empty-handed. Was everything to be blown by a damn contact lens?

"Yes, we did some heredity tracing and found some of her ancestors came from the Caucasus. Allah blesses us in different ways, does he not?"

The inspector nodded. He scanned their passports into the computer and handed them back. *"Mosaferate khoobi dashteh bashid."*

Zara returned the man's smile with a shy nod and submissive smile of her own and followed Ibrahim out the door.

As they neared the bridge, Zara glanced around to see they were alone. "We're almost there. We need to walk across this bridge," she whispered.

"Look," Ibrahim said, "there they are." He nodded to midway across the bridge.

"Yes, I see them." Shira and Mustafa were ahead of them but walking slowly. They must have lingered, waiting for them to catch up. "Let's go." She'd had enough. Zara couldn't wait to get out of Iran. All of the fear and anxiety couldn't be good for the baby, and it needed to end. She quickened her pace, forcing Ibrahim to do so as well. She felt in her pocket for the gun. Funny how the instrument of death felt like a lifeline.

Later, she wouldn't recall what made her turn around. But the shock of what she saw sent a jolt through her system. Three police vehicles pulled onto the bridge with lights flashing. Six men jumped out of the car and began running toward them, shouting for them to stop.

"Run!" Zara screamed. Around them, people panicked. Everyone who'd been making their way across the bridge began running and shouting. Confusion and fear took hold. The older people hit the ground, knowing they couldn't outrun the police. They put their hands up in surrender. Others made a mad dash to the border. Zara and Ibrahim ran with them. Mustafa turned, his face a tableau of disbelief. He stood fast, waiting for Zara to catch up. She waved him on. "Run!" she screamed. "Get to the Azerbaijan side."

She could hear the officers closing in on them and yelling for them to stop. They were so exposed. Suddenly the weapon was useless to her. She faced too many men and their were too many innocent bystanders around them. All she could do was run and pray that on the other side, Mossad agents waited to help them. Fear and anxiety tore through her in a rush of adrenaline. They were so close. Her thoughts turned to the baby growing inside of her, and she ran faster.

A vehicle screeched to the Azerbaijan end of the bridge. A group of men in combat body armor jumped out with weapons drawn and began running toward her. Tears slipped down her cheeks, not from fear, but from helplessness.

A gunshot spun her around.

No pain. Only shock. *You're going to die — you're going to lose the baby!*

Zara tumbled to the ground. She registered continuing gunfire, people screaming with fear, people shouting in anger. She could smell her own fear, and it made her want to vomit. She raised her head and saw Mustafa restrained by one of their rescuers. Mixed emotions assaulted her, joy that he was desperate to save her and horror that she couldn't say goodbye, that she would die alone a few yards away from him on this damn bridge.

Zara's fingers brushed across her chest and came away warm and bloodied. She'd smelled it before, the smell of rusty metal. On the bright side, she didn't feel any cramping, but if she died, so would the baby. Their baby. Waves of nausea overwhelmed her. *No, I can't give up. Breathe. The baby needs oxygen.*

The chaotic scene faded away as she focused on taking deep, even breaths. Strong arms lifted her, cradling her, and then they were running. Searing pain as she bounced against a broad chest. The pain was so great that her body fought the only way it knew how, by slipping into unconsciousness. "Save my baby," she whispered before everything went black.

CHAPTER FORTY-FIVE

Saturday, February 15
Tel Aviv, Israel

Aryeh stood outside the ICU, his gaze fixed on the woman with so many tubes and monitors attached they gave her the appearance of an alien from outer space. It was his fault she lay precariously poised between this world and the next.

Why didn't you tell me you were pregnant?

It was no use lamenting what was done, but guilt ate at him, and he barely maintained his composure.

Mustafa, Shira, and Ibrahim had all given him an accounting of what had occurred. But he took little comfort in knowing that Zara was the only casualty of the mission. The *sayeret matkal* team, an elite commando team of the IDF, had managed to get everyone away from the border. The extraction had the secret blessing of the Azerbaijan government. Israel had long maintained a covert military base located 70 km northwest of Azerbaijan's capital Baku in Sitalchay, and their relationship with Azerbaijan was excellent.

Iran wasted no time lambasting the Azerbaijanis and accusing them of green-lighting the Israelis and helping a wanted traitor defect in possession of damaging materials. Azerbaijan denied all complicity and claimed to be searching for the criminals that shot up the Astara border crossing, damaging their relations with Iran.

A diplomatic quagmire was unfolding, but as with most things diplomatic and without resolution, it was more hot air than repercussion, which meant that basically, Iran had bigger things to deal with than starting up trouble with its neighboring country.

Leave that to the politicians, thought Aryeh.

He had enough worries.

His tortuous thoughts revolved around Jazmin's narrow escape, her remorse over the assassin's death, and Zara's near-death at his own hands. Jazmin had been released from hospital yesterday with a cracked rib, her only reward for her death-defying jump from the helicopter. The prime minister and the Ramsad had agreed that she should recover at the safe house, watched over by Cyrus and Layla.

Cyrus had called and texted with updates on Jazmin's convalescence, letting him know that Jazmin had asked for him, but Aryeh was too worried about Zara and too caught up in the emotional letdown of the mission to talk to her. But mostly, it was Jazmin's reaction to the death of her nemesis that continued to plague him. He didn't know what to say to her or how he'd react to her empathizing with the man who killed her family. He also didn't know how he'd get past knowing if the monster had violated her willingly or unwillingly.

"Thanks for keeping watch, Aryeh." Mustafa joined him, handing him a cup of black coffee. "Any change while I was gone?"

Aryeh shook his head. He still hadn't gotten used to the strange bonding he and Mustafa shared.

Mustafa patted Aryeh's shoulder. "I know you're blaming yourself," Mustafa said. "but it isn't your fault. She didn't tell me about the pregnancy, and you know how she is — proud and stubborn. If anyone is to blame, it's me —" His voice cracked, and he ran a shaky hand through his hair. "Such an idiot I am, thinking only of myself. I told her how much I wanted us to be free, not to hide from the world. And this mission would set us free. Us. Zara was always free. She gave up so much for me. And here, I was pushing her to give up even more. I was the one who let himself be ruled by selfishness."

It was Aryeh's turn to offer a comforting hand on Mustafa's shoulder. "Zara is going to recover, and the doctor says the pregnancy is fine. You'll have a lifetime to make it up to her."

"I will make it up to her. I will spend the rest of my life making it up to her and our child and, God willing, our future children."

Aryeh nodded in agreement. Zara was the kind of woman who inspired that kind of devotion. His regrets about their relationship were his own. Not hers. She'd been right all along. They were never meant to be. But Zara's friendship meant the world to him, and he didn't want to lose that. "Do you think she'll talk to me when she wakes up?"

Mustafa took a sip of his coffee. "I know you want to bury the hatchet with her, but I think she'll need time. And I am worried about upsetting her when she has such a road ahead to heal."

"I know you're right, but we've been friends for so long. Losing her friendship would be like losing my right arm."

"Let me talk to her. It may not happen right away but give me time. Give *her* time. I want to be by her bedside when she wakes up. Why don't you get some rest? From what I understand, you've had your own harrowing experience."

Aryeh nodded. "You have my number. Keep me posted."

THE SAFE HOUSE in Ramat Ha Sharon was tucked away on a quiet residential street. The two-story Mediterranean sat behind imposing gates, set back from the street and landscaped with a high hedge offering privacy. Outside the gates, a revolving team of security agents monitored the comings and goings of visitors.

Inside the house on the second floor, Jazmin lay awake, staring at the ceiling. Everything in her life had fallen apart, and on top of all the chaos, she was wracked with guilt. Adding to her emotional turmoil was her future, which was clouded with uncertainty. She didn't know whether she was more distraught over the assassin's death or the disappointment she'd seen on Aryeh's face. She couldn't help weeping when she realized she'd lost the chance of revenging herself against the man who paid for her family's destruction. She felt sure Aryeh would never understand and forgive her for what appeared to be her betrayal.

It was in this state of depression that Jazmin heard the door to the bedroom inch open. She expected to see either Layla or Cyrus checking on her. Her awareness sharpened when she saw a cloud of red hair and green eyes gaze at her uncertainly. Her surprise visitor brought a ray of sunshine with her as she tiptoed into the room. Behind her followed a puppy with its pink tongue hanging out.

"Are you awake?" Cerise asked. "*Ima* said I'm not to disturb you, but you're not disturbed, are you?"

Jazmin bit back her smile. If she was disturbed, it was too late now. "No, come in."

The tiptoe became a jump and a hop as the little girl bounced up onto the bed. Jazmin breathed through gritted teeth at the stab of pain in her rib. Luckily the puppy's whine gave her cover. She didn't want to make Cerise feel bad for causing her pain. Cerise heaved a deep sigh, got down from the bed, picked up the little dog, and hopped back onto the bed. The puppy squirmed out of Cerise's arms and dashed toward Jazmin, licking her all over her face.

"*Aba* said you are a beautiful princess from a faraway land. He said you lost your Mommy and Daddy, and I need to be kind to you." Cerise's voice revved up several decibels with her excitement. "I've never known a princess before. Did you live in a castle? Are you waiting for your prince to come and get you? Is he going to come here on a white horse and take you away? *Aba* told me that's what *he* did with *Ima*."

Jazmin laughed as much from Cerise's words as the rambunctious puppy that continued to lavish her with kisses. "I'm not a real princess, but don't tell your daddy. He might not let me stay if he finds out. I'm a girl like you, and I wish I had a prince, but I do not have one."

Disappointment filled Cerise's face. "You don't look like a girl like me. You're beautiful like Snow White, and when you speak, you sound different than me."

"Well, that part is true. I am from a faraway land."

Cerise's brow creased. "*Ima* says you *have so* met your prince, but you don't know it yet. Mommy also says you will see him soon and fall in love, and you'll live happily ever after."

Jazmin shook her head and looked around the room. "Where is he? I don't see him, but I do see you, and I'm very happy to meet you."

Cerise smiled. "Me too! Do you know how to swim? Maybe we can go swimming together. The pool is so nice. I told Daddy we need a swimming pool, too. Norit really needs one. She's only a puppy, as you can see, and she's learning how to swim." Cerise wrinkled her brow, her voice carrying a commanding intonation. "Norit, sit!" The puppy reluctantly abandoned her licking and sat on the coverlet, her gaze shifting from her mistress to Jazmin. The yellow ball of fur's tail thumped back and forth. From the hallway, Layla called, "Cerise, I told you not to bother Jazmin. She needs to rest. Come here. I want to talk to you."

"I have to go. Please come swimming with Norit and me." Cerise dragged out the "ee" sound in "please."

"Okay, I promise I will." Jazmin watched the bubble of energy scamper from the room, closing the door behind her. She sighed. Cerise had managed to do what no one else had. She'd lifted Jazmin's spirits and made her forget her troubles, at least momentarily. She laughed, remembering Cyrus and Layla talking about their child's irrepressible spirit. In a few minutes, the child had accomplished something miraculous, and Jazmin felt herself step a few feet back from the abyss and the darkness that consumed her.

CHAPTER FORTY-SIX

Saturday, February 15
Tel Aviv, Israel

Layla and Cyrus were taking a siesta before getting ready for the afternoon barbeque they'd planned. At Layla's insistence, Cyrus had invited Aryeh, and he agreed to come. Layla was back on track pushing the two broken hearts together. She claimed her woman's instinct told her that Aryeh and Jazmin needed each other and were a perfect match. He didn't see it as clearly as she did, but then he'd hadn't seen that he and Layla were fated to be together, either.

Cyrus lay back against the pillow with his arms crossed behind his head, enjoying the warmth and relaxation after a much-needed interlude of lovemaking with his muse. Making love with Layla accomplished what hours in therapy could never do. It decompressed him and sent the Mossad agent back to where he belonged — compartmentalized. Living with that part of him daily was too dangerous. It wasn't the man he wanted to be, but he knew it was the man he had to become when on a mission. But now was not the time to think of killing or assassinations, now was the time to indulge in desire. His love for Layla was the deepest well. Only she could replenish him and make him whole.

The bathroom door opened, and a naked Layla hopped onto the bed with the most tantalizing, teasing smile on her face. She snuggled into his shoulder, and every cell in his body sprang to life.

"*Eshgham.*" He ran his hand down her hip to her thigh. "you're not giving me much time to recover my strength." His eyes gleamed with rekindled craving. "But I'll do my best."

"No, that's not why I'm smiling."

He couldn't hide the look of disappointment on his face. "Okay, what am I missing?"

He hadn't noticed that she was holding something in her hand. She lifted it and waved it in front of his eyes. "Notice the color of the line in the window?"

It took a moment for him to catch up. He yanked her on top of him so he could look up into her turquoise eyes. "We're pregnant?"

"Yes, we are." She grinned.

He grabbed her face and kissed her with all the love inside him. His happiness was exponential. "I can't believe it, considering all that's happened."

"Maybe Cerise is right after all. What we needed was to kiss more."

He laughed, fisting the hair that draped her face. He brought her mouth to his. Maybe they had time for a quickie before their daughter woke them up. He nearly burst into laughter, anticipating Cerise's reaction when they told her.

ARYEH PICKED up a newspaper from the stand on Dizengoff street and shook it open. The headline announced a series of explosions occurring in Iran. He read the article about the mysterious attacks around the country. A new centrifuge facility at the Natanz nuclear plant had been destroyed, followed by the predictable denial of sabotage by the Supreme National Security Council. The regime also claimed to have thwarted a cyber-attack on the country's water supply but was not successful in averting an attack on Shahid Rajaae, a company that shipped more than fifty percent of Iran's imports and exports in and out of Iran. In addition, it was reported there had been numerous attacks on nuclear facilities, oil refineries, power plants, major factories, and businesses across the country. Another explosion and fire had occurred at the Ahwaz power plant, and a chlorine gas leak at the Karoun petrochemical plant in Mahshahr were all reported to be of a suspicious nature.

A group calling themselves the "Homeland Cheetahs," a revolutionary paramilitary group dedicated to the overthrow of the regime, claimed victory for the strikes. Innuendos coming out of Iran placed the blame on Israel. Aryeh couldn't help but grin when he read the cryptic response from Israel's foreign minister when questioned about the attacks. "Our actions in Iran are better left unsaid."

Aryeh took note of one special casualty, the Iranian General Davood Choudhury. The man was thought to have been inspecting the tunnels beneath the Karoun facility when the explosion occurred. Word had leaked out from the Homeland Cheetahs claiming that the general and stockpiles of missiles had been destroyed in the conflagration. Aryeh hoped news of the man who ordered the hits on Jazmin's family would bring peace to the woman whom he couldn't get out of his mind.

Ramat Ha Sharon, Israel

Jazmin lay on a lounge chair watching Cerise and Norit swim. The sunlight warmed her skin to a golden bronze. She was so focused on the child and puppy she was taken by surprise when a shadow fell over her, blocking the light. The bright sun behind him cast his face into shadow, and for a moment, she didn't know who he was. Her heart skipped a beat, and for less than a breath, she had a vision of Khalid hovering over her.

She recovered her senses and realized the man's identity. "No one told me you were coming."

"I guess Layla thought you'd enjoy a surprise. Sorry if you're disappointed."

"Why would you say that? Of course, I'm not disappointed."

He reached out his hand to her. "Can we talk alone for a few minutes?" He pulled her up out of the lounge. Cerise called from the pool to Jazmin. "Jazmin, come in the water, pleeeeeeze."

Cyrus dove in the water and scooped Cerise up, tickling her. Her laughter rang out as the puppy paddled toward them with ferocious little strokes.

"Cerise, let's leave Jazmin alone while she and Aryeh talk. Play with me, *motek sheli.*"

Aryeh gave Cyrus a thumbs up and took Jazmin's hand in his, then pulled her inside the house.

"Where are we going?" she asked. He pulled her into the TV room and shut the door behind them.

"This'll do." He turned to her, not letting go of her hand. "I want to apologize for the way I reacted when you broke down. I was wrong, and I'm sorry. You had gone through a devastating experience. Whatever happened between you and that thug is none of my business."

Jazmin did something that she couldn't imagine herself doing. She closed the distance between them and took his face in her hands. "Nothing happened between us." She stared up into his eyes, waiting for his response.

"How —?"

"Give me some credit. I fell apart because he'd promised to kill the general in Iran who purchased my family's murder."

"Why would he do that?"

She dropped her eyes. "I said he didn't touch me. I didn't say he didn't want it to happen. But I thought you were d-dead…I-I thought the only thing left to me was revenge. I lost my family, my fiancé, my future, and you. I think I lost myself, too." She looked up again, and the pain she saw in his eyes mirrored the pain inside her heart. "I couldn't think about anything except my own vengeance." She couldn't stop the sobs from escaping. "I was lost. So lost."

Aryeh's hands encircled her waist, and he pulled her closer. "Hush, love, it's going to be all right." He tucked her head into his chest, and his hands rubbed her back in soothing circles. "You got your revenge, Jazmin. The general *is* dead. Our people worked with the two flash drives to locate targets, and Ibrahim figured out who killed your family. The strike blew up a missile facility at Khojir while the general was at the facility. Apparently, he was underground in the tunnels, and that's where he'll remain for all eternity."

Jazmin gasped and pulled back so she could look at Aryeh's face. His thumb gently wiped her tears away.

"Aryeh, when I met you again at the hotel in Zürich, everything began to change for me. I was starting to come out of the stupor that had me in a stranglehold at the embassy. You did that. You helped me. You made me laugh. You made me think about things. I believed that I was perhaps helping you too."

"You did. You made me examine my life and confront my failures. I realized so much of what I thought was important meant nothing. I know now what I've been missing. What I want," he whispered in a ragged voice.

"Aryeh, I want to tell you everything, to share everything that happened with you. Some things I don't understand myself, but I need you to understand and help me understand. Because if you're not in my life, I think I truly will go mad."

Aryeh clenched his jaw, and she could feel the sharp tension in him. Without thinking, she caressed his face, and he sighed.

"I argued with him in that helicopter," Jazmin said. "I told him either land it, or I would jump. And he refused. So, I jumped."

She had more to tell Aryeh about those last desperate moments when she argued with the assassin — Khalid or Gurga — or whatever his name was. The cat and mouse game at the mansion had been her revenge. Even if she'd won that game, she would have lost her soul in the end.

She needed to share everything with Aryeh, but there would be time enough for that.

A lifetime, in fact.

"You are one daredevil woman." Aryeh grinned.

"I knew you would catch me." Jazmin grinned back.

"I want to spend the rest of my life catching you," he said.

Aryeh pulled her into his arms and kissed her, and she knew her soul was not lost after all.

EPILOGUE

Ramat Ha Sharon, Israel

"Oh, Superman, my love."

"Shalom, my only one," Cyrus replied with a grin. He never got tired of hearing Layla call him Superman. And like that superhero's alternate persona, Clark Kent, Cyrus had happily returned to his role of husband, father, and official head chef, minus the black-framed glasses.

He turned the kabobs on the barbeque, inhaling the aroma of grilled vegetables, almost ready to be plated, while the skewers of lamb, beef, and chicken were still marinating on an oversized platter on the prep table. He wanted to get those morsels on the grill. On the table, a tall, fluffy stack of homemade pita that he'd baked that morning waited, ready for their last-minute char. He couldn't wait to fill a bunch with fixings, then drench them with tahini, hummus, tarator, and hot spicy *schug* sauce. The thought made his mouth water. Layla called them Middle Eastern tacos. Whatever you called them didn't matter because they were finger-licking good.

All around the patio and pool, the team mingled in celebration of the successful end of another mission. For the moment, the world was a peaceful place and they could enjoy a respite from the usual demands of their boss, the Ramsad.

"Everything looks great!" Layla sidled up beside him and gave him a peck on the cheek. "I brought you some refreshments while you're on grilling duty, my love." She set down a plate of hummus and pita chips and an icy margarita.

"Thank you, *eshgham.* Everyone seems to be having a good time, especially Cerise." He glanced over to Cerise and Levi, whose heads were bowed together in concentration. Levi was teaching Cerise about the small drone he'd brought for her. Cyrus could only imagine the trouble that lay ahead when his curious daughter figured out what she could do with this high-tech toy. He would have to remember to close the drapes every night, or he and Layla would know no privacy.

Layla giggled. "Don't ask. She already declared she wants to grow up to be a gamer like Levi."

"Oy!" Cyrus took a deep swig of the margarita. "I think I'm going to need another margarita after that comment." He returned to the task at hand of turning the kabobs on the barbeque. "You didn't think she was going to become an artist or an art historian, did you?"

"No, it's your brain and my father's brain she inherited, not mine. She's a scientist of some sort, that's for sure." Layla swept her gaze around the patio. "By the way, have you noticed my matchmaking success?"

Cyrus rolled his eyes. "Yes, I think we can safely confirm Aryeh and Jazmin are an item." Aryeh hadn't budged from Jazmin's side since he arrived. Cyrus had never seen Aryeh look so happy or relaxed, and Jazmin simply glowed every time the big lion looked at her, which was often. They were chatting with Nira and Ash, another budding love story in their group. Nira, who'd missed the mission to Malta because of the gun wound she'd received courtesy of Hezbollah in the Beqaa Valley, had finally acknowledged her attraction to Ash. The two, who were noted for their back and forth jabs, had finally called a truce and, damned if the rose didn't start blooming shortly thereafter. Nira was as thorny as ever and had given everyone a piece of her mind at being left behind and having to forego Malta. She was a high-octane woman for sure, but oddly, Ash didn't mind being the butt of her cantankerous personality. He seemed to revel in it and usually gave as good as he got. Hell, Cyrus recalled, he and Layla had started out pretty much the same way. Fireworks in a relationship kept the party going.

Layla followed the direction of his gaze. "Sometimes love blossoms in the most unlikely places and between the most unlikely couples. Don't you think, honey?"

"Hey, I just flip the burgers."

"Admit it. You know very well what I'm talking about, and you're as happy about it as I am."

Cyrus chuckled and kissed the tip of his beloved's nose. "I admit nothing, except that I adore you, now and forever."

"Good comeback, Superman."

"Speaking of which, Mustafa checked in with me, and Zara is progressing well."

"Is she still pissed off at Aryeh, or is she willing to talk to him?"

"She's still pissed, but since her rehab will keep her here for the next couple of months, Aryeh will no doubt hang outside her door begging like Norit over there until she forgives him."

"Do you think she will?"

"Eventually. They share too much history together to cut the cord."

"Hey, Layla, you settle who's the winner." Daniel waved Layla over to where he, Ben, Yitz, and Zvi were sitting around a table drinking beer and arm wrestling.

Layla made her way to them. Cyrus called, "Don't get between that crew of nudnicks. And Daniel, don't you bust any stitches and ruin my party, or your sorry ass is in a heap of horse sh—" Cyrus's gaze collided with Cerise's "— horse manure." He winked at his daughter.

"Daddy horse manure is stinky."

"That it is *metuka,* that it is. Remember Cerise, you need to keep an eye on Norit and see that she doesn't eat something bad for her."

Cerise turned her head and gasped, running to stop the puppy vacuum cleaner from inhaling all the crumbs on the patio.

"No, Norit! You're going to throw up all over the place, and then everyone's gonna leave the party, and there won't be any cake." Cerise wagged her finger at Norit, who cocked her head and gave a little *ruff* of agreement. She led the puppy to Levi and commanded her to sit. Norit looked none too happy to being pulled away from the fertile feeding beneath their guests' feet.

Cyrus caught Noam eyeing Aryeh and Jazmin and noticed the trace of a smile that curved the old fox's lips. Having no children of his own, Cyrus knew Noam cared for Aryeh like his own son and would be overjoyed to see him marry and settle down. Cyrus wouldn't have minded being a fly on the wall listening to the ongoing debate between Layla's father, Aleck and the aging warrior. Although Aleck's work in nuclear physics was for the benefit of Israel's security, he remained a peacenik at heart. Cyrus could only imagine those two haggling over military or diplomatic strategies

Cyrus smiled to himself as he watched everyone around him enjoying the sunny afternoon. The world was full of uncertainty and looming threats of violence and chaos could erupt in a month or a year or even tomorrow, but he was certain of one thing—he would continue to fight for justice and protect the people he loved.

A MESSAGE FROM BELLE AMI

I hope you enjoyed reading *Exposed.*
I welcome any and all reviews. If you'd like to write a review please *click here.*

ALSO BY BELLE AMI

OUT OF TIME THRILLER SERIES

The Girl Who Knew da Vinci

Book 1

The Girl Who Loved Caravaggio

Book 2

The Girl Who Adored Rembrandt

Book 3

The Girl Who ...(Coming in 2021)

Book 4

TIP OF THE SPEAR THRILLER SERIES

Escape

Book 1

Vengeance

Book 2

Ransom

Book 3

Exposed

Book 4

THE BLUE COAT SAGA SERIES

The Rendezvous in Paris

Book 1

The Lost Legacy of Time

Book 2

The Secret Book of Names

Book 3

The Blue Coat Saga Box Set

THE ONLY ONE ROMANTIC SUSPENSE SERIES

The One

Book 1

The One and More

Book 2

One More Time Is Not Enough

Book 3

Sign up for Belle Ami's newsletter at belleamiauthor.com

Follow Belle Ami on BookBub and Amazon

ABOUT THE AUTHOR

Belle Ami writes breathtaking international thrillers and compelling romantic suspense with a touch of sensual heat. A self-confessed news junky, Belle loves to create cutting-edge stories weaving world issues, espionage, fast-paced action, and of course, redemptive love.

Belle is the author of the ongoing international espionage thriller series *TIP OF THE SPEAR,* which includes the highly acclaimed *Escape, Vengeance,* and *Ransom and Exposed.*

She is also the author of the ongoing bestselling *OUT OF TIME* thriller series, which includes the #1 Amazon bestseller—*The Girl Who Knew da Vinci* and #1 Amazon bestseller—*The Girl Who Loved Caravaggio* and *The Girl Who Adored Rembrandt.*

Belle is also the author of the romantic suspense series *THE ONLY ONE,* which includes *The One, The One & More,* and *One More Time is Not Enough.*

Recently, she was honored to be included in the RWA-LARA Christmas Anthology *Holiday Ever After,* featuring her short story, *The Christmas Encounter.*

A former Kathryn McBride scholar of Bryn Mawr College in Pennsylvania, Belle, is also thrilled to be a recipient of the *RONE, RAVEN, Readers' Favorite Award,* and the *Book Excellence Award.*

Belle's passions include hiking, boxing, skiing, cooking, travel, and of course, writing. She lives in Southern California with her husband, two children, a horse named Cindy Crawford, and her brilliant Chihuahua, Giorgio Armani.

Belle loves to hear from readers—you can contact her at: belle@belleamiauthor.com

Connect with Belle Ami online:
belleamiauthor.com
BookBub
Amazon
Twitter: @BelleAmi5
Facebook
Instagram
Newsletter Signup

www.ingramcontent.com/pod-product-compliance
Lightning Source LLC
LaVergne TN
LVHW091110080826
845145LV00008B/1867

* 9 7 8 1 7 3 5 9 4 2 3 5 3 *